Voyager 2.0

E. M. Denison

Voyager 2.0

First paperback edition May 2025

Design by Nick Mosher

ISBN 979-8-9905292-2-9 (paperback)
ISBN 979-8-9905292-3-6 (ebook)

Published by E. M. Denison
emdenison.com

Dedication: To my husband, the brightest star shining in my whole sky.

Acknowledgments:

Thank you to Marie Marley for your excellent, thorough copy edits and for being a wonderful friend.

Thank you to my alpha reader Rebekah Zemansky. Thank you for your encouragement and your thoughts about this novel.

Thank you to Nick Mosher for your fantastic cover design. I am so impressed with your ability to convey exactly what was in this strange, strange book.

Voyager 2.0
E. M. Denison

1

The lights were low, and the shades were drawn, which was fine. It was almost midnight and too dark to see anything out the window anyway. Jess was lying tucked into one of the twin-sized beds in the guest room. Lavender scented votives flickered on the dresser next to framed pics of Jess and Vince. Smiling on their wedding day. Dressed up as ketchup and mustard on Halloween. Jess had wanted to be the ketchup that year, but Vince had called dibs, and she hated to kick up a fuss.

New Age electronica hospice music permeated the room. Jess didn't care for it, but the palliative technicians insisted that it promoted oneness with the cloud. Jess hated to contradict them. They were trying to be helpful, so she held her tongue and endured the music, which was only mildly irritating after all.

The technicians were gone then, though. Only Vince remained at her side. He sat on an ottoman by her bed, rubbing the back of her hand anxiously. His handsome, navy-blue face rendered even more compelling by his expression of worry. "Do you regret not having children?" he asked.

"No," she lied.

The truth would only make Vince feel bad. And he was being so nice. Fussing over her, making sure she'd had a happy life and that he had contributed properly to her thriving as a dutiful husband ought to. It was important to Vince's deep programming to perform as expected. And he had. He had.

"Everything in our marriage was as we had agreed at the start of it," she assured him. It was okay. She was about to get a new life anyway. She lay back, spreading her long magenta hair across the smooth silk pillowcase. The thick comforter was warm and heavy over her body. Her flannel pajamas were warm and fuzzy against her rose-pink skin, though the red and green plaid clashed with her complexion. But at a time like this, who cared? Only dear Vince would see her in them anyway.

Maybe in her next life on the next server, her partner might agree to children. Children were fresh eyes with which to see the world. Perhaps with children she wouldn't get so bored with her next life so quickly. She wouldn't remember how much she'd wanted them in this life, though, so she might not appreciate them as much. But that was a worry for future Jess. Or whatever her name was going to be next.

"Welp," said Vince. "I suppose it's about that time."

"I suppose," she said.

She released his hand and poked both her eyeballs. A projection appeared in the air in front of her with three buttons labeled, 'Restart,' 'Sleep,' and 'Shut Down.' Her lips twitched up. Every night of her life, these three buttons had offered themselves to her. Until today, she'd always selected 'Sleep' or 'Restart.' Each time, the third button had morbidly called to her, like the edge of a high cliff. What would happen if you stepped off? What would happen if you pushed the third button?

Everyone found out eventually. Today was Jess's turn. "To die will be an awfully big adventure." A quote from her mother's Peter Pan book. Her mother had crossed over to another server years earlier. Perhaps Jess would run into her mother's code in the next life. It was unlikely. The Voyager 2.0 housed thousands of server dimensions, each one home to several billion digital souls. And even if Jess and her mother happened to meet again, they wouldn't recognize each other. But it was fun to fantasize about.

Crossing over didn't mean deletion. But it did mean saying goodbye to everything you knew. "Never say goodbye because goodbye means going away and going away means forgetting." Another quote from Peter Pan. But Jess wanted to go away. She wanted to forget. Her spirit had grown tired and restless from too long and unbroken a life. A common problem among mortal souls who lived immortal lives. Crossing over was the technical solution to a spiritual problem. It was time for a new world. She pushed the 'Shut Down' button, wrapped all four of her arms around her torso, and imagined a caterpillar falling asleep in a cocoon. The world went black.

The next morning Jess woke up. She sat up. Her body was supposed to have vanished in a puff of chlorine-smelling vapor. Her soul was supposed to have waited on the servers until midnight when she was assigned a new Incarnation in a new dimension. She was supposed to be an infant. She was still an adult lying in the twin bed in her guest room. She remembered her name and her life. Everything was the same. "Oh, bother," she said.

***

Morning light glowed behind the closed window shade. A songbird program chirped cheerfully outside. The smell of lavender votives was gone. Replaced with the nose-stinging lemon-pine of Vince's favorite antivirus. The bored, restless feeling in Jess's chest remained, squirming. Struggling to move on. To push its way into a new life.

She poked her eyeballs for a forced shut down. Nothing. She poked them again. Nothing. This was most inconvenient. It happened sometimes. She'd heard of this on Bugs, the popular 30-minute TV program about rare code diseases. Like everyone ever interviewed for the program, Jess never thought something like this could happen to her.

She looked at her feet to where her four canopic jars were spread. Each was the size of a wine bottle made of dark-colored glass with a miniature bust of one of the four sons of Horus as a lid. Inside were her most prized NFTs, the code that represented possessions, skills, or knowledge that all digital souls got to bring along to the next life. Birthday presents for your future self. Everyone got to take four. Some people took the ability to play the cello or speak another language. Others took a lot of money.

Jess opened the lid of a green glass bottle that had a jackal head for a cap and a hiss of creamy-orange smoke escaped. Jess coughed at the pungent anise smell of the canopic vapors. The smoke ball coalesced on the foot of the bed and took shape. Her big, fat, orange cat, Hippopotamus, stretched languidly and flicked an irritated ear back at her.

"Sorry I disturbed your nap," she said.

He yawned in response and licked his paw. The other jars could stay closed, but it wasn't fair to her cat to keep him bottled up like a genie. She hoped she could get him back inside the jar and take him with her once she got this 'not dying on time' problem sorted out. She'd completed her crossover paperwork properly, after all, and filed it with the district court of her dimension. Weary souls who crossed via the legal route had the right to take their jars. It was only that once the hospice nurses extracted them from your code and laid them at your feet, you usually didn't open them again until your next life. But Jess was sure the bureaucracy would be sympathetic to her situation and do their best to help her.

She swung her legs out of bed. Her feet fished for her slippers, but they weren't there. Oh, right. All her stuff would be gone. Vince had tagged all her NFT possessions in the weeks leading up to her death. Naturally, when she hit 'Shut Down,' the estate-sale software would have plucked anything of hers from their homepage and auctioned it off overnight.

She looked around the room. Sure enough, the pic of their honeymoon at Crystalwater Falls was missing. There was a placeholder asset—a tasteful lily bouquet—where it used to be. The homepage environment was inviting Vince to redecorate following his widowerhood. It warmed Jess's heart that he hadn't yet found replacements for all her things. It was an unexpected gift, learning how attached Vince had truly been to her all along.

Vince was a dear and he might be able to help her. She smiled to herself, thinking how grateful Vince would be for the unexpected additional time to spend with her. She went to look for him in their bedroom. She found him having sex with their neighbor, Anne.

***

She stared at the startled couple who were gaping back at her.

Vince and Anne were covered in rumpled blankets, thankfully. But also, there were strappy, leather undergarments on the floor, and the ambiance software was playing a cliché Marvin Gaye song. The stench of patchouli incense hit Jess's nose, and her eyes began to water. From the smell, she told herself. Jess's hot pink lava lamp bubbled on the end table next to the smoldering patchouli twig. Vince had kept that item of hers, at least. But this was not Mr. Lava's intended purpose. The lamp was a meditation assistant for unfrazzling herself after stressful workdays.

"Oh, hello!" panted Vince. "You're still alive. Um. I wasn't expecting that."

"Lovely to see you, Jess!" said Anne from below him. Her graceful, alabaster arms were draped around Vince's neck.

The caught lovers did not fly apart, despite Jess's sudden appearance in the bedroom. Through her shock, she remembered that she was supposed to be dead. Vince and Anne were behaving normally. It was her own presence that was the anomaly there.

Vince chewed his lip and gave Jess a sheepish smile. "Err…I want to talk to you. I really do. But would you mind waiting until we're through?"

Jess found her voice at last. "Oh! Of course not. Take all the time you need. My calendar is wide open today. Obviously."

She forced a chuckle to make Vince and Anne feel more comfortable. They chuckled back in return. Having smoothed things over socially, Jess turned around and closed the door behind her. It was fine. Experience told her she wouldn't have long to wait.

***

She padded numbly to the kitchen and was greeted by the aroma of brewed coffee. The kitchen of their homepage looked much the same as it had the previous night. Cheerful yellow walls. White cabinets. A rounded 1950's-style refrigerator painted robin's-egg blue. A rectangular breakfast table seated with four chairs stood under a spiky art deco light fixture that Jess had always felt looked pleasingly like a sea anemone.

There were subtle differences though. The magnets featuring cat butts that Jess had bought on their last vacation were gone. Vince had always thought they were tacky. Perhaps he'd always felt Jess was tacky too. A headache pressed in at her temples. She needed coffee. But when she opened the cabinet, her favorite mug was missing, which was disappointing, but unsurprising. She selected the placeholder mug—a creamy orange one like her cat—and poured herself a cup. She sat at the breakfast table and waited.

Vince joined about 20 minutes later, and an uncharitable part of Jess imagined that he'd been hanging out in the hall for most of that time to give the illusion of bedroom stamina. But there she went again, thinking everything was about her. She could be awfully self-involved sometimes.

"I really wasn't expecting to see you again," he said, seating himself in the chair beside her.

Obviously, she wanted to say in as scornful a voice as possible. But she knew it wouldn't be fair to him.

"I know. Me either," she said. "I didn't know you'd already identified a new partner. You must have done so even before I died." She tried to keep the accusation out of her voice. There was no call for it.

He shrugged. "I knew I was going to run through all my grief cycles the night you crossed, experience each stage fully, and come to terms with my loss, a healed and integrated man. So, why wait?"

He seemed a little embarrassed, though he had no reason to be. His behavior was acceptable and normal. Most widowers and widowers-to-be secured a future partner before their current spouse died to minimize time spent without companionship. But Jess had always romanticized the couples who didn't do that. The ones who chose to spend years sad and alone before finding new love. It was silly, and girlish of her. There was no practical reason to expect Vince to spend time lonely. It would only be a token gesture of loyalty to a dead woman who would never feel the impact of the sacrifice. Except…there she was…feeling the impact. It was bad luck and nobody's fault.

"So…," she said, careful to keep her voice neutral. "You selected Anne after all."

In addition to being their neighbor, Anne worked alongside Vince at City Hall, processing birth, marriage, and death certificates, cataloging applications to cross over, and logging complaints about local elections.

Jess had never had reason to be suspicious of Vince, but she'd felt Anne had always been overly friendly with her husband. She had other unflattering opinions about Anne that she was careful to keep to herself. Words like 'strong-willed,' 'extroverted,' and 'shameless' came to mind. Apparently, she'd been right.

Jess remembered the morning Anne had first threatened to move in with Vince once she was gone. It had been Garden Time yet again in their suburban neighborhood. You could tell because bees were buzzing, and the city's automatic sprinklers had activated on the lawns of all the homepages. When this happened, Vince made her drop everything and go mulch because the servers rewarded any horticulture work done at Garden Time with a double yield of blossoms. Hot diggity dog.

There was a blue sky overhead and the air was warm. Another perfect day. The weather in Garden, the dimension Jess and Vince called home, had been irreproachably beautiful for more than 40 years. Never a storm. Never a chill. Never a cloud unless it was crisp, white, and fluffy.

Sometimes there were random monsters, though.

The Pilot of the Voyager 2.0 spaceship had started dropping those into the dimensions around the same time the weather had gotten peculiarly nice. But so far there were none of those today. The distant skyline of Cyber City was Kaiju-free. The blue, gold, and purple glass of its graceful faceted towers sparkled in the sunshine, peaceful and unshattered.

Jess and Vince were weeding their geranium bed when Anne had waved to Vince over the shared fence and said, 'Hey big guy! I hear Jess decided to cross in a few weeks. Want to couple off with me once she's gone?'

'I'll think about it,' Vince had replied.

Jess had been about to make a tart remark when a bright blue ring of crackling energy opened over the distant city skyline. A preying mantis the size of a cruise ship fell through, crashing into one of the buildings and breaking half its windows. Sirens wailed on the alert system poles that stood on every street corner, even out here in the 'burbs,' so far from the action.

In the distance, police hovercopters converged on the tower where the predatory insect clung. Jess sighed heavily. It was the Pilot's way of 'spicing things up.' Praise Be Unto Him, and all that. Long easy lives made people terminally bored. Without conflict and drama, people gave up and crossed over, hoping that a new life in another dimension would refresh their souls—like Jess was planning to do.

To keep people on their toes and in their dimensions as long as possible, the Pilot killed people randomly, forcing them to cross over without their canopic jars so that the rest of the populace might savor more dearly the sweetness of their own lives. Whatever.

If Jess had been at work, she would have been called to deal with the Kaiju. But it was her day off, and she was off the hook. Which was great. She didn't fancy punching a mantis any more than she wanted to prune a hydrangea. However, the attack meant that Jess, Vince, and Anne had to retreat to their respective Kaiju shelters, and Jess never got to use her snappy comeback.

Jess had assumed Vince had only been being polite when he had told Anne he'd 'think about it.' Personally, Jess had been scandalized at Anne's proposition. Mannerly people don't just ask for what they want using out-loud words. At the time, she didn't believe such a brazen tactic would actually work on Vince. But perhaps Vince wasn't as smart as she'd always thought. Because there he was. Coupled off with Anne. And completely over her.

"You know I don't get out much," Vince explained. "I hadn't gotten any other offers, and Anne was right next door."

"Practical," she said, approving of that aspect of the match, at least.

"You know, I read a book like this once," he said. "A woman thought her husband died in the war and she remarried. But he'd only been captured, and he showed up on their doorstep years later, still expecting to be married."

"How did they solve it?" she asked.

"Well…," he said, shifting uncomfortably. "It was erotica, so…"

"We're not doing that," she said firmly.

"Of course not," he said quickly. "Some things are fun to read about but would just be a mess in reality."

"Very true," she said. For some books, she supposed. Other books Jess longed to fall into. Vince didn't know this, but her job had taken her to dozens of the other thousand dimensions. They were all much the same as Garden, but some were wildly different, full of strange people. Jess had a secret hope that some of the dimensions were fashioned after storybooks, and she'd wake up next in Narnia or Neverland. Though, if that were true, then Mordor was also a possibility…especially given the current mental state of the man in charge of the dimensions.

Most people didn't know this, but the Voyager 2.0's Pilot, Max, could be a real pest sometimes. And he was getting more erratic by the day, using his godlike powers for pranks and mundane amusements. Like a child using a Stradivarius violin as a golf club.

Jess was one of the Pilot's Agents—a superpowered enforcer at the highest level of the spaceship's government. A job so elite and secret, Jess couldn't even tell her husband about it. And Max sent Jess with all her skills and expertise on pointless tasks into bland dimensions like she was some kind of intern he was hazing.

But Jess didn't want to think about work just then. She had left that particular headache in her Task Manager's lap when she'd given her two weeks' notice. The boss had been distraught. Had begged her to stay. Lately, Jess was the only Agent who was able to handle Max. Work was the only place she had been certain would miss her.

"Vince?" she said. The question she wanted to ask was difficult to speak aloud because she was sure she already knew the answer and didn't like it. "Were you sad when I died?"

"Oh yes," he said. "But it's like the old adage says, 'Grief cycle software heals all wounds.' I still love you, but it's like…there is healed tissue over the place you held in my heart."

The answer was what she had expected, though she still found it disappointing.

"That's exactly how the grief processing software is supposed to work," she nodded.

"My feelings for you were so strong, I had to spring for the premium Griefbegone Plus™ software," he said.

"I'm touched," she said.

"I thought you might be," said Vince. He raked a frustrated set of fingers through his hair. "This is all so damned inconvenient. And you are the most inconvenienced of all, my poor Darling." He took one of her hands and squeezed it warmly. Her heart fluttered like always when he did that. He was being so kind. She looked into his big, navy-blue eyes and began to regret leaving him to start over.

"So, what do we do?" she asked.

Anne burst into the kitchen just then. She looked relaxed, happy, and effervescent. Her auburn hair was wet from a shower and her graceful, elflike figure was wrapped in Vince's bathrobe. The blue color looked good against her alabaster skin. Anne had paid for a re-skinning to a 'natural human' Incarnation. It was the latest edgy fashion to harken back to the days when people had bodies and lived on planets. Jess considered the trend a useless extravagance. Expensive and purely aesthetic, which was pointless, in Jess's opinion.

Jess's own augmentations—two extra arms—were practical. She was learning piano, and she couldn't play Duke Ellington Extreme™ remixes without them. Unlike Jess, Anne did not have any extra arms, so new-wave jazz charts were out of the question for Anne. Perhaps she had other interests or skills, though Jess wasn't aware of any.

Anne slid into the third kitchen chair and took one of Jess's other hands. She patted it sympathetically. It took all Jess's willpower not to jerk the hand away. Jess knew she was reacting like someone who was supposed to be alive, which she was not. Anne was only trying to be friendly. Jess ought to cut her some slack.

"Well, we certainly won't hear of you getting your own place," said Anne.

"No one said anything like that," said Jess. Why would she leave her own homepage? Oh. Because it was Anne's homepage now. That was why. Jess stared at the orange coffee cup. Placeholder assets like this were everywhere, waiting for Anne to add her personal touches. Jess was the only item that no longer belonged.

"I've got to cross over as soon as possible," she said.

Vince squeezed the hand he was still holding. "We will get to the bottom of this, Darling. Err, Jess," he amended, noting the brief scowl that flickered across Anne's face.

"It will be our second priority!" said Anne, with forced cheer.

"Second?" said Jess.

"After planning our wedding. Right Pookie?"

"Of course, Schnookums," said Vince. He dropped Jess's hand and leaned across the small table to nuzzle Anne's nose with his own. Then they gave each other rapid kisses punctuated by 'mwuah' noises.

"My own place…" muttered Jess. That sounded like the way to go.

Anne broke off the kisses. "Oh, don't leave! I promise you wouldn't be in the way. You could even help us wedding plan, seeing as how you don't have anything else going on in your life."

Jess shook her head. "I really want to concentrate on figuring out what's wrong with me and fix it."

"Ha!" said Vince. "I wish you'd done that before you decided to die." He laughed heartily and elbowed Jess in the ribs below her lower left arm. Anne gave a courtesy laugh to acknowledge the joke. Jess did not.

2

The analog clock ticked into the silence, a lonely sound which always set Jess's teeth on edge. The chrome faucet of the little doctor's sink dripped just out of time with it. Maddening. A stinging, antiseptic tang of antivirus software pervaded the environment, threatening to make her sneeze. She had been waiting in the examination room for two hours by then, worrying, with only a couple of patronizing medical advice posters to divert her from her dark, spiraling thoughts.

"Battery low?" asked one. "Switch to sleep mode and save energy!"

"Is your software bloated and sluggish?" asked the other one. "Browser cookies may be to blame. Accept them only on special occasions."

She'd read the posters over and over, trying to silence her ruminations. Will I ever be able to cross over? And What if I'm stuck here forever? And, most hauntingly, What if this is only a harbinger symptom and I'm going to get deleted?

A nervous dryness gathered at the back of her throat. She eyed the stack of paper dixie cups next to the sink, wondering if she ought to risk getting up for a drink. Dr. Barnes could barge in at any moment, and Jess had already stripped out of her unflattering red and green plaid

pajamas as instructed and replaced them with an even more unflattering paper gown that gapped in the back.

Jess licked her dry lips. What were the chances that the doctor
would come now after all those hours of waiting? Pretty low, she esti-
mated. She decided to go for it. She peeled her butt cheeks off the sticky,
blue vinyl examination table and padded over to the sink.

The door banged open. Jess wheeled, quickly pressing her exposed
rump against the cold medical cabinets.

"Hello!" said Dr. Barnes. His voice was ebullient and also muffled
by the visor of his level-five software hazard contamination suit.

Jess's knees became weak. He was wearing an alarming amount of
protection against an ailment she had been hoping would be a quick,
easy fix. He was holding a medical scanner in one gloved hand that displayed readouts of Jess's deep code across a five-inch screen.

"How bad is it?" she croaked, steadying herself against the sink
counter. She still hadn't gotten that drink of water, but she couldn't
turn around then with the gap in the back of her gown and the doctor
in the room. No matter that he probably saw a hundred butts a week.
This was Jess's own personal butt, dammit.

"My, my," he said. "Aren't you a medical curiosity. It's all very
exciting. I searched the medical journals for two hours and couldn't
find anything like what you've got…not even in the journal Anomalous. That's the rag we medicos secretly call 'Sideshow Freaks.'"

"Good job keeping that secret," said Jess. Her heart sank. She
searched the face of the man visible through the visor's splash-proof
plexiglass. He looked like a textbook 'Doctor.' Clean-shaven and
soap-opera handsome, skin coded a soothing, medical light blue. No
extra- cutesy body augmentation frills like horns, wings, cat ears, or
extra arms. Jess's extra arms were for piano, so they were not frivolous.
Dr. Barnes appeared to be a man fully committed to his identity as a
doctor. A man who lived for this kind of stuff.

His gaze went through her, not at her, as he looked back and forth
between Jess and her readout on his handheld device. His eyes were
dancing with the avarice of a new, rare condition and he was grinning
like a maniac. The device beeped.

"Oh, Praise Be Unto the Pilot," said Dr. Barnes. "You're not contagious. Mass quarantines are a logistical nightmare."

Jess frowned. She knew the Pilot personally, and he hadn't done anything ever worth praising him for. But she couldn't say that kind of sacrilege out loud. There were only a few people in the whole Voyager 2.0 who didn't hero-worship the Pilot. They were the people he worked most closely with.

Then Barnes pressed a button on the handheld and the air around her wavered like a mirage on a hot day, and Jess heard the 'wum' of a force shield powering down.

"You had me in a force cage?" she said.

"You can never be too careful."

"Actually, you can," she said, annoyed. Force cages were extreme prisons reserved for the most dangerous germs, monsters, and even people. There was always a risk of a force cage getting stuck in the 'on' position and trapping the person inside forever. Jess and the other Agents had the Pilot himself in one of these cages back in the Agency.

"That's what ex-Nurse Shelly thought too," said Dr. Barnes. "Once I had a vomiting patient—a clear cut 'use the force cage' case, mind you—but Nurse Shelly said it would be 'wrong' to put a preschooler alone in an energy prison and use remote drones to treat him, so against my better judgment, I…touched the patient." He shuddered. "I caught the dang virus and had to miss my vacation."

"How terrible," said Jess, dryly.

"Ghastly," he agreed. "That's why Nurse Shelly doesn't work here anymore!"

Barnes removed his protective helmet and placed it on the counter behind Jess between a glass jar of cotton balls and a box of tissues.

"So, as I was saying. You have a very rare and serious problem!" he said happily.

"But…but I saw something like my problem on an episode of Bugs…," she started. That was all she got out before Dr. Barnes rolled his eyes and waved dismissively.

"Oh, that show. People watch that sensationalist med-ertainment poppycock and then come and tell me my business. But you're quite right. You're not the first soul who's had trouble crossing over. The difference is the underlying cause. There's an anomaly in your code never before documented in this dimension. I'd love the chance to study you more."

He rubbed his gloved hands together and leered at her in a greedy way that reminded Jess of a fly preparing to eat a dropped sausage link. She wrapped all four arms around her body, feeling uncomfortably visible all of a sudden. But his enthusiasm might work in her favor. Perhaps she'd found a champion in Dr. Barnes. Perhaps such a determined doctor would be able to solve her problem, even if it was more out of ambition than compassion. What did that matter?

"Can you help me cross over?" she asked.

He frowned; his face was suddenly sad. "Maybe. But tragically we are unlikely to ever find out."

"What do you mean? Why not?"

"We've hit a snag in the billing department," he said. "My front-office staff informs me that you don't have active health insurance."

"Well, of course I don't! I don't officially exist in this dimension."

He nodded. "So, you see the problem. We can't treat you, or even further consult with you without payment. If I had but known, I wouldn't have spent nearly two very expensive hours researching your condition, exhilarating though it was. I'm afraid this little exploratory evaluation is going to cost you as many credit chits as a new luxury hover sedan."

Jess's jaw dropped. She scoffed audibly. This couldn't be right. There had to be exceptions made for extraordinary circumstances. "But…can't the government cover the cost of a medical novelty? Can't you? You're so curious about me. Isn't it worth it to you to have your name on some groundbreaking white paper in the journal Anomalous or something?"

"That's bribery you're attempting," he said, his lips flattening into a disapproving line. "It's not ethical to cover medical treatment of people who aren't competent enough to maintain active health insurance. Unfair to the competent. I swore oaths, madam." He sniffed self-righteously.

"Right. The hypocritic one," she said, deadpan.

"Exactly," he said brightly, missing her irony. Most people missed Jess's irony.

She was so finished with this dimension. She'd spent ten whole decades here and still hadn't made what she'd wanted out of her life. Choice after choice had set up like concrete until she'd found herself stiff, hard, and stuck in a position she'd put herself in. A pose she was uncomfortable holding even a moment longer. She didn't know any way out of it but to start all over again somewhere different. Someone different.

"What do I do?" she said, trying to keep the despair out of her voice.

He puffed out his cheeks and blew. Then he leaned against the examination table and looked her up and down. "Well, without insurance, you just…keep living, I guess. You'll go slowly, restlessly mad from being unable to move on. Then you'll find a nice bridge to live under with some other gone-batty sideshow freaks like yourself—hopefully friendly ones—and… exist."

A strangled squeak escaped Jess's throat. She clutched her chest, wondering if she'd always had this bug, and this fate had been waiting for her since she'd been born. Or whether she'd done something to mess herself up. Picked the wrong time to cross over? The wrong pajamas to shut down in? Chosen the wrong assets for her canopic jars?

She was starting to spiral on those thoughts when Dr. Barnes at last noticed that his patient might be experiencing some emotional distress. He rose and placed a gloved hand on her shoulder. He gave her a sympathetic 'bedside manner' smile.

"Oh, hey," he said. "It sounds more hopeless than it is. On occasion, the universities will round up some of the under-bridge dwellers for an impromptu clinical trial, and some lucky fellow or other will cross over. Medicine advances every day! You never know! Here, take this. My nurses tell me I should hand these out instead of talking to patients myself."

He fished in his lab coat pocket and produced a pamphlet. It had a picture of a bald, cerulean-blue man on the cover. Clean-shaven and clear-eyed. A wise and benevolent-looking man. Jess recognized the iconic image immediately. It was supposed to be the Pilot. The real Pilot, Max, looked nothing like that. The pamphlet said Chicken Soup for the Cyber Soul: 'The Pilot Loves You' and Other Comforting Platitudes for Times of Personal Trouble.

The tears finally came. "No. No. That can't be my future," she said. Her nose filled instantly with snot. She hated this feature of her dimension. She knew there were other dimensions where Incarnations didn't mimic the bodily reactions of their carbon-based human ancestors. She envied the civilians of those dimensions often. "What if I get my old job back," she pleaded. "I'd have insurance then."

Dr. Barnes gave her a sad smile and a shoulder squeeze. "Perhaps if you'd gotten the job back first and then come to see me. But now that I know about your ailment, it counts as a pre-existing condition, and I have to report it."

"Ah, yes," she smiled, wiping her nose across her forearm and sniffing hard. "Because of ethics."

"Exactly so," he said. He handed her a tissue from the box on the counter next to his helmet. "But if I were you, I'd get that job back anyhow, or you're going to get terminally, insanely bored much faster. If they pay you under the table, you won't have to pay taxes, and all that money can cover some proper diagnostic tests. Maybe you'd have a chance."

"Pay me under the table to avoid taxes? Isn't that unethical?"

He shrugged. "You'd be the one violating the ethics codes, not me. It'll be expensive, though. You might end up under a bridge anyway because I don't know how you're going to afford healthcare and rent. Do you have any family you can stay with?"

Jess sagged against the counter and nodded. She did, unfortunately. Anne had made it clear that Jess was more than welcome—desired even—as a sad third wheel in the new love nest she shared with Jess's former husband. Jess's eyes were stinging again. Antivirus antiseptic had never agreed with her. She sniffed.

The truth was, Vince had moved on, but Jess had not. The irony of that was darkly hilarious, and she appreciated it very much. Even more so because it was happening to her and not some pitiable other person who might crumple like one of the dixie cups she still hadn't gotten a drink from. As long as Jess could find amusement in her situation, she could keep moving forward.

"Hey," she said. "While I'm here, could you prescribe me some Griefbegone software? I need to cycle through some things. Add it to my tab?"

"I imagine that would be very helpful, given your circumstances," Dr. Barnes said, poking his handheld device to make a note in her chart. "But you don't get a 'tab.' You have accumulated an overwhelming amount of medical debt here this morning and you must pay it off before you get any new treatment.

"If I were you," he said. "I wouldn't waste a single credit chit on your 'feelings' when you can always do a little something we doctors like to call 'sucking it up' until you've solved your main problem. Which is going to cost a lot of money given that no one in this dimension knows anything about the bug you've got, and I'll be researching this from scratch."

Jess perked up at his last sentence.

"You said this dimension. What about other dimensions?"

Dr. Barnes laughed and shrugged. "Who knows what treasures of medical knowledge await beyond the veil? But it's impossible. Only the Pilot and his Agents have access to the other dimensions."

Jess threw back her head and laughed. For the first time, she saw a light at the end of this nightmare tunnel. She could tell the doctor, she realized. Medical issues were one of the extenuating circumstances her employer specifically called out in the handbook for revealing her real job. Even poor Vince thought she was a low-level secretary at the interdimensional Agency. But Barnes, being her doctor, would have to know the whole truth.

"Can I count on you to maintain doctor-patient confidentiality?" she asked.

Dr. Barnes nodded. "You know how seriously I take my professional promises."

"Then I will tell you that I am in luck. Because that's the job I've got to get back. I was one of the Pilot's Agents."

Dr. Barnes's jaw dropped, and he began to look at her with new, more respectful eyes. Somewhat wary eyes, too, she noted. Jess tried not to smirk. She was used to this. She was soft-spoken and agreeable. It was easy for people to dismiss a demure, pink woman. Until she dropped her big 'Credential.' Then the room would go quiet. No one knew what to say next to a pan-dimensional Super Agent.

"It is possible, then," he whispered. "Yes…yes…the tests could move so much faster if I had extra-dimensional information and knew where to aim my research." He had started to tap the fingertips of his protective gloves together in a scheming hand steeple. Then he stopped. "Wait. Isn't the cross-pollination of knowledge across dimensions forbidden?"

Jess deflated. So much for that plan. There were old rules to ensure the dimensions stayed different from one another. If every sub-world on the Voyager 2.0 shared the same knowledge, they could become so alike in their technology, art, and philosophy that the souls crossing over would grow bored far more quickly. People would need to cross more often, and the dimensional cultures would destabilize from constant soul-turnover.

From what Jess had seen as an Agent, most of the dimensions were already so similar they might as well be the same. Her boss, the Task Manager, liked this. Clarise thought the similarity made the worlds easier to police. But Jess harbored misgivings she couldn't quite put into words.

"It's true," she said miserably. "I swore oaths."

Dr. Barnes tapped his chin. His eyes narrowed and Jess could almost see fast wheels turning behind them, powered by intelligence and ambition and unencumbered by a moral center. "You know...I believe the rules don't apply to canopic jar contents. So, anything you take with you in your code is fair game. You couldn't download an article in another dimension and bring it to me. But you can read it and remember. There's no specific prohibition against that."

Jess's eyes narrowed. "That's...kind of a 'letter of the law' interpretation. Not in line with the spirit."

"It shouldn't be. That's what most people put in their canopic jars. Learnings brought from one dimension to another. The key difference is that the knowledge you bring must be something you learned for yourself. Stored in your own memory circuits."

With a jolt, she realized Dr. Barnes had a point. She'd memorized the copy of Peter Pan her mother had left her...a strange book from another dimension that was otherwise unavailable in her own world. The entire text was waiting in her second canopic jar at the foot of the twin bed on her former homepage.

She met the doctor's eye and smiled. "I think this is going to work," she said.

He shifted uncomfortably. "Are they going to want you back, though? That was a pretty prestigious job you just up and quit. You might have offended them." He shook his head, unable to understand why someone might walk away from status. Getting her job back wouldn't be a problem, though.

"Oh, yes," she said. "I'm the Pilot's favorite. Lucky me."

Dr. Barnes looked even more impressed, if it were possible. "Is it true, the things they say about him?"

Jess sighed. "Which things specifically? They say a lot of 'things' about him."

"That he's a genius beyond our understanding," whispered Dr. Barnes, low and reverent.

Jess snorted. "No."

Dr. Barnes looked disappointed. "But…the choices he makes governing our universe often don't make sense. I'm a bit of a Pilot enthusiast and I've studied his seemingly random dimensional augmentations. I'm convinced he has a strategy with all those Kaiju attacks that we of more limited minds are too simple to grasp."

She shook her head, cringing inwardly. The Mystique of the Pilot was thick by design. The Agents encouraged legendary rumors among the dimension-dwellers. It was safer for the populace to believe such grandiosities than for them to learn the truth about the man in charge of the multiverse, who was only an ordinary man after all. Worse than ordinary. The truth was that there had been a terrible mistake. The Agency was doing its best to cover it up until they found a way to fix things. But the Pilot who held everyone's lives in his hands was really a petty criminal totally unqualified in both intelligence and character to captain a ship of souls.

"There are explanations other than 'genius' for why a person might do things you don't understand," she said.

3

Jess typed all 40 digits of the Agency's comms number into the handheld Dr. Barnes had loaned her. She no longer had a handheld of her own, of course. It had been lost to the previous night's estate sale, so she had to borrow the doctor's device to call to get her job back. Dr. Barnes leaned against the dripping examination room sink, scrutinizing her as she typed. Probably trying to memorize the comms number.

On the counter behind him were her neatly folded red and green flannel pajamas—the only clothes left in this dimension that were still tailored to her Incarnation code. If she tried to put on anything else, the NFTs wouldn't recognize her, wouldn't bind, and would crumple uselessly to the floor leaving her naked until she could purchase them and claim ownership. Exceptions were one-size-fits style assets like the gap-backed paper medical gown she was wearing. But you couldn't go out in stuff like that. Dr. Barnes knew that and was holding her PJs hostage pending the return of his device.

"You might be tempted to make off with it, given your situation," he'd said. "I need assurance you'll give my handheld back."

Jess suspected that what he really wanted was to get the device back with the number for the Agency's direct comms line stored neatly in its recent contacts folder. It was enterprising of him, and Jess admired his chutzpah. But there was no way in Desolation she would allow it.

She finished entering the number and hit 'dial.' On the other end of the line there was a click, then the irritated voice of Clarise, the Task Manager.

"Who are you? How did you get this number," she demanded, her voice crisp and angry.

"I memorized it," Jess said.

"Jessamae? Is that still you?"

"Yes. Still."

"You're supposed to be dead," said the Task Manager. She sounded put-out and irritated.

"It didn't take, I'm afraid."

"Well, if you're not dead, why in Desolation aren't you at work?"

Jess blinked. She hadn't been expecting sympathy from the Task Manager. Nor joy at a potential reunion. But a lambasting for failure to clock in was a step too far, in her opinion.

"I thought that, given the circumstances, a day off to figure out what went wrong was logical," said Jess. "That any reasonable person would understand…"

"That's ridiculous," said the Task Manager, cutting her off. "Get in here. If you're not dead, you've got obligations to this ship. Max is in a mood today and we need all hands on deck."

Jess sighed. She should have seen this coming. "Will I get paid?" she said.

"Debatable. You won't have a bank account anymore, and HR's going to have to sort that nightmare out. Glad it's them and not me."

"I really need money," Jess said. She had Dr. Barnes's research bills to pay, and she really needed to buy some new clothes.

"Why does a dead woman need money?" said Clarise. "Just come in and do your job. We'll sort the little mundanities of your employment out later."

Jess ground her teeth. The little mundanities like her paycheck. But she knew further argument was futile. At least, as an Agent she could search the dimensions for the data Barnes needed. She sighed. "Be there in ten," she said. She hung up.

"So?" said Dr. Barnes, holding his hand out for the handheld. "Did they rehire you?"

"They did," she said. His face broke into a smile of avaricious delight. He was set to receive forbidden knowledge, plumb the depths of a new medical mystery, and have a direct line to the Agency itself. Things were going well for Dr. Barnes at this moment.

Then Jess crushed the handheld with her supernaturally strong fist. It crumbled like a graham cracker, and she dropped the little bits to the floor. Barnes grabbed fistfuls of his hair, his eyes wide in disbelief.

"I…my…you just…how did you? I'll call security!"

"Using what?" Jess asked, glancing down at the scattered device shards.

Barnes frowned at her. "You'll have to pay for that."

She shook her head. "Like I said, they rehired me. I'm a full Agent again. Consider your handheld 'commandeered.' You can apply to the Agency to reimburse you for your loss. They have hundreds of detailed forms to complete that will help you on your journey."

She gave him a bland smile and hopped up from the examination table. Barnes shrank back from her and her strong, crushy fists, acutely aware in his medical knowledge that his Incarnation's bones weren't nearly so sturdy as the handheld had been. Jess grabbed her pajamas and unfolded them.

Usually, she had the code to Jump back to the Agency, but not since she'd quit. There was one daily transport that took civilians from the dimensions to visit the outer shell. It departed City Hall in an hour.

"Now get out," she said. "I've got a bus to catch, and I can't be breaking any decency laws."

Barnes fled for the door. But he stopped in the entryway. "You'll be back with that data though, right? Still want to cross over, yes?"

He looked hopeful, despite his terror. Jess was amazed. Barnes's curiosity about her condition outstripped his fear of her and her super abilities. He was a true and dedicated maniac.

"Yeah," she said. "I do not love my job. And I don't see any other way that I will be allowed to quit."

***

Jess paused outside the locked door in the industrial-looking

23

hallway of the Voyager 2.0's outer shell. The walls there were gray metal. The floors, shiny and black, kept clean by a janitorial staff and a fleet of ankle-high vacuum bots. Four metal utility pipes ran the length of the tubular corridor-red, grey, blue, and black stacked on top of each other at about eye-level. The sickly-sweet tang of welding fumes and ozone filled her nose. A nearby vent hissed an outgassing of built-up steam into Jess's hair. Great. Insta-frizz, she thought, smoothing her magenta waves before they rebelled.

The droning of the ship's propulsor engines vibrated through her body, adding momentum and substance to her gathering headache. Somewhere in the world of matter, the ship's engines were drinking the cosmic radiation that permeated the space between stars. All the fuel they'd need to power the ship on its aimless road trip to infinity. Traveling toward what? The souls aboard living for what? Was it that no one knew the answers or was it that no answers to these questions existed?

The outer shell had seemed thrilling to her once. The neutral place between dimensions from which the Agency controlled the multiverse. The dimensions had the feel of full-fledged worlds. But the outer shell felt like living on a spaceship. It was all a lie though, like everything else.

Even the outer shell was just another kind of dimension. A digital overlay so cyber souls could understand it. The material world of atoms existed just beyond, a hairsbreadth away, but completely untouchable. It baffled Jess that she'd once been excited to work here. As with everything, the job had worn on too long and had gotten old. The itch between shoulder blades that she could never reach to scratch. The uneasy feeling that all of this should have been over by now, a wearying sensation that wore you out even faster once it settled into your bones.

Reincarnation seemed to be digital humanity's cure for the malaise of a too-long life. An idea as old as humankind, familiar and easily accepted. If humans of old could believe in it, so could Humanity 2.0. After all, they were Just like them, only digital.

Here at the end of her frazzled lifeline, Jess understood that it was all just a cosmic shell game to distract the masses. Move this soul here, move that soul there. Recombine the personalities in different configurations and hope it sparked something fresh and new. Maintain the illusion that there was a purpose to all this. Jess knew better now. It would always be the same old, same old.

But the illusion was all the hope she had. Once she gathered enough money and enough data, it would be her turn at last to pull the wool back over her own eyes and pretend to begin again. Because maybe it would all work out differently this time.

She pressed her hand to the entry panel of the locked door. The indicator light by her thumb blinked from red to green, and the double doors hissed open, sliding along their tracks. A puff of cool air hit her face, and Jess entered a room she used to find astonishing.

It was a hundred-foot-high transparent globe, and outside burned the infinite stars of deep space. Jess stepped onto the metal walkway that ringed the equator of the spherical room. There was a computer station every few feet, and a woman with bubblegum pink skin and a Shayla scarf the color of blue-raspberry candy floss stood by one of them poking at buttons and frowning. She wore the standard-issue black, skintight Jumpsuit the team used when visiting the dimensions. Jess's own Jumpsuit had probably disintegrated into spare code the previous night, so she still couldn't change out of her pajamas. Her locker had probably already been reassigned too.

Special Agent Amira Darwish turned from the console, and her face broke into a delighted grin.

"Oh, thank goodness," she said. "I was so glad to hear about your bug."

"You already heard?" said Jess. But of course, Amira had. She was something of a busybody and a gossip. The former was a great trait in a secret Agent. The latter, not so much.

"Yeah," she said. "Sorry for you, though, but glad for us. Max has been impossible since you left. He's increased the number of stupid errands by 50 percent. And, I'm not supposed to say…"

"So don't say," said Jess, knowing Amira would say anyway.

Amira rose and whispered in her ear, unable to contain any sort of gossip. "Clarise has been even worse," she said. "Honestly, between the two of them we've been walking on eggshells. Max, so he doesn't notice us and give us extra work. And Clarise, so she doesn't jump down our throats. You should go tell Max you're back and get a new Jump code if you're going to be here a while. Which I hope you will. It's become kind of obvious since you left how much you were holding this place together.

Jess had had an inkling. All the office stress came down on her. She raised her gaze to where Max sat contained inside his invisible force cage.

Four metal walkways led from the equatorial catwalk to a central hub at the core of the room, like the spokes of a wheel. The hub was bounded by railings, filled with the supercomputer panels that administrated the dimensions, and littered with juice boxes, candy wrappers, and crushed soda cans. The Pilot's detritus. In the center of the hub platform was a spinning office chair, and in the chair was Max, Pilot extraordinaire of the Voyager 2.0 and the reason Jess had to stare at a hot pink lava lamp for at least 30 minutes after every workday, doing deep breathing exercises and trying to clear her mind.

Most people put in at least a little effort keeping up their Incarnation's appearance, but not Max. He had bright yellow skin, the color of a school bus, an attractive shade in Jess's opinion. Only he neglected his sleep cycles and had prominent grey undereye circles. His eyes had corner wrinkles as well, because he never bothered to apply smoothing treatments. He had a five-o-clock shadow of carrot-orange stubble, and his unkempt carrot-orange hair had faded to almost grey in patches, again, due to neglect of basic hygiene.

He was shortish and unmuscular and wore a dingy white tank top, striped boxers that hit just above the knobby knees of his hairy, chicken legs. He thought his round, red-lensed sunglasses gave him a 'dangerous edgy' appearance, but they only made his head look like a marigold. He wore a faded maroon bathrobe over all of this nonsense and slippers shaped like bear feet.

Once he'd told her, "I'm going 'bear foot!' Get it? You have to laugh because I'm basically your god."

"You are not," she'd replied, unintimidated. By then, she knew him. The other Agents were still frightened of him. Rumor was that he had collapsed an entire dimension full of people and now it was a howling wasteland populated by monsters. There was a dimension like that, sure. Desolation. But she doubted Max was responsible. Max was the most irresponsible person she'd ever met. He didn't have the organizational capability to destroy that much stuff.

At the sight of her, Max leaped out of his spinning office chair and bounded down the metal walkway spoke toward where she was standing.

He was grinning in a delighted way Jess knew spelled trouble. She folded all her arms and waited for whatever fresh hell Max was bringing.

He skidded to a halt a few feet in front of the invisible containment shield that kept him prisoner in the globe room hub and stood, bouncing on his toes. He put her in mind of a retriever at the window when its owner's car pulled up at home. The likeness to a pet was unsettling. As Pilot, Max was supposed to be competent enough to care for a whole starship full of souls.

"Hey! Dead woman walking!" he said. He gave her obnoxious double finger guns. "Couldn't go through with it, eh? I get it, I get it. You didn't want to forget me. This is marvelous. I've got so many things that need fetching, and you are the best."

She rolled her eyes. "I didn't intend to stay. I've got a bug. I'm going to fix it."

He chuckled. "Hope you fail. It wouldn't be the same around here without you, Jess." He grinned and she could just picture the long list of pointless tasks he had in store for her.

"Hang on," he said. He held out a finger and poked the air in front of him. A flash of blue electricity spread from where he'd touched the containment shield. It crackled up 50 feet to the apex of the dome and down 50 feet to its base. She heaved a weary sigh. He always did this. "Alas," he said. "The force cage is still working."

"It's always working," Jess said.

"Can't blame a guy for checking. Someday the bottle's going to break, and this genie will be free! You cannot even imagine the chaos I've got planned for that day." He winked at her over the top of his stupid red shades like he was cool or something.

"Oh, I can imagine," she said. "It's why we divert most of the ship's spare power to keeping you in."

"Which is flattering," he said. "Speaking of flattering. Those pajamas. Yowza. They are a good look for you."

She frowned. She could never tell if Max was being serious. The red and green of the shapeless flannel garments clashed horribly with her pink skin. She hadn't thought it would matter, since she was supposed to have crossed over the previous night. Jess decided there might be something to the adage, 'I wouldn't be caught dead in that outfit,' after all.

"That's not an appropriate statement to make to a coworker," she said mildly. "I'll make a report to HR."

Max chuckled and rocked back on his heels. "What are they gonna do, fire me?"

If only it were that simple. The Pilot was code-locked into his role. You couldn't remove a code-locked Pilot without his consent, and you couldn't delete him. The Pilot was powerful and un-killable. This is why the Agency only installed Pilots who had passed dozens of ethics tests—people with that much power had to be paragons of virtue. But there had been a mistake with Max.

So, the Agency had trapped him where he could only affect the dimensions remotely, using the server interface controls on the hub platform. He was supposed to manage dimensional entropy so the eternal souls living in them didn't grow bored and wish for death.

Pilots of yore accomplished this through natural disasters and subtle cultural shifts. Processes so intricate they were like symphonies of mathematics and chance, played by the flapping butterflies of chaos theory, the Pilot conducting it all as maestro. But to Max's simple mind, his work with the dimensions boiled down to 'Keep it fresh. Drop monsters in.' And Jess was still stuck doing this guy's bidding.

"I need a new Jump code," she said.

"Gotcha covered," he said. "Just use your birthdate."

"That was my last code."

"Your new birthdate," he said. "Which should have been today."

Jess shook her head, disgusted. "That's just taunting," she said.

Amira rose from her place at the console, carrying a yellow slip of Pilot assignment paper. The daily list of canopic jars that Max forced the Agents to bring him from various dimensions. They had to comply, or he refused to drop monsters into the dimensions, and the cultures inside them would start to fall apart.

Amira handed the paper to Jess. "Ignore him," she said pleasantly. "It's what I do. I think of him as a siren, calling from a rocky shore. I know it's awfully tempting to sail on over and quibble with him. But much safer to just stuff your ears and carry on manning the rudder. By the way, how's Vince taking your failure to dearly depart? It's got to be awkward, what with Anne and all."

"How did you know about that?" asked Jess.

Amira's eyes slid briefly to Max, then she cleared her throat and looked away. Jess narrowed her eyes at Amira. "You ignore him, do you?" Jess said.

"Heh, want to talk about your feelings?" Amira offered sheepishly.

Boy howdy did Jess ever not. She wheeled on Max instead. "You fished around, looking for that information!" she said, pointing an accusing finger.

Gratifyingly, he took a step back. "Don't be mad at me," he said. "I'm a godlike superbeing with infinite brain capacity and unlimited information. I can't help but know everything."

"You do not have infinite brain capacity," she said. "You might have access to all the knowledge, but your mind is just as limited as the rest of ours. You only know what you think to look for. And you were thinking of checking up on me and my situation."

He stuffed his hands into his pockets and refused to look ashamed of himself. "Fine. You got me. I was curious where my favorite minion was going to end up, is all. I didn't mean to see anything about your marriage. It came out automatically with the information I was looking up. Is new baby Jess going to get good parents or not? Is little Jess going to be born in the Octopus Dimension? All that. Can you blame me? It's distressing, losing a person. Imagine my delight this morning when I awoke to find your code signature still pulsing merrily away on the server where you still remember who I am."

"Where was I headed?" she asked, suddenly curious. Max would know what awaited her in the next life, wouldn't he? "It wasn't the Octopus Dimension, was it?"

"Some secrets are not for you mortals to know," he said primly.

"I'm not mortal. That's my problem," Jess growled.

Amira laid a hand on her shoulder. "Ignoring. Ignoring works best," she advised.

"You're late," said a voice from the entryway. Jess turned. A tall, angular woman the color of a palomino horse stood in the doorway. She had dusty gold skin and cream-colored hair cut into a severe bob. She wore tan riding breeches and an olive gray, tailored foxhunting jacket spangled with more than a dozen chest medals. An exacting frown sharpened her graceful features, and her eyes gleamed disapproval. She started toward them, a riding crop held in two hands behind her back, her shiny black gestapo boots banging against the metal walkway with every step. The Agency's Task Manager, Clarise.

"I'm not late either," muttered Jess. "That's my other problem."

Max snorted, though no one else noticed Jess's double-meaning for 'late.' It was always like this.

"I see you've already got Max's list," said Clarise. "So. Where am I sending you today?"

Jess casually handed off the yellow paper to her boss. At one time, she would have flinched from the commanding woman, terrified to make a mistake. Now, the mighty and powerful head of the Agency seemed a mere frustration. Time and experience had dulled Jess's world; the sharp bits had worn to bumps. Eventually, everything hard would weather to smooth, easy sameness, on and on forever. She couldn't cross over soon enough.

"Dimension X," said Clarise. "Max, how tough is the Syndicate in Dimension X?"

"Creampuffs," said Max. "It's a one-Agent job." He scratched his chin and looked thoughtful. "Maybe two," he amended. "Those Dimension X'ers get nasty when they're hungry. You shouldn't need a lethal gun, though."

Clarise nodded curtly. The Agency kept a safe full of seldom-used lethal firearms. Most weapons simply crossed people over, but there were rare assets that could delete a soul, erasing it from existence. Only a few Syndicates were dangerous enough to warrant bringing such weapons on a mission. As little as the boss trusted the Pilot, everyone knew Max would never send an Agent on a mission with bad intel. He wanted his data packets too much to risk the lives of any of his glorified errand boys.

The Canopic Jar Syndicate had somehow threaded its tendrils through every dimension. No one knew how. The dimensions were supposed to be separate. In each dimension there was an underworld buying, selling, trading, and stealing canopic jars from those about to die and from those newly born.

When you were about to cross over, hospice workers extracted your jars from your code and laid them at your feet. When you materialized in your crib as a brand-new baby in another dimension, your jars materialized along with you. The jars were vulnerable to thieving in those first few weeks, until your parents had bottle-fed you the canopic fluid and you'd integrated your old skills and possessions into your new Incarnation.

Hospices and maternity wards were popular Syndicate targets. It was a lucrative crime ring. Canopic jars frequently contained blueprints for revolutionary technology, exclusive financial knowledge, and of course, Agency secrets. Ways to game the system.

Every dimensional branch of the Syndicate was different. Most were little better than petty criminals. Down-on-their-luckers who were basically decent, but on the wrong side of the law. Some, however, didn't just steal jars. Some crossed people over unprepared and pocketed the jars when they materialized. The worst Syndicates were metaphorical monsters—the kind of brutal mafias that deleted the very souls of their enemies.

"Jess, I'm putting you on this one," said Clarise. "You can bring someone else if you want to."

"I don't have a Jumpsuit," she protested. "I can't dimension-hop in my pajamas."

If she Jumped with anything that wasn't a specially coded Jumpsuit or a canopic jar, it disintegrated once she hit the portal. All part of the anti-cross-contamination protocols that governed the dimensions.

"Get a one-sizer from the equipment locker," said Clarise.

Great. A one-sizer. Jess was hard to fit. At 6'1" she was tall for a female and 'well-endowed' was underselling it in the pectoral area. Plus, there were her extra arms.

"I'm going to have to cut two more arm holes," she warned the Task Manager.

Clarise frowned. "I'll have to dock the damage from your pay."

Jess brightened. "Oh! I get paid, then?" she asked slyly.

"We're still figuring that out."

Jess put all four fists on her hips. "Have you even told HR I'm still here?" she asked.

Unreassuringly, Clarise looked away and didn't answer. She spoke into her wristwatch instead. "Jerome, are you back yet?"

A heavy sigh like a sarcophagus lid scraping closed sounded from the comms. "Yes, Task Manager."

"Get up here," said Clarise.

"We're nearly 'up there' anyway," said Jerome's weary voice. "Moments away, in fact. Your micromanagement is only delaying our entry."

"Did they get my jar?" Max asked, hopefully.

Clarise waved him to silence. "You can hold your horses," she whispered. "Don't interrupt."

A moment later, the door to the globe room hissed open. The petite, rabbity woman on the other side flinched away from the noise. She had dark indigo skin and sparkly silver hair done up in a corkscrew ponytail. She wore a black, skintight Jumpsuit and round, brass spectacles over large, nervous eyes. Agent Netta Pine was the keyed up type who shied from shadows. Which was understandable. She came from a dimension with predatory, bloodsucking shadows. She was constantly in fight-or-flight mode, which made her a total beast on missions.

Behind her loomed Jerome, a lean, fit man with the essence of a living obelisk. Hard, grey, and humorless. He held a canopic jar in an ashen fist large enough to cover most of the bottle. His hair was the same gray as his skin, and his face should have been handsome. By all accounts, the proportions were right for movie stardom. But the unchanging dour expression he wore snuffed any spark of charisma before it could flare up. Also, today, there were angry red sucker marks on his forehead and cheeks, which was new. He and Netta must have just come from the Octopus Dimension.

Jess suppressed a flash of jealousy. Jess almost never got missions in the nonstandard dimensions. Clarise disapproved of them. The Task Manager thought she was 'sparing' her favorite Agent the annoyance by never assigning her there, but secretly Jess always wanted to see the really weird worlds.

Max burst out laughing. "Get frisky with one of the locals, eh?" he teased.

Jerome only shook his head. "That's always the easy joke with tentacles, isn't it? Well, it turns out the octopus people get equally as furious as bipeds when you abscond with their possessions." He held up the little canopic jar. It was made of black, shiny glass and had a falcon-shaped lid. "I hope this hard-won trinket satisfies your offering quota and you will perform some feats of power for us, oh guardian of the multiverse." Disdain practically dripped from Jerome's tone.

Netta poked Jerome in the side and shook her head, warningly. "Don't antagonize him," she said. "He could snap you in half."

Jerome rolled his eyes, unintimidated. "The force cage prevents that." Jerome and Jess were the only Agents who weren't afraid of the Pilot. Jerome didn't experience intense emotions like fear. And Jess, for reasons she couldn't articulate, just didn't think Max had it in him to hurt someone on purpose.

"Sometimes I don't know about that," said Netta. "Sometimes I think he's faking being trapped. I see him watching me with those dead, criminal eyes and I know he's hiding something."

On cue, Max poked the shield. A blue wave of electricity crackled up to the top of the dome. "Ah. Still trapped," he said. "But you're right, Netta. I am hiding something. Look who's back from the dead! Ta-da!" He made jazz hands in Jess's direction.

"We know," said Netta. "Amira already told us."

From her console by the equator wall, Amira cleared her throat. She was blushing furiously. Jess understood. It was hard sometimes to be a gossip at a top-secret Agency. You had to keep a lot of juicy tidbits all bottled up. Jess's bug and Vince's engagement were the perfect pieces of irrelevant scuttlebutt that Amira could spread around without worrying about destabilizing the universe.

"Hi, Netta. Hi, Jerome," she said.

Netta narrowed her eyes at Jess. "Your bug isn't contagious, is it? I don't fancy crossing over right now, but I'd hate to have that option removed. It sounds like a nightmare."

"It is," Jess agreed.

"Glad it's you and not me. Well, I'm not glad it's you, to be clear. I'm just glad it's not me."

Jess nodded. She understood what Netta meant, though tact was not the woman's strong suit. HR had forced the Agents to attend a 'Relating to People' seminar some weeks earlier after Jerome made a supplies clerk cry. He'd regaled the poor man with a hopeless description of the inevitable heat death of the universe as grounds for why he ought to be allowed to borrow the label maker without signing for it. Netta had been awake for the meeting. But that was all you could say for her. Change was hard. Especially when you weren't trying to change, and you'd only attended because your boss required it.

"Your unexpected return is crushing to me on a personal level," said Jerome. "I had thought one of us had finally escaped the Agency's cycle of suffering. But alas, you are here, and the flame of hope I keep lit for myself dwindles once again."

Jerome had also failed to benefit from the 'Relating to People' seminar. It was okay. Jess was used to her coworkers and their personalities.

Max frowned sharply at Jerome. "Are you going to gab all day, or are you going to give your mighty god his offering, minion?" He held out his hand for the canopic jar.

"As you wish," said Clarise. Her voice carried a sadistic edge.

The Task Manager drew a thin, chit-card sized remote from her jacket pocket and held it aloft. The elephant tranquilizer of tech, specially coded to the Pilot's personal signature. The Disruptor only worked for two minutes, though. Just long enough for Agents to safely enter the force cage to deliver the canopic jars.

Max's eyes widened. He held out his hands in a 'stop' gesture, knowing what was coming. "Hang on!" he said. He started to lie down on his own. "Give me time to—"

But Clarise pushed the Disruptor button while he was still standing, like always. Max collapsed like a puppet with its strings cut. His head hit the metal walkway with a resounding 'bang.' Jess winced. It wouldn't damage him, but the Pilot still felt pain. His face assumed the vacant 'not there' look it always did while his personality was suppressed. Jess stifled her visceral shudder. She should be used to this by now.

"Let's move people!" Clarise shouted. "Two minutes!"

The team sprang into action. Jess sighed and moved automatically to her accustomed position at the console beside Amira and the Task Manager. Her first job was to offer two-factor Agent authentication. Amira typed furiously on her console, jaw set, fingers flying. One console over from them, Netta pulled up the file tree that contained all the dimensions.

"Where is he sending us today?" she asked.

"Dimension X," said Jess, recalling the directions on his yellow slip of paper.

"They could use a good Earthquake over in Dimension X," said the Task Manager. "That'll really shake things up."

The female Agents chuckled politely. Clarise always made that joke when they were starting an Earthquake. Jerome maintained silent focus, abstaining from any affectation of humor.

This was the secret they kept from Max. The only way Clarise had found to subvert the man who held the Agency hostage to his mercurial whims. Whenever Max was unconscious for a canopic jar delivery, they hacked his brain and used his Pilot powers to send natural disasters instead of a stupid Kaiju to one lucky dimension.

One disaster in a single dimension among the thousands was all they had time for—yet. But the team was getting better with every test. And Clarise had found ways to suppress Max's personality for longer and longer periods of time. A decade earlier, the Disruptor only knocked him out for a single minute.

"A minute 50!" Clarise called. "Shield status?"

"Ready!" said Amira.

The Task Manager placed her hand on a green-glass panel on Amira's shield console. Jess placed her upper left hand on the one beside it. The scanning lasers moved up and down below the glass, reading their code fingerprints. The console beeped, and the 'wum' of the containment shields powering down echoed in the globe.

Jerome took off, sprinting down the metal walkway toward the hub, the canopic jar clutched in his hand like a relay race baton. He deposited the jar in Max's chair and sprinted back, making sure to step on Max's back with his giant boot on his way out of the containment zone. Jess winced again. Jerome was not a small man.

"Shields up!" barked Clarise.

A few clicks of Amira's keyboard and the walls of the Pilot's force cage 'wummed' back on again. The others clapped Jerome on the back, as though he'd been brave as well as fast. Clarise looked especially pleased. She encouraged antagonism toward Max. Anything to get back at him was good in her view, whether it was productive or not. Jess patted Jerome lightly, not as impressed as the rest. She'd been in the cage with Max once herself—when he hadn't been unconscious, even. The others couldn't know that though.

"We've got a minute 38, people," said Clarise. "Let's make this Earthquake happen."

The other Agents swarmed the consoles, inputting instructions into Dimension X's digital environment. Jess took up her usual post on the other side of the barrier from Max to watch him for signs of wakefulness.

She watched the Agents select the quake's focus and epicenter, dial up its magnitude and select how long the period of motion would last. The number and frequency of the aftershocks. The amplitudes, troughs, and arrival times of the seismic waves.

"This is our best-planned Earthquake yet!" said the Task Manager.

"Just like in nature," Jess remarked.

The rest of the team missed the irony. Max would have caught it if he weren't busy drooling on the floor. The Agency loathed Max's Kaiju-induced brand of chaos because it wasn't 'natural.' The carbon-based humans of old faced earthquakes, hurricanes, wildfires, and tornadoes. Not actual Godzillas. It was important to digital beings to be Just like them. There were many religions aboard the Voyager 2.0. Some of Earth origin; some new. But 'Just like them' was a refrain that had taken on the tenor of a Universal creed across most of the dimensions.

It was why Incarnations had to eat, burp, and use the bathroom. The more digital humans lived like the carbon-based humans of old, the more humanlike their souls would be, or that was the theory anyway. There were the nonstandard dimensions, of course. The octopus people and the sentient rhombuses, for instance. But those were the rare, form-breaking exceptions that upheld the rule.

Most dimensions were populated by bipedal hominids who could catch colds or get the hiccups. Sometimes Jess wondered if the Agency had gotten it backwards. The 'natural' disasters they forced out of Max were highly controlled. Manufactured, even. An inauthentic brand of chaos. True, no carbon-based human had ever encountered a Kaiju. But Max's monsters had personalities and wills of their own. Once he dropped one into a dimension, it did as it pleased—totally beyond even his control. And wasn't that more chaotic than a designer Earthquake?

"Data's coming in!" said Amira. "How long can I keep collecting it?"

"We've got 42 seconds left on the clock," said Clarise. "Unless he's waking early. Jess?"

Jess stared hard at Max's slack, lifeless face and considered. Her instincts about Max were often more reliable than the timer. She could always tell when his personality was beginning to surface from whatever depths it had been shoved down into.

The others wondered how she did it, but it was easy. She could feel him return somehow. When he was 'back,' but not yet awake, he reached this sort of in-between place. He always reminded her of a shipwreck survivor, soaked and spent and suspended in a moment of peaceful oblivion between the past terrors of the sea and the future lonely grind for survival on hostile, uncharted shores.

"I think you've got about 30 seconds," she informed the team.

"Quick, cut the download," ordered Clarise.

Amira's eyes were glued to her console. The green light from racing lines of code flashed across her face. "Just a second, just a second."

"You've only got about 26 of those," Jess warned. Max's color had improved.

"The data's so good on this one," Amira chattered. "It's almost like Max would make a good Pilot after all. If we could just get the 'Max' out of the way."

Amira kept collecting. A sudden resounding 'whack' echoed in the globe, Clarise had smashed the kill switch with her riding crop. Amira's screen went dark. She grabbed her Shayla scarf in frustrated fists and groaned.

"My data!"

Clarise spun Amira's office chair so that she was facing her and held the end of her riding crop underneath Amira's chin, her expression deadly calm. Amira froze, only now realizing that in her obsession with Earthquake data, she'd been insubordinate.

"Obey me, Agent," Clarise said. "If the Pilot discovers what we are up to, he will destroy everything we hold dear back in our respective dimensions."

The room fell quiet, save for the sound of Netta hyperventilating. Clarise's riding crop wasn't a simple accessory. It was one of the rare, deadly lethal assets. Only Agents were allowed to use such things, though bad Syndicates had them as well. If Clarise were to deal a killing blow with this crop, she wouldn't just cross the victim over. She'd delete their whole soul.

Jess misliked the way Clarise had touched the deadly crop to Amira. The Task Manager ranted and raved at Agents. She insulted them, belittled them. That was normal. This was a secret Agency after all. But threatening Amira like that was an alarming new level of intensity. Something had set Clarise off. So far, Clarise had only ever hit Jess with the crop. Nonlethally, of course, just a tap. And Jess totally had that one coming. But Amira had done nothing to warrant a threat to her very existence.

The room was tense as a taut, vibrating string. Jess itched to relieve the building pressure. That was her unofficial other role on the team, after all. Attract the Task Manager's attention onto herself like a rodeo clown leading a raging mustang away from a fallen cowboy. She counted down aloud to distract Clarise.

"Max is almost awake, people!" she said. "Ten…nine…"

"Act causal!" Clarise said, letting the riding crop drop from Amira's chin. Amira rubbed her jaw, and Jess released her breath. Amira's eyes slid gratefully to Jess. It was these sharp, painful moments when Jess understood how important she was to the team, though it wasn't safe for them to acknowledge it out loud.

"I said casual, Agent Pine!" barked Clarise. Netta pulled her smelling salts from her utility belt and began hyperventilating into them.

"That is casual for Netta," said Jess. Clarise wheeled on her, crop in hand, expression furious. Jess kept her face neutral. Rodeo clown, she reminded herself. "Max won't notice anything's off."

Max groaned then, and Clarise turned her head to look at him. He pushed himself up to his knees and held his head. His sunglasses had been knocked off, and Jess could see his undereye circles had darkened. Every time they used the disruptor and hacked Max's brain, they pushed him closer to his breaking point. The hoped-for day where he'd finally crack under the strain and beg for release from his station.

The trouble was, Max said there were Syndicate crime lords waiting to delete him the moment he became a common mortal again. That fear had kept him in the Pilot's chair since before anyone in the Agency could remember. Everyone who worked here now had inherited the problem of Max from their grateful-to-crossover-at-last predecessors.

Over the years, Jess had tried to convince Max that he was safe. That he could step down. "I'm sure whoever wanted you dead has crossed over by now," she'd assured him on more than one occasion.

His answer was always the same. "Doubt it. If I'm still here, then so are they."

Once she'd even asked him how old his present Incarnation was. He'd always laugh and make a joke. "So old and forgetful I can hide my own Easter eggs," or something similar. But he never gave her a real answer.

Max replaced his red sunglasses and forced a smile. "Let's see what you brought me," he said. He struggled to his feet and staggered down the walkway toward his chair. He picked up the glass falcon canopic jar, uncorked it, and peered inside. He sniffed the contents, frowned, and took a drink.

Jess tensed involuntarily. Drinking straight from another soul's canopic jar was poison to anyone but Max, who could not die. You couldn't just drink a jar straight and become a piano virtuoso. The Syndicates ran distilleries to refine the contents of the canopic jars they trafficked into drinkable, though less potent, versions that gave you a small competence boost in whatever cultivated talent had been in the jar.

Max swallowed his sip and made a face. "Drat. No good. Not the right one."

A ring of blue light opened in the air beside him. A rift to an uncharted dimension not found in any of the branches of Netta's dimension file tree. A feat of processing power so astounding it might as well be magic, and Max used it as a cosmic trash bin. He tossed the disappointing canopic jar inside. There was a sound of shattering glass and the ring of light irised closed again.

Jess shook her head at the waste. Someone's carefully cultivated talent or special knowledge. Their dreams for themselves in the next life stolen, then discarded. She'd tried to convince Max to return the unwanted jars to their original owners, but he'd insisted that would be too awkward. It ground her gears.

"Welp," he said, cheerfully, rubbing his hands together. "Octopus Dimension was a bust. I hope that jar wasn't too difficult to obtain."

Jerome said nothing, but a muscle jumped in his jaw below a red, ring-shaped tentacle welt. Max stuffed his hands into his robe pockets and nudged the platform floor with a bear- foot slipper.

"Man, I need a win today," he said. "Dimension X it is, then! Chop, chop! Look alive, people. Ope. Sorry, Jess." He grinned at her.

Before she could stop it, a soft groan escaped her throat at Max's terrible joke. Unfortunately, he'd heard her, and his smile only broadened. Once again, she'd given him the satisfaction. She shook her head, frowning, and turned to go suit up for the Jump to Dimension X.

4

The Agency employed a whole custodial department. Five people who cleaned and organized the rooms of the outer shell, though Jess would never know it, judging by the equipment closet. That was because Security kept all non-Agents away from the room where the high-tech, top-secret gadgets were stored. The Agents were in charge of cleaning this nook themselves, and all of the other Agents were slovenly chaos gibbons, so the room was a pit.

The walk-in closet was dim and cramped. The shelves were cluttered with spy gear. X-ray lenses, intra-dimensional comms watches, manacles and quad manacles, fingerprint replicator gloves, tracking devices, and wiretaps lay piled on top of one another, threatening to spill over the edges and onto the floor—which was littered with unwashed disguise garments.

At the back stood a black vault-style wall safe where the Agency kept its lethal guns. Jess wouldn't need one of those for Dimension X. But she would need clothes. Jess pawed through the rack of one-sizer Jumpsuits that stood next to the safe. The smell of mothballs and baked-in sweat radiated from the whole array of her unappealing clothing options. The men's suits couldn't hope to accommodate her curves, the women's suits were all too short, and none of the one-sizers had extra arm holes. At last Jess settled on a women's Jumpsuit that would work for her torso but would hit her legs at the mid-calf like a pair of capris.

She shimmied out of her flannel PJ's, folded them, and laid them on a shelf covering some random espionage bric-a-brac. Then she pulled the skin-tight black spandex Jumpsuit on and zipped up the front as far as it would go.

She'd just finished cutting slits for her lower two arms when the door behind her banged open. "You're not authorized for the equipment closet!" said a low, male voice.

Jess wheeled. Behind her towered a square-jawed, carrot-shaped man with skulls, snakes, and spiders tattooed across most of his lilac-purple skin. He wore his hot-pink hair in a buzzed high flattop, and his tactical vest was sleeveless to display bulge-veined shoulder muscles the size of cannonballs. Oh, goody. It was Dick Veden, Chief of Security.

"Dick, it's me, Jess," she informed him, in case he'd forgotten, which was possible. He scowled harder, unmoved by the argument.

"You're not on the list," he said. He tapped a data pad with a dainty, three-inch stylus that looked absurd in his giant gristly man fist. Jess's heart sank. 'Stickler' did not even begin to describe Veden's devoted relationship to the Agency's rules. And he was always spoiling for a fight.

"I should be," she insisted. "Clarise rehired me. HR was supposed to get that memo." She knew this wouldn't satisfy the Security Chief. She'd have to face him in single combat. After all, what was the point of all his gym reps and enhancement substances if he never got to use those big muscles, right?

As she expected, Veden shook his head. "Not on the list, not an Agent."

He placed his data pad on a spy gear shelf and attacked. Jess sighed tiredly as he lunged for her. This was tedious. She didn't have the energy to dodge, so she allowed him to plow right into her and seize her upper two arms like he always did. Veden's combat training was baked into his nerves. He was a fighting machine. But his training had never covered opponents with extra arms, and he seemed incapable of learning new things. But this was never a fair fight to begin with. Veden wasn't simply attacking her. He was testing her claim to Agent-hood the only way that made sense to his martially-inclined mind.

She grabbed one of his wrists and wrenched his arm behind his back, forcing the huge man to his knees with her unnatural strength. He sank to the floor, grinning at the pain. Jess's innards squirmed a little. Normal civilians couldn't beat Veden in hand-to-hand, so he enjoyed being dominated by the Agents. A little too much in Jess's opinion. She tried to avoid fighting him whenever possible.

"Ahh," he breathed, immense satisfaction in his voice. "You are an Agent."

"As I said."

"I lasted longer than I usually do," he said, panting.

That's what he said, Jess thought automatically, though she did not say it out loud. That was the kind of thing Max would say out loud.

"You are improving," she said, encouragingly. She didn't know, though. She hadn't been paying attention to the fight. She just wanted to do her job and get paid, and all these extra hangups were getting tiresome.

"Do you think Clarise will accept my application this year?" he asked, blinking up at her with beady, hopeful eyes.

"I keep telling you, Dick. It isn't about strength. The servers just give you the powers when you become and Agent."

"What is it about then? I must know," he said. He grabbed her leg with his free hand and wrapped his legs around her boot like a kid whose parent is trying to get out the door on time.

"Clarise screens for a special sort of psych profile," she said.

"Courage?" he asked "Tenacity? A cool head in battle?"

"You'd think it would be something like that," she said.

"Tell me."

She paused, considering. It was a secret, but it wasn't an oathbound secret. She wavered a moment before deciding against it. She didn't want to give Clarise any reason to dock her pay once HR got her file up and running.

"Can't tell you," she said. "It's classified so applicants can't tamper with the selection process."

Veden sagged in disappointment. She released his arm. The truth was that all the Agents had something deeply wrong with them that worked to the Agency's advantage. Veden would be a shoo-in if only he could pass the creative thinking portion of the test. Jess wasn't holding her breath on that, though.

"So now that I've proven I'm still an Agent, you go tell HR to get my file up and running."

Veden hopped to his feet and saluted. "I would, ma'am. But the Task Manager has given the HR staff the rest of the week off in honor of HR Appreciation Day."

Jess frowned. "That's not a real thing."

"The Task Manager declared it so this morning. There's a cake in the break room for it and everything, lest you doubt my word. What's left of a cake anyway. HR ate a great deal of the monstrous pastry before they went home." He shook his head in a disapproving way.

Jess closed her eyes and groaned. This was deliberate. Clarise had vacated the entire department of the only people who could get her paycheck up and running again. Why? Her salary wasn't breaking the Agency's budget or anything. The musty stench of Jess's used one-sizer Jumpsuit filled her nostrils. She couldn't keep living like this.

"Then you go get my file. I'll reinstate myself," she said. She didn't know if she could do that, but she was going to try. It was all just bank accounts and health insurance policies, surely. Dr. Barnes wasn't going to pay himself, after all.

"Yes, ma'am!" Veden said. He retrieved his data pad from the shelf he'd stashed it on and turned to leave the room. "Ma'am? I'm sorry. But you can't leave those there." He pointed to her folded pajamas.

"But my locker combination has changed. Where am I supposed to put them?"

"I can't say, ma'am. But rule #8,439 of the Outer Shell Comportment Codes prohibits the cluttering of shared workspaces with personal effects."

Jess blinked. Those were a lot of rules he'd memorized. With the numbers attached, even. She eyed the strata of gadget detritus that covered the shelves.

"We wouldn't want to clutter shared workspaces, would we?" she said dryly.

"No, ma'am," he agreed.

She pinched the bridge of her nose and wondered if she could borrow her meditation lava lamp from Vince and Anne's love nest when she returned to her homepage. Their home page, she reminded herself. Then she realized that Mr. Lava might not be able to soothe her anymore, given what the happy couple had been using it for.

"The file, Dick," she snapped. She hated to be rude, but she was past the end of her patience, though it was mostly not Veden's fault.

"Yes, ma'am!" He gave her a smart salute and exited the equipment closet. Jess followed after; her pajamas tucked under her lower left arm.

***

Jess and Veden walked together down the long, tubular corridor until the hallway bifurcated. Veden continued left toward HR, the break room, and whatever was left of the appreciation cake. Jess turned right toward the portal room.

At the end of the hallway stood a thick, impenetrable door made of tempered steel and outfitted along the outside with three authentication panels. Jess sighed and prepared her patience for the tedious security rigamarole.

"Fingerprint authentication," said a computerized voice from the little comms panel. Jess pressed her palm against the green glass fingerprint plate and waited for the lasers to finish their scan.

"Accepted," said the voice. "Retinal scan."

Jess bent and placed her chin on the cold, smooth, contoured plastic chin tray and tried not to flinch as the computer flashed a bright burst of light into her eyeballs.

"Accepted," said the voice. Jess stood, rubbing her stinging eyes, and blinking against the dancing blue and black dots clouding her vision.

"Blood sample," said the voice. She put her top left index finger inside a little hole between the retinal scanner and the fingerprint panel. There was a sharp, stinging prick and the scraping sensation of the sampler.

"Accepted." Jess removed her finger. "What is your bra size?" asked the computer. Ah. The password and voice portion of the authorization gamut. The portal room was the most high-security area of the outer shell besides Max's force cage. It hadn't always been such a pain to get in, but after that incident with the school field trip, Clarise had installed some precautions.

"None of your business," Jess replied coolly.

"Accepted," said the computer. "Welcome to the portal room!"

The light above the door blinked from red to green. Jess ground her teeth. Clarise had greenlighted her for all the security clearances she needed to do her job. But not the paperwork she needed to get paid for it.

The doors hissed open and Jess's nose was hit with a lemony astringent blast of the strongest antivirus software aboard the Voyager 2.0. It was important software for the hub that connected all the dimensions. Jess sneezed several times before stepping into a room with shiny black floors, walls, and ceiling. The black interior was a plastic, antiviral composite, but it looked like polished obsidian. Glowing lines and dots of pure white light ran along the walls and ceiling in a geometric pattern that reminded Jess of the traces on a circuit board.

The floor had only one light line to break up the black. A thin circle with a 12-foot diameter. The dimension portal. Jess strode forward and stepped inside the portal ring.

Netta was already in the room waiting for her, seated behind a row full of computer consoles, ready for the mission to Dimension X.

"Give me your pajamas," said Netta. "No contamination between dimensions."

"Sorry," said Jess. "I don't have a locker anymore."

Jess tossed the flannel garments to Netta who laid them over a console. She approached Jess with her head cocked to one side and her shoulders braced in a state of tense alertness.

"Are you okay?" she asked.

She stopped short of the portal circle and waited for Jess's reply before going any closer. Jess realized all her dark, angry thoughts about her paycheck must have given her a furious scowl. Always on her guard, Netta was probably debating which fear response would be most adaptive to this 'angry coworker' situation. Fight, flight, freeze, fawn…and so on.

Jess definitely didn't want to start a mission with Netta in 'fight' mode, so she arranged her features to look friendlier.

"I'm cross with Clarise, not you," she said.

Netta's shoulders unwound. She stepped inside the portal circle. "Why are you mad?"

Jess sighed. "I need my paycheck or insurance to cover my medical bills so the doctor can fix me, and I can finally cross over."

Netta nodded sagely. "It makes sense that she's blocking you, then. Clarise really didn't want you to cross over. She was spitting nails when she found out that was your plan. I hid under my desk until after Clarise went home that day."

Jess laughed bitterly. "Right. Because I'm the best at getting Max to cooperate."

"True," Netta agreed. "But I think it's more than that. I think she doesn't know how to show that she cares."

"Oh," said Jess. She considered this. Clarise took it very personally whenever one of her Agents disobeyed or disappointed her, just like a mother would. True, she'd just touched Amira with a lethal riding crop, and Jess didn't approve of that. But Amira had been out of line, and physical threats were a more intimate and familial way of gaining compliance than mere citations.

Jess was familiar with non-demonstrative love. The kind of love you had to read between the lines to feel. Her own mother's affection had been subtle as well. The faintest star in the constellation, but a steady star, nonetheless. Easily recognized when you knew what you were looking for.

"I'll think about that," said Jess. "Are we all set?"

Netta nodded and relaxed, apparently satisfied that she'd smoothed over any threatening, angry feelings that might be brewing between Clarise and Jess.

"Max already set the coordinates," said Netta. "By the way, "I am sorry you couldn't cross. But I was starting to worry how things were going to be around here without you."

Jess didn't know how to reply to that. It was something she knew Netta could only confess now when they were alone. In the weeks leading up to her planned crossing, Jess had struggled with a lot of guilt about leaving her coworkers without their rodeo clown, stuck between Clarise and Max.

"Dimension X, here we come," she said. "Energize."

A deep, resonant humming began and built to a crescendo that grew both louder and higher in pitch. Jess's skin began to tingle as the servers prepared to cut and paste her soul into a new context. The lines of light in the floor, walls, and ceiling intensified until a dazzling whiteness surrounded the Agents and the black walls of the portal room dissolved into a whole different world.

****

The tingling sensation of the Jump began to abate. Jess kept her eyes closed while the servers pasted her code into Dimension X. Otherwise, the sensory overload of a sudden, new environment might freeze her systems, sending her into buffering mode, where she'd be vulnerable to attack.

She was aware of noise, lots of noise. But she'd parse it later. She'd learned that if she focused on sound first it could knock her out entirely. She concentrated instead on integrating touch. It was warm in Dimension X. A perfect, sunny afternoon temperature. She wondered if it was always so tediously beautiful here, like it was back in her home dimension, Garden. Perhaps not. Perhaps the Dimension X'ers were lucky enough to get occasional rainstorms. Judging by the gentle breeze playing with wisps of her hair, she hoped that it might be so.

Besides the weather, the ground was vibrating below her feet. A subway perhaps? Or an aftershock from Amira's pet Earthquake? Jess stuck her tongue into the crown of her control molar to begin data collection. Amira would want to know about all her dear little aftershocks.

Jess tried smells next, inhaling deeply the scent of warm blacktop, tire rubber, and street cart tacos. So. They'd landed in a city. That was good, since Max suspected his target canopic jar was hidden in the X City branch of the Syndicate.

Now that she was accustomed to the feel and smells of Dimension X, it was time to listen. She focused until individual sounds emerged from the undifferentiated roar of auditory input. An emergency siren wailed. The car alarms of Earthquake-jostled vehicles beeped, convinced they were being stolen and crying foul with repetitious blarings.

Human sounds emerged from the cacophony next. Hundreds of close-packed voices cheering wild and loud. Whoopings and joyful shouts sounded in the warm air. Cries of "A real Earthquake!" and

"It wasn't another stupid Kaiju; Praise Be Unto the Pilot!"

Jess smiled. "That's a beautiful sound," she remarked to Netta.

"Shh," said her co-Agent. "I'm listening for threats."

"Of course you are," said Jess. But she wasn't going to let Netta's paranoia ruin the mood for her. Jess was going to savor this feeling. This is why she'd joined the Agency. This is why the Agents defied Max with their secret tests. Jess rarely felt like she was making a difference as one of Max's glorified go-for lackeys. But thanks to the Earthquake, the Dimension Xers were invigorated and glad to be alive. And the damage had been minimal. Amira's readouts indicated only 102 civilians had crossed over in the quake. Max's Kaiju never claimed fewer than a thousand.

Of course, 102 families would be purchasing Griefbegone software that night. Their loved ones' orphaned canopic jars would be distilled for next of kin. One hundred and two souls would awaken as infants the next day in a new dimension without any of the knowledge or talents they'd hoped to bring with them. Born at a disadvantage, some of these babies would end up in state care as many parents didn't like to accept children without employable canopic jar skills. Unfortunate casualties of chaos. But at least not senseless chaos, as with Max's Kaiju.

Jess was almost feeling fresh and new herself, but then she opened her eyes. The fresh feelings vanished. It turned out that X City looked like yet another twin of her own Cyber City. Sure, there was a big Earthquake crack running down the middle of the street. And okay, the broken fire hydrant next to the bank was spraying jets of sparkling water into the clear air. But it had the same graceful skyscrapers made of violet, light blue, and golden glass. The same warm-toned brownstone row homes with window boxes full of purple petunias.

Hundreds of Dimension Xers were out celebrating in the streets, hugging, dancing on car roofs, and waving excitedly to strangers. The few people who noticed Jess and Netta materialize on the streets gawked a moment and quickly looked away. Jess was used to this from civilians. When an Agent Jumped in, normal people knew to leave them alone and let them go about their Agency business undisturbed.

Jess had never met an Xer before, but the people here looked the same as Garden's civilians. Sure, there were more body augmentations in Dimension X. Jess spied at least a dozen revelers with more than two arms. Three shirtless men sporting decorative devil's wings raced past them, high-fiving each other. But everyone was bipedal and colored the same rainbow of bright and cheerful hues as the people in her own dimension. Like most people in most of the dimensions.

There were some differences between Dimension X and Garden that hinted at a little cultural and technological diversity, at least. Here, for instance, hovering multicolored lantern globes lined the avenues in honor of some local festival or other. Not HR Appreciation Week, Jess was pretty sure.

True, the hovering lanterns did defy the laws of physics. But it was only a trivial sort of defiance, like a toddler insisting he eat soup with a fork. How else could physics respond to such minor insubordination but to say 'Well, fine! I supposed if you must.'" Physics had bigger fish to fry than these fool lanterns.

Most of the dimensions were like this. The same or nearly the same. Trying to mimic Earth as it was when the carbon-based humans launched Humanity 2.0 to the stars. All in the name of being Just like them.

Jess sometimes wondered if the creed wasn't holding digital humans back. Technically, the servers' environments were limited only by imagination. The ship ought to be crawling with Middle Earths, Starfleet Federations, Xianxia Dimensions, and Perns. But in the hundreds of Jumps she'd made, Jess had mostly seen small, polite bendings of the rules that governed nature. Only a few truly original dimensions existed aboard the Voyager 2.0. Jess really wished she'd accompanied Jerome on the Jump to the Octopus Dimension, tentacle welts be damned.

She looked down to see that her Jumpsuit had chameleoned itself to fit in with the local fashion. Even the clothes here were similar to Garden's. Breathable cotton pants in light, neutral colors and solid-color dark wash tops. Jess had ecru trousers and a navy turtleneck. Netta wore khaki slacks and a wine-red V-neck.

Their spy gear utility belts had even disguised themselves to mimic the locally favored fanny packs. The two Agents would blend in seamlessly, unless you were law enforcement and knew what you were looking for. Jerome would have already alerted Dimension X's precinct that Agents were arriving so an officer could meet them.

Sure enough, a woman with butter yellow skin, a cherry-red

ponytail, and a silver shield pinned to her navy-blue uniform pocket was picking her way through the happy crowd. She was smiling big, with the kind of fresh-faced expression that pegged her as a rookie who still thought she could make a difference.

A pair of green glass virtual reality goggles hung over her eyes, which was how she recognized Jess and Netta as Agents through their disguises. The goggles let users peek behind the scenes into the underlying code of the digital environment to see how things really were, despite how they appeared. Jess and Netta both had their own pairs stashed in their utility belts-turned fanny packs.

It was the same technology doctors used to diagnose bugs. Only medicos and police were allowed to have them, and they took years of training to master. The kind of skill you cultivated over lifetimes in canopic jars. The approaching officer probably didn't really know what she was looking at, only that Jess and Netta somehow looked different from other people, and she'd been told to expect Agents in the area.

The woman stopped a few feet away from them and leaned forward with conspiratorial excitement. "Agents?" she whispered.

Jess nodded. She poked her eyeballs, and a projected image of their Credentials flashed from her pupils and hovered in the air in front of the officer. Projections like these were skills all Humanity 2.0 had, but rarely used in public. Because carbon-based humans couldn't project from their eyeballs, it was considered a minor social faux pas, like an overloud belch.

The officer read the text, and Jess hoped the woman wouldn't notice that Jess's certificate listed the previous day as her last date of employment. But the number was small and off to a corner. The officer nodded, satisfied, and Jess blinked to close the image.

"Wow," said the woman, dipping a star-struck little bow. "I'm officer Eden, and it is an honor to meet real Agents. I begged Captain Felix for this assignment and I'm super glad to meet you! Wow, what a day, huh? It was a beautiful Earthquake. Praise Be Unto the Pilot!"

Praise Be to Amira, Jess thought. "I'll pass along the compliment," Jess said.

Officer Eden's eyes grew wide. "That's right! You work with him. Oh, my gosh. What's that like? What is he like?"

Jess and Netta exchanged a glance. "Completely indescribable," said Jess. It was the well-rehearsed answer for whenever a civilian asked this question. The Pilot's mystique had to be maintained.

"I can imagine," said Eden.

"No," said Netta, shaking her head. "You truly cannot."

Officer Eden's eyes grew even rounder. "Do you know why the Pilot made the change today? I mean, we've all come to expect Kaiju, so this Earthquake was a delightful surprise. I mean, one event and boom. Done. Even with the aftershocks. Normally, my department gets tied up chasing a monster over a week-long rampage before it lays its eggs and flees for the ocean. But with this Earthquake, people don't have to cower in the shelters, waiting for the all-clear. Our economy can keep clicking along. This is just so much better."

She stopped suddenly. Her yellow cheeks flushed tangerine orange, aware that what she was saying could be construed as disloyalty to the Pilot.

"What I mean is," she amended, "I like it better. Just personally. But what do I know? The Pilot knows best, of course. Praise Be Unto Him."

Jess frowned sharply, and Eden cringed away from the expression, assuming the frown was about her. She needn't worry. The officer wasn't going to be in trouble or anything. It was only that Jess had noticed that civilians had started using the phrase 'Praise Be Unto the Pilot' almost ironically, often following a statement about how erratic he'd become. Civilians used the dictum as a screen to obscure dissident thoughts.

To Jess, it signaled a cross-dimensional trend of questioning the Pilot, a growing anxiety concerning the stability of the worlds. It was as though the whole starship were coming awake to the problem of Max, and their trust and devotion were beginning to erode.

Not that she blamed them, but it spelled trouble for the Agency. When the civilians at last lost faith in Max, anarchy would reign. The Agency would be stuck struggling to control Max on one front, and rebellious dimensions on another. Like a big, chaos sandwich with Jess and her fellow Agents as the hapless bologna in the middle.

But that was a future problem. And if she could cross over, future Jess wouldn't have to deal with it at all.

"We need your help," she said. She produced Max's yellow slip of paper and handed it to Eden. The officer took the slip with Max's scrawl reverently in both hands like it was a holy relic. Which, in a way, it was.

"In the Pilot's own handwriting, even," she breathed. Her eyes were round and dewy. Jess hoped she wouldn't notice the chocolate thumb smudge in the lower right corner from Max's candy bar breakfast.

"Oh," said Eden, her face falling. "You need to get to Earl's. Why am I not surprised? Are you sure you want to go there?"

"What do you mean?" said Netta, her eyes growing wide. "Is it really dangerous? Should we call for backup?"

Eden rubbed the back of her neck and looked away. "No...not dangerous. Definitely not dangerous. It's just...there are a lot of other places to find canopic jars," she suggested. "Nice places."

Jess frowned. "We got the address from the Pilot himself."

"Right," said Eden unhappily. "I just...well. Don't judge. Hop in my squad car. I'll have you there in a jiffy."

***

They pulled up in front of pile of rubble that used to be a brownstone office building. The adjoining buildings were severely damaged as well, but their target was in ruins. A broken pipe sprayed water across the debris, and the strong, black licorice smell of distilled canopic jar fluids permeated even through the squad car doors.

Officer Eden killed the siren and exited the vehicle. Jess and Netta tried to follow, but they were in the backseat where the criminals were kept, and the child locks were still engaged. Jess rapped on the windows for assistance.

"Oops! Sorry!" said Eden, blushing furiously and fumbling with her keys. The young rookie's nerves were endearing. She was convinced she was botching this when in fact she was doing fine.

Once free of the car, the three women surveyed the destruction. A dented metal sign lay at their feet that read: "Earl's Neighborhood Syndicate and Distillery. We won't tell if you won't. Cash only."

Jess relaxed, finally understanding Officer Eden's reluctance to take them here. The rookie was embarrassed on behalf of her precinct for allowing the Syndicate to flourish out in the open like this. But Jess had seen the same setup dozens of times.

Some Syndicates were peaceful small-timers who bought off the law with good behavior. They kept thieving to a minimum, never forced a crossover, and pumped so much money into schools and hospitals that it was better for the community to keep them running than to shut them down. In return, the cops looked the other way when the Syndicate stole things.

It was a gray area, but very light gray in the Agency's opinion. The Task Manager had more pressing matters than cracking down on mostly harmless Syndicates. But Officer Eden probably didn't know that. She was probably wondering how much trouble she was in. Jess wanted to put her at ease.

Jess elbowed Netta and pointed to the sign. "Hey, you can relax, it's one of those Syndicates," she said. Jess pulled her VR goggles from her fanny pack and started scanning the area, hoping Eden would take the hint and feel better.

Netta pursed her lips and pushed her glasses more firmly onto her face. "Relaxation goeth before a fall," she said.

"What do you mean, one of those Syndicates?" asked Eden.

"Let me guess," said Jess. "Earl's a popular guy. Does a lot of favors for a lot of people. If he ever went to court for some reason, he'd have 100 character witnesses ready to take his part."

Eden nodded vigorously. "He paid for the local homeless shelter when the city didn't have the funds."

"Right," said Jess, turning on the goggles' 'life-form detection' feature. "So, when a tip comes in to dispatch about some of the big, muscly folks Earl employs, your captain makes it low priority. Bottom of the pile."

Officer Eden's chin drooped, and she stared hard at the rubble by her feet. "Captain says we're charged with keeping the peace. He says you can live peacefully with a wasp nest in your room, so long as you don't start throwing stones."

Netta clucked her tongue. "Tale as old as time," she said. She was frowning at her handheld. Scanning the rubble as well.

Eden rubbed the back of her neck. "So…you two don't seem too worked up about our…corruption." She whispered the last word.

Jess noticed the woman said 'our.' Unwilling to distance herself from her fellow officers, her lot thrown in with them, despite that their unspoken truce with the Syndicate, made her uncomfortable. Jess put a sympathetic hand on the rookie's shoulder.

"This is corruption with a small 'c.'" she assured Eden. "You can relax about your captain. He's still a man worth following." Provided he doesn't take a riding crop to any of his officers, Jess thought darkly.

Netta tutted and shook her head. "There you go again with that 'r' word. It's a dirty, dirty word, 'relax' is."

Jess's VR goggles beeped, and the display inside her lenses pointed to a mound of shattered concrete on the other side of the pile from where they stood. It looked like it had once been the top of a stairwell leading down to a basement.

"There's someone alive under the rubble," she said, pointing to the stairwell. "In a Kaiju shelter maybe?" Only a reinforced bunker could have survived the concentrated code tampering at the quake's epicenter.

Netta nodded. "That's where most Syndicates keep their distilleries, too. The Pilot's canopic jar is probably down there—if it hasn't already been smashed to bits."

Jess nodded. "Let's go."

Jess and Netta picked their way across the unstable rubble field, upright and steady. Officer Eden followed behind the surefooted Super Agents, reduced to scrambling on all fours over blocks of broken brownstone that slid treacherously underfoot, threatening to crush a toe or twist an ankle.

At last, they came to the top of the stairwell where the back of the destroyed building used to be. The entry was buried under rebar, concrete, brownstone chunks, and drywall. Uncovering it would require a bulldozer. Or a couple of Agents with super strength. Being an Agent only seemed prestigious from the outside. The reality was that having superpowers meant Jess had to do a lot of physical grunt work.

She squatted and grabbed a chunk of broken concrete the size of a bedroom door. She tossed it over her shoulder as easily as chucking an empty soda can, if Jess were the sort of person who littered.

Officer Eden's eyebrows climbed. She mouthed a voiceless 'wow,' at the display of strength. Jess looked away, embarrassed. She lifted the next piece of debris less grandly, trying to ignore how good it felt to impress someone. She had schooled herself not to let people's reactions to her status and powers go to her head. Better that Jess see herself as mundane and unmiraculous and avoid the temptation to show off.

Sweat prickled her back between her shoulder blades. Powers or no, this was hard work, and she was the only one doing it. Her co-Agent stood to the side of the stairwell, alternating between furtive glances at their surroundings and peering at the readout on her handheld.

"Are you going to help?" she asked Netta.

"Not with you bending over like that," she said. "Mountain lions attack most frequently when joggers stoop to tie their shoes. They find the exposed backs of necks irresistible."

Jess quirked an eyebrow. "You're expecting mountain lions in X City?"

"I don't know what to expect," Netta said primly. "That's the whole point of vigilance. Tell the back of your neck I said, 'you're welcome.'"

Jess sighed. The paranoia bred in Netta's home dimension with the carnivorous shadows was an asset, she reminded herself. But to benefit from it, Jess had to tolerate the times that it was completely unnecessary. She hoisted a nine-foot-long steel I-beam and threw it aside like a Scottish Highlands caper tosser, then she wiped her forehead on her sleeve. Her back was already wet with perspiration. Her clothes only looked light and breathable. They were still a hot, black-plastic Jumpsuit underneath. But whatever. It was easier not to kick up a fuss. Jess could handle the heavy lifting by herself.

Presently, Jess finished clearing the debris from the stairwell. Miraculously, not even one mountain lion had attacked during that whole time. They were ready to search the basement for fresh shadows Netta could jump at. Jess put a foot on the first stair, but Netta grabbed her shoulder.

"Hang on," she said. "Eden, what's this 'Earl' person like? Is he the angry, hot-tempered sort of violent? Or is he more of a cold, detached sort of monster?

Eden burst out laughing. "He's kind of like Santa Claus, actually. Super jolly. Everyone's best friend."

Netta nodded knowingly. "That's exactly the image the most Machiavellian crime bosses aim to project. Keep alert, Jess. We're dealing with ice here, not fire."

Eden raised a finger to object, but Jess gave her a curt headshake and the officer dropped the issue.

Jess led the way down to the Kaiju shelter and banged the stuck door open with a firm shoulder blow. A rolling cloud of anise-scented canopic jar fumes billowed past. Jess covered her face against the nose-stinging vapors until they dissipated.

She ducked through the doorway into a dim, low-ceilinged room lit with red emergency lights. The others followed, fanning out. Netta slunk into a shadowed corner, and Eden remained by the door. Jess blinked as her eyes adjusted to the darkness to take in the scene. The room was still structurally intact despite its location atop the quake's epicenter—a testament to the sturdiness of Kaiju shelters.

The shelves that lined the room stood mostly empty; the canopic jars that once filled them lay broken at their feet, their slick, oily contents spilled across the concrete floor. Four steel apothecary tables stood empty too, their surfaces spotted with corrosion from years of spilled canopic jar fluids.

Jess wondered vaguely if Max's target jar lay among the broken ones, or if it had been important enough to keep in a safer place. But first things first. They had to find the survivor.

"Hello?" she called into the darkness. She received no answer.

Jess pushed a button on her VR glasses to locate Earl. Three little triangles flashed in her lenses and darted from one inanimate object to the next—a squat, squashy armchair, an overturned desk, an unlit wall sconce. Nothing pointed to Earl. Jess was disappointed, but unsurprised. While the Agency's gear worked across all the thousands of dimensions, it was never as accurate as the locally built tech that only worked in one.

She pushed the VR button again to clear the unhelpful locator triangles, and Netta hit her in the face with a steel table.

Jess staggered back but did not fall. She went numb. Her mind dropped into a deep well within herself where her training guided her actions unburdened by conscious thought. Somewhere up on the surface, Jess was feeling pain and surprise. It would soon morph into betrayal and a desire for revenge.

But the Jess of this deep place knew to listen. A noise. The click of a crossover gun trigger far off in the shadowed shelves of the Kaiju shelter. The whine of a gathering energy burst. Netta hadn't attacked her at all. The table was protective. The deadly, blue-white nimbus of the weapon's discharge erupted on the other side of the steel slab before crackling harmlessly into nothing.

"Take cover!" Netta cried. She dropped the table onto its side and pulled Jess down behind it, using its thick, metal surface as a shield, its legs pointed toward their attacker. A second burst erupted against the steel, and Jess did two things at once.

First, she started counting the shots. A crossover gun only had six charges before it overheated. Second, she somersaulted low to the entryway where Eden stood openmouthed, too confused to act. She grabbed the officer and tossed her safely behind the table next to Netta. A third bolt crackled against the wooden doorframe where Eden had stood only an eyeblink earlier.

Jess rolled back to join the others and lay panting while her mind resurfaced up the deep well waters. She didn't want to come back up; her training mode made such good decisions. But it burned through so much energy that it fizzled after only a few seconds.

"You'll never take me, you filthy monsters!" called a male voice from the darkness.

Jess elbowed Eden. "Does that sound like Earl?"

Eden nodded. "That's him."

"So, he's jolly, is he?" said Netta dryly.

Eden's shoulders hunched. "I'm sorry. I messed up again."

"Yes, you did," said Netta. Eden curled tighter in on herself, putting Jess in mind of a sweet, guilty puppy with its tail tucked between its legs.

Earl fired another blast at the apothecary table. Something stung Jess's shoulder. She looked down. There was a corrosion hole in the table where she'd been leaning against it. The edges glowed red from the gunfire and widened ominously like a spreading cigarette burn. Across the whole surface of the table, all the little rusty holes were widening. And Earl still had two shots left.

Netta cranked the dial of her own crossover gun from 'sleep' mode, which did not always work in the dimensions, to 'crossover,' which nearly always did. Agents reserved that setting for life-threatening situations, which this surely was. Netta was not out of line. Earl's soul would be fine if Netta crossed him over. He'd arrive safe in his next life, only without his canopic jars; his kith and kin of this lifetime left to mourn. Harsh. But that's what you got from firing on law enforcement. Still, Jess hated to go 'whole hog' on a civilian if she could help it.

She put a hand over Netta's wrist. "Whoa! Let's de-escalate. Earl might just be frightened."

Another round of laser fire nibused on the other side of the table. The burning holes sped their widening. Jess swore. Earl was not helping his case here.

Netta set her jaw and peered over the edge of the table, preparing to fire. "Spoken like a chump who wants to get crossed."

Then Jess realized. "Hey," she said. "I do want to get crossed. That's what I want most in the whole world, actually."

Netta met her eyes and swallowed, catching Jess's implication. "Are you sure? What about your canopic jars?"

Two of the widening holes met and formed a larger hole. Soon, the table wouldn't offer any protection at all. Jess thought fast about what was in her four canopic jars and weighed whether the contents were worth risking the current Incarnations of three people.

She'd let Hippopotamus out of his jar that morning. He was the most wonderful cat she'd ever met. Worth discarding the library of code languages she'd brought from her previous life. But he'd be alright without her. Vince was good with animals and would never rehome a pet. As a bonus, Anne was even allergic.

Then there was the random handyman knowledge. Plumbing, electrical, heating and cooling. The kind of mundane work Jess's mother thought beneath a child who she just knew had greatness hidden somewhere deep inside. But it would pay the bills, at least, her mother admitted.

Jess had been keeping the handyman jar as a backup for when she inevitably failed as a professional piano player. She'd dumped her third jar with the spreadsheet skills to fill it with long hours of secret etude practice. At first, she'd only meant to impress her mother. Jess suspected she'd been an impossibly dull person in her previous life. The kind of soul who brought spreadsheets, coding languages, and home maintenance skills with her from another world. The kind of person she didn't want her mother to think she was. Piano was the sort of artistic pursuit her mother would appreciate. But Jess hadn't expected to love music so much, just for herself.

She'd planned to surprise her mother with her piano playing, but her mother had crossed before Jess got good enough to perform. Jess still wasn't good enough to perform. Perhaps next life, she'd always told herself. But if she crossed over in this unplanned way, she'd have to start all over again. And future Jess might not know she loved music.

Then there was the hardest jar to discard. Peter Pan. They weren't supposed to have the book in Garden. It was one of the Earth-written books, relegated to certain dimensions to maintain cultural diversity, as though that protocol was working at all. But her mother had crossed into Garden with a copy as an infant, and she took it with her when she crossed away. It was so special to her mother that she didn't even leave it for her only child. Good thing Jess had memorized the story for herself.

Jess always pictured her mother as a hummingbird. Flitting from one flower to the next. Sipping vitality from a new hobby here, a new social circle there. A club. A cause. An organization. Burning so fast through the nourishment she drew from them that she never came to rest. Except to lean back on her daughter's pillow for 20 minutes every night and read about Neverland. To lose her memory of Peter Pan would be to lose her mother.

Something spiky stuck in the base of Jess's throat. She found she could not answer Netta. Netta nodded, as though Jess had already decided against it. There was no judgement. People who couldn't cross over naturally chose to go slowly crazy and live under bridges rather lose their canopic jars. You didn't just throw them away. Netta's gun whined, warming up to shoot Earl down.

But Jess hadn't decided. She'd only hesitated. Earl still had one shot left, and there was more corrosion hole than tabletop left between Netta and Eden and the coming deadly nimbus. Three people's Incarnations verses some jars. What kind of choice was that? Jess was ashamed she'd even paused to consider. She breathed a prayer that her new parents wouldn't mind a talentless infant. Then vaulted over the table and charged into the line of fire.

5

Earl's final bolt caught Jess in the chest, knocking her back into the table; the impact of her body split the hole-riddled metal. Stinging pain crackled across her torso like a high-dive belly flop.

Netta rushed past her toward the row of far shelves. She tackled the man crouched waiting on the other side. Eden grabbed Jess's upper left hand, rubbing the back of it soothingly with calloused fingers and saying words Jess could not hear.

The world around her turned colorless and unfocused. An all-consuming image of a red, shut down icon glowed in the center of her awareness. Numbers below the icon counted down from five. This was it. The end had come.

Jess had expected to feel the same way she'd felt when she'd tried to shut down the previous night. Relief to be done with it all mixed with a drop of resentment that it hadn't been better and the hope that next time would be different. But an entirely different emotion took her instead.

It was like her mind was always filled with thick, low-hanging gray clouds that dulled the light and muffled the world with unfallen rain. But now a sudden crack parted them and a stinging shaft of the blinding clear blue beyond stabbed through. Like a chord of music so beautiful it hurt.

A fierce curiosity tore her forward to the next life. An eagerness spread in her limbs. Anticipation of the new world that awaited her. But an equal and related feeling pulled her back to the life she was so keen on leaving. What was she leaving behind unfinished and unexplored?

She knew, she knew, that she had wasted her years in Garden, skimming along the surface, never sinking deep into her own life. If she'd already thrown away the gift of one such life, why wouldn't she do the same with her next one? A line from Peter Pan sprang to mind. 'All of this has happened before, and it will all happen again.'

A seed of survival sprouted; its fine white stalk pushed achingly free of the shell as the timer counted down. Jess felt more alive than she'd felt in the decade since the day she'd met Max and mistakenly thought the world might be brighter than it really was. Then the timer reached zero. Jess held her breath.

Her vision turned into a white page with a message in the center:

```
404 Next Life Not Found Error
Can I offer you a game while you wait?
```

Without waiting for permission, her vision switched to a primitive 8-bit black and white desert scene populated by rectangular cacti. A pixelated T-Rex appeared in one corner and 'ran' as the desert side-scrolled toward the primitively-coded succulents. The T-Rex slammed into the first one it met and dissolved.

```
Oops you lost.
Try again?
Your day can't get much worse anyway.
```

Jess wasn't so sure about that. She blinked away the distracting video game. She was still in the Kaiju shelter. Her bug wasn't letting her cross over at all—not even by force. She wondered if Dr. Barnes had ever seen anything like that before. In Jess's mind, the low heavy clouds had closed back over the piercing blue feeling of aliveness and she began to doubt the feeling had even been real. She'd seen crazy people recounting their near-crossover experiences on those hokey TV shows that also interviewed 'eyewitnesses' to interdimensional alien abductions. They usually mentioned some kind of bizarre emotional upheaval right before the end. What Jess had felt was probably that.

Jess sat up, her vision clear. Eden was still holding her hand.

"Agent! You're alive!"

She helped Jess to her feet with trembling hands. Jess prodded her chest where the blast had taken her. No damage, but still an ache.

In the corner by the shelves, Netta had her knee pressed firmly between the shoulder blades of a handcuffed, facedown man. Earl was clover green, short, and plump. He had an upturned nose and a cute sort of bearded leprechaun face that would have made him look jolly indeed, had he not been foaming at the mouth.

"I'll see you in Desolation, you Agency monsters!" he snarled, squirming under Netta's knee. His struggles were actually jostling the super strong Netta. Jess wondered if he were hopped up on some local stimulant drug.

Netta pulled a credit chit-sized device about the same size as Max's Disruptor remote from her fanny pack and pressed it to his lips. "Quiet you," she said.

Earl continued to hurl inaudible curses at them. Jess could still read each one from the shape his muted mouth made as he spat them out. Netta turned to her, her expression both grave and impressed.

"So," she said. "Not only can you not cross over willingly, but other people also can't cross you either."

Jess wrapped her left two arms around her right two and hugged them against her body for comfort. A future flashed in her mind of sitting under a bridge, rocking back and forth, and clutching her canopic jars while muttering absurdities.

"It would appear so," she said quietly.

Netta beamed at her. "I'm sorry," she said, smiling. "That must be so hard for you."

Netta was quoting a phrase from the 'Relating to People' seminar. She meant well, Jess knew. But her delivery was off.

Jess pinched the bridge of her nose. "Netta, when you're trying to convey sympathy, it helps to not smile."

Netta smiled even bigger. "Okay, but you've got to admit this is kind of awesome. It's like you've gained a bonus Agent power—a power I very much covet. You're uncrossable! You are going to be the best field partner ever. You can take the most dangerous mission roles while I stay relatively safer. We can really surprise the big bad Syndicates with an uncrossable Agent."

Jess shook her head. "Not the big bads," she said. "Those guys don't cross folks. They delete them. I have no idea if my bug can protect me from deletion, and I'm not keen to find out."

At this, Earl thrashed with such intensity that he threw Netta off and kicked himself to standing. Jess lunged at him, wrapping all four arms tight around him. He was shockingly strong. Netta scrambled up and helped Jess hold him.

Only a handful of times had it ever taken two Agents to control a single civilian. Earl's face was mottled and he was screaming a stream of frantic, muted words. His strength made sense at last. Fueled by the adrenaline of emergency, old ladies had lifted whole cars off their husbands. Earl was nearly out of his mind with terror.

Eden started toward them. "I can help," she said.

Netta shook her head. "You've done enough," she said. "You'll only be in the way." Eden's shoulders slumped. Jess winced on her behalf. Netta could be harsh sometimes. She should talk to both women. But later, after they dealt with the struggling Syndicate boss.

"We're going to need a sedative," she said, tightening her grip. Netta nodded.

She pressed her little command remote to the back of Earl' neck and pressed the 'half speed' button to calm him. His thrashing stilled, his skinny legs buckled beneath him, and Jess caught him under the arms of the yellow suit jacket that was too tight to button over his Santa paunch. She eased him to the floor where he sat, watching them with an expression of loathing.

Netta pressed the command remote to his lips and unmuted him. "Start talking," she said.

"Talk?" he said. "To you?" He turned his head and spat.

"You're in a lot of trouble," said Jess. "You fired on two Agents and a local officer. You're looking at a century of jail time minimum. I'd like to know why."

Earl's eyes slid to Eden, then quickly away. He looked deeply unhappy. "I didn't know you were one of ours," he said to Eden. "Sorry, lass."

Eden tilted her chin up. "I'm an officer of the law, not one of your lackeys. No matter what 'understanding' you think you have with the precinct," she said.

He shook his head. "I meant you're an X'er. Not some extradimensional slime. We're in this together against them," he said, pointing at Jess and Netta. "What are petty differences like 'criminal' and 'cop' in the face of an outside threat?"

Jess and Netta exchanged thin-lipped glances. It was not good when a civilian viewed the Agency as an 'outside threat.' Even a minor Syndicate boss like Earl. Only the big bads painted them that way, and those dimensions had become lawless and unpredictable. Terrible for the stability of the starship.

"We came here to rescue you," Jess explained.

Earl scoffed. "I don't know what you twisted creatures are playing at. Deleting people, then pretending you're here to save the day. You're mad or sadistic or both."

"Deleting people?" Jess said. That was serious. If Earl had witnessed an actual deletion, it would explain his terror. It also meant this mission just got a lot more complicated. If Earl had really seen what he thought he'd seen. Jess was reserving judgement. "Who got deleted?" she asked.

Earl laughed bitterly. "My boy, Mac. Watched him dissolve before my eyes, crying out for the Pilot's mercy while his code unraveled."

"Your son? I'm so sorry," said Jess. She didn't need the 'Relating to People' seminar to look properly grim. She hated that the Pilot the dying man called on was really just Max. Sure, Max would show mercy if he could. But he wasn't that kind of god. There wasn't a divine line of code in his entire matrix.

"Not my son," Earl said, as though she were stupid. "My boy. We're a family here at Earl's Syndicate and Distillery. We take care of our own." There was a tilt of pride to his chin. But then he tucked it down. "But not well enough, apparently. I'll have to explain to Mac's mother." He closed his eyes and sighed.

"Who shot him?" Jess asked. There would be a thorough investigation. Deletion was a class one felony. It carried a sentence of immediate forced crossover.

But Earl was shaking his head, a dark and bitter smile on his face. "No one shot him. Don't you even know? It was your Pilot's goddamn Earthquake."

***

Jess guided Earl up the stairs from the Kaiju shelter into the light golden glow of early sunset. The Dimension X wind had grown chillier, and fireworks celebrating the Earthquake sounded across the city, adding bangs and crackles to the continued blarings of car alarms. Jess gulped fresh air, glad to put some distance between her and the strong anise scent of the basement.

Earl was sullen but cooperative. She and Netta each held one of his elbows on the trek back to the squad car. Officer Eden brought up the rear, tripping over rubble as she went. Earl's feet slipped only occasionally as they led him across the debris field that had once been his lair of low-grade, mostly harmless crime.

"How'd your boy die?" Netta asked, with no 'if you don't mind me asking,' preamble as the 'Relating to People' seminar would have recommended.

"Pinned by a falling wall," said Earl. She and Netta exchanged skeptical glances.

"Only lethal assets can delete a soul," said Netta. "Special weapons. Pieces of the environment can't delete someone."

"I know what I saw," he insisted. He nearly turned an ankle on a brownstone block. Jess steadied him and felt him trembling, though his voice had been calm.

"Oh yeah?" said Netta. "Describe how his body looked while he died. Anything stick in your mind?"

It sounded cruel, but Jess understood what Netta was doing. She was trying to catch Earl in a lie with her outrageously insensitive demands. The technique was effective at flushing out falsehoods, though it was hard on people who had actually been traumatized. But Agents' jobs were to uphold order, not coddle victims.

Earl glanced over his shoulder at Eden. "She's all tact and compassion, this one is," he said. Eden only frowned, intent on proving that she was law enforcement first, a Dimension Xer second, no matter what Earl wanted.

"I'll get you some Griefbegone software, old man," Netta said dryly.

Earl stopped cold a few yards from the squad car. "The Hell you will. Mac didn't 'cross.' He got deleted. And I'm damned if I'm not going to feel every drop of that agony."

Jess felt a stirring of deep respect for the man, provided he wasn't delusional or lying. Netta muscled Earl forward again.

"Describe it," said Netta.

He turned his head away, pursing his lips to a thin line. They reached the squad car and stopped Earl outside it while Eden fumbled awkwardly in her pockets, searching for the keys. Netta rolled her eyes. At last, Eden found the fob and unlocked the car. Jess opened the door and Netta started to shove Earl inside.

"Wait," he said, "I tell you how it happened. Mac said he could see the word 'delete' in his vision. He cried that the timer was counting down. He prayed to the Pilot, then…he disintegrated. He turned into a smoke made of black, glittering 1's and 0's, and then even the smoke vanished. And there was this smell. Vomit and brimstone." He trailed off. A sick, yellowish tinge colored Earl's clover-green cheeks and he looked away.

Netta only smirked. "Funny. That's just like how they delete someone in all the TV programs," she said. She put a hand on Earl's head and shoved him down into the back of the squad car and slammed the door.

But when she straightened up, she locked eyes with Jess and frowned. Yes, it was how deletions happened on TV. But the dramatized versions looked remarkably like the real thing, And Jess hadn't experienced a movie yet that captured the smell.

Netta pursed her lips. "I still don't buy it," she said. "Deletion from an Earthquake? It's preposterous."

Jess shrugged. "Earl knew about the smell," she said. "That doesn't come through on the TV programs."

"He's Syndicate!" said Netta. "Sure, he's small-time. But I'm sure he's communicated with the big bads at some point. They could have told Earl how it smells when you unmake a soul. Seems like the kind of small talk they'd make before a meeting."

Jess felt Netta might be grasping at straws. She leaned against the squad car, feeling old and used up. She didn't even know where to begin processing the day's events. She'd tried to cross over twice and failed both times. She didn't even officially exist in her own life anymore. And Vince, the one person who might have offered her sympathy, had already moved on into someone else's arms.

Now there was this possible deletion to contend with, which was going to divert focus from her efforts to cross over.

"There's going to be a big investigation," she said unhappily.

"Which Early probably knows all too well," Netta said. "I know what's going on. I bet he's got a bigger scam going on than what the local police are aware of. He thought we were here to bust him on it, so he shot at us. When he found out different, he invented this deletion nonsense as a smoke screen to cover what's really going on."

Jess rubbed her chin, considering. What Netta was saying made sense. If she were right and there was no deletion, it meant a lot less paperwork and a lot more time Jess got to spend researching code bugs for Dr. Barnes. But somehow, as much as she wanted to avoid red tape and headaches, she wanted to believe in Earl. A criminal, yes, but the head of a crime family? And one who refused the quick, easy way out of grief. And besides, if he were right and the environment could kill, it would mean no one in Dimension X was safe.

"Well, either way, it means a lot of paperwork for us."

Netta nodded gravely. "Do we...take him back to Clarise for questioning?"

Jess locked eyes with Netta, catching her full meaning. Clarise conducted interrogations in the little windowless rooms in a deserted hallway of the outer shell. The Agents stayed far enough away not to hear the screams. The Task Manager always got to the truth, but always at a cost.

"That won't be necessary," said Jess. "You ask the questions. You're plenty intimidating."

Netta looked relieved. Eden stepped forward, shifting from foot to tentative foot. "What can I do to help?" she asked.

"You can stay out of the way," said Netta. "I'm going to record Earl's statement. Then we take him to the precinct holding cell and go back to the Agency. Clarise is going to want to know everything."

Netta ducked into the car and started talking to Earl. Jess was not going to have much unaccompanied time here in Dimension X to access the local medical journals for Dr. Barnes. Even with Netta occupied, there was still Eden standing a few paces away, watching Jess expectantly and hoping for an assignment. Suddenly she had an idea.

A way to kill two birds with one stone.

"Can you do me a favor?" she asked.

Eden's head snapped up, eager and hopeful like a puppy when its owner mentions walk time. "Anything."

"The Pilot sent us here for a specific canopic jar," she said, drawing the slip of yellow paper from her fanny pack and handing it to the officer. "We think it's down in the Kaiju shelter still. Can you look for it while I, err, take some readings?"

"Glad to!" Eden said.

Jess nodded and gave Eden her handheld as well. The device started to beep and a trio of locator triangles on the screen pointed toward the shelter stairs. "This will help," she said, knowing that it wouldn't. But the slow, imprecise Agency tech would buy Jess the time she needed to do her research. If she worked fast. Eden scrambled away from her, slipping on the treacherous, uneven ground.

Jess switched on her VR goggles and connected to the ambient Dimension X Wi-Fi network. She searched the most prestigious local medical journals, clicking through articles on rare code diseases.

A couple of cases caught her attention. One patient's whole appearance changed every time he sneezed. There was another case of two souls crossing over into the same infant Incarnation. The child—children?—grew up with one body and six canopic jars full of talent. They had been valedictorian of their high school and were currently the mayor of a small town about 50 miles south of X City. Interesting stuff, but not applicable to Jess's situation.

At last, she found a list of people in Dimension X who couldn't cross over. Attached to each name was a description of the patient's code anomaly. She didn't understand any of it. Jess couldn't copy the medical charts, but she could keep them temporarily in her RAM and relay what she'd seen to Dr. Barnes verbally, provided she didn't clear her cache.

She'd started another search when the ground lurched beneath her feet and she lost her footing. The earth rolled under her as she clung to a steel I-beam like it was the side of a life raft on a stormy ocean. A rumbling vibration shivered through the ground. Next to her, the squad car's alarm began to honk. Just as suddenly as it had started, the motion stopped. An aftershock from Amira's Earthquake, she realized.

Then her VR lenses flashed bright red.

`Warning! Deletion Detected!`

Three locator triangles blinked on and zeroed in on the top of the Kaiju shelter staircase. Eden. Jess dropped into the deep well of her training, vaulted up and ran, feet flying over shifting rubble. In this mode the terrain did not slow her down. Her legs pumped, burning through her energy, but it didn't matter. She had to get to Eden.

She stopped at the top of the shelter stairs. The rush of her training mode vanished in the face of impossibility. She was already too late. The deletion had already happened. Rubble filled the stairwell down to the now-collapsed shelter. The sickly-sweet smell of anise mixed with another horrible scent; the detail the multi-sensory TV programs never got right because you had to witness a real deletion to know. The bile and brimstone smell that always lingered for a minute or two after a human soul had unraveled forever.

6

The white light of the Jump back to the outer shell spread in Jess's vision, obscuring her view of Dimension X. She was glad to be leaving the place. What had begun as a diverting mission to a happy city filled with celebration had turned into tragedy.

She and Netta had brought Earl to the local Justice Center and handed him over to Eden's precinct captain—a tall, thin, sober fellow named Felix, with onyx black skin and a bushy, metallic gold mustache. They'd told him about Eden's deletion. He'd accepted the news with quiet gravitas and thanked the Agents for their work. Earl had then asked Captain Felix if he would be using Griefbegone that evening. Captain Felix said, 'surely not,' and the two Dimension X'ers had shared a look of understanding solidarity before a jailer had marched Earl away to his new cell.

She and Netta had dismissed themselves from the Justice Center, pressed their control molars, and transported back to Agency headquarters. Now, the familiar vibrations of the outer shell were rattling Jess's bones. A sharp smell of astringent and lemon hit her nose. The whiteness of her vision cleared, and the shiny black walls, floors, and ceiling of the portal room surrounded her once again.

Netta materialized beside her. The indigo woman put a hand on Jess's shoulder. "You look terrible," she said.

"Gee, thanks."

"What I mean is, why don't you go home? I'll report to Clarise about the deletions. Amira's going to want to know everything Earl said."

"Clarise sure isn't," said Jess. "This is the kind of thing she very much doesn't want to know about. She's going to doubt any report of potential problems with using Max's powers behind his back. It's her pet project. The reason she gets up in the mornings."

Netta grimaced. "I know," she said. Netta looked a little sick to her stomach. She started toward the exit. Jess followed.

"Brave of you to offer, then," said Jess. "Are you sure?"

Taking on such a risk was unlike Netta. Netta looked away and shrugged. "I was really snippy with Eden that whole mission. I made her feel so bad about herself. Really mucked up her last hour alive. I think maybe I owe…something."

Jess nodded. She felt similarly guilty. She'd sent the rookie back into that Kaiju shelter so she could do her selfish research in peace. If Jess hadn't been so wrapped up in her own problems, Eden might still be alive.

But she knew she didn't have the energy to give Clarise bad news right now. Tangling with the Task Manager meant guarding her emotions. Watching her words carefully enough not to set the boss off. And today had been the worst day of Jess's life since the day her mother had crossed over.

"Alright," she said. "I will take you up on your generous offer. I just have to get something from Veden first."

She pressed the exit panel, and the door hissed open. Dick Veden stood on the other side, his purple face set in a hard scowl. He was holding a file in one hand and a gallon-sized plastic evidence bag in the other. Inside were the red and green flannel pajamas Jess had left draped over the portal room console.

"Hey," she said. "Give those back!"

He held them above her head so she couldn't reach them unless she wanted to jump around like an idiot. Veden was the only person in the outer shell tall enough to pull this stunt with Jess. She tensed her jaw and glared at him. She was tired and spent and felt far, far too old for this nonsense. She considered punching him, but that would be 'wrong' since he hadn't officially challenged her to single combat.

"Really, Veden?" said Netta, giving voice to Jess's irritation.

"I am only doing my job," he said. "Leaving personal effects on Agency equipment violates Workspace Order 72. I had no choice but to confiscate these."

He stuffed the evidence bag with Jess's only clothes under his hairy armpit. Jess suddenly wanted the PJ's back a whole lot less. She wondered if the plastic evidence bag was enough to guard the garment from Veden's body odor.

The Security Chief riffled in his pocket and handed her a blue slip of paper.

"Here's your violation citation," he said. "One more, and I send you to the Penalty Box."

Jess took the paper and frowned. "I thought it was three strikes," she said.

Veden puffed out his chest. "It was until two months ago," he said. "HR finally ratified my suggested protocol changes. It's two now, and that's two too many, if you want my opinion. I hate second chances for rule breakers, let alone third chances. It's a crime against the universe to keep Lady Justice waiting."

Jess folded all her arms and jutted a stubborn hip out.

"Look, Dick," she said. "I have to go home, and those are my only clothes. Rules say I have to return my borrowed Jumpsuit. Rules also prohibit nudity outside the locker rooms. Which of the rules do you want me to violate?"

Veden's mouth fell open. He shook his head, disbelieving. "The rules..." he muttered. "They shouldn't contradict each other. If the rules are correct, there should always be a clear path forward..."

"But there isn't, is there?" Jess said coolly. Netta was smirking beside her. Veden's lower left eyelid jumped. His mouth moved wordlessly as he performed inscrutable, regulatory calculations in his head.

Finally, he focused on her. "Okay," he said. "Keep the Jumpsuit for now. It's technically still allowed out into the other dimensions, and so it is a lesser rules violation than nudity or returning your garment and therefore tampering with evidence."

He reached into his pocket and pulled out a notepad full of blank violation tickets. He began writing another one.

"That's not fair!" said Jess. "You can't put me in the Penalty Box for something you're making me do."

"Oh, this ticket is for me," he said. "I, Ricardo K. Veden, am guilty of attempting to coerce a fellow employee into violating two separate outer shell rules. This citation will serve as a lesson to me. Motivation to amend the rules into a more harmonious symphony of lawfulness."

"A wha--?" she said.

"Oh, and here is that file you ordered ma'am." he said. "He handed Jess her HR folder and marched off, muttering ordinance numbers to himself. Jess watched him go, shaking her head.

"I am really glad he keeps failing his Agent exams," said Netta. "I feel like he would complicate our workdays." Jess nodded in whole-hearted agreement. "Listen," Netta continued. "I have to go report the deletions to Clarise and our failure to recover the canopic jar to Max. You better go home before I chicken out. Something tells me we'll need you at the top of your game tomorrow."

"Okay. I'll just Jump home then, since Veden took my clothes, and the only thing I needed in the outer shell is this file."

Netta nodded and left. The door slid closed behind her, and Jess was alone in the portal room. She was probably too worn out to do her paperwork, but she ought to try anyway. The sooner she could rein-state herself as an Agent, the sooner she could get her salary and health benefits back. She could pay Dr. Barnes and hopefully be done with this Incarnation, including her new, horrible memories of Officer Eden.

She moved to the console and spread the file across it. Another violation probably, but what Veden didn't know wouldn't trouble him. She leafed through the papers. Her resume. Numerous commen-dations from her teammates. Even more numerous censure reports from Clarise, each with a yellow slip of paper stapled to the top and 'You can't fire her, she's my favorite,' written across them in Max's childish scrawl.

At the back of the file was her resignation letter. The word 'Approved' was stamped across it in green ink. But there were two extra pages clipped to the back—a formal protest against Jess crossing over. A judge's red stamp marked the protest as 'Denied,' which was unsurprising, since almost no one questioned the crossover plans of someone who had lived past 100. Jess had reached a full century two months before.

She skimmed the document. It was politely worded. "Just not sure it's appropriate, given Jessamae's arguably young age…" and "…rather rash and hasty decision," and "…all due respect to her autonomy, but…" Jess frowned. Who would dare?

She turned to the signature page and gasped. Vince.

A small flash of anger heated her cheeks. How dare he? It wasn't his decision to make! And yet…and yet. It felt good. He hadn't really been ready to let her go after all, no matter how often he had assured her that the choice was hers entirely. That he supported her decision. That he was satisfied that she'd fulfilled her marriage agreements. Her husband had wanted her still, and had tried, and failed, to hold on.

***

Jess didn't use the portal room to Jump home. She pressed her belly button instead. It was a feature of digital humans that if you triggered a sensor inside your belly button, you returned to your home dimension. Most people never left their home dimensions. But it was a failsafe installed to ensure people could get back home again if they got lost.

Jess materialized in the living room of her former homepage. There was a lingering aroma of spaghetti sauce and noodles, but the ticking wall clock read 8:23. Well past dinner. It was fine. Jess had no appetite anyway.

The living room looked just the same as it had when she'd been lady of the house. Lemon yellow walls; a white sofa with navy blue sailboats, anchors and compass rosettes patterned across it; and a thick, soft teal carpet. Anne had yet to redecorate. Jess had expected the interloper to have put her personal stamp on everything by now, like a cat scent-marking her new territory. But perhaps Anne was too wrapped up in wedding planning. She'd get around to it, though. Jess was sure.

She took a step toward the sofa and froze. Her Jumpsuit boots felt heavy, dirty, and damaging pressed into the luxurious carpet. Normally, Jess wouldn't give a fig about tromping around in the living room wearing work boots. But this was Anne's plush, teal carpet now. Jess was a guest/intruder, and what were Anne' rules about shoes on carpets?

She would have to ask. Then Jess noticed her outfit and realized she maybe might not have to. Her Jumpsuit had automatically chameleoned itself to fit the local environment. Her heavy-duty tactical boots appeared as medium-sized slipper socks that looked like they were made of purple Muppet pelts. And, of course, her skintight black Jumpsuit looked just like the only piece of Jess's clothing the environment recognized—a pair of red and green flannel pajamas.

"Sonofa—" she muttered, but didn't finish, because swearing was rude.

Maybe she could fiddle with the Jumpsuit settings manually. It probably wouldn't go well, though. Her e-tailoring skills left something to be desired. And Veden would probably write her up again for tampering with the matrix of borrowed equipment. Her heart sank a little. Not even her clothes belonged to her anymore.

A mrrrrow! sounded at her feet. She looked down. Hippopotamus was nudging her, weaving between her ankles with glad greetings. She felt herself smile. This little guy, at least, was well and truly hers. An unexpected blessing from not having crossed over back in Dimension X.

She bent and scratched his head. He seemed lonely. If Vince were there, the cat would have him pinned to a chair and left him unable to get up lest he disturb their four-footed master. Which meant Vince must not be there.

Jess found that she was sad about that now that she'd seen his appeal letter. She wanted to talk to him about it. And then what? Patch things up? What a dreadful bother that would be for Vince at this juncture, with Anne and the wedding and everything.

She felt a sharp twinge under her breastbone, like a lashing from a snapped violin string. An echo of the blinding-blue feeling she'd experienced in the Kaiju shelter when she thought she was about to cross over. She had left so much undone in this lifetime. Perhaps she ought to speak up, despite the inconvenience.

A jangly sound of piano keys startled her from her reverie. Hippopotamus was sitting beside a vase of begonias atop Jess's upright piano, blinking slowly at her with big, orange-brown eyes. He'd apparently played a few notes on his way up. She smiled fondly at the little goober.

Then she realized. Her piano. The one with JK for Jessamae Kensington inlaid into the rosewood fallboard. Or 'Just Kidding,' she thought automatically. She wished her mother had paid more attention to what Jess's initials would spell when naming her. Vince hadn't tagged the instrument for the estate sale after all. She wondered what it meant that he hadn't auctioned it off. Her piano was the most personal item she owned that she hadn't placed into a canopic jar. Vince didn't play and neither did Anne. What did he want it for?

She pictured him in the days before the Griefbegone software, tagging her possessions like a dutiful husband preparing for widowerhood. But finding himself unable to part with something so dear to his wife's heart. Conflicted and torn. Anguished at the coming goodbye but knowing that he must not interfere. Then, writing the appeal letter in secret. Vince's quiet ways of screaming 'no' at the abandonment to come. Jess had always 'loved' Vince as she ought to, but she'd never let herself feel him deeply. She'd never felt anything deeply—except the music. Perhaps it was time to change that.

She sat down at the piano and lifted the fallboard. She placed all four hands on the cool, smooth keys and began to play. She began with Thelonius Monk's 'Round Midnight.' A jazz- age piano standard written with two-handed performers in mind. Introspective, melancholy, and simple enough to play. Jess didn't think she had the energy for a more challenging piece. As her fingers fell and chords sang out, she found the beauty of them made little cuts through the gray soul fog, and on the other side was a light so bright it hurt, but a good hurt. A living hurt. That feeling had always been in the music. She just hadn't paused long enough to feel it.

"Oh, how original your sound is!"

Jess stopped playing and turned. Anne stood in the doorway cradling a sample page of fabric swatches in her pale 'natural human' arms. The squares were lacy or beaded. Some of them embroidered. But all of them were a wedding white. A moment later Vince rounded the corner. He was carrying a shoebox filled with various sample boutonnieres. Carnations, roses, and stargazer lilies.

"Jess sure does love piano," he said.

"I was thinking," said Anne. "If you haven't crossed over by the wedding next week, would you consider playing our ceremony music?

It would be a nice way to smooth things over. Neighbors are starting to talk because you're still here when you shouldn't be. It's a bit awkward, but if you were part of the wedding it would show everyone that you approve. That there aren't any hard feelings. That we are all perfectly happy." She paused a moment. "And I like how you play."

Nice of her to tack that on at the end.

"Next week?" Jess said.

Her voice squeaked. That didn't give her much time to reach Vince's heart…if that's truly what she wanted to do.

But Vince chuckled. "Gracious of you Pookie, but Jess will be there anyway, because she hasn't got any hard feelings. And wouldn't you rather have a professional play for our wedding? One with a lifetime or two of canopic experience? Besides, I know Jess. She loves piano, yes. But she's just an amateur. A private hobbyist. She never plays outside the house. Isn't that right, Dar—Jess?"

Jess nodded. Numb. She didn't want to play in any public, much less at Vince and Anne's wedding. But she couldn't deny it stung to hear Vince call her 'just an amateur.' Though it was the truth.

"Pity," said Anne. "I quite like your style, actually. Raw and authentic. Not at all polished. But that's what makes it interesting. Oh, well. We probably shouldn't count on you being here anyway."

Jess's ears burned. She wanted at least another lifetime of canopic talent cultivation before performing. Of all the outsiders to overhear her practicing, it had to be Anne listening and judging. 'Not at all polished' and 'raw and authentic' were polite synonyms for 'bad.' Everyone knew that. She pulled back from the keyboard before she could further disgrace the instrument.

Vince and Anne didn't seem to notice her humiliation though. They were rubbing noses and kissing. Each lip-smacking 'muah' noise hit Jess like a dart sticking in a dart board. Only with bonus nausea. And something else. A wistfulness. Vince had never been that affectionate with her. He might have been if she'd let him. But she'd made clear that she considered this sort of behavior to be childish nonsense. Which it was…and yet.

It put her in mind of Wendy's mother in Peter Pan. "She was a lovely lady…and her sweet, mocking mouth had one kiss on it that Wendy could never get, though there it was, perfectly conspicuous in the right-hand corner." She'd felt that way about all kisses, ever since she was a child. Not the physical act of lip-smushing. She had plenty of that starting in middle school. But the metaphorical kind from the book. Something intimate and personal. Something mysterious that other people kept secret in themselves except to share with those they especially treasured.

That kind of kiss, she felt, was never meant for her. And it would be crass and boorish of her to chase after them. They were out of reach, and best to leave it that way. But now she found that she had always longed to be the person that the precious, held-back kisses were for.

Watching Vince and Anne canoodle in the doorway made her think she had maybe been right not to get too close to Vince, because here he was with Anne now. Happy and free. In love and allowed to show it, as he'd never been with her.

The pair of them left the living room and giggled and flirted down the hallway, clutching wedding planning supplies and chatting happily. Jess was all alone in the living room with the piano Vince had kept.

She felt like she'd been too late. The piano. Vince's cross-over objection. These were the unspoken love letters from a man who was already gone. His heart for her lost, changed by the Griefbegone software. It seemed the real Jess and the real Vince had missed each other by mere moments. Like Juliette, Jess had awakened at last from a too-long soul slumber, ready to love. Only to find Romeo poisoned and cold on the floor of the catacombs.

There was a scraping noise and a crash. Hippopotamus had pushed the delicate vase of begonias off the top of the piano and was twitching his tail angrily. Staring at the interesting wreck he'd made on the floor.

"You said it, boy," she said.

7

Jess leaned against the cold wall of the stark, sterile examination room staring at the obnoxious medical advice posters and waiting for Dr. Barnes. She was not there as a patient, so she would be damned if she was going to climb up onto that blue vinyl examination table with the flimsy, tissue paper aisle runner. She'd rather stand, thank you, no matter how long it took.

The antiseptic smell of antivirus software assaulted her nose. The ticking of the wall clock assaulted her temples in throbbing bursts of rhythmic time. Her sleep mode the previous night had been fitful. Officer Eden haunted her dream cycles. The dreamscape ground rolling under her feet from the replayed aftershock, the scraping noise of a debris field shaken from below. It disturbed her stomach and set her teeth on edge. Then, the VR goggles flashing a hopeless red with news of the rookie's deletion.

When Jess awoke from the nightmares to find she hadn't miraculously crossed over, she'd gone to Barnes's office to give him the list of Dimension Xers with crossover bugs before heading back to the Agency with her newly refreshed HR file. She hoped the papers she had filled out the previous night would work. Unless she got officially reinstated, she didn't have the health insurance or salary to pay Barnes. She wondered if he'd even try to charge her for merely dropping off the list. If anyone could find a billing code for 'Patient told me about an interesting article,' it would be him.

There was a knock at the door. Before Jess could answer, Dr. Barnes burst through. The light-blue man was wearing a normal, white lab coat this time and smiling with far too much cheerful enthusiasm. What if I'd been changing? she thought, annoyed.

"Oh, good," he said. "You didn't take a paper gown this time."

"Why would I want one?"

"Sometimes people get confused and think they're freebies. But they're specialized medical supplies for paying custom... err—patients—only."

Jess rolled her eyes. "Really expensive, are they?"

"They cost 50 credit chits apiece," he said.

She couldn't believe her ears. The one-sizer gowns spooled out of a box of 100, like low-budget, wearable toilet paper. The scratchy kind. They couldn't cost that much, could they? "Fifty!" she exclaimed. "That's as much as a calamari dinner in the Octopus Dimension."

"The Octopus Dimension? So, the rumors are true!" Barnes gasped. He hopped up onto the examination table and leaned toward her, hands folded under his chin like he was waiting for a bit of hot gossip. "Are they cannibals, then? The sapient octopus people? If we cross over to that dimension, will we grow up partaking in their brutal customs and simply accept them as normal?"

Jess bit her tongue. This was how salacious inter-dimensional rumors began. People were curious about what awaited them in their next lives. It was only natural that speculation abounded, and the Agency allowed it to flourish. There was no reason to crack down. But sometimes a particularly wild story would spread so wide that the Agency got angry letters complaining about amoral dimensions and demanding that the Task Manager 'fix those barbarians' so that nice, normal civilians didn't cross over into some lawless backwater world and become degenerates. She thought she'd better set Barnes straight with the boring truth.

"No. Calamari is squid. Not the sentient octopi with the human souls. The squid creatures are actually descendants of the Pilot's Kaiju that assimilated into the local ecosystem."

"Fascinating," said Barnes. "I'd love to see that."

"Me too," Jess said, wistfully. When she had joined the Agency, she thought she would be seeing all the most interesting places inside the Voyager 2.0. But Max was always sending her on fetching missions in the snoozeville dimensions. "But I didn't come here to talk about the Octopus Dimension," she said. "I came to show you what I found in Dimension X."

She poked her eyeballs and a transparent, blue-green hologram of the list she'd memorized beamed from her pupils and hovered in the air two feet in front of her. Barnes read it with interest. Then he sighed heavily and seemed to deflate.

"Oh. This. I've read it already," he said. He sounded disappointed.

Jess blinked the hologram away and narrowed her eyes. "How did you already read this? It's from another dimension."

The doctor reached into his lab coat and produced a Frankenstein-ish electronic device that was held together with digi-tape and scrolling code across a broken screen. It looked like it might have been a handheld sometime in the past. It was difficult to tell.

"What's that?" she asked.

Barnes leaned back with an air of exaggerated casualness and fixed her with a hard smile. "I'm surprised you don't recognize it. You crushed it, after all."

Could it be? Barnes's handheld with the Agency's comms line in the cache? It had been nothing but bits the last time she'd seen it. It would take a true master to piece that thing back together.

"You rebuilt it?" she asked.

He picked some lint off his lab coat and shrugged. "It was nothing," he said. Jess thought Barnes knew full well that it was not 'nothing.' "Just a little canopic skill I've been cultivating over several hundred lifetimes. All it takes is a little persistence. Tending the canopic gifts you were born with, crossing over with them. Anyone could do it."

Jess knew she was oddly fickle for dropping three of her four inborn canopic jar skills in exchange for a cat, a book, and an amateur piano aptitude. Most people did just what Barnes had done, arrive as newborns and let the canopic jars they came with direct their lives. Everyone got better at what they were already good at and took their skills with them to their next lives.

However, a talent like Barnes had just displayed meant that his soul was very old indeed. Perhaps one of the original souls that the carbon-based humans had programmed into the Voyager 2.0. Something still didn't make sense, though.

"How did you see the Dimension X list? All you had was the Agency's comms number."

"I used the comms line to reverse hack the pan-dimensional ansible system. Now I have access to all the medical journals in all the multiverse of worlds!"

His eyes glittered with the avarice of limitless, forbidden knowledge. Jess's stomach lurched. This was very bad. She'd meant only to feed him memorized tidbits of information. A manageable amount of contamination. Less impactful than a canopic jar. Jess was lucky the doctor was too myopic in his focus on code bugs to realize it wasn't only medical journals he could access. It was everything.

"You're engaging in the cross-contamination of dimensions," she warned.

"Which isn't illegal for us civilians," he pointed out. "Only for you pan-dimensional Agent types."

"Because it shouldn't be possible!" she said. "There shouldn't have to be a law against the impossible."

"That is not my problem," Barnes said primly.

She shook her head, disgusted. "And you pretend to be so moral."

"Not moral," he said, wrinkling his nose. "Moral people follow personal, internal codes, which are shifting, amorphous things. You never know where you stand with moral people. They can 'just decide' they'd been mistaken and completely reinvent themselves. I'm ethical. I follow external principles that I don't have the power to change. You're on much firmer ground with an ethical person than a moral one."

She was not sure that was how ethics and morals actually worked. Dr. Barnes reminded her of a scheming fae lord in a fairy tale. Completely adherent to the letter of the law, but slippery as hell in matters regarding the spirit of it. She would have to deal with him and his illegal ansible. But later.

"Okay, smart guy. What did you find, since you already saw my list."

"Has your health insurance been reinstated?" he asked.

Jess cleared her throat. "Heh. As soon as I get back to the Agency and file the paperwork."

He shook his head. "Not good enough. It would still be unethical to tell you anything. Which is a pity. I have information that would blow your mind, if only you could afford to know it."

He turned from her and looked down at the code that was scrolling across the screen of the Frankenphone. Jess recognized an opportunity.

"Ethical this!" she said. She snatched the device from his hands as fast as a striking mamba. He leaped to his feet.

"Hey, that's mine!" he said.

"Want to fight me for it?" Jess made a fist, cracking the knuckles of her lower right hand. Barnes took a step back, remembering who he was dealing with. "Besides," she said. "I seem to remember commandeering this gadget on behalf of the Agency last time we met. Unless you filled out your paperwork and had it approved, the handheld is technically still mine."

He rubbed his chin and looked thoughtful. "What if there was a way I could tell you what was wrong with you. Ethically, I mean."

She folded the three arms she wasn't using to hold the device. "Is this a real loophole in your code of conduct? Or did you 'just decide' to reinvent yourself?"

He waved a dismissive hand and chuckled. "No, no, no. You see, if I tell you as a doctor, I have to charge you. If I leave out all the technical jargon and tell you as a friend, well that's another matter. That kind of consultation could be free."

Jess raised an eyebrow. "And we're friends, are we?"

He flashed her a cutting smile. "We are if you give me my handheld back."

"I'm listening," she said. There was no way she was giving the device back. But Barnes didn't need to know that.

He perked up and gave her a more genuine grin. "Okay!" he said. "This is what's going on. Open that device you stole from me and hit the middle green button." She did as he asked. The screen displayed some numbers that Jess didn't understand.

"What's this?" she asked.

"This is a really bad code tangle. Worst I've ever seen." He was smiling very wide. She guessed the enthusiastic maniac had been bursting at the seams to tell her what he'd found. "And here—and I'll spare you the technical details because I'm ethically obligated to—is the jammer signal responsible."

"Jammer signal?" she asked.

"We can't make them here in Garden, but the Syndicate in the Noir Dimension can. They invented the jammers to keep people who owed them money from crossing over and defaulting."

"Clever," she said.

"I thought so too," he said admiringly.

"What does it mean for me?"

"It means someone put this in you on purpose. You're tied to that person and only they can untangle you."

"What?" Jess said. She felt crawly under her skin. This was worse than merely being code sick. Someone had infiltrated her systems, and now, in some capacity, they had her. Like she was a fish with a hook in its mouth, waiting for an unknown fisherman to reel her in."

"Any idea who it could be?" asked Dr. Barnes.

"How should I know?" she whispered, still reeling.

"They'd probably have tried to blackmail you," he said. "Get you to do something for them."

"Nobody's done anything like that to me," she said. She thought about who would want to keep her in Garden. Could it be Vince? But if it were him, he wouldn't have taken the Griefbegone. Then she knew.

"Clarise," she said. "The Task Manager really wanted me to stay and wrangle Max."

"Who's Max?" asked Dr. Barnes.

"Nobody," said Jess. "But the Task Manager wants me here so much she won't reinstate my health insurance."

"I thought you said that was coming along. Any day now," Dr. Barnes accused.

"It is. I went behind her back," said Jess, stowing the device and preparing to leave. How was she going to get Clarise to release her jammer signal? Would the boss even admit what she'd done?

"Hey," said Barnes. "My handheld. You said you'd give it back."

"I said I was listening," said Jess. "I agreed to nothing." She felt a little pleased with herself. There was something of a tricksy hairsplitting fae in her as well, she decided.

Dr. Barnes scowled and folded his arms. But he looked merely annoyed, rather than defeated. Jess groaned. "You don't seem too upset," she said. "You've got backups, don't you?"

He rolled his eyes. "Well of course I have backups. I'm not an idiot."

Jess pinched the bridge of her nose to combat the gathering headache. She'd have to call in a raid as soon as she got back to the Agency. It would be a pain and would generate additional heaps of paperwork.

Then Dr. Barnes's device vibrated angrily in her hand. A red warning message flashed across it.

Agents: Emergency meeting. All butts back at HQ by 1100 hours.

It was from Clarise. Dr. Barnes should very much not have access to the private Agency comms line. He could learn the truth about Max, decide to tell people, and throw Garden into chaos.

"You spied on the Agency's comms," she said. "You are in big trouble."

"There's nothing in the medical regulations about that," he said. "No one's going to revoke my license."

"It's not a medical regulation. It's a pan-dimensional law. You could face jail time," she said.

Barnes's eyebrows went up. His mouth formed a round 'o,' shocked to remember there were ethical schema that had nothing to do with medicine. But it was almost 1000 hours and Jess wanted to get back to the Agency well in advance of Clarise's 'emergency meeting.' Something had set the Task Manager off. It was probably to do with the Dimension X deletions. And now that Jess knew what Clarise had done to her code—what the woman was capable of, she thought it wise to go early and ask the other Agents what they thought the meeting might be about.

"I'll deal with you later," she said to Barnes. "Don't touch any of your backup devices until you hear from me. Your freedom may depend on it."

Barnes nodded. For the first time, he looked unsure of himself.

8

The white light of the dimension Jump faded from Jess's vision, and the shiny, black portal room walls came into focus. She was so mad at Clarise that one of the little veins in her forehead was already throbbing. The low-level vibrations of the propulsor engines and the pervasive astringent of antivirus software further stoked her headache.

If she bumped into Clarise just then, she'd probably start shouting accusations. The Task Manager would deny them and tell her she was crazy, and Jess would never learn the truth, much less get Clarise to release the jammer signal. It was best to avoid the boss until Jess had a chance to cool her head and learn what the 'emergency meeting' on Dr. Barnes's handheld was supposed to be about.

She walked to one of the computer consoles to consult the active map of the outer shell. She stared at the layout. The diagram showed every room and office of the outer shell with icons representing each employee. The HR office stood empty. Jess rolled her eyes. Apparently 'HR Appreciation Week' was still in full swing. Max's icon was turning circles at the center of the globe room. He must be spinning in his office chair. Typical. Veden was in the upper right corner of the gym where the new Buttocks 5000™ machine was. The six engineers were all at their desks. The cleaning staff moved through the hallways like Pac Man ghosts. Amira and Jerome were in the break room.

At last, her eyes rested on the briefing room. Two icons indicated that Clarise was inside with Netta. A pulsing, purple rectangle surrounded Netta's icon. Uh oh. The Penalty Box.

Clarise reserved the transparent prism-shaped cell for the really bad mess ups. It looked like the Penalty Boxes they used for hockey matches, only the walls were made of an energy-reinforced plexiglass. It was a sort of cosmic time-out Clarise put employees in to shield them from her own wrath until she'd calmed down and decided whether to demote them, fire them, or cross them over. Netta's icon wasn't moving. The poor thing was probably catatonic with fear.

Jess downloaded the active map onto Barnes's Frankenphone and hurried out of the portal room. She turned down the left branch of the hall toward the break room to talk to Amira and Jerome. She pressed her hand to the panel and the door hissed open, and the smell of cheap, Agency coffee wafted out. An industrial-sized pot of the stuff was percolating wetly on the chrome kitchenette counter. Jerome and Amira sat on folding chairs around one of three round, polyvinyl breakfast tables, holding steaming mugs and looking miserable.

Jess was struck with a sense of foreboding. She rarely saw Amira looking troubled about anything. Jerome just looked normal. Amira noticed her then.

"Thank goodness you're back!" she cried.

"What happened?" asked Jess. "Why is Netta in the Penalty Box?"

Amira tugged nervously at the hem of her Shayla scarf. She motioned for Jess to take the third chair at the table. She entered the break room, the door hissed closed behind her, and she sank into the seat to listen.

"Netta claims my sweet little Earthquake deleted two people," said Amira.

"Poor parenting, if you want my opinion," muttered Jerome.

Amira whapped him lightly on the shoulder, but otherwise ignored him. "It can't be true, can it?" she asked.

"There were deletions," Jess said. "I saw one of them on my own VR headset. We don't know the cause for sure, but it's possible."

Amira shook her head. "No. I won't believe it. Everyone knows our tech makes mistakes out in the dimensions."

"That's exactly what Clarise said before she put Netta in the Penalty Box," said Jerome. He picked absently at a bit of lint on his Jumpsuit.

"There was also a local witness," said Jess.

"He's just a Syndicate boss though, right?" said Amira hopefully. "Clarise thinks he might have been lying. Or delusional. Or even responsible for the deletions himself?" Her voice went up at the end like a question. Amira was clutching at straws. There was nothing she hated more than putting the brakes on a science project.

Jess shook her head. "I don't think so. He was already in custody when the second deletion took place."

Amira looked deeply unhappy. "That's what Netta said. Then Clarise…hit her with the crop." She buried her face in her hands. Even Jerome winced.

Jess's bulging temple vein throbbed harder. It had been bad enough when Clarise had merely touched Amira with the lethal asset. But to actually strike Netta with something that could delete her. Just for delivering bad news?

Clarise had hit Jess with it once, but the threat of deletion had been warranted in her case. Jess had forgiven Clarise even before she'd been hit. However, deserving the blow hadn't made it less frightening.

"Amira," Jess said, as gently as she could. "If something is wrong with the natural disasters, wouldn't you rather know than proceed anyway and maybe delete some people?"

Amira wiped her nose on her Jumpsuit sleeve and nodded. "Yes, yes, you're right. But it isn't up to me. And I don't think Clarise is going to let us back off the project."

Jess frowned. "Why? What's got her so hyped up about this? Hitting Netta. Ignoring warning signs. This is bordering on unhinged."

Amira sighed heavily. "I shouldn't be telling you this," she said.

"And yet it sounds as though you are about to anyway," muttered Jerome.

"We weren't supposed to tell you since you're so close to Max…," said Amira.

"I am not close to Max!" Jess protested.

Jerome and Amira shared a knowing smirk. Jess ground her teeth.

"Anyway," said Amira. "Given the circumstances, I think you ought to know. We've had a breakthrough. Clarise had me working on the Pilot's Disruptor remote. She wanted me to fix the shock effect you broke."

Jess nodded. Ah yes. The reason Clarise had hit her with the riding crop two years earlier. The Pilot's Disruptor remote was an ancient bit of code. A fail-safe to neutralize an all-powerful Pilot, should something like what had happened with Max happen. Which it had. The remote still knocked the Pilot unconscious, but previously, it delivered an agonizing electrical charge too.

Jess had gotten tired of watching Clarise zap Max whenever he pissed her off—which was often. The remote was meant to be a one-time safeguard, not a continuous, button-pushing anti-Pilot extravaganza. The pain served no purpose, so Jess had broken that particular feature.

She understood why Clarise had hit her. The remote was a one-of-a-kind artifact from the dawn of time. The carbon-based humans had built it into the ship's operating system themselves. It was completely irreplaceable, and Jess had risked destroying the whole device when they had a dangerous Pilot who very much needed to be controlled remotely. She had never once regretted the choice, though.

"Did you get it working again?" Jess asked.

She tried to sound casual. To appear uninterested in the answer. She would break the damn thing again if she had to.

"No," said Amira. "But I discovered a way to keep Max in a permanent coma so we can use his powers."

"What?" Jess said.

"No more two-minute typhoons. No more sprints to the hub of the globe room to deliver canopic jars. Heck, no more missions to fetch Max his canopic jars in the first place. The Agency can run the ship the way it was meant to be run, with controlled chaos. Only we'll do it by committee instead of relying on a single, godlike mastermind. It's everything Clarise has been working toward. We were scheduled to put him under tomorrow."

Jess blinked. She wasn't sure she was hearing right. To be honest, most of the plan sounded great. Only she didn't want Max under forever. Just long enough for the rest of them to get work done.

"Permanently comatose?" She said. "Would he ever wake up again?"

"I don't know," admitted Amira. "And Clarise doesn't care."

"Actually, she'd prefer it if he didn't," said Jerome, taking a sip of his coffee. Jess must have made a face because Jerome said, "See, Clarise knew you wouldn't like it."

"That's why she threatened me with the crop yesterday," said Amira. "I almost let it slip right in front of you."

"What about you two?" Jess asked. "Are you okay with Max just… being gone forever?"

"He won't be gone," said Jerome. "But he will be quiet for once."

Amira shrugged. "Look, I feel bad for the guy, I really do. He's just a petty little idiot who got caught up in something too big for him to handle. But he's become a danger to the ship. I wanted to give him a choice, you know? See if he'd step down on his own. But Clarise doesn't want to lose the element of surprise. Max can delete people with his thoughts if he wants to."

"It's a wonder he hasn't already," said Jerome. "Given how much he and Clarise antagonize one another."

What Jerome had just said was always in the back of Jess's mind. Before Jess had arrived at the Agency with her uncanny ability to tell when Max was about to wake up, Clarise had gotten caught inside the force cage with a fully conscious Max. He could have deleted her, but he hadn't, despite the electrical shocks and social isolation. The worst Max had done when his chief tormentor fell under his power was to zap Clarise's underwear onto the outside of her pants and give her a wedgie. It gave Jess hope for Max that he was not half the monster he could be if he so chose.

And she hated how dead he looked when he went under. She couldn't explain it, but Jess felt like a mother hen to all the Agents—and to Max too. Protective, like a herding dog. Whenever Max was knocked out, Jess sensed a nagging absence in her flock where he ought to have been. When he at last resurfaced from the deep waters, she felt like one of her sheep had finally wandered back home.

But the good of the whole Voyager 2.0 did outweigh one irritating little man. Only…

"But now we don't know whether unconscious Max is even more dangerous than awake Max," she said.

Jerome nodded. "This deletion accusation is rather inconvenient," he said.

"It could all be coincidence," said Amira. "Maybe we're just flinching at shadows."

"You've both met Netta," said Jess. "She would never have risked Clarise's wrath unless she really believed there was something wrong."

Jerome closed his eyes and nodded. "Unfortunately, it is so. I am certain of few things, but if Netta considered Clarise to be the lesser risk, then we are indeed dealing with something serious. Amira, I'm afraid your brain children might be a bit too naughty to be playing unsupervised on our servers."

"Amira chewed her nail. "I wish we had more data to be sure. But you're right. It would be wrong to proceed without knowing."

Jerome patted Amira's shoulder in the comforting manner they taught in the 'Relating to People' seminar. "There is enough blood on all your hands already," he said.

"All our hands!" she protested. "You were part of it too!"

"You were the one playing mad scientist," said Jerome. "I merely delivered the Pilot his canopic jar as requested, as is my duty. My conscience is clear."

"Clarise isn't going to let us stop," said Jess.

The others stopped quibbling and looked serious. They knew it was true.

"What do we do?" said Amira. "Talk to her? I suppose she can't put all of us in the Penalty Box."

"It would take weeks to change her mind," said Jerome. "Maybe months. In that time, how many more civilians will get deleted? It would be our own version of the Desolation Dimension. We must act now."

"But there's no one above her in the chain of command," said Amira. "Except Max, and he doesn't count. We can't overpower her. She has the crop and she's as strong as six Agents combined."

Jess rubbed her temples. She hated that she hadn't crossed over, and this was her problem now. But it was her problem. She'd sworn oaths. And besides, she owed it to Eden to fix whatever had cost the young officer her life.

So Clarise wouldn't give Max the choice to step down, but Jess would. She couldn't tell Amira and Jerome, though. First, because if the plan failed, Clarise would cross every single one of them over...or worse. And second, they might try to stop her. They still considered

Max a bigger threat than the deletions.

Everyone else approached the guy like he was a bomb about to go off. But to Jess, he was more like a fussy printer that had to be soothed and babied if you wanted it to do any work at all. She believed in the little weirdo, despite herself.

"I'll handle it," said Jess.

"How?" asked Jerome.

Jess shook her head. "It will be safer for you if you can deny any knowledge of my plan if something goes wrong."

Jerome and Amira exchanged a relieved look, glad their mother hen seemed to have things handled. Jess wished she had their confidence. "We see nothing. We know nothing," said Amira, smiling.

She had to hope she was right about Max. Because she was certainly right about Clarise.

9

Jess entered the globe room with the stars outside. Max was slumped in his chair at the center of the hub, reading a book. She couldn't tell which one from afar. It could be literally any book. To keep the dimensions distinct enough to refresh the reincarnating populace, some creative works were only available in one or two dimensions. Some worlds had Sun Tzu but no Shakespeare. Others had Virgil but no Valmiki. Only here in the outer shell could a person access all of them. It was Jess's favorite aspect of her job, and why she intended to take Peter Pan with her to her next life.

Max looked up. He looked annoyed. "Hey," he said. "Where has everyone been? Where's that canopic jar I ordered? What do I even pay you minions for anyway?"

He snapped the book out of existence and snapped a candy bar into it. He unwrapped the bar and took an overly large bite. A drop of chocolate got stuck in the overgrown red-orange stubble by the corner of his mouth. Jess wrinkled her nose. Slovenly.

"You've got something right there," she said, pointing.

He grinned. His teeth were coated in slimy chocolate. "I'm saving it for later. So come on. Where's the jar? Everyone's acting weird."

"You are one to talk," Jess said, raising an eyebrow.

"Touché."

"Max, you are in trouble."

"I know," he said, his mouth unflatteringly full of candy bar. "That's why I need that jar. Do I have to do a double Kaiju drop in your home dimension to convince you that I mean business?"

Jess folded her arms and ignored the threat. "What I'm more afraid of is your Earthquakes," she said.

"Earthquakes," Max scoffed. "I don't do Earthquakes."

"You sure did yesterday. And plenty of others in the past."

"What!" he said. "How?" He swallowed a too-big lump of candy bar and let the wrapper drop into the pile of so many others at his feet. Max had a trash can a mere two feet from his chair. He also had a physics-defying pocket dimension where he threw priceless canopic jars. But did he use them? No. He littered.

"When Clarise knocks you out with the remote, they use your powers to make natural disasters that are much more controlled than your rampaging Kaiju," she said.

His eyebrows drew together in uncharacteristic anger. "They?" he whispered. The accusation in his voice echoed in the dome.

"We," she amended, owning it. She was part of it, after all.

Max hurried toward her down the metal walkway spoke from the hub, his face serious. He pressed his palms against the barrier shield, sending a wave of sparkling energy up and down to the poles of the globe.

"Jess, this is a bad idea," he pleaded. "It's so dangerous. I can't even tell you how dangerous…"

"There were deletions," she said. "In Dimension X. Two of them."

Max looked like he'd been punched. He actually sank to his knees. His school bus yellow complexion paled to a warm butter shade. But he did not seem surprised to hear this. Jess felt a cold dread spread from her chest.

"You can't do that anymore," he said. "It's not safe."

"Clarise intends to keep doing it," said Jess. "She's going to put you under permanently and use your powers as they were intended to be used. For natural disasters—the kind that might have befallen real, carbon-based humans."

"No!" he cried. "More people will get deleted. You have to stop her." His eyes were wide, and he was breathing hard.

Jess noted without comment that Max's first thought was for the people who might get deleted—not concern for himself. She tried not to feel smug for being right about him. Ironic that the Agency' secret, behind-Max's-back project might be the leverage they'd always needed to get him to step down.

"That's really all up to you," she said, playing 'good cop' to Clarise's 'bad cop.' "Clarise just wants to knock you out. But I came here to give you a chance to step down willingly."

Max laughed bitterly. "No way, no how."

"What have you got to lose?" she said. "Sure, you'll be arrested immediately, but how will a prison cell be different from this place?" She poked the containment shield and let the crackling silver energy make her point for her.

He shook his head. "Can't. The Syndicate will delete me as soon as I'm mortal."

The poor guy was really scared. Jess felt for him. He was a small fry in over his head with dangerous people and being asked to leave a place of certain safety. This couldn't be easy for him.

But she believed Max would do the right thing, if only he could trust that he'd be okay. She hesitated. She really wanted to cross over. But if she could get Max to step down, it would be worth the cost of her future. All those souls weighed against one measly Jess. It wasn't even a contest.

She knelt beside him on the other side of the barrier. "I will keep you safe," she said gently. "I promise I will personally watch over you until I go mad from boredom and end up gibbering under a bridge. I swear."

There. She'd said it. Max brightened and gave her a genuine smile. "I mean…that does sound entertaining, watching you lose your mind and all," he said. "I know you mean what you say. But you don't know what the people who want me deleted are capable of."

She scoffed. "I'm an Agent. I'm sure I can handle it."

"You can't," he said. "I'm not stepping down."

"Really, Max?" she said. She couldn't keep the anger out of her voice. She'd been so close. "More people are going to get deleted if you don't."

"People who aren't me. Which is what is important here," he said.

"What kind person are you anyway?" she said.

"The self-interested, weaselly kind, naturally," he said. His fake, devil-may-care smile was back, and she knew she'd failed to appeal to his better nature.

"You really care more about your own hide?" she said. "For a moment I thought...I thought..."

"Let me out instead," he said.

Jess burst out laughing. "I guess it's my turn to say it. No way, no how."

He raised an eyebrow at her. "Oh? So, you'll stand by while innocent people get deleted when you could have done something to stop it?"

"Hey!" she said. "That isn't...that's not..." she felt the tables turning. Narratives shifting. Max slyly slipping her into his own bad-guy role. "I am not the problem here," she said.

"Not if you let me out, you're not," he said. "I'm not stepping down. And Clarise isn't backing off. The fate of the whole Voyager 2.0 comes down to the choices of our very own Jessamae Kensington!" He did little jazz hands.

"You can't put this on me," she protested.

"And yet I just did. Come on, whaddaya say? You and me out in the dimensions. I'll take you to the really fun ones for once. You look like you could use a vacation."

"Vacation..." she scoffed. "It'd be absolute chaos."

"But no deletions, I promise. You won't get that bargain from those Tornadoes and Earthquakes." He winked at her over his round, red sunglasses, like some sort of deal-making demon.

"No deletions?" she whispered, hardly able to believe she was considering this.

He put his hand up in a three fingered, 'scouts honor' sign. "None. Not even my worst enemy. You know me, Jess. The others don't, but you do. You know I'd never delete someone on purpose. Can you say the same thing about her?"

Jess hesitated. He was like a genie begging free of its bottle, promising the world, but powerful enough to destroy it. She should turn him down and find some other way. The trouble was, she believed him when he promised he didn't want to delete people, because a decade earlier, on her first day at the Agency, Jess had seen a side of him the others hadn't.

10

It was Jess's first day at the Agency. She was a shiny, brand-new intern. It said so right on the yellow sticker badge affixed to her black spandex Jump uniform. There was a picture of the bald, blue, benevolent-looking Pilot in the corner. She was very proud of the badge. She'd spent two entire decades of college training to serve the Pilot. Taking and re-taking exams. Tweaking entrance essays. Running conditioning obstacle courses. Deep in her heart, all Jess wanted was to matter. And there was nobody more important to matter to than the Pilot.

She was in an orderly, industrial-looking room with gray metal walls and utility piping leading from floor to ceiling. Cheerful red and green buttons blinked in wall panels. Occasionally a mechanical vent would hiss an outgassing of built-up steam. Jess inhaled deeply the sweet smell of welding fumes and the pleasant metallic tang that filled the air. She had lived her whole life on the Voyager 2.0. But only here in the outer shell did it feel like she was really, actually on a spaceship.

The exciting hum of the Voyager 2.0's propulsors vibrated through her, as they sipped the cosmic radiation that permeated the stars, the fuel that powered the debris shields and sent the whole ship hurtling on its adventure into deep space. They'd never run out of this resource. Enough energy to last forever. The Voyager 2.0 was eternal so long as it had a steady hand to guide it. Praise Be Unto the Pilot.

She stood at attention, shoulder to shoulder with two people, the only other applicants to make the cut. The man on her right was a pale orange ectomorph with a sort of vacant air about him and unfocused blue eyes. The young woman on her left was slightly built like a horse jockey with deep indigo skin, sparkly silver hair, and perfectly round brass spectacles. She kept bouncing on her toes, twitching, and inhaling deeply from a little pouch of smelling salts to calm herself.

Neither of the other interns was the type Jess was expecting, but she supposed extreme talent must come in strange packages. Jess herself was a six-foot-tall woman with four arms. Probably not what her cohorts were expecting either. It looked to Jess like the Agency had selected a stick insect, a hyperventilating rabbit, and a discount circus girl as its newest employees. Jess aspired to make 'Agent' but that was a pipe dream, she knew. Only the very best made that cut, and given who she had been grouped with, she doubted the Agency thought she was up to the task. But you never knew. She had her foot in the door, and that was the first step.

Speaking before them was a tall, angular woman colored like a palomino with sandy skin and cream-colored hair cut in an angular bob. She wore riding breeches and an olive gray, tailored foxhunting jacket spangled with more than a dozen chest medals. An exacting frown sharpened her graceful features, and her eyes gleamed challenge as she paced in front of the new interns in her black and shiny equestrian-looking boots, holding a riding crop in two hands behind her, lecturing them on protocol, and laying down ground rules. It was Clarice, the Agency's famed Task Manager. The organizational captain who handled the mundanities of running a spaceship so the Pilot didn't have to.

The Task Manager was flanked by two full Agents, who stood behind her at parade rest with mildly bored expressions. One was yet another woman with pink skin, hers a shade approaching 'bubblegum.' She wore a teal and gold Shayla scarf over her hair. Her nametag, which was not a paper sticker, but a more permanent, plastic badge with her picture on it and everything, said 'Amira.'

There were a lot of pink and purple women around thanks to Humanity 2.0's digital cure-all for racism. Racism had been a big problem for the carbon-based humans of old. But there was no human problem an AI-generated blanket solution couldn't fix. Nowadays, the color of digital people's skin wasn't tied to their parentage, but to their favorite color when they entered kindergarten. Babies started out with skin like the fluctuating rainbow of an oil slick. Then, when they started school, they got to choose what color they were going to be for the rest of their lives. People could change it later, but the procedure cost a lot of money.

The handsome but aloof-looking male Agent named Jerome had gray skin and matching gray hair. It said a lot about the kind of person he was that he'd chosen to be gray as a kindergartener.

The Task Manager stopped lecturing and pacing. She clicked her gleaming bootheels together and faced the interns. "Well, any questions?" she demanded.

"Can we meet the Pilot?" asked the orange intern, whose badge said 'Frank.' Jess was surprised he'd spoken. He didn't look like he'd been paying attention.

The rabbity intern named 'Netta' with the brass spectacles gasped. "You want to meet him?" she squeaked. "He could squish me like a bug. I think I'd die of terror." The indigo woman started breathing faster. Jess worried that she was going to hyperventilate and faint right there on the briefing room floor on her first day. She put a hand on Netta's elbow to steady her.

The Task Manager laughed a bitter sort of laugh. "The Pilot could indeed squish you like a bug. He is as terrifying and dangerous as he is powerful. Some have been driven to madness by simply comprehending the truth about him. But if you're strong enough to survive all your tasks, you might be strong enough to meet him."

Netta whimpered. But Jess had a question. The Agents' badges triggered misgivings in Jess's head. They had permanent badges. But the interns only had paper stickers. Plus, their Jumpsuits were ill-fitting. The legs of Jess's standard issue Jumpsuit fit like capris instead of the full body catsuit they were intended to be. This meant the Agency hadn't yet paid to link the clothing to the interns' Incarnations. Put together, these clues pointed less to 'intern' and more toward 'temp.' Jess breathed deeply to calm her anxiety. She'd worked so hard to get there and she craved assurance that the Agency wanted her for the long-haul, even if only to fetch coffee.

But the word 'survive' changed things. 'Survive' might mean 'didn't get fired or quit.' But the Task Manager's warnings about the Pilot put a different spin on things. 'Survive' might mean 'don't cross over or get deleted' too. Jess had joined the Agency for meaningful work and the feel-alive thrills. A chance to see the wonders of other dimensions. The clarity that came with skirting the edge of death every day. She welcomed a certain amount of risk.

But the Pilot had become more dangerous lately. It was something everyone knew at an almost subconscious level. He used to send earthquakes or floods. These would force maybe 50 to 100 people to cross over prematurely, without the chance to fill their canopic jars. But lately, the Pilot, in his wisdom, had been sending Kaiju. Praise Be Unto Him. Just the previous week a land-Kraken fell into the middle of Lambda City, forcing more than 700 souls to cross over at once.

"What tasks do we have to complete?" Jess asked, her mouth running dry.

"You need to chaperone a school field trip," said the Task Manager. "Don't worry. All the little darlings are coming from standard dimensions, thankfully. All humanoids. All normal. We don't have to accommodate any bizarre, jazzy body plans or cater to fussy, non-humanish diets."

Jess blinked, stunned. This was not exactly coffee-fetching, but it was not the sort of work she had been expecting either. "I don't understand," she said. "If the Pilot is so dangerous, why do we bring children to the outer shell? Why risk it?"

"Tell me something, err…" The Task Manager studied Jess's name sticker. "Jess-a-mee…"

"Jess-a-mae," Jess corrected, wishing her mother had chosen the more traditional 'Jessica' for her daughter's full name.

The Task Manager scowled at the correction. "We'll see before the day is done whether you're still here and I need to remember that very particular name pronunciation. Tell me, Jess-a-mae, did you visit the outer shell as a schoolgirl on a field trip?"

Jess's face flushed hot. She was making a mess of this.

"Um, yes?"

"Ahh. And do you care about our spaceship and its inner workings, now that you are an adult? Do you feel like you have a responsibility for our collective futures? Hint, hint, you wouldn't be here in my briefing room if you didn't."

"Yes, ma'am," Jess said, ducking her eyes in what she hoped was a humble, not-lay-offable way.

"We need civilian buy-in," said the Task Manager. "If the younger generation forgets how important the Agency is to the survival of Voyager 2.0, they won't follow instructions. Local dimensional law enforcement won't cede precedence to our Agents when we visit their worlds. We will lose our ability to control them.

"Agents have powers in the dimensions, but not limitless ones. We need the intangible influence of authority if we are to keep the satellite stable for all eternity. If anything can threaten an eternal existence, it is the natural entropic forces that reign in the human soul. So, go! Mold their young squishy minds toward a future of civic duty! And keep their sticky little fingers away from all the buttons!"

The Task Manager flipped a switch on the panel beside a double sliding door. The doors hissed open to reveal an expansive, gray-walled arrival bay. Bright, industrial bay lights shone down from between the spidery bars of the ceiling structural grid, lighting seven cheerful yellow transport buses. The bus doors burst open, spilling forth a rainbow flood of chattering, squealing kindergarteners. They chased and gambled around the arrival bay floor, their tennis shoe soles squeaking against the polished concrete. Harried teachers climbed out behind them, blowing unheeded discipline whistles and waving their arms.

"I'll just leave you too it, then," the Task Manager said over the cacophony. "Amira, with me. Jerome, mentor the interns."

Jerome rolled his cold, grey eyes. "Very well, ma'am," he said. His voice dull, low, and longsuffering.

The Task Manager handed Jerome a data pad clipboard, turned on her squeaky booted heel, and stalked down the back corridor toward the control bridge and away from the onslaught of little humans. Bubblegum pink Amira followed, free and clear and off the hook, with almost a spring in her step.

Jess plugged her ears against the auditory assault, but a firm, grey fist seized her wrist. She glanced up to find Jerome frowning.

"Don't cover your ears in front of the ankle-biters," he said. "It betrays weakness."

She took her fingers from her ears and sized up the seething tide of activity and noise. Jess liked children. But she liked individual children. Not a roaring ocean of ever-moving little entities. The phrase 'too much of a good thing,' came to mind.

"What do we even do with them?" she asked, hoping her experienced mentor would provide some help or at least a clue.

"Well, since your hands are free…," Jerome said. He shoved the data pad clipboard with the field trip instructions into Jess's hands. "This is your problem now. Perfect task for a fresh-faced ambitious, young intern to cut her teeth off."

"You mean on?"

"No. Better get cracking, whelp. I have more pressing matters to attend to."

"This seems pretty pressing," she said, gesturing to the invasion.

"Mmm," he said in his resonant baritone. "Too much for you? I understand. Not every intern has what it takes."

He walked away, turning in the opposite direction the Task Manager had gone. Jess ran after him.

"Wait!" she called. But the door slid shut in her face and the red lock indicator above the frame lit. Her 'mentor' had shut her out, leaving her with the Clipboard of Responsibility, seven transports full of kindergarteners, and no guidance. Jess ground her teeth. Netta and Frank stared at her, as though she were now in charge. As though she had the first shred of a clue what to do. Well, she wanted to make Agent, didn't she?

Just then a mint green teacher wearing a cardigan with a tight hair bun atop her head ran toward her through the river of school children, her face set in a furious scowl. "Is this how you run things at the Agency?" she demanded. "We've been here five minutes and already a little girl got lost down one of your mazelike passages! This is all your fault." She jabbed her pointed nail into Jess's chest. She had the clipboard, right? So, she must be in charge.

I just got here, Jess wanted to protest against the unjust accusation. But 'passing the credit chit' wasn't how an Agent was supposed to respond. Agents were in control of their emotions. They shelved their own needs, and they didn't whine about what was 'fair.'

But not even an Agent could be in two places at once. Jess couldn't manage the field trip and find the child. The kid could have gotten anywhere by now, smearing some sensitive spaceship instrument with the sticky hand jam of childhood. Or worse, bothering the Pilot. That thought gave Jess a nasty start. The Pilot was a cosmic force. Limitless power. Infinite danger. He was supposed to be all-wise. He wouldn't harm a little girl, would he? She thought about all the Kaiju and decided it was not out of the question.

"I need a description of the child," said Jess. The teacher pulled out her mobile and showed Jess a picture of a little girl named Sirita with rose pink skin, the same shade as Jess's, only with rainbow pigtails. When Jess had entered kindergarten, her actual favorite color had been a bright, golden yellow. But her mother loved pink, and Jess wanted her mother to delight in her, so when her turn came, Jess had picked 'rose' on the pantone palate.

Jess shoved the clipboard into Netta's hands.

"Here, you're in charge while I find the kid," she said. Jess was shocked at how easily she'd assumed authority among the group of interns. And equally shocked at how quickly she was passing off unwanted responsibility. Perhaps this was a 'leadership thing.'

"Me?" gulped Netta, her eyes blinking rapidly behind the spectacles. "Why me?"

"Because I'm going to find that kid before she blunders into the Pilot."

Netta's mouth formed a round, impressed 'o,' and she clutched the data pad and nodded vigorous acceptance of a more challenging, but less terrifying task. "I'm glad it's you and not me," she whispered.

Frank nodded too. He held out his hand for a firm, goodbye hand-shake. His orange skin had gone creamsicle pale, and his expression was sober. "Good luck to you, ma'am. Any next of kin?"

Jess shook her head. Her mother had crossed over when Jess was in fourth grade. She had no husband. No boyfriend. There was a per-fectly acceptable young gentleman named Vince she had planned a second date with that night. But they were hardly on 'emergency con-tact' terms.

But she wasn't afraid. She'd joined the Agency for adventure and meaning. She was definitely getting the better end of the deal. She hustled across the arrival bay, down the corridor where little Sirita was seen last, in the direction of all things new and interesting. Behind her she left Netta and Frank the same way her mentor Jerome had left her—lost in an ocean of invading kindergarteners with only a sad digital clipboard as a life raft. Lesson learned, Jerome. Perhaps he was a better mentor than she'd originally thought.

***

The corridor the girl had disappeared down was a starkly lit circular tube. The walls were unpainted light-gray metal, and utility pipes ran down the left side of them the whole length of the hallway. Four stacked on top of one another - gray, blue, red, and black. Different cables ran inside each one. Jess didn't know their function, but engineering would. You didn't have to know everything about a spaceship to work there. You just had to know who to ask.

Every 20 feet there was a door or a hallway leading off into a different section of the outer shell. Jess would explore them all. So many doors to open. So many new things to see. How could she ever get bored?

Jess jogged down the center of the corridor as fast as she could go while still watching the screen of her handheld for any signs of little Sirita. She passed the decontamination showers where Agents returning from different dimensions would wash so as not to spread any native viruses across worlds. That's when she heard it: a child screaming.

A cold dread dropped into Jess's stomach. She had grown up listening to tales about the power of the Pilot. The wisdom of the Pilot. She hadn't really believed he would hurt a little girl. But something in him had changed. The Kaiju drops. More casualties. Everyone could feel it, even on a level they couldn't acknowledge out loud.

She broke into a dead run, all four arms pumping at stiff, right angles, feet flying. The beginning prickles of exertion sweat started up in the hollows of her four armpits. She rarely regretted selecting the 'curvy' Incarnation option at puberty rather than 'svelte' or 'athletic,' but this was one of those times. Jess's mother was already two years gone when she had to make the choice and she had no older, wiser female to advise her, so she optimized herself for maximum social approval. At the time, Jess's reasoning was that she liked boys and boys liked boobs. Never mind that the boobs misbehaved terribly when she tried to sprint.

At the end of the hall, Jess burst into a room so astonishing that she skidded to a halt. It was spherical and a 100-feet high with transparent walls looking out into deep space at billions of steadily burning stars. Jess knew she wasn't really looking into space. This was all a simulation for the benefit of digital beings. But this is what the real, round body of the Voyager 2.0—the one made of atoms, not code—was actually flying through.

Jess stood at the sphere's equator on a metal platform that ringed its whole circumference. Fifty feet up to its apex, 50 feet down to its base. Four metal walkways like wheel spokes led to a central circle platform suspended in the core of the sphere of glass. The platform was bounded with railings and furnished with blinking instrument consoles. There was a spinning office chair in the middle of the platform.

A man the exact golden yellow color Jess would have chosen for herself as a kindergartener stood at the platform's edge with his back to her. He had disheveled carrot orange hair that stuck up at odd angles and was wearing a maroon bathrobe and bear-foot slippers. He was not the Pilot. The Pilot was blue and bald. But he was dangling a rainbow-haired girl over the railings by her ankles anyway. He let go.

"No!" Jess screamed.

The child plummeted screaming toward the bottom of the globe. Suddenly, a ring of blue light opened in the air below her and swallowed her up before closing again. Sirita's murderer turned and cocked his head. He wore a puzzled, innocent look on his stubbly face as though he hadn't just dropped a child out of existence. A choking mix of fear and rage gathered at the base of Jess's throat. She whipped her newly issued crossover gun from its holster and aimed it at the man's chest.

"How could you?" she demanded.

His eyebrows climbed slowly, and he raised his hands in tentative surrender. His robe flapped open when he did, revealing a stained, white tank top and striped boxers that hit just above knobbed knees. He didn't even look afraid of her. His expression was bemused. The bemusement made Jess's temples throb with her climbing blood pressure. Angry tears gathered in the corners of her eyes.

"Nothing can justify that!" she shouted. "The Agency may have its secrets, but there's nothing that child could have seen that warranted killing her!"

"What?" he said. Then he laughed. "Oh! No. This isn't what it looks like."

Just then another blue ring dilated over the office chair at the center of the platform and he dropped Sirita into it, safe, alive, and shrieking with delighted giggles.

"Again!" cried the girl.

Oh. Sirita's screams had been screams of fun. Jess's face flushed hot, and she sheepishly holstered her weapon. She'd drawn on an Agency employee. And a pretty high-level one too, given the grandeur of his office.

"Sorry, I thought..." she trailed off.

"Thought I was murdering some kid? I know. I know. I totally look the type." He ran a rasping palm over his chin stubble and grinned. Jess was in big trouble. She didn't know who this guy was, but only really important people got to come to work in basically their underwear.

"No, no of course you don't," she said. She started down the walkway spoke toward the hub to collect the child, but a few paces in she hit a strange force shield. It sent a wave of blue energy crackling across the room. It was only a mild shield, so she pushed her way through it and continued on to join the strange man and the child on the central platform.

The man's eyebrows climbed as she approached. "Say, you're new here, aren't you?" he said. "You don't know who I am yet."

Jess swallowed hard. Yep. He was important alright. "No," she said. "I'm so sorry. I probably ought to."

He held out a friendly hand for a shake. She shook it. "Well, all you need to know is that I'm Max, and I'm in charge of physics. And I'm also in charge of fun. Right Sirita?"

The child ran up to him and held up her leg, offering. "Right! Ankles again, please."

Max obliged. He held Sirita over the railing and let go. The girl fell into another blue light ring and disappeared.

"And you are Jessamae," he said, reading her nametag correctly. Jess cringed. She had hoped to scuttle away from this encounter unnamed and anonymous so she couldn't be directly called out in an incident report.

"Just Jess," she said. "Sorry for the trouble."

So. This Max fellow was in charge of physics, he said. He was important and irreverent. He was unworried enough about being disciplined or replaced that he was playing with a stray kid while on the clock. Jess deduced he must be one of the ship's engineers. Maybe the chief engineer. Some of those folks were fanatical enough about their work to basically live at the office. It very much looked like that was what was going on here.

"Oh, no trouble," he said, stuffing his hands into his robe pockets and rocking back on his heels. "Miss Sirita burst in with about nine thousand questions while I was working, and not a chaperone or mute button in sight. I had to start throwing her through portals just so I could hear myself think."

"A much more reasonable solution than calling someone to come get her," said Jess. She winced. Why had she said that? Her smart mouth was going to get her into further trouble.

But Max only grinned at the sarcasm, which few people did. "See? You understand," he said.

She tucked a strand of hair behind her ear and blushed. Max seemed jovial and not at all like a man fixing to file an incident report. She allowed herself to feel more at ease. She'd expected the Agency to be a high stress working environment. But Max seemed one of the few new coworkers who wasn't standoffish, domineering, or a total nervous wreck. She decided she'd come visit this room more often, as long as she wasn't bothering him.

The blue ring opened over Max's chair, and he deposited Sirita inside again. She cackled with laughter as she spun in the chair from the momentum of her drop, her head tossed back, kicking her penny loafers.

"Welp," said Jess, "There are kids running all over the satellite like squirrels on cocaine. I should go help before another one breaks from the pack and interrupts you again."

"Nah, it's fine," he said. "I like both of those things."

"Which both?" she said mildly.

Max barked a laugh, explosive and undignified. "The squirrels and kids, smart stuff. But I'll try the cocaine and let you know."

This was unusual. Few people picked up on Jess's humor. She always kept it subtle in case someone didn't like one of her jokes so she could deny she'd been trying to make one.

"You're a lot of fun," she said suddenly. "It's been a pleasure meeting you. Maybe I could come back here sometime?" she said. She bit her tongue, afraid she'd gone too far. Her ears burned, shocked at her own brazenness.

But Max's face broke into a delighted smile. "I'd love that," he said with feeling. "It's been a while since I've had such good company as you two. Or a compliment. Clarise isn't exactly an encouraging sort of Task Manager." He grimaced.

Jess wanted to stay, but she was certain that she'd say something even more cringeworthy than she already had if she continued to try to be clever with Max. Then he'd discover she wasn't really fun company after all.

"Well, come on, Sirita," she said. "Let's get you back to class."

The girl groaned and hopped down from the chair, dragging her feet as she made her way toward Jess. A pained expression flickered across Max's face. "Do you have to take her back so soon?"

"Yeah, let me stay," said Sirita, turning her big eyes up at Jess. "I'm learning so much more here than the rest of the class. Please?"

Jess narrowed her eyes. Sirita was one of those kids who understood too well what arguments held sway with grownups. "I don't know…," Jess started.

"Please?" Max said, turning his big eyes on Jess as well, chewing his lip in a hopeful sort of way.

Jess decided she liked his disheveled appearance. His unkempt hair and stubble. His easy, frequent smile, the tired circles under his eyes, and the way they crinkled at the corners. Most people smoothed away all the code imperfections that built up over time. But Max's flaws lent him a sort of compelling vulnerability. And they made her think he had more important things on his mind than impressing other people.

She found she didn't want to leave. The stars were beautiful outside the glass dome. And Sirita was a delightful, manageable amount of child in comparison to the tidal waves of chittering wee beasties she'd left Netta and Frank with. It might be worth the risk of staying and revealing herself to be dull, stupid, and uninteresting. And besides, hadn't she earned a break? She'd found the kid and saved the day. No jam hands on buttons, no almighty Pilot interrupted. Not bad for an intern on Day 1.

"I suppose we could wait a few more minutes…," she said.

"Hooray!" said Sirita. She bounced out of the chair and ran for the railings again. But Max caught her hand. The girl skidded to a stop and looked up at him expectantly.

"Wait," he said. "You want an education on this field trip? I'll teach you something few people know anymore." The girl's eyes grew wide; she nodded. "Once upon a time," he said, "our carbon-based ancestors used to name the stars. They would look up from the surface of their one little world, the only place they had ever known, thinking it was special, and they were special. They would imagine that the stars formed pictures called constellations made just for them."

"That's silly," said Sirita. "The pictures would go away if you looked at the stars from a different angle."

Jess agreed with the kid. It was impossible for someone born aboard a moving deep space starship to imagine that groups of stars formed an image. She wondered where Max was going with this. A lesson in perspective, perhaps? It sounded exciting, whatever it was going to be.

Max laughed. "True. Knowing what we know now, they sound like idiots. But back then, they didn't know any better. And here's the thing. It's easy for us to think our ancestors were stupid. But then we miss their wisdom. Because the constellations weren't just pictures. Our ancestors made up stories about the pictures, and told them to their children and grandchildren, assuming the constellations were fixed and firm. And generations of humans looked up at the same pictures in the sky and told each other the same stories. Civilizations were nurtured on these tales. And their species grew, assuming they were the center of everything, and the universe was personal and given to them to tame with words and understanding.

"They eventually learned they weren't special. Their world was only one of trillions just like it. The universe wasn't built for them. It was cold, inhospitable, and deadly to creatures made of flesh and far too vast for their frail bodies to traverse. They knew eventually their whole kind would wink out, unnoticed by a universe infinite in both its size and its indifference."

"Right!" said Sirita brightly. "So, they made us to survive for them. Smarter and smarter computers until we could think and feel things Just like them."

Just like them. The girl was well-steeped in the unifying refrain of their people.

Max ruffled her hair. "That was the idea," he said. "But we aren't Just like them."

Sirita's jaw dropped, and Jess gave an uncomfortable laugh. There were many religions aboard the Voyager 2.0, but no official one. Even so, the doctrine of Just like them had taken on some of the trappings of a Universal creed across all the dimensions. What Max was suggesting felt dangerously heretical.

"No, we are Just like them," Sirita insisted, her tone distressed. "My dad said we have souls. I know we have souls!"

"It's not our souls that are the problem," said Max. "It's our location. To us in this ever-moving ship, there can be no constellations, no home base, no shared stories to unite us. The humans of old launched thousands of cyber ships—all in different directions, and we fly farther and farther apart across light years. We have an ansible to communicate with our sister ships, but it would take a miracle for two cyber ships to find one another in this vastness.

"We live as though the stars aren't part of any larger picture. They burn in the black—solitary and isolated. Too many to name. Too many to even count. And we fly past them in these ships without saying hello. And so, we agree tacitly that the universe is impersonal and there is no story to connect the dots. We have abandoned the delusions that made us shine."

"What do we do?" Sirita asked.

Jess was honestly wondering the same thing. An ache had started growing in her chest as Max spoke. A loneliness and an inadequacy. A deep-down anxiety permeated all digital beings that they weren't 'real,' that they weren't truly feeling emotions the way the carbon-based humans had, and everyone was only fooling themselves. That the authentic humans were all dead, and all that remained was a cheap imitation.

"Name some stars with me," said Max. "Do what our ancestors

did. Stare the universe in the face and insist that it is not indifferent. It was made for us, and we for it. The stars are part of our story, and so we ought to be on first-name terms."

"We can do that?" asked Sirita.

Max shrugged. "I do it all the time, between my other tasks. It might just be me anthropomorphizing, but I feel like the stars shine a little brighter when I give them a name. Come on. I'll show you."

Max took the girl's hands and gently placed them on a toggle joystick sticking out of one of the console instrument panels. A neon purple selector rectangle appeared on the glass dome above them. Jess watched Max help Sirita highlight a star.

The girl turned to him. "What kind of names do stars get?" she asked.

"Well, the old Earth ones had names like Aldebaran, Deneb, and Betelgeuse," he said.

Sirita wrinkled her nose. "Those are silly," she said. She pointed at the one she had highlighted. "I'm naming that one Rainbow Sparkle."

Max snorted. "Which is not at all silly," he said.

Sirita rolled her eyes. "Rainbow Sparkle is a beautiful name. And it's my star," she said.

"Fair enough," he said.

He showed her how to speak into the microphone to tag the star. Sirita moved the toggle to the next star over and named the highlighted red giant 'Cupcake.' To an adjacent white dwarf, she bestowed the moniker 'Princess Galaxy.' Then she moved excitedly to another, and still another. Max stepped back from the girl, who remained absorbed in her star naming, and stood alongside Jess, staring out with her into an ocean of stars.

"You ever think about where we're going?" he asked suddenly.

With some embarrassment, Jess realized that she hadn't ever given it any thought. The universe was infinite. Digital lifespans were eternal. She'd assumed there was no destination, only journey. Here's where I unmask myself as a dull-witted idiot, she thought.

"Heh, I trust the Pilot has something amazing in mind," she said. It was always a sure social bet, invoking the Pilot. It signaled humility and a civic spirit.

But Max just scoffed. "Oh, that guy," he said. "That idiot couldn't find his own buttcheeks in an outhouse."

Jess gasped, scandalized. From the console, Sirita paused her steady stream of new star names to giggle, as all children will do when they hear the word 'buttcheeks.' Predictably, the next highlighted star got named 'Buttcheeks.' The one after that was simply called 'Butt.' The following star, a bright blue supergiant, was more imaginatively named "Sandy Bootycheeks."

"I need to watch my language," Max muttered.

Again, Jess wondered what exactly Max did aboard the Voyager 2.0. He was certainly important, but there was a shiver of something dangerous about him. He spoke heresies; he referred to the Pilot with total irreverence. Jess would have been lying if she'd said there wasn't something exciting about him.

"Okay, mister 'I know better than the Pilot,'" she said. "You look at space all day. Where do you think we're going?"

He grinned. "No idea. That's what the Pilot's for. But I know where I'd take us…" He pointed vaguely at the stars beyond the glass dome. "Second star to the right and straight on 'till morning." He gave her a crooked grin.

"What did you say?" she whispered.

"Ah, nothing," he said. "It's a line from a book you don't have in your dimension. Beautiful in places but err…flawed. You wouldn't know it. I probably sound like a crazy person quoting it."

Oh. Jess knew that book. It was important enough to Jess's mother that she'd brought it with her in a canopic jar from her previous life. She'd read it to Jess a hundred times. Its words could slice through Jess's masks and layers and shields and lay her bare and able to feel something for once. When she'd lost her mother, she'd lost the only other person who knew this book. The only other person who had understood the ache that Jess could never quite put into words. She didn't know what he meant by 'flawed,' but she supposed everyone had their own literary tastes.

She decided right then to cancel that night's date with the perfectly acceptable Vince fellow and come back to name some more stars with Max. She was certain there was a pulsar out there just itching to be named 'Wendy.'

She was about to come right out and ask Max when the comms on her handheld pinged. She pulled it out and glanced at it. It was

Netta calling. She unmuted the device, and a racket of children's chatter poured forth from the small speaker. Over the commotion, Jerome's voice sounded. It was loud, harassed, and buzzing with irritation.

"You found the girl yet? We are sending all the transports back now. A boy climbed into the portal room and was about to send himself to another dimension."

"Which one?" Jess asked, afraid of the answer. If the field trip had been cut short, it could have been only one Dimension.

"The one we don't talk about," Jerome said darkly.

She met Max's eye. The merriment had gone out of his face as well. If an untrained child had Jumped through the portal into Desolation… Jess shivered at the thought. The Pilot, in his wisdom, had collapsed a whole dimension. It was devoid of people now. Populated only by monsters. The Pilot had done it for the good of the ship, the Agency insisted, and Jess believed them. The civilians of the dimensions believed them. To believe otherwise was…unthinkable.

"I've got Sirita," said Jess. "I'll bring her shortly."

"Praise Be Unto the Pilot!" came Netta's frazzled voice. "Where did you find her?"

Jess started to answer, but Max made a slashing motion across his throat that was the universal sign for 'cut the mic.' Jess pushed mute.

"What is it?" she asked.

"Don't tell Jerome McDowerpants you found her in here with me," he said seriously.

Jess snorted. "McDowerpants? Is that his real last name?"

"It ought to be," Max said, a faint wry smile playing at his lips. "But this is a sensitive area of the ship and Clarise will ban all non-Agents if she finds out. I'll only have Amira and Jerome to entertain me, and I get really obnoxious when I'm bored." He gave her a winning grin, once again cheerful and full of mischief.

"Well, we wouldn't want you to get bored," she said, smiling back. She unmuted her mic.

"In the decontamination showers," she said, shocked at how easily she'd lied to her superior. "I'm on my way with her now."

Sirita hugged Max goodbye and took Jess's hand. Two thirds of the way down the metal walkway, they ran into that strange barrier again. Light crackled all the way up to the ceiling and all the way down to the base of the globe. Jess lowered her shoulder and pushed through once more. She glanced back at Max. He gave her a two-fingered salute and a smile. She smiled back and left the astonishing room, wondering if Max got off work at the same time she did.

***

Later, once the school buses had departed safely with the children aboard, the Task Manager ordered all the interns back to the briefing room, which meant it was to become a de-briefing room, Jess supposed.

The interns assembled. Jess stood in a row alongside Frank and Netta, who both looked frazzled and pushed over the edge from the stresses of the day. The de-briefing room looked much the same as it had that morning back when it had been a briefing room. Clean and industrial with utility piping and outgassing heat vents. But there was one key difference.

In a corner of the room, Jerome stood in a clear plexiglass cuboid enclosure the size and shape of a personal shower stall. His arms were folded tight against his body, and he was scowling at the floor. Jess wished Max were here so she could joke about how Jerome was 'in prism' and someone would get it. She was pretty sure he would.

Amira stood outside the containment unit staring straight ahead with a smile as sweet as artificial sugar. The Task Manager paced in front of them, her riding crop held behind her and a fierce, disapproving expression on her fine-boned face. Clarice, Jess thought, recalling the irreverent, overly familiar way Max referred to the fearsome commander of the outer shell.

The sandy gold woman stopped pacing and fixed Jess and the others with a demanding stare. "Perhaps you are wondering why Jerome is in the Penalty Box," she said. "Well Jerome is in there to reconsider his 'sink or swim' approach to mentoring interns."

Jerome sighed heavily. "I was hoping," he said in a voice dark, surly, and dripping with resentment, "That by stepping back I would allow the natural competence of our recruits to shine through."

"And shine through it did!" said the Task Manager. "And thank goodness, because the day was nearly a total ronching disaster."

"Don't thank goodness," he sniffed self-righteously. "Thank me and my hands-off style of mentorship."

"I haven't decided about that yet," said Clarise. "It's why you're in the Penalty Box and not in the interrogation cells for near-catastrophic negligence of duty. An untrained person in Desolation could destabilize the whole rickety physics setup and send the contained monsters rampaging across all the populated dimensions."

Jerome only rolled his eyes at this. Apparently bored with the tedium of imprisonment.

"As for you interns," said Clarise. "You may be wondering why I selected you from among the millions of hopeful applicants, given your obvious misfittishness. It really seems as though the Agency could do better, doesn't it?"

Netta nodded vigorously. "It really does," she said.

In other circumstances, Jess might have felt insulted, but honestly, she was wondering the same thing. She'd done her best to get into the Agency, of course. She was smart and diligent. Totally above average. But the best of the best? Absolutely not. Who in their right mind would have picked her? Or Netta? Or Fank?

Clarise nodded knowingly. "Your physical capabilities are a nonissue. The Agency bestows superpowers on its Agents. Intelligence is a wonderful asset, but it isn't everything. The real key is your psych profiles."

Jess recalled the psychological examination she'd sat for as part of the application. Five thousand True/False questions long. She'd agonized over most of them. 'True or False?' it would ask. 'I like the color blue.' Of course it didn't specify what shade of blue, so Jess had to consider whether she liked all shades of blue or only some of them, and whether liking only some of them meant that she should answer 'True' or 'False.' And further, what did it say about her if she were the sort of person who liked blue? Was liking blue something a good Agent did?

Then there was 'True or False: John Keats is a poet I like.' Jess didn't know who John Keats was. She worried that she would appear uneducated if she answered 'False.' But on the flip side, what if this was a trick question and she'd never heard of John Keats because he didn't exist? And wouldn't she look a fool if she answered 'True.' But then, the question didn't ask about his poetry, but whether she liked the man himself. It was all very confusing.

Occasionally there was an easy question. 'True or False: The blood of my murdered ancestors cries out to me for vengeance.' She'd give those a fast 'False' and move right along.

"What about our psych profiles made you choose us?" she asked.

"There was a different reason for each of you," said Clarise. "Netta!" The spectacled woman flinched at the sudden attention from the commanding Task Manager. "Your anxiety score was nothing like we've ever seen. You exist in a sweet spot of constant terror and constant vigilance. Always on high alert, yet somehow still able to act. With you on our side, no threat will escape the Agency's notice."

"Golly," said Netta. She inhaled deeply from the bag of smelling salts in her hand.

"In fact," Clarise continued, "It was this obsession with danger that saved us all today. I understand it was you who intercepted the boy in the portal room before he jumped into Desolation."

Jess regarded the twitchy woman beside her with a newfound respect. Netta nodded vigorously. "I just asked myself 'what's the worst thing that could happen here today?' And I knew I had to go wait in the portal room just in case. 'Prepare for the worst.' That's my motto."

"And hope for the best," Jess finished automatically.

Netta gave a nervous laugh and shook her head. "No. That would be foolish."

"Frank!" said Clarise, startling the vacant-looking ectomorph from his reverie. He focused his glassy eyes on the Task Manager and swallowed.

"Ma'am?"

"You are too unaware of reality to know when to quit. Often that's a weakness, but in your case, it translates to the sort of doggedness that keeps you digging yourself into a hole until you pop out the other side of your problem."

"Err…when you're going through Desolation, keep on going?" he said, uncertain.

"Exactly. Today, for instance. You finished the school tour alone and amid the chaos of missing children. A more cognizant person would have quit. But not you, Frank. No. You kept to the schedule, blissfully oblivious at the helm of the tempest-tossed field trip, despite that reason demanded you send the busses home. And somehow, somehow, you saw us all through the storm.

"The teachers won't blab about the kids going missing, the parents won't think to ask, I won't get 200 angry messages from public relations, and we can all put this disaster of a day behind us." Clarise blew out a relieved, lip-flapping breath like a horse and shook her head, amazed.

Jess realized that the quirks she had thought made her fellow interns seem like odd choices for Agency recruits were exactly the traits the Agency had been looking for in the first place. She resisted the urge to chew a fingernail as an old anxiety gripped her. What idiosyncrasy had they discovered in her? She knew she had one, she just didn't know what it was. She had always tried to cover up the unknown flaw by being as unobtrusive as possible.

Clarise stopped in front of her then, with her hands clasped behind her back holding the riding crop. She looked Jess up and down appraisingly. Jess fought back the urge to squirm. With growing mortification, she realized she'd been referring to the Task Manager by the overly-familiar 'Clarise' in her head because that's what Max did. Here, face to face with this sharp, naked blade of a woman, Jess the intern understood that she hadn't yet earned that right.

"And Jess-a-may," said the Task Manager, correctly this time but with acrid mocking. "It seems I shall have to remember the absurd pronunciation of your name after all. You performed admirably today, though your actions in recovering the girl had nothing to do with why we chose you.

"Why—," she began, but she found her throat too dry to finish the question.

"Your psych eval revealed an unprecedented aptitude for both secrecy and self-sacrifice. There's no limit to the disturbing knowledge you can keep tucked away to spare others' feelings. You let even the people who supposedly love you believe comforting lies, though you know better. Though the secrets you keep from them eat you inside."

The Task Manager beamed at her with an approving expression. She was pleased with this unflattering description she'd just presented of Jess's soul? Jess swallowed hard, her esophagus so dry it felt like sliding her tongue down a belt sander.

"But that doesn't sound like a good thing," she said.

"Oh, it's terrible for civilians, but it's the skill we value most in an Agent. Here at the Agency, we guard a terrible secret. A secret so devastating we lose more Agents to the despair of it than to Kaiju or Syndicate operatives combined. Perhaps an Agent accustomed to such burdens won't burn out so quickly and apply to cross over. That's what we hope for from you, Jess-a-may."

What the Task Manager spoke of sent shivers up Jess's spine. But also, she couldn't help but notice that the commander had said Agent.

"You said Agent?" Jess whispered, hoping she was right.

"Congratulations," said the Task Manager. "You've all been promoted."

Jerome looked up from the Penalty Box. "The fastest promotions in Agency history, I might add. That is what skilled mentorship can do," he said.

"The jury is still out on that," the Task Manager called back. "So," she said to the three interns. "Do you accept your new roles? Will you learn the secret we keep, though it will surely cost you your happiness to know it?"

"It's better for me to know the danger I'm in than to speculate about what it might be," said Netta.

The Task Manager nodded gravely. "I'm not sure even you could imagine something worse than this. You see, there is something wrong with the Pilot. He is indeed all-powerful. But he is neither wise nor good."

Silence bloomed in the room thick and heavy. Jess felt protestations well up in herself. Urges to defend the honor of the blue, bald godlike man who guided them through the stars and renewed the worlds and souls of all. But her objections, died before they reached her lips. Max had derided the Pilot openly as well. And Max was deep in the know there at the Agency.

Then there was that indefinable dread that spread its stain across her mind each time a Kaiju attacked. 'Refreshing the dimensions,' they said. 'Sanity-prolonging novelty,' they said. Something was deeply wrong aboard the Voyager 2.0. A swooning feeling of vertigo overtook her as the heresies fell on her ears and she found them plausible.

"There is a rigorous screening process to choose a Pilot," continued the Task Manager. "Far more rigorous than the trials you went through to become interns. When a Pilot is at last selected, the good, self-sacrificing civilian leaves their life behind to be installed into the deep code of the Voyager 2.0. They assume godlike powers and the exhausting task of managing the dimensions until the day they step down to let a fresh, new civilian take their place. They cannot be crossed over, and until they cede their spot to another, they cannot be deleted."

Everyone knew this protocol. But the Task Manager was using it as preamble for the giant 'other shoe' Jess felt was hanging over their collective heads waiting to drop. Netta and Frank sensed it too. They both grabbed Jess's hands and squeezed in anticipation of the world-rocking secret.

"But the system failed," said the Task Manager. "The intelligence screenings. The ethics tests. Everything. Somehow a petty criminal, a low-ranking rascal in a canopic jar Syndicate got through all the trials. No one was the wiser until he'd already been installed as Pilot and it was too late.

"He refuses to step down because he double-crossed his Syndicate bosses. The mafia wants vengeance and they're waiting to delete him the moment he gives up his title and becomes mortal again. So, the ship is stuck with an immature, emotionally bankrupt nobody installed in its highest office.

"The Pilot and the Agency are locked in a mutual stalemate. The Pilot has this little project collecting data packets from canopic jars across the dimensions. He insists that once he collects all the ones he needs, he can bring down the Syndicate that's hunting him. But we trapped him in a force cage here in the outer shell. He can't get out and wreak havoc with his godlike powers in person. He's limited to influencing the dimensions only virtually, through the consoles in the Pilot's office.

"But he's got us by the throat here as well. He refuses to do his dimensional-maintenance jobs unless we Agents go fetch those little thingies he wants. Without the Pilot refreshing things, we mortal souls with immortal lives will grow restless and unhappy. Crossover applications will pour in. Societies will destabilize. Misery will reign here on the Voyager 2.0.

"And of course, running the ship takes its toll on a soul. The energy required to be Pilot is wearing on him. He's getting crazier and crazier. Our hope is that eventually, our 'Pilot' will grow so uncomfortable that he'll snap and step down voluntarily. So, we do his bidding. But we also push him closer to his breaking point so we can get rid of this guy and install a proper Pilot at last. That is our secret. That is what the glorious Agency has been reduced to. I'm sorry. Welcome to the burden of knowing."

Netta's quiet sniffles filled the stunned silence of the briefing room. Frank's eyes were wide. Jess's throat was threatening to close off. She wanted the Task Manager to be lying. For this to be just one final test. She waited for her superiors to say 'Just kidding! You should have seen the looks on your faces.' But as the uncomfortable silence stretched, Jess's hope for a 'gotcha moment' faded.

Some of the details in the Task Manager's description were even more disturbing. The Pilot was trapped behind a shield, she'd said. Max's office had a shield. But that easily permeable barrier couldn't be a cage for an all-powerful entity, could it? A kindergartener had gotten through.

But also, the Task Manager said the Pilot was in charge of physics, as Max had said he was. But the Pilot was a bald, blue man. The Pilot was deranged. Max was insightful, good with children, and cheerful yellow. But Jess knew she could be awfully good at lying to herself.

"Is the criminal Pilot really that dangerous?" she whispered.

The Task Manager nodded. "He set the portal to Desolation today, despite knowing there was to be a field trip. We'd made sure it was on a safe setting this morning. But I am encouraged. This could be one of the symptoms of his fraying sanity. Perhaps he's closer to snapping than we thought." The Task Manager forced a grim, thin-lipped smile. "Well," she said at last, "Are you ready to go meet the man behind the curtain?"

The interns looked at one another. They nodded. What other choice was there? They left Jerome in his Penalty Box in the briefing room and followed Amira and the Task Manager across the arrival bay and down the round corridor Jess had already explored in her search for Sirita. A growing dread gathered in her stomach as they followed the four vertically stacked utility pipes down the length of the hallway. Gray, blue, red, and black. The ship seemed to be vibrating awfully hard now, Jess thought. Then she realized that she was trembling.

Once they reached the decontamination showers without veering off course, Jess was certain. The Task Manager pressed her hand to a panel by a door Jess knew would open onto an astonishing star-filled room. The door slid open, and Jess followed the others into the glass globe, boots dragging on the metal walkway that ringed the sphere, numb except for the feeling of being a very foolish girl indeed.

Max was in the chair in the middle of the central platform. He spun to greet the open door, the bright smile on his face that Jess had found so charming only a few hours before. His robe and undershirt had been replaced with crisp khaki pants and a royal blue button up that complemented his skin tone. He still wore the bear slippers. This monster had set the portal dial to Desolation with a child inside.

Max's smile vanished when he saw the Task Manager. He rolled his eyes. "Oh, it's just you. Hello, Clarise."

"Of course it's me," she said. "You're wearing clothes for once. Who were you expecting?"

His gaze darted past the Task Manager and fell on the group behind her. He locked eyes with Jess. She glared at him to show she knew the truth. His face fell, sad to see his little game of 'toy with the ignorant intern' spoiled.

He sighed heavily. "No one."

He snapped his fingers, and the nice clothes morphed back to the bathrobe and tank top as if by magic. Netta screamed. Jess blinked. Her stomach twisted with a strange after-the-fact kind of fear. She felt like she'd been a child playing in a lovely garden at the local zoo, never realizing she'd fallen into the tiger enclosure.

Max's countenance changed then. He gave Jess a jaunty grin and winked. She wrapped all four arms around herself and looked away. She realized she might be in a whole lot of trouble if Max decided to tell the Task Manager she'd been inside his force cage. He'd made a fool of her. He was a bad man. Criminal scum. And she'd been flirting with him. She'd allowed a child to stay near him. She was as disgusted with herself as she was with him.

Netta was rocking back and forth and hyperventilating. "Don't worry," said Olivia, patting her. "There's a failsafe for when we have to go in there with him."

Netta gulped. "We go in there with him?" she asked.

"We have to hand-deliver his little packages so he can inspect them," said the Task Manager. "He won't say what about them he's looking for, but 99 percent of the canopic jars we spend our blood, sweat, and Agency resources retrieving for him, he throws through some blue ring into an unknown dimension."

"I so enjoy our little games of fetch," said Max. He steepled his fingers and twirled in the spinny chair like Sirita had done. Childish, Jess thought. How had she been impressed with this man?

"Does he…try to kill you when you get in there?" Netta asked.

The Task Manager smiled. "I have ways of controlling him," she said.

She drew a slim, chitcard-sized remote from her uniform pocket. Max's eyes widened. She pushed the pause button, and his body went slack. He pitched forward from the chair onto his face, hitting the metal platform with an echoing 'clunk,' and laid still. Jess winced. He'd be fine, probably. He wasn't conscious to feel any pain. Serves him right.

The Task Manager strode down the nearest metal walkway spoke toward the hub, slowing only to push through the mild barrier shield that held the Pilot captive. Electricity ran up and down from where she'd disturbed its surface. She walked to Max and placed a booted heel on his prone form.

"See?" Perfectly harmless. Work quick, though. Get in, deposit the package here," she indicated one of the consoles with an intake tube sized just right to accept a canopic jar, "and get out in under one minute. He's too powerful to be stopped for longer than that."

She ground her heel into Max's back for good measure before walking back toward the group. Jess grimaced. He had it coming, she assured herself. The Task Manager emerged through the shield and pushed 'play' on the little remote. Max pushed up to his knees, rubbing his face with one hand and the small of his back with the other.

"Ow. Was that strictly necessary?"

The Task Manager folded her arms and raised an eyebrow. "Was it necessary to set the portal to Desolation this morning?" she asked.

Max raked a sheepish hand through his hair. "Heh. Well, I went to my console to inject some good, wholesome chaos into the dimensions and, wouldn't you know? Fresh outta Kaiju. Gotta drop Kaiju or the population atrophies, you know? I'm only being responsible. So, I thought I'd copy/paste a new batch from the monster zone. Field trip slipped my mind."

"Or you could send natural disasters like the Pilot's manual says to," said the Task Manager, pointedly.

Max waved a dismissive hand. "Snoozeville, baby! Monsters are far more diverting. You're lucky you've got me. This satellite had been languishing from boredom, waiting for me and my rare and special brand of entropy."

"Yes. Your special entropy," said Clarise, coldly. "Not only is the Pilot a criminal, he's from a nonstandard dimension. The ones that just have to be different, no matter how much harder it is for the Agency to manage them."

Amira turned to them. "That's what Clarise thinks," she said. "I think the Pilot's just too dimwitted to perform the probability calculations for proper natural disasters. But rather than admit his own shortcomings, he zaps the Kaiju in like a child playing with dinosaur toys."

"That is also plausible," the Task Manager conceded.

Max stuck out his tongue.

"Ignore him," said Amira brightly. "I do. And I stay happy. So that's it then. We fetch him canopic jars for his little 'collection.' He refreshes the dimensions and the world limps along none the wiser. He insists when that console is full of the right canopic jars, he'll step down."

"I don't buy it," said Clarise. "I don't think he'll ever step down. We're working on a way to rein him in. His monsters cross too many people over early. He is on a trajectory to start destabilizing the dimensions more than he stabilizes them. We only have a couple of decades before the balance tips. And he's getting worse all the time."

As if on cue, Max leaped from his kneeling position, formed his hands into claws, and charged toward them, snarling and drooling. Netta fainted. She fell forward toward him, and Jess rushed to catch her before she plummeted off the walkway. Max hit the shield, just in front of the pair of them. But he couldn't push through. He bounced back onto his butt, cackling.

Jess scowled at him and tried to shake Netta awake. He leaned toward the barrier with a wicked smile and whispered. "Surprise," his tone glib and mocking. "Don't worry. What went on between you and me is our little secret." He winked.

She wanted to shout and scream at him. But she'd only make herself into a bigger fool. He had it over her that he'd hoodwinked her. No

Agent worth her salt should have fallen for his tricks. She was already inadequate for her new job. But she wouldn't allow him the satisfaction of thinking he'd ruffled her. Dark and low she pitched her voice so only he could hear.

"Figure out where we're going yet? Or are you still looking for your own buttcheeks?"

Annoyingly, he guffawed, and his smile widened. He pointed to her, nodding in admiration. "You're going to be a fun one, I can tell. I like my reluctant little minions to be game and lively."

She smoothed her hair primly. "I'm here to serve the ship. Not you," she said, shaking her head in disgust. The truth was of course that she had come to serve the Pilot. To matter to the man who mattered the most. Jess could not even begin to process the depths to which this con man and fraud had let her down.

"Keep telling yourself that," he said. "Congrats on the promotion, Agent. I'm sure we'll be seeing a lot more of each other."

Jess kept the second date with Vince that night and the rest was history.

It turned out that the Task Manager had been wrong about Frank not knowing when to quit. The following day, he had turned in his new laminated Agent badge and applied to cross over, unable to carry on under the burden of the Agency's terrible secret. Yet another casualty to lay at Max's feet. It wasn't his direct fault of course. Frank's choice was Frank's choice. Jess hated that she recognized that fact. She did not want to be fair to Max, but she was anyway. It was probably why she remained Max's favorite to this day.

Netta had only stayed because she was frightened that in her next life she would know nothing of the danger the ship was in.

Jess stayed because…because she couldn't think of anything else to do. The Voyager 2.0 needed her, whether her heart was in the job or not. As with most endeavors in life, what mattered were the motions you went through. Jess trusted that, when you added it all up at the end, you could see if the motions had amounted to anything good at all.

Over the years, she'd found Max to be more an irritant than the threat the other Agents thought he was. A childish prankster. Not evil, but an imp with enough power to make him dangerous.

She looked him up and down, wondering what damage he would cause if she let him out, weighing her ability to keep him under control.

The Disruptor remote would help. But would it be enough? Max might have been sincere when he promised to be good, but his ability to keep that sort of promise was like an inbred Chihuahua puppy: tiny, fragile, and easily distracted.

In the back of her mind, Desolation loomed. Everyone thought Max had collapsed it. What if everyone was right? But even Desolation had only crossed people over. The Task Manager's determination to ignore the deletions was far more worrisome in Jess's opinion. She was certain more would follow if she stood by and did nothing.

"I'll do it," she said. "Hang tight. I'll get you out of there."

Max did a victorious fist pump. "Oh, yeah!"

Jess shook her head. "I wish you wouldn't do that."

11

THE PRESENT DAY

Jess had gone back to the dim, stuffy equipment closet to fetch some needed gear. She was surrounded by the smell of mothballs and the baked-in sweat of loaner Jumpsuits. She eyed the dark safe full of lethal guns and decided against bringing one. Her crossover gun had always been enough. She rummaged through the spy stuff on the cluttered shelves until at last she found a box of fingerprint replicator gloves. She removed a pair and started for the exit.

She eyed the clipboard with the sign-out sheet hanging by the door. She was supposed to log her name when she took equipment from the closet. She was already just one Veden citation away from the Penalty Box. But given that she was about to spring the Pilot from his force cage, a Veden citation seemed like small potatoes. It was best not to leave Clarisse a clear, signed admission of her guilt.

She brushed past the clipboard and down the hall to the globe room, checking the active map on her Frankenphone as she went. Clarise was still in the briefing room with Netta. Her way was clear. She pressed her hand to the door panel and stepped back into the globe room to free the genie from his bottle.

At her entrance, Max leaped to his feet. He bounced on his toes at the edge of the containment shield. "You're back!" he said. "Come on, let's blow this popsicle stand!"

Jess walked to the computer consoles that lined the equator of the globe room. "What does that even mean—'blow this popsicle stand?'"

"Leave this place and go somewhere else, duh." said Max.

"Yes, but why does it mean that?" she said. "I've never understood. What does the popsicle stand represent?"

"Do not question the popsicle stand," said Max. "It just is."

Jess rolled her eyes.

"So how are you going to get me out?" Max asked. "You need Clarise's handprints in addition to your own to satisfy the two-factor authentication."

"Pish," she said. "I can do this single-handedly."

"Funny, since you've got four of them."

"Exactly," she said.

Jess was the only person in the outer shell who could free Max by herself. She slipped the fingerprint replicator gloves onto her two lower hands. She knelt and placed her hands on the locker that held the Pilot's Disruptor remote—a surface she'd seen Clarise touch with her bare hands many times. The gloves beeped as they acquired the fingerprints and morphed to conform.

"Bingo," said Jess. She was about to stand when Max spoke up.

"Hey. Is the Disruptor really necessary?" he said. "Don't you trust me?"

"About as far as I can throw a Kaiju," she said.

"Which is a lot, since you are so strong?" Max said hopefully.

"The Disruptor remote comes with us," she said firmly. He sagged.

Jess grabbed the handle of the locker, flexed her bicep, and broke the cast iron door off its hinge. There was, Jess realized, a high degree of internal trust there in the Agency. That was probably because the Chief of Security hero-worshipped the Agents. Veden would never have expected her to break into a vault. The poor guy was going to beat himself up over this for a solid month. But that was not Jess's problem.

She tucked the remote into her utility belt and moved to the computer console. She pressed her gloved, Clarise-print hands to one panel and her own Agent hands to the other.

"Oh!" said Max, finally catching on. "That's quite bright of you, Agent Kensington. Well done."

The console offered a two-button choice menu.

```
Lower Pilot Containment Shield:
Yes   No
```

Her hand hovered above the 'yes' button. She turned over her shoulder. Max was shifting from foot to foot, wringing his hands.

"Go on then," he said, nervous and eager.

"Don't make me regret this," she said.

"Me? Never! I am offended that you would even think you might have regrets. This is undoubtedly the best decision you have ever made in your entire life."

She covered her face with two of her palms and muttered. "Dear God, why?"

"I am kind of godlike," mused Max.

"Do I at least get three wishes or something?" she grumbled.

"Oh-ho! Three? Baby, I'm the kind of all-powerful genie who will let you wish for more wishes, even."

"I am going to regret this. And don't call me 'baby.'"

He only grinned. She pushed 'yes,' and the computer flashed a second message.

```
I hope you know what you're doing.
```

She did too. A 'wum' echoed in the transparent dome, and the shield went down. Max stepped across the line into freedom. He turned back toward the hub.

"In your face!" he shouted at his former cell.

He reached into his bathrobe pocket and threw a handful of nothing into the air. It exploded into a glittering shower of blue, gold, and magenta fireworks. That should have been impossible, but of course none of the rules of reality applied to Max. It began to settle in just how outgunned, outclassed, and out of her depth Jess was. She had a tiger by the tail and had to pray he didn't turn right around and bite her.

12

Max turned right around and bit her. Not literally, but meta-phorically. As soon as the glitter from his freedom fireworks faded, he turned pointed at her utility belt. The compartment that held his Pilot's Disruptor remote came open as if by magic and, before Jess could figure out what was happening, the device sailed through the air and into Max's hand.

"Hey!" she said.

He stuffed the remote into his robe pocket and gave her a jaunty grin. "In case I have any trouble falling asleep, what with all the excitement I'm about to cause."

"You never used that power before," she said.

Her face burned. Over the previous ten years, Max had lulled her into a false sense of security. He had fooled her again, just like the day she'd met him.

"Not in front of you Agents, no. That's very much on purpose. I only ever do two things in front of you. One, I store my canopic jars in my personal dimension. And two, I materialize food for myself because I have to eat. I don't like to remind people how powerful I am, lest someone have second thoughts about, say, letting me out of my cage, heh, heh. But now that I'm out of the bottle, I'm going to start granting wishes—my own wishes—starting with that canopic jar you failed to bring me."

He started toward her. Jess shrank back against the locked double doors as Max reached for her, unsure how to stop him, or even if she could. Noting her reaction, he pulled back.

"Hey, you should probably come with me," he said. "When they find out what you've done, they'll throw you in the Penalty Box. and it's crowded in there at the moment, what with Netta and all."

She hesitated. She could do nothing to stop him.. What was the point of going along? Just to hang around as he wrecked the dimensions, pleading with him like an unheeded shoulder angel?

Her Frankenphone beeped. She glanced down. The Active Map was still running on the screen and an icon labeled 'Clarise' hovered right on the other side of the double doors Jess was leaning against. Great.

The door light turned red. The globe room doors locked automatically whenever the containment shield was down—even to authorized personnel. There was a furious banging outside.

"Hey!" Clarise shouted angrily. "Anyone in there?"

"Where else would I be?" Max called back, his eyes lit with humor. Jess's stomach turned over. She couldn't try to pretend she hadn't freed Max..

"Besides you, jackass," Clarise snapped. "I'm getting readings that the containment shield is down. It shouldn't be down."

There was beeping on the other side of the door. Clarise was inputting the emergency access codes. Jess was out of time. The door hissed open and Clarise was right in Jess's face, riding crop in hand, wearing a furious expression. Then she saw Max and her eyes boggled.

"What have you done?"

Clarise reflexively brought the riding crop down on the nearest person. Jess's training mode kicked on. The world slowed and data fed itself to her brain in manageable packets. Her knees crumpled out from under her so that she could avoid the blow. It had been the wrong move. In her slowed down state, Jess could see the crop had gained enough momentum to become a death blow. It was coming for her head, and, as fast as Jess was, the Task Manager's arm was faster. Clarise was made of much more advanced code than the Agents. Jess didn't even have time to close her eyes.

Max stepped between them; somehow, he was even faster than Clarise. The death blow cracked hard against the side of his skull. A nimbus of electricity crackled in a sphere around his body, but he stayed upright.

"That stings," he said, frowning.

Clarise gaped at him. Her body might be fast, but her brain was clearly still struggling to catch up with the new situation. An all-powerful Pilot on the loose. One with a shaky, broken mind and a very large grudge against her personally. The great Task Manager froze like a cornered prey animal.

Max snapped his fingers and Clarise was suddenly trapped in a five-foot-tall Christmas pudding. There was a dollop of cream on her head and a maraschino cherry on top of that.

"What?" said Clarise, blinking in numb confusion. Jess shared the sentiment.

Max reached down and grabbed Jess's upper left arm. "Welp," he said. "You've got no choice now. I obviously can't leave you here with Clarise."

He snapped his fingers again, and the white light of a Jump clouded her vision. It shouldn't be possible, Jumping outside the portal room. But then, once again, Jess had forgotten who she was dealing with.

***

Jess and Max materialized in an out-of-the-way alley just north of Ponzing Avenue in X City, leaving Clarise and her riding crop safely behind in a pudding back at the Agency. Jess hadn't got the impression that Clarise meant to delete her. The near-death blow felt like a reflex triggered by seeing Max free. But the Task Manager ought to have cared enough about Jess's soul to be careful with her deadly weapon. She tried not to feel betrayed. The Agency only seemed like a little family to her because she didn't really have one of her own to speak of. It was her own fault for forgetting that the Agency was a workplace, not a home, and Clarise was a boss, not a mother.

She blinked away the lingering Jump whiteness and looked down. Her Jumpsuit had morphed back to the ecru trousers and navy shirt with long sleeves. Max was still in his bathrobe and underwear. It could have been worse. If Agents Jumped in street clothes, they'd find themselves naked in a new dimension. Max didn't have to wear Jumpsuits to stay clothed, thank goodness, another rule that didn't apply to the Pilot. Praise Be Unto Him, Jess thought with utmost sincerity for once.

She and Max made their way out of the alley onto the shattered avenue. Yesterday's Earthquake revelers had mostly dispersed. The street was still full of abandoned vehicles, though the horn honking had stopped. Whether this was because the owners had disabled the alarms or because the cars had simply run out of batteries, Jess didn't know.

Orange-vested X City workers milled about the wreckage, frowning at the various structural damages and making notes on digital clipboards. Jess ducked under the line of multicolored globe lanterns that still hovered all along the street in honor of some Dimension X festival or other. Max gaped at the spheres. He batted one like it was a balloon. It bobbled out of place for a moment before retaking its position in the line.

"Incredible," he said, grinning. Through his red lenses, Jess could see his pupils had fully dilated. He batted at the next lantern and the one after that, laughing louder with each swipe. He reminded her of Hippopotamus when she gave him a catnip mouse.

"This place is amazing!" he cried.

The city workers looked up from their clipboards and eyed the maniac in the bathrobe. Then they quickly averted their gazes.

"Spoken like someone who has not 'got out' in a while," Jess said, taking Max's hand and leading him away from the lanterns before he could violate some local conduct custom. He was wrong. Dimension X was boring. It was one of the most vanilla dimensions Jess had ever visited. There was nothing special here.

"This is just the same as every other dimension," she said. "Which it wouldn't be if you'd do your job properly."

"Are you kidding? There's never been another place quite like this one. I know I'm not the most conventional Pilot in history…"

"Or the most competent," she muttered.

"That too," he said, grinning. "But it is totally everyone else's fault if they get bored with a place as fantastic as this! There's so much cool stuff right here in front of our noses. It's not too long a life that's y'all's problem. It's a lack of imagination."

She folded her arms. "So, you're blaming everyone else for your own shortcomings as Pilot?"

"Shh," he said. He sniffed the air. "Oh, boy. Dimension X is about to get even better. I detect tacos!" Max tore off down the street toward a corner taco cart. He was track-star fast of course.

"Wait!" she cried.

She ran after him, hoping he wouldn't do anything too terribly stupid. By the time she caught up to him, he was already at the cart, pulling something out of his robe pocket that looked like a bar of solid gold. She seriously hoped it was not, but given that the taco vendor was planting kisses on either side of Max's cheeks and shaking his hand, she bet that it was.

"Hey," she said, breathless from the sprint.

"Keep the change!" Max told the vendor. He turned, a platter of five tacos in each hand, and made his way to the curb in front of the taco stand where he sat down and picked up a taco. "I'm sorry. Did you want any? I should have ordered for you too."

"You have got to cool it with the powers," she whispered. "You're going to mess with the local currency. You're drawing all kinds of attention to yourself. Just look at your clothes."

He raised his fingers to snap-change his garments.

"No, no, no, no," she said, pushing his hand back down. "Don't snap into something different. That'll attract even more attention. Right now, you're just a simple weirdo."

"A simple weirdo with tacos," he said. He took a huge bite, and some rusty red sauce dribbled down his chin. Jess shuddered. She walked to the taco cart and asked for wet naps. She returned to Max with two handfuls of the little pre-wrapped squares. He was going to need them.

He gave her a smile that was both metaphorically and literally saucy. "Now that's what I call service. Good minion. I owe you a Scooby snack or something."

"You could stand to eat a little neater," she said.

"But I enjoy it more when I can savor the juices. Besides, I only ever get food I make myself. It's completely exhausting. It's so nice to have someone else cook for me for once."

She snorted. "You snap your candy bars in and out of existence by magic," she said. "How hard can it be?"

"A true master makes the impossible look easy," he said primly.

"Like that Christmas pudding?"

He cracked a smile. "That was a good one, eh?" He licked each of his fingers one by one to clean them of sauce, despite the pile of wet naps on the pavement beside him.

"The pudding was…unexpected," she said. She plopped herself down on the curb and fixed him with a stare. "So, I find myself at a loss," she confessed. "I studied for years the things that normal Pilots have done in the past. I know exactly how you don't measure up to them. But there was nothing ever in any training manual like that Christmas pudding. You've been hiding your powers. What else can you do?"

"'What can't I do?' is a better question," he said. "My power is only limited by my imagination and my knowledge. Unfortunately, I am not all-knowing. I still use search engines and read books to learn things. I'm even going to need directions to that Syndicate den where my canopic jar should be."

"Can you finally tell me what's in those jars we fetch? Now that we are fugitives together?"

Max hesitated. "Debt ledgers," he said at last. "If I can collect all the records of the money I owe the Syndicate and delete it," he said, "the Syndicate will lose its memory of me, and I'll be free."

Jess frowned. "How do they have records across dimensions? The dimensions don't mix."

"That is the mystery," he said. "But the data are like head lice. If I leave even one egg out on the servers, there'll be a new infestation of knowledge concerning me and my debts across the multiverse, and I won't be safe anywhere."

Jess wasn't too sure about this story. In her ten years at the Agency, they had never uncovered any evidence that the various Syndicates were connected. But then, they'd been heavily preoccupied with Max's pointless errands and Amira's natural disaster experiments.

"So, if you get all these debt ledger jars, then you'll step down?"

"I promise to think about it," he said.

"Let us get a new Pilot," she said. "You're not good for the ship, you know."

"How can you say that? Look what's happened because of me!"

He pointed to the taco cart. Jess noticed the bright yellow text that said '100% lean ground Kaiju meat!' She buried her face in her upper palms.

***

The location of Earl's Syndicate was burned into Jess's memory. She had no trouble leading Max to the site that had been the epicenter of Amira's Earthquake. When they arrived, the rubble field lay in the shadow of the neighboring buildings looking much the same as it had the day before. Only now there were two memorials by the entrance to the Kaiju shelter.

Officer Eden's face smiled at Jess from the middle of an oval-shaped flower wreath. She was wearing a navy uniform and cap with brass buttons and looking every bit as earnest as she had in life. Dozens of miniature X-City flags had been planted around her wreath and roses and a plush toy newt lay at the base of her portrait stand.

The other memorial wreath held a picture of a big red guy with a square jaw and metallic silver hair. There were no flags around his portrait, but there were seven teddy bears at the base of his wreath and a sign that said 'We love you Uncle Mac' beside them.

Jess imagined the police and the Syndicate running into each other as they set up these memorials. She wondered if the members of the two organizations had comforted one another in their shared loss or whether they gave each other wide berths and the side eye.

She noted with distaste that someone had placed a brochure stand between the two wreathes full of flyers advertising Griefbegone. 'Tired of feeling sad?' The ad copy asked. 'Ready to move on already? Let us help you process your loss! We'll see you quickly through all five grief stages. For added thriving, try Griefbegone Plus™, now with bonus Double Acceptance Stage!"

Jess fought the urge to uproot the brochure stand and fling it across the debris field. She didn't know why she fought it, given that she was now a fugitive and was no longer obliged to adhere to the Agency's minimal dimension interference policies. But old habits died hard, she supposed.

She glanced at Max. His expression was serious for once, his hands stuffed unhappily into his robe pockets.

"It was my fault," she confessed. "I sent Eden down to the shelter for your jar because I wanted privacy so I could look up ways to cross myself over."

Max looked at her sharply. "I hate deletions," he said. "But I hate crossovers almost as much. It's just another kind of death. Everyone who ever loved me crossed over long ago, citing boredom as their excuse. Their souls are happy and alive on new servers. They're loving new people and making new families. But they've all forgotten one another, and they've all forgotten me."

In all the years she'd known Max it had never occurred to her that he'd had a life of some kind before he'd stumbled into the Pilot's role. She wondered if the people he'd lost were his parents, or a spouse and even children. She hesitated, then put a hand on his shoulder.

"When they crossed, did you use Griefbegone?" she asked.

"Oh, heck yes," he said. "I'm too much of a weenie to sit around and feel unnecessary pain. But it doesn't work on Pilots, it turns out."

"I'm sorry," she said, not knowing what else to say.

"I don't get it. Why cross over at all?"

She shrugged. "Our souls are just like those of the carbon-based humans," she said, using the official line. "We weren't meant to live so long."

"It doesn't have to be that way," he said. "Take me, for instance. I have lived for several centuries in a containment unit with only grumpy Agents for company and I still love my life. I have my memories. I have my awesome personality. I even have all the books and movies I could ever hope to consume. And ten years ago, I hit the Jackpot. You showed up and everything got even better."

Jess's ears burned. The compliment was an uncomfortable amount of positive attention, like a hot, bright spotlight glaring down on her. All she wanted was to crawl off center stage and back into the anonymous shadows.

"I don't know if you've noticed," she said. "But you are a bit unlike everyone else. The rest of us grow weary of our lives."

"But why? You had everything. A husband. A job. Music. A cat.

What made you get tired of all that?" he asked.

She sighed heavily. How to describe the gray feeling? She didn't know if she could. "I don't think I was wanted here to begin with," she muttered under her breath.

She blinked in surprise at her own words. They had tumbled automatically from her lips like she'd dropped into combat mode and they'd just…happened. She'd never meant to say them, but since she had, she felt the truth of them sink into her like a barb into flesh.

Max cocked his head and leaned forward to hear better. "What was that?" he asked. "I didn't catch it."

"I said '100 years has been long enough for a single Incarnation.' Everyone knows that. You're just weird."

Max rolled his eyes. "Fine," he said. "Be that way. But you're not fooling anyone. I know you've got an imagination. You've just been conditioned not to use it."

He bent down and touched the piles of rubble blocking the Kaiju shelter entrance. The bricks began to tremble and scrape together. Jess swallowed, uncomfortably reminded of the Earthquake. The rubble moved away from the stairs as though by magic until the door stood open before them. Max started walking down toward the basement. Jess grabbed his arm.

"What?" he said.

"Oh, right. You can't be deleted. I just…bad memories," she said.

He grinned. "Thanks for your concern. I'll be back in a jiffy!" He disappeared down the stairs into the shadowed Syndicate lair.

As soon as he was out of sight, Jess pulled out her Frankenphone and dialed Jerome's direct line. She had to know how things were going back at the Agency. How much trouble she was in. How much trouble the others were in. Whether Clarise had got out of the pudding.

Jerome answered. "Doom," he said. A fairly typical greeting for Jerome. "You have brought doom upon us all."

Then in the background, Amira's voice. "When you said you had it handled, I thought you meant something helpful! What were you thinking?"

"I had to do something," Jess said defensively. "I tried to offer Max a choice—step down or go under. But he forced my hand."

"Well, Clarise is about to force Max's hand," said Jerome. "Once we got her out of the pudding, she decided she was through with him and a forever coma wasn't enough. She Jumped to the Noir Dimension. The Syndicate there has created a viral serum that can delete even Pilots, and Clarise wants to use it on Max."

"What?" said Jess. "That shouldn't be possible."

"Humans are awfully inventive," said Amira. "And I suppose the Syndicate got tired of waiting for Max to step down to kill him."

The Noir Dimension. That was where Dr. Barnes said her crossover jammer signal had originated. The Noir Dimension boasted the most advanced code tech in the whole spaceship. They also had the biggest, baddest Syndicate in all the dimensions.

"I've got to warn Max," Jess said.

"But…why?" said Amira. "If Max is gone, whatever is going wrong with his power that's deleting people will go away too. It sounds extreme, but sacrifices must be made for the greater good. This is safer than putting him under forever."

Jess hesitated. What Amira said made perfect sense. But she hated it. She could do with never smelling the bile and brimstone of a human deletion again. And she'd feel that absence in her flock where Max was supposed to be and know that she'd made the hole herself.

"Jess?" Netta's quiet voice sounded across the comms.

"Netta? Clarise let you out of the Penalty Box?"

"Uh huh. She is going to pardon anyone who helps track Max down and delete him. Even you. Lucky for us, you know right where he is."

Jess swallowed hard. "I do at that." Nothing in her wanted to help them. But if what they said was true, if it was the only way to unseat Max the Agency had found after several centuries of trying. She felt caught between her duty to the Voyager 2.0 and some other, nameless duty she had to her own soul.

"Clarise said you stole Max's Disruptor remote," said Netta. "You can knock him out and Jump to the Noir Dimension. We'll call you when we have the virus, and you can meet us there. Max won't feel a thing."

"I can't!" she said happily, feeling a rush of gratitude that Max had immediately betrayed her upon being freed. "He took the remote from me. I'm honestly just following him around, doing damage control as I can."

"I can imagine," said Jerome. "Can you trick him into going to Noir voluntarily?"

She smiled. A glad relief washed over her. She didn't have to choose between her duties because she had no power to act.

"Unlikely," she said. "I can't get him to do anything whatsoever. I can't even get him to wipe taco sauce off his chin."

"I see," said Jerome. "I cannot say that I'm surprised. It seems capturing Max is to be a long and tedious task."

Down in the Kaiju shelter Max whooped. Presumably he had located his jar.

"I've got to go," Jess said. "Max will be back any moment."

"We'll contact you when we have the virus," said Netta. "Try to get him to us. I know you'll think of something."

"Will do," said Jess. Not sure if she would. She pressed the hang-up button on the Frankenphone just as Max emerged into the sunlight holding a glass canopic bottle with a baboon head. He smelled strongly of anise.

"Victory!" he declared, grinning. "This is the second-to-last jar I need. One more and all my troubles will be over."

This was great news. If Max could erase himself from the Syndicate's memory, he could step down at last, and the Agency would have no reason to delete him. Perhaps her duties need not be in conflict after all. She just had to help Max achieve his goals before Clarise found him.

"Do you know where the last one is?" she asked.

"Oh, yeah. Didn't I promise you I'd take you to all the fanciest places? Well, brace yourself. Because you and me are headed to the Noir Dimension!"

Jess pinched the bridge of her nose. "Of course we are."

13

The whiteness of the Jump faded, and Jess blinked in the warm, humid Noir Dimension night, trying to understand what she was seeing. They were on a street corner in what looked like an old, American city, but the world was black and white like Earth movies made before the carbon-based humans had the tech to record in color. Or the films made after that whenever the director wanted to be artsy.

Jess felt a thrum of excitement. She'd rarely seen dimensions with physics that were fundamentally different from Garden's, and Noir's didn't have a color spectrum! Plus, she found even more wonderful weirdness all around.

The smell of tire rubber and fully-leaded gasoline emanated from a street filled with an anachronism of cars. A Cadillac with fins swerved past a round-fendered Buick convertible. An even older car followed them. One with conical, chrome headlights, a square top, and a radiator grille. The avenue looked like an antique car festival was driving past, but this was probably just everyday traffic in Noir.

On either side of the street, buildings stretched up to lose themselves in low, muggy clouds. Even the architecture looked like she'd gone back to a time when businesses, theatres, and nightclubs were made of stone and concrete, rather than the graceful, colored glass of so many other dimensions. Jess got the impression this was a tough, edgy city with sharp angles and a blunt personality. Nothing like the cities she'd visited before that tried to make you feel comfortable and safe.

In front of them was an electric lamppost with three speakers underneath like the Kaiju sirens in Garden. Only these speakers were playing a slinky saxophone number that lent even more gritty ambiance to the black-and-white street corner.

It was nearly 8:00, and the street-level restaurants were beginning to lose their customers to neighboring nightclubs. The people moving between venues astonished Jess even more than the cars and music.

A Noirian couple passed by, but Jess couldn't tell what color their skin was. Light gray and dark gray? Or was gray an approximation for a color that Jess's outsider eyes couldn't discern? She was so accustomed to divining a little of someone's personality by observing what color they'd chosen to be. It was jarring when she found couldn't get a feel for these two folks the same way.

She wondered if, instead of colors, Noirian kindergarteners chose favorite shades of gray for their skin. Or if Noirians even had a concept of color at all. For instance, did Noirian children's books say, 'the apple is red?' Or did they say, 'the apple is grayscale #45?'

So many questions exploded into her brain, and she realized she'd been missing this sort of zest and interest for too long. This is why it was a shame the dimensions weren't more different from one another. And why it was a shame most people would never visit more than one of them in a lifetime. The Voyager 2.0 was supposed to be optimized for digital beings. But Jess felt it only offered the civilians the worst of both worlds. It would be okay. That's what she and Max had come there to fix.

Besides their skin, Jess was fascinated by the Noirians's clothes. The man of the passing couple wore a light gray zoot suit with black pinstripes and a wide-brimmed, white fedora. The woman on his arm wore an ash-colored popover dress with black polka dots, a feathered pillbox hat, and tall high-heeled shoes.

Nearby, two giggling women burst out of a restaurant wearing glittering flapper's dresses with long strands of round beads around their necks. One was a doppelganger of Josephine Baker, the other of Myrna Loy. Arm-in-arm, they ducked into a nightclub called Harry's Happy Hour Hideout.

Since arriving in Noir, Jess had seen styles spanning the entirety of the Jazz Age and on into the Big Band Era all smashed up against each other. The Noir Dimension boasted all the historical accuracy of a Renaissance festival, it seemed. Various flavors of 'back-then-ness' mixed together to create a very enjoyable, nostalgic atmosphere.

Jess looked down at herself, eager to discover what outfit her Jumpsuit had morphed into to blend in with the locals. For the first time since she'd failed to cross over, Jess was not disappointed with her clothing. She wore a form-fitting, off the shoulder pencil dress made of shimmering black rayon. She had delightfully useless black-lace gloves with pointless wrist ruffles on all four hands. Her utility belt had morphed into an evening clutch and her combat boots had chameleoned into four-inch-high pumps.

The shoes gave her pause. Max would look out of place enough in his shabby bathrobe and bear slippers. But standing next to an Amazon woman in heels, he'd be nigh-unforgettable. Which was bad news on a secret mission. She turned around to advise him to change and pulled up short.

He was grinning up at her like a kid watching fireworks. "Wow," he said, appreciatively, taking in her outfit.

Jess blushed and tucked a stray curl back into her updo. She had almost said the same thing right back to him. Max looked amazing. His neck was shaven for once and the stubble he still had looked dashingly intentional. His hair was clean and coifed and mostly hidden by a dapper bowler hat. He wore a crisp white shirt with a bowtie at the collar. There was a smartly tailored silver vest over the shirt with a chain leading into the pocket—presumably attached to a pocket watch, though it was best not to make assumptions with Max. His pants had a sharp crease, and his bear slippers had been replaced with wingtip dancing shoes.

He looked an inconvenient amount of attractive. Teenage Jess always had a weakness for cute boys that rendered her unfortunately open to suggestion—an instinct she'd worked hard to suppress over the years. She made note of her reaction to Max. Best to be aware of it lest it cloud her judgement on their mission.

She hadn't told Max about the Agency's plan to delete him, and she didn't plan to. She feared that if she did, Max's self-preservation instincts would kick in and he'd flee the Noir Dimension, losing the chance to capture his last jar, free himself of the Syndicate, and step down at last. Risky, but worth it, in Jess's estimation. She just had to make sure they didn't run into Clarise while they were there.

"The city is a woman," said a low, husky voice out of literally nowhere. Jess nearly jumped out of her skin. Her mind shifted into combat mode and she dropped into a fighting stance—no easy feat in a pencil dress. All her senses went on high alert, burning through the flood of adrenaline she'd just released as she tried to pinpoint the source.

"But a woman can be many things," the voice continued. "For every Madonna, there's a Dark Mother. For every Sunday Church Girl, there's a veritable ally cat—all purrs and silk, but don't forget the claws." It sounded male. But Max's lips weren't moving. No one was nearby. What in Desolation? "What kind of woman is the city? Well, it all depends what side of the tracks you landed on when the stork brought you."

Max was bouncing on his toes, a look of sheer delight on his face.

"You hear it too?" she asked, plugging her ears and shaking her head to clear the voice. He nodded vigorously, reached over, and pinched her earlobe. The voice shut up and Jess relaxed.

"I've heard of this!" he said. "I have always wanted experience it!"

Jess felt a rush of relief. She wasn't crazy, then. "What is this?" she asked, a little shamefaced to be using Max as a sanity yardstick.

"It's the hard-boiled detective voiceover narration!" he said, vibrating with giddy enthusiasm. "An informative ambiance feature of the Noir Dimension. The software offers residents insight into the digital environment, all filtered through the personality of a world-weary private eye with a shady past and a drinking problem."

"Is it always going to sound like budget Sam Spade's in my head?" Jess asked.

Max laughed. "You can shut it off or dial it back. I just dialed your narration back with the earlobe trick. The voice should only interrupt your thoughts when the dimension has something really important to show you. This is fun, eh?" he said. "Something different."

"And how!" she said. This was going to be cool, now that she understood what she was dealing with.

"You should hear mine," Max said. "Here." He took her upper left index finger and stuck it in his ear, which was really super weird. The voice returned.

"She was a leggy dame, with gams that went all the way up, if you know what I mean. But there were only two of 'em. Arms were another story. She had four arms. And forearms too, for all you wordplay-minded mooks. I had to hand it to her. She was the best-looking dame I ever laid eyes on. And I had to hand it to her no less than four times…"

Jess removed her finger from Max's ear and wiped it on his vest. She laughed despite herself.

"That is something," she said. "I almost wish…" she started. Then stopped herself. Noir would be a total playground for her—if she had time to play. But she hadn't come here to indulge herself.

"Did someone start a wish?" said Max, temptingly. "You did let a genie out of his bottle, after all. I think you get three of them or something."

Jess snorted. Well, what the hell? She might as well tell Max what she really wanted, even if it was frivolous and selfish. These past few days, she had become aware that she had never really lived her own life. Like her life was too fragile for her to touch it, lest she mess everything up or disappoint someone. It was, in retrospect, an absurd attitude. She had messed her life up anyway; she just hadn't had any fun doing it. She figured she owed it to Officer Eden and Mac to live a little while she was there.

"Maybe when we have finished finding your canopic jar, of course," she said. "Maybe we could go to one of the nightclubs. Just for a little bit. Maybe go dancing."

"Oh, ho!" said Max. "You are in luck. The Noir Syndicate runs a nightclub, so we get to do both at the same time."

14

Arm in arm they walked for several blocks past glowing nightclub signs. Lively music and the smell of gin and rye spilled out of the inviting, open doors. Over the din of loud-talking tipsy revelers and dance music, the ever-present slinky saxophone solo emanated from the street corner speakers, accompanying their footsteps.

Warmth from Max's arm spread to Jess's, and she felt herself flush. Probably the warm, summer air, she reasoned. She kept hold of Max's arm despite the heat. After all, all the other Noirian couples walked that way, and it was important to blend in.

Max only let go when he stopped them in front of a tall, darkened office building with a brightly-lit nightclub at its base. She touched her inner elbow absently where his arm had been and regarded the club.

There was a half-block-long line of sharply-dressed patrons waiting behind a velvet rope to enter. Two hulking bouncers in pinstripe suits with white lapel roses were accepting cover charges. The illuminated sign over the door said, "The Denial Club: Ignore your worries for a while."

"What is this place?" she asked.

"Griefbegone headquarters," said Budget Sam Spade, suddenly

and uninvited. Jess startled but kept herself from dropping into combat mode this time. "The best-selling medical product in Noir and across all the dimensions. I never touch the stuff myself. You have to have a heart for it to break. But there was this one dame—"

Jess pinched her earlobe before Budget Sam could get started on the poor dame.

"Across the dimensions?" she asked. "People didn't invent Griefbegone independently in multiple worlds at once?"

"Nope," said Max. "It's a contaminating meme."

This surprised her. Jess had always assumed Griefbegone's ubiquitousness owed to that weird human tendency to invent or discover the same things at the same time in multiple places. Like how the crossbow emerged independently on four different continents at once. That's how Clarise had explained it anyhow, and why the Agency didn't crack down on Griefbegone.

"How did it spread then?" she asked.

Max stuffed his hands into the pockets of his crisp pants and rocked back on his heels. "How do you think? Oh, pan-dimensional Super Agent?"

"The Agency?" she said. "But this is exactly the sort of contamination the Agency is supposed to prevent! Griefbegone's been around since before I was born in Garden. Who could have done it?"

"There were Agents before you were born, you know," said Max. "But you already know the culprit. The one person who's been at the Agency since before any employee can remember. Besides me, I mean."

"Clarise?" she said. Max nodded. "But...why?"

She couldn't understand it. The Task Manager had always been harsh, had always had an edge to her. But Clarise had always been the staunchest defender of the dimensions' integrity.

Max shrugged. "Money."

"Money? That's it?"

Jess could hardly believe it. All the rules Clarise had drilled into her. All the hours she'd trained and the oaths she'd sworn. The Agency was a calling, and the woman who'd been the heart of it was only a hypocrite who wanted money?

"Boring, huh?" said Max. "She's trying to set herself up for her next life. She wants to be born as some dimension's richest infant ever. She plans to enjoy life aboard a floating sky yacht for as long as she can until the world ends."

"World ends?" said Jess.

"Oh," said Max, nonchalantly. "Just the standard, inevitable heat death of the universe stuff, I mean. We can't power the Voyager 2.0 once all the cosmic radiation fizzles, heh."

Jess crossed all her arms and glared at him. "All those years, you could have said something about Clarise and the Griefbegone!" she accused.

"And you'd believe the guy in the force cage over the Task Manager of the Agency?" he said, raising an eyebrow at her.

"Touché," she said.

But she decided she didn't believe him. Clarise was an idealist. She'd never shown the slightest inclination toward material goods. And besides, Max had that 'eyes sliding away' look he always got when he was lying. He was hiding something. Jess just couldn't begin to guess what or why. She narrowed her eyes.

"And besides, it doesn't matter," he continued. "The dimensional damage was done long ago. Everyone's adapted."

"What do you mean 'it doesn't matter?'" she said. "It's corruption of the highest order."

Max laughed dismissively. "Pish. Small potatoes. There's even higher-order corruption at play here."

"What could be higher?"

He tipped the brim of his bowler hat and grinned. "Me, for one."

"Ah."

"So, what matters most is that we get that jar," he said. "And remember, the Noir Dimension Syndicate is dangerous. Some of their goons carry lethal assets. Your bug keeps you from crossing over, but I don't want to find out if you can get deleted."

"Me either," she agreed. "Let's go."

She started toward the velvet rope line, but Max grabbed her hand to stop her.

"No, no," he said. "I don't know where in the Denial Club they're keeping my jar, but I guarantee we won't find it in the areas where they allow the regular customers. We're going to have to go behind the scenes to find it."

"How?"

"You're going to get a job!" he grinned. He nodded at an A-frame sidewalk sign with an arrow pointing down the alley to a Denial Club side door that said, "Piano Tryouts Tonight!"

"Oh, no," said Jess. "No, no, no. Maybe next life. My piano skills are not at performance level."

"What's the big deal?" said Max. "It's just trying out."

"Trying out…to then perform. Also, the judges would have to hear my audition. And they're probably people. With ears."

Max chuckled. "Very likely so."

Jess folded an arm. "Look, you want a big heavy thing thrown? A criminal punched unconscious? I'm your girl. But playing music? In front of humans? I only just started piano 90 years ago! Audiences expect performers to have had at least a couple of lifetimes of practice before they sit down to enjoy a concert. I'd only let everyone down if they heard me."

Max shook his head as though he didn't understand, which of course he wouldn't. He never lived up to anyone's expectations. It was his whole thing. But Jess? She couldn't let people down. It was the worst feeling in the world, looking into someone's disappointed face, and knowing it looked that way because you hadn't measured up.

"I don't think they'd notice your mediocrity," said Max. "But I noticed. These past ten years I've observed that you, Jessamae Kensington, are merely okay-ish on piano."

"Gee. Thanks."

"You're welcome!" he said. "Because it's brilliant. From my Pilot's eye view, I see how everyone acts, the general behavior trends aboard the starship. Most people stick with what they're good at. The familiar, safe canopic jar skills honed over lifetimes. Almost no one is ever brave enough to try something new, not even for passion. But you? You found something you loved and jettisoned a seasoned, multi-lifetime skill to make room for it. That's dazzling. And it's why I think you can do this. At least—I think you'll be passable enough as a musician not to rouse the Syndicate's suspicions."

She narrowed her eyes. "Well, this is filling me with confidence," she said. But deep down, it felt good to be called 'brave' and 'dazzling,' though she felt neither of those things.

Max chucked her on the upper right arm. "Come on, what do

you say? The multiverse is depending on you and your lackluster piano skills."

Jess heaved a heavy sigh, remembering her oaths and the debt she owed to Officer Eden. At least her mother wasn't around to be embarrassed by a publicly incompetent daughter. That was something.

"For the multiverse," she mumbled.

Max grinned and led her toward the side door of the Denial Club. She wondered if Dr. Barnes had figured out a way to unjam her jammer signal. Or whether the simple embarrassment of her audition would be enough to cross her over. Barnes would probably find a billing code for that, too, though.

***

Jess had heard the Noir Dimension Syndicate was bad news, but the seedy, backstage lounge where piano tryouts were held really brought the idea home. Mostly, it was the failed piano applicant with a gag in his mouth dangling on a chain above a 20-foot-long Kaiju tank. An eight-foot long croctopus—a creature whose front half was a crocodile head and back half was a mass of tentacles attached to it—circled expectantly below the poor talentless fellow.

Jess was no expert on Kaiju anatomy, but it didn't look like the croctopus had nearly enough belly space to fit the pianist. However, judging by the gleam in its eyes and eager snapping at the musician's feet, it was going to give it a try. Two other failed applicants sat beside the tank, bound and gagged and awaiting their turn. The Syndicate was picky about its music, it seemed.

Adding to the outrageousness of the overwrought execution was the casual atmosphere the Syndicate goons had created in the lounge. Other than the Kaiju tank, the room looked like a dive comedy bar. Cigar smoke and alcohol smell wafted from eight two-person tables in the darkened 'audience' section of the room. Syndicate henchmen wearing the same black pinstripe suits with white lapel roses that the bouncers outside wore sat at them, drinking and talking, their nonchalant conversation din punctuated by the muffled shrieks of the gagged pianist.

In front of the audience tables and to the right of the aquarium stood a raised plywood stage at the center of which stood a white, upright piano. It shone painfully bright under the glare of a hot spotlight that reminded Jess of the confessional lamps back at the Agency's brig. The music judge who'd decided the last guy's act wasn't good enough would be back any minute, and Jess's audition was next. Sweat started to prickle all four of her armpits.

In the shadowed corner where she and Max were standing, Max elbowed her; she startled.

"Oh, hey!" he said. "It's Chester." He pointed at the tank.

"You know that poor guy?" she asked.

"No, no. Chester's the Kaiju. I dropped him and about 100 more of his kind into Noir's floating river market a couple of years back. Nice to see he's landed on his feet. A gig in show business, even."

She blinked. "You…you know all your Kaiju by name?"

He shrugged. "Well, sure. I named them, after all. I form the Kaiju from little bits of my own code and other random data bytes and set them to grow up back in my home dimension. I know I'm not good at this whole 'Pilot' thing. But I am doing my best. Adding my own personal touch. Destroying things…but with love. Just like any god, really."

She shouldn't have been as surprised as she was. After all, the day she'd met Max, he'd been naming stars as the Voyager 2.0 sailed past them. But she and the other Agents had always assumed Max's Kaiju were his flippant, lazy way to fulfill the Pilot's chaos duties. She had no idea how much care he'd been putting into his random, ham-fisted monster attacks.

It was kind of sweet. Like, when a preschooler brings his mother an unrecognizable drawing and she says, "tell me about your picture," rather than, "what the hell is this?" Because it was all done with an earnest heart. All those years, she and the other Agents had been asking Max, "what the hell is this?" she realized, with some shame.

"Chester's kind of small for a Kaiju," she observed. Mostly they were at least 50 feet tall.

"I was really into swarms of miniatures at the time. It was a phase. Like my 'blue period' or something," said Max. "Hey, did you ever hear about the Kaiju who was only three feet tall, but gruesome?" He grinned at her.

Jess sighed heavily. She was going to have to perform a piano solo in a few minutes and she was in no mood to humor Max.

"Yes," she said simply, hoping that would be the end of it, but knowing it wouldn't be.

"Grew-some? Gruesome?" he said, elbowing her. "Get it? It's a homophone."

She stared flatly at Max. How had Budget Sam Spade put it again? Oh, yes. 'Wordplay-minded mook.'

"Forgive me if I'm not in a joking mood," she said, gesturing to the piano stage and Kaiju tableau before them.

"Come on. You'll be fine. You're a Super Agent to begin with. And also, you can't cross over. So even if you bomb on the piano, the worst Chester can do is gnaw on you a little."

She looked at Max like he was insane. "I'm not worried about the croctopus, Max. I'm worried about the audition."

Max returned the 'you're insane' gaze. "Your priorities might be a smidgen screwy, I think."

"Look at those audience tables. Two henchmen are sitting at each one. Plus you. Plus the judge when he returns. Plus the previous piano applicants. Oh, and I forgot - Chester. I know you're not a 'math person,' but that's 40 total ears about to hear me suck it up onstage."

"Well, I'll be off looking for the canopic jar while you distract them with your playing. And Chester doesn't even have ears."

"So, 36 ears and two crocodile auditory holes, then," she said miserably.

"And I really don't think you need to care what that fellow dangling over the tank thinks of your playing. He is in no position to judge."

"Speaking of," she said, "What's the plan for rescuing him?"

"I'll pocket him when they lower him into Chester's tank, so it looks like he got eaten."

"Pocket him?"

"That trick I do where a ring of light opens, and I toss a canopic jar into the dimension beyond."

"It's safe for humans, then?" she asked.

He gave her a sly grin. "I mean, you've seen me toss a kindergartener inside."

She recalled the little girl, Sirita, from her first day at the Agency.

All her giggles. How nice Jess thought it might be to have her own child. But Vince hadn't wanted kids, so that had been that. "Oh, yeah," she said. "And the other two prisoners?"

"When I get back," he said. "I don't have to be so slick when I save them. Once I have the jar, we don't need to worry about concealing our identities."

An ominous shaft of light pierced the dim lounge, illuminating the clouds of cigar smoke. A man stood silhouetted in the open door.

"It was Mr. Styles, the Entertainment Judge and right hand of the Noir Syndicate's boss," narrated Budget Sam Spade. "He was stocky and squat like a fireplug with a face like the bulldog that was peeing on it. He had an underbite like a piranha and the personality to go with it."

"Cool it, Sam," Jess muttered. She dialed her earlobe back to the minimum setting—'emergency interruptions only.'

Mr. Styles entered the room, swirling a three-olive martini in his hand. The pinstripe suit he wore was the photographic negative of his goons' outfits—white with black pinstripes and steel-gray lapel rose. He nodded toward the Kaiju tank, and the chain began to let out slow inch by slow inch as Chester swirled eagerly below the piano applicant. Styles raised a micro-toast to the man and approached the corner where she and Max were standing.

Max stepped up to Mr. Styles and reached out to shake his hand. Styles stared at it, like it was a rancid fish. "I'm Max," said Max, withdrawing the disdained hand and wiping it on his vest. "We hear you've got an opening for a pianist?"

"You heard right. Our regular guy left the organization suddenly. Finally caught his big break."

"Point of context for your safety," interrupted Budget Sam. Jess's nerves came alight. She'd just dialed his settings back to 'emergency only.' "The 'big break' he's referring to happened last week when Mr. Styles caught the pianist canoodling with his third-favorite girlfriend and broke every bone in both their arms, from the phalanges to the funny bones. Which they failed to find humerus."

Unbelievable. She'd just muzzled Sam, but he'd interrupted anyway to deliver some terrible bone puns and the information that Mr. Styles was a bad dude. Seemed that Sam was a bit 'mookish' himself.

Then he interrupted again.

"Further point of context for your safety," he said. His voice was quieter and serious that time. None of the hard-boiled personality accompanied his words. "The gun tucked in his waistband is a lethal asset. And Mr. Styles has never been shy about using it."

Max locked eyes with her, a grim, pursed-lipped expression on his face. Budget Sam was probably whispering the same thing to Max right then. The presence of a weapon that could delete people shifted the power dynamic here considerably. She'd trained for this, but Max sure hadn't. She hoped the Pilot didn't wind up doing something rash or foolish with such a dangerous weapon so close. And in the hands of such slime too.

A splash sounded from Chester's tank. The piano applicant was only about four feet above the tank surface now, and the Kaiju was trying to jump out of the water and start dinner early. The other two failed applicants shut their eyes and huddled together for comfort. Styles chuckled darkly, then turned toward Jess. He squinted at her with dark, piggish eyes and frowned.

"This your girl?" he asked Max.

"Uh, I'm her agent, yes?" said Max.

"She's a freak," Styles said.

Jess felt her mouth drop open. She hadn't expected gentleman-ly behavior from Styles, given Budget Sam's warning. But this was beyond the pale. She hadn't seen much body augmentation in Noir, but she'd seen at least some. There'd been a dead ringer for Grace Kelly standing in line behind the velvet rope with angel wings on either side of her head where ears ought to be. Jess couldn't be the first augment Styles had ever seen.

"The arms help with piano," she explained calmly, trying to keep the anger out of her voice. She could crush this little pugdog of a man with one of her pinky fingers. But that would be bad for the mission.

Styles ignored her and turned to Max instead. "I mean that she's tall. Freakishly tall. Can't stand broads taller than me. But she's damn good-looking at the same time. I'm having a hard time deciding how to feel about her."

Jess was suddenly very glad she was wearing four-inch heels. She wished they were five or six inches tall, in fact. She wished to positively tower over this nasty man.

Max cleared his throat awkwardly. "Er. She is here for the piano job, not you. And I don't know how many concerts you've seen, being the entertainment judge and all, but she will in fact be sitting down when she plays the piano."

Jess was glad Max was there to explain this to Mr. Styles, because her brain was on too high a boil to respond coherently. But then Styles went on.

"I mean…when I look at your girl," he said, "I get this weird lust/revulsion combination that's very interesting. Like I wanna go visit her Netherlands, but I'd have to take an antiviral shower after. I'm sure a lotta other guys would feel the same. It's unique. Maybe workable for an act. I'll listen to her play after all." He chucked Max on the arm and grinned horribly, as though he'd given Max some sort of honor.

Max put a quiet hand on her shoulder and squeezed. His gaze slid to her, his expression horrified on her behalf. But he needn't have worried. Jess was accustomed to schooling her emotions. She'd developed many tactics for this over the course of her life. Just then, in fact, her brain had been playing a little head movie about punching Styles over and over to see just how much flatter she could make his pug face.

But Jess was a trained Agent, Styles had a lethal firearm, and she and Max had a mission to complete. She smiled back at Max to indicate she was not about to start a brawl, though she certainly deserved to.

"Your girl takes the stage as soon as the last guy gets eaten," Styles informed them. "I wanna give her audition my full attention. It is an embarrassment to me to put a bad performer on the main stages. One I take very personally, as entertainment Judge. I wouldn't want to miss a single foul-up just because I was relishing the demise of that cold fish on the chain."

Styles walked to the audience tables. The pair of black-suited goons sitting at it scrambled up and away, allowing their very dangerous superior his own space. Max took her elbow and led her toward the stage.

"As soon as I pocket that pianist, I'm going to go look for the jar," he whispered. "I wish I could stay to watch your audition."

"I don't need your moral support," she said. "The audition is to serve the mission, not the other way around."

Max chuckled. "No, I mean I wish I could watch because I can tell you're going to be great."

"How?" she asked.

"Right now you are so furious with Styles that you look like a Valkyrie. I know you're going to knock everyone's socks off."

Perhaps she would. Her fear seemed to have evaporated in the heat of her anger, and now there was an eager sensation of licking flames tickling up and down all 20 of her fingers. She wanted to play. She'd show them. She'd show them all. It was a new emotion. A different sort of crack in the gray fog. One with red behind it, rather than blue. She could use it.

A splash from the tank caught her attention. Chester had leaped from the water and locked his jaws onto the pianist's ankle. The man screamed through his gag.

"Uh oh," Max muttered. "It's going to be hard to hide the light ring if Chester eats him above the surface of the water. I've got this."

Max made a subtle pointing gesture at the dangle chain, and one of the links snapped. The pianist fell into the water, splashing the closest two tables. Chester surged toward the pianist, kicking up a view-obscuring number of bubbles.

"My drink!" cried one of the Syndicate goons.

Jess caught a ring-shaped flash of light through the disturbed water and tentacles. Chester thrashed a few more seconds before breaching the surface. He keened dismay, robbed of his dinner. The Kaiju's cry was like the sound of a walrus making love to a bassoon. The table goons clapped, unaware that they'd actually been cheated out of their execution. Jess turned to congratulate Max, but he was already gone.

"The stage is yours," came Mr. Styles's voice from the audience section.

Jess stepped onto the raised platform, sure and steady atop her towering shoes. She pulled out the bench and sat down. The spotlight overhead shone down hot on her, but Jess was already full of fire. She and the light were kindred now. It was there to stoke her, not to wilt her.

She placed all four hands on the white ivories and the black ebonies, thinking what song she would choose. Noir's music was her kind of music. Its style was her kind of style. If there was anywhere she wanted to belong, it was here.

The pent-up energy coursing through her fingers itched for something fast with syncopation. She chose the Lawrence Cook version of Bugle Call Rag, took a deep breath, and began to play.

She slipped into a mindset then, that she often fell into when practicing. Where the outside world went away, and her universe became the rhythm and the pitches and the gathering phrases. She moved through the music, placing her emphasis on just the right notes to tell herself the story of the song.

Every song had an underlying form, and the musician was a beam of light, illuminating the structure that the little black dots perched on staff lines suggested. Like sunrise light descending down a mountainside, revealing the majesty of what had stood all night in cold darkness awaiting something living to bring it back to life. It was the composer's story, narrated in her own voice and she and he touched across time and death and light years of space and together made music.

She finished the song and remained seated at the piano, breathing. She had done well. It had been raw and flawed, but her performance had fire. In the past, she would have wished her mother had been with her to witness what Jess had felt had been a triumph. But she found herself wishing it had been Max there instead. Silly of her. They were there for a mission.

Several of the table goons clapped enthusiastically into the post-performance silence, confirming her suspicions about how well she'd done. They were quickly hushed up by their compatriots, she supposed so they could await Styles's verdict.

"It's passable," he said from the back. "You won't embarrass me, at least. That's something. Run-of-the-mill piano skills coupled with your weirdly compelling figure, I bet you could fill a room. I can put you on the Depression Stage."

Such flattery.

"Depression Stage?" she asked.

"We've got five stages, each named for one of stages of grief. Get it? It's hilarious," he said deadpan. Like Styles himself hadn't named them, but someone above him in the Syndicate hierarchy had, so officially he loved the names.

"You've got to be a whole lot better to make the Acceptance Stage," he said. "But Depression is just fine for a small-timer oddball act. Maybe Anger once you've got more shows under your belt."

"What stage is this?" she asked.

"Bargaining, obviously," Styles said, gesturing to the Kaiju tank. A bell sounded over the door. Styles looked suddenly worried. Jess wondered what could make this cold killer fearful.

"Ah," he said. "The boss is here. She'll want to meet you."

Jess turned and her stomach went cold. Clarise stood framed in the doorway, light streaming in from behind her, banishing the concealing shadows.

15

The Task Manager's cream-colored bob shone white in the colorlessness of Noir. Her Jumpsuit had chameleoned into a fox-hunting-style jacket, as she preferred, but with a pencil skirt and pumps instead of riding breeches and boots. Her legs were spread in a wide, strong stance; her fists were planted on either hip, her riding crop clutched in her left hand.

Chair legs scraped away from tables as 16 Syndicate goons scrambled to their feet and fell into attention before the big boss. Jess noted with some satisfaction that even Styles looked intimidated in Clarise's presence.

But the stirrings of Jess's Agency pride were undercut by the sinking knowledge that Max hadn't been lying about Clarise heading the Griefbegone Syndicate. The Task Manager had been dedicated to upholding the laws and the integrity of the dimensions for as long as Jess had known her. Clarise's crime-boss identity was so incongruous with everything Jess knew of her that she almost couldn't accept it. So, what had Max been lying about? Clarise's motivations?

"Styles!" barked Clarise. "There's been a break-in at the lab. Quit playing around with the club entertainment and go do the important half of your job."

Jess assumed the break-in had been Max. A sudden worry prickled its way down her spine. She hadn't told Max about the viral serum that could delete him. Was it back at the lab he was stealing from? Or did Clarise have it on her person?

"Yes, ma'am," said Styles, moving to leave. But then Clarise spied Jess.

"Jessamae?" she said.

Jess prepared to drop into a fighting stance, but Clarise's free hand flew to her mouth and her face softened. "My very own Jessamae? Safe and alive?"

"Uh," said Jess.

Clarise rushed forward and caught her in a tight embrace. Jess struggled for breath as the Task Manager's arms constricted around her ribcage.

"Point of context for your safety," interrupted Budget Sam. "I don't know what the Hell this thing that looks like a woman is. But it has a lethal asset and is ten times stronger than you. You better hope the crush it's got on you doesn't turn literal."

'Thing that looks like a woman?' Jess wondered. What did the ambient narration software see that Jess could not? But Budget Sam needn't have worried. Clarise released her and wiped her eyes, seemingly overcome with emotion.

"How did you escape from Max?" said Clarise. "I was so worried when that untethered brute kidnapped you!"

"Uh, you know our new pianist?" asked Styles.

"Know her?" said Clarise. "She's my finest Agent, and like a daughter to me."

Styles pulled uncomfortably at his collar. He'd been the height of rude to someone much more important than he'd believed. Jess did not smirk at him, which would have been childish. Jess was above that.

But Clarise's reaction was interesting. She seemed to think Jess had been Max's victim, not his liberator. Whether the Task Manager truly believed this, or whether it was an act to get her guard down, she didn't know. The other Agents knew the truth of what Jess had done. But she didn't know if they'd told the boss.

On another level, she tried to ignore how good Clarise's welcome felt. How nice it was to feel fussed over and cared about and how much she wished Clarise's feelings were genuine. Like a daughter, she'd said. But it didn't add up.

"You almost hit me with your riding crop," said Jess. "As hard as you could?" She tried to make it sound like a question, rather than an accusation, to invite Clarise to explain herself.

"Combat reflexes, dear. I know you understand what it's like. Besides, my control is excellent. The blow wouldn't have been dangerous if you hadn't flinched away." There was a note of indictment in Clarise's voice. "Besides, at the time, it looked like you might have been Max's accomplice. Given the risks that man poses to the ship, I had to act."

Jess nodded. Clarise was right on both counts. Agency training emphasized that it was dangerous to hold back in a deadly situation, no matter what the collateral damage. It didn't sit well with her, but Jess could stuff down her personal feelings of betrayal in the face of logic.

"Max?" said Styles. "Wasn't that the name of your short, scrawny talent scout?"

Clarise's eyes flashed with the predatory interest of a cat that's just seen something small and wiggling.

"Max is here? You brought him here?"

Jess swallowed. There was no denying it now. She nodded mutely. Clarise gave her a wide, white smile.

"Max is the Pilot, Styles, for your information," said Clarise. "To think I ever doubted you, Jessamae! You don't know how perfect this is. I have a viral serum that will dissolve Max bit by byte. When he escaped, I thought we would be locked into a tedious manhunt across the dimensions. But you, my brilliant girl, you brought him right to me. Everything I've been working for comes to fulfillment at last!"

"I thought you were only going to put him in a coma and use his power," Jess said.

"Max is like a Hydra," said Clarise. "You can't have just one plan for dealing with him. The coma was what I had the Agency working on. It was all 'above-board.' No deletions. Nothing illegal. Something my pure-hearted Agents could do. But I couldn't put all the Voyager 2.0's safety eggs in one coma basket."

"That's another thing," said Jess. "You've been contaminating the dimensions. Selling Griefbegone everywhere. That's breaking every Agency law."

"In service of the larger goal of unseating Max."

"Not making money for yourself personally?"

Clarise scoffed. "The money was for research and development. The Pilot-dissolving serum wasn't easy or cheap to create. Surely, you can see that, Jessamae. It was Max who forced me into this terrible position. And now I find myself the unwilling head of a criminal organization. When this is all over, I promise you can arrest me. I will go willingly, satisfied that I've done my job. Only help me finish it."

Clarise extended her hand for an agreement handshake, a rare pleading expression on her face. Max had been wrong or lying—about Clarise's motivations, at least. She didn't want money. She truly thought she was doing what was right for the ship. And she was correct; Max was dangerous. But so was a leader so consumed with regaining control she ignored the dangers she herself was creating.

But Clarise didn't need to know that was what Jess really thought. Jess accepted the handshake. Clarise looked relieved.

"I don't suppose you managed to steal his Disruptor remote?" asked Clarise. "Max is unlikely to sit still for the injection."

Jess shook her head. "He stole it as soon as he escaped."

"Blast," said Clarise. "But it's alright. I have other ways of subduing him."

"How?" Jess asked. "Max can bend reality. He put you in a Christmas pudding!"

Clarise smiled. "Look through your VR goggles, dear," she said.

Jess opened her clutch purse and riffled through her spy gear. She nudged her gun aside. Under the gloves with Clarise's fingerprints, she found her goggles. She put them on and gasped. Every single one of the Syndicate goons had full Agent powers.

"All these men are Agents," Jess breathed.

"Not just these 17 gentlemen," said Clarise. "Every one of Noir's Syndicate Henchmen are superpowered and highly trained. I created an army capable of taking Max on. Yet another backup plan for dealing with the Hydra."

"How many are there?" Jess asked.

"A hundred and fifteen," said Mr. Styles.

"That's not going to be nearly enough," said Max.

Jess turned. He was seated on the edge of the Kaiju tank, petting Chester's crocodile head with one hand and clutching a large, dark-glass canopic jar that had a jackal-shaped lid with the other.

"Get him!" Clarise shouted.

The lapel-rose goons rushed toward Max. They'd only gotten a few steps before lurching to a stop, unable to lift their feet. Jess looked down to see the soles of their shoes had melted to the hardwood floor. Their lapel roses morphed into animated Venus flytraps that snapped at the goon's chins with cartoonish, serrated teeth.

The corner of Jess's mouth tugged up. Max was a walking nonstandard dimension. A living Narnia. A portable Hogwarts. Who needed to escape to Neverland when you were with Max?

She shouldn't have worried about the Syndicate's deletion serum. As long as Max was conscious, there was nothing anyone could do to stop him. She started toward him so they could escape, but Styles grabbed her lower left arm. She tried to twist away, but for once, she found herself in the grasp of someone stronger than she was. It was a new experience.

Styles's hand moved to his waistband, and his pistol emerged in a silver flash.

"Point of Context for your safety," said Budget Sam. "You're too close to Mr. Styles. The gun he's got is deadly. And his cologne is trying its best."

Styles pointed the barrel toward the Kaiju tank, taking aim at the leftmost failed piano applicant. He squeezed the trigger, and the man exploded in a spray of sparkling 1's and 0's like confetti. His bindings and clothes fell empty to the floor, and the stomach-turning smell of bile and brimstone rolled over Jess like a wave, dragging her under toward dark, unknown thoughts of death. Max leaped to his feet and started toward Styles.

Styles put the gun barrel to Jess's head. "Don't move, Mr. Pilot. Or I put a new window on the top floor of your skyscraper."

Max skidded to a halt, a wild look in his eyes Jess had never seen before. His image on Jess's VR lenses went strange. Fuzzing in and out in bursts of static.

"Good work, Styles," said Clarise. "I know he has a little crush on our girl here."

The Task Manager's eyes gleamed in triumph. She winked at Jess, as though this was a ruse to trick Max, and Jess was in on it. A fake hostage. Jess didn't think Styles saw it that way, though. She swallowed and kept still, trying not to throw up from the smell.

"Do you realize what you've done?" Max said. "That pianist. There was only one of him in the whole universe."

"That's nothing," said Styles. "People are a half-chit a dozen. Too many of 'em crammed in all these thousands of dimensions anyway. Me and my boys don't mind making more elbow room for the rest of us."

The other goons chuckled darkly, feet still stuck to the floor, but feeling more confident now that their side had some leverage at last.

"All those souls," Max panted. "I swore oaths to protect them."

Clarise scoffed. "You did no such thing. You weaseled your way into power and sat there like a bloated tick, feasting on us all. Now, as Mr. Styles said, he has no qualms getting his hands dirty. If you know what's good for Jessamae, you'll hold very still until this is finished."

The Task Manager drew a syringe from her foxhunting jacket and cocked her head at Max, awaiting his response. Max nodded. Jess's stomach dropped. Max didn't know what the serum would do to him.

"Max don't!" she said, throwing her lot in publicly with the Pilot. But Styles clapped a hand over her mouth. She bit Styles's hand and tasted blood, but the bulldog-faced man only grunted and held tight, accustomed to pain.

Clarise turned to Jess, a look of betrayal on her face that hardened into a cruel sneer.

"It'll be fine, Max," said Clarise. "Just hold still, and everything will go right back to the way it was before your little adventure."

Max was shifting nervously from foot to foot. Something wasn't right. When Jess looked over the top of her VR lenses, he looked crazed. He was sweating, his chest was heaving, and his eyes were wild. But when she looked through them, he barely looked human at all. He was a man-shaped shadow of static. There was a low, tingling vibration emanating from him, pulsating through the air.

"Do what the lady says, Mr. Pilot," said Styles. "Praise Be Unto

You, and all that."

He cocked the lethal gun and pressed it hard to Jess's temple. Max came unhinged. A bolt of lightning erupted from his eyes and struck Styles. Jess found herself in a cloud of glittering confetti. 1's and 0's. The smell of brimstone and bile. She gagged and sank to her knees as Max rose into the air. The canopic jar tumbled from his hand and shattered, adding the tang of anise to the vile deletion smell.

"Point of context for your safety," said Budget Sam. "I have no idea what's going on. But this is bad."

Several of the goons screamed. Clarise pocketed the syringe and ran to Jess's side.

"Come on, Jessamae," she said, tugging at her shoulder. But Jess couldn't find her feet. Max had deleted Styles. Jess had been in the middle of a dissolving human, touching the man who, though no great loss to the world, was now simply gone. She felt coated in slime and darkness, and she didn't know if she'd ever be able to wash the feeling away.

Max turned his electric gaze on Clarise, a charge gathered where his pupils ought to be. Clarise left Jess behind and bolted from the room. Max released the lightning strike into one of the goons with the stuck shoes. The others shouted with terror and tried to pull their feet free. Max deleted another man. Then another.

"Max!" she called. "Stop!"

He turned to look at her. His eyes were full of electricity and empty of his soul, and she was struck with the feeling of missing a sheep. Max wasn't home.

Trembling, she approached his hovering form and reached up to touch his foot. He stared down at her, cold, distant, and unfamiliar. His footwear was phasing back and forth between a wingtip shoe and a bear foot slipper. The sight of the slipper gave her hope that perhaps Max was in there somewhere, just submerged for the moment. She had to try to bring him to the surface.

"Hey," she said. "This is a fancy nightclub. You can't go bear foot in here." His expression didn't change, but his lightning eyes blinked. "Come on," she said gently. "This isn't how you are. Clarise? The Agents? They think this is how you are, but I know better."

This was completely illogical, she knew. Max had literally deleted four people right in front of her. It was very much 'how he was.' And yet, she believed her own words. If Max could choose, he would not choose this. So, she very much needed the real Max back.

Suddenly, the sensation of vibrating air vanished. Max sank to the floor, the lightning gone from his eyes. His feet touched the ground, but he kept on sinking until he was lying on his back, gasping like a fish on a riverbank.

His eyes were glassy and unfocused, and she still felt like she was missing a sheep. Max's soul had not yet returned. She was almost out of time. Several of the goons had freed one of their feet from the stuck shoes. Shouts sounded down the hall, accompanied by enough heavy footsteps to be a miniature army. Clarise's voice rose over the noise.

"He's in there! This is what you've trained for. Don't kill the four-armed woman, if you can help it."

Jess was out of time. Clarise was coming back with the deletion serum, and Max was unconscious and couldn't Jump them away. But she could Jump them home to Garden. She started to reach for her belly button, then stopped. There were people she cared about in Garden. Hippopotamus, for one. And Vince, and even stupid Anne. Max might be unsafe for them.

She poked Max's belly button instead and held tight to him as the world turned white and Max's 'home key' programming took them to whatever dimension he had been born into.

16

Jess blinked as the Jump light faded. She raised her head from Max's chest where it had been buried, and her heart sank at what she saw. There was only one dimension this could be. She might have known Max would hail from Desolation.

It was daylight in this world and hot, but it was a grim daylight dulled by a haze of choking dust kicked up across the wasteland by a relentless howling wind. The ground was gray dirt-baked hard under a rainless sky and shot through with so many desiccation cracks the earth itself resembled a floor of hexagonal bathroom tiles.

In the distance, the ruins of a modern city loomed forlorn against the horizon. The graceful spires of abandoned skyscrapers had been reduced to exposed structural skeletons, devoid of colored glass and bent at disturbing, unstable angles.

The biggest giveaway that this was Desolation, however, was the brachiosaurus with a cobra for a neck and head they'd landed under. It was the biggest Kaiju Jess had ever seen in all her years as an Agent, and its foot was coming down on them.

Max lay on his back on the hard earth. Back in his underwear and bathrobe, but still staring blankly upward, not comprehending.

"Max!" she cried, shaking him.

But he didn't respond. She leaped to her feet and stood astride his prone form. She raised all four of her arms to catch the descending pillar leg, praying she was strong enough. She'd never be able to stop the foot, but maybe, just maybe she could knock it off course.

As soon as the rough, scaly foot pad touched her palms, she pushed. Her combat boots scraped against dry ground as the weight of the beast pressed down on her. She thrust sideways to the left and her tendons strained painfully, threatening to snap. This is what her powers were for. Until this moment, she'd always thought her superstrength had been a bit overkill. Now she was certain it wasn't enough.

And it wouldn't have been, except that the Cobrachiosaurs bellowed in surprise and jerked its knee up. It lurched awkwardly and then brought the foot down about six feet to the left of them with an earthshaking thud. Jess collapsed onto her knees beside Max, breathing hard, aching, and with a pain in her left upper elbow that made her worry she'd torn a ligament.

Then the Kaiju's cobra head snaked back toward her, its slitted eyes glowing red. Jess curled her body over Max. She had no energy left for a fight or even to run. Her code bug kept her from crossing over, and Kaiju didn't delete people. But this was going to really, really hurt. And then she and Max would be too wounded to escape when Clarise found them at last.

But the Cobrachiosaurus only flared its hood at her and hissed reproachfully before ambling off into the hazy dust storm. The annoyed, almost offended expression it had worn reminded Jess of herself when she tripped over Hippopotamus in the dark.

Max coughed then, and a missing presence filled her like a sheep returning to her fold. She looked down at him. His yellow skin was butter pale, but his eyes were focused, and he was smiling weakly. He looked like himself again. She almost threw her arms around him and hugged him from the immense relief of it all. But that would be unprofessional.

"Wow," he wheezed. "That was really impressive."

"You were awake? It would have been reassuring if you'd said something."

"I was too groggy," he said. "I'm still too groggy. Gosh this wind is annoying. Hang on." He snapped his fingers and the howling ceased. The dust began to clear from the air. Jess tried not to gape. Another reminder of how powerful Max was.

"Would have been nice if you'd been awake to do something too." She rubbed her strained elbow. She could have done with some god-like assistance with that Cobrachiosaurus.

"I hate to kibitz about your amazing rescue," he said, "but I have to say, you really did things the hard way. I am not that big a guy. I know I ate a lot of tacos back in Dimension X, but it would have been way easier to drag me out from under Lydia's foot."

"Lydia?"

"The Kaiju," he said.

Oh. Of course. But it was a fair point. She could have dragged him, but some instinct had warned her not to.

"I didn't know whether I should move you. I had to Jump us away, but your soul didn't seem to be in your body at the time. I worried that somehow, if I moved you, you couldn't find your way home."

"That doesn't make any sense," he said.

She shrugged. "Sorry. I've just never seen anything like what you did back there. I am way out of my depth, and I am so glad you're back."

His brows furrowed. He struggled to sit up, failed, and sank back to the dirt. "What do you mean, what I did back there?"

"You don't remember?" she asked. She sized him up. He was acting far too jovially to be aware of what he had done.

"The last thing I remember was…petting Chester. Melting every-one's feet to the floor. Then…that poor pianist. Then…" His eyes wid-ened. He put a hand over his mouth, squeezed his eyes shut, and curled away from her into the fetal position. "Oh, God. What have I done?" he mumbled softly.

She put a hand on his shoulder and felt him trembling. "It's okay now. You're safe. You're back."

"How many did I delete? Four," he said, answering his own ques-tion. "My God - four. You stopped me, Jess. Thank you for stopping me. This is why the Agency can't keep knocking me out and using my powers. I can barely control them when I'm conscious. And now, I've started slipping into that mode, even when awake? This has to end now." He sat up and looked around wildly. "The jar…"

"Broken," she said.

"No," he whispered. "Oh, no."

"Why?" she asked. "The contents are spilled. Unless someone thinks to sponge up the liquid before it evaporates, wouldn't that mean you are in the clear? That the Syndicate will forget you?"

He stared hard at her, as though considering something. After a long moment, he nodded, like he'd reached a decision. "Sure. I can tell you. Now that the last jar's broken, I'm going to need help. And you want to cross over anyway, so nothing I can say can damage you further." There was a touch of censure in his voice.

"What do you mean?" she asked.

"I lied. About the jars. My past. I lied because the truth is that I am so much worse than some petty criminal. The truth is that this - this," he waved his arm to indicate the barren wasteland of Desolation, "is all my fault."

"What?" she said.

She looked across the wasteland to the destroyed city on the horizon. The readout on her VR goggles indicated there was no human life anywhere there. She hadn't believed Max was truly capable of such destruction. She struggled to believe it now, even as he offered to confess.

"What did you do?" she asked.

"Here is the truth. I was never a criminal. I never tricked my way into the Pilot's chair. That was the story I made up. I started off as a normal Pilot—a good Pilot—so many centuries ago. I was a math genius with a shiny, irreproachable morality record. For 200 years, the Voyager 2.0 thrived under my command. Until everything went wrong."

Jess stiffened. His words should have been shocking. And yet, so many things seemed to fall into place. How the all-powerful Max would never harm Clarise or the other Agents no matter how they tormented him. The way he'd acted the first day she'd met him. Max had always kept secrets. But these words, at last, felt like the truth. She leaned toward him.

"What went wrong?" she asked.

"I had served my term and was preparing to rejoin my family here in my home dimension—which was called Spring back then. But when

I tried to step down…I couldn't."

"Couldn't?" Jess said.

"It turns out, I have a code bug. I can't fix it—and I have tried every-thing. You know how it is," he said.

She nodded. She did indeed. "What a piece of rotten luck, installing a Pilot with a hidden code bug."

Max nodded ruefully. "At first, it was alright. I soldiered on past my 'expiration date.' My team of Agents had my back. I kept on man-aging the dimensions, inserting chaos with skill and finesse. It seemed like things might be alright until we found a solution.

"But the decades dragged on without a cure. One by one, members of my family came to me. They wished me goodbye and crossed over. My team members did the same. I replaced them with new Agents, whom I liked and who liked me. And all seemed okay. I never told the new people about the code bug, and I carried on like all was normal.

"Then I started making mistakes. There were information bleeds between dimensions. My natural disasters deleted people. So, I made the Kaiju—chaos with a little bit of soul, so the monsters could stop themselves from going too far, even when I could not.

"The truth is, I've been Pilot for over a thousand years, and I'm wearing out. Coming unraveled. I don't know how much longer I will have before I lose it altogether and start deleting people. I mean, I guess I already have. And I can't step down to get rid of this power. I can't even get deleted. The ship is stuck with me."

Jess thought about telling him that Clarise had found a way to delete him. But instinct warned her to keep that information close to the vest. Max was truth telling now, and the less she interrupted, the more she was likely to learn.

"You know?" Jess said, "When I first met you, you didn't seem like a criminal or immature screw off. You seemed…deep."

He gave her a pale smile. "Thanks for that. And you're right. I had dropped the act that day because you were new and didn't know the lie yet. Which was actually a bit selfish of me, I realize. I want-ed you to like me because I'd gotten so damn lonely existing as 'Max the Criminal.'"

"I don't get it," said Jess. "Why didn't you tell anybody? Why let us think you were a selfish little bad guy? You didn't have to be so alone.

We could have helped!"

He laughed bitterly. "Because the last time I told my Agents the truth, it destroyed this dimension. The Voyager 2.0 is doomed because of me. This secret is apocalyptic, Jess. Eventually, I'm going to snap and kill the ship and everyone aboard it. The truth of this is so heavy, that people who learn it apply to cross over."

"Just because they know?"

Max nodded. "At first it was just one of my Agents. A guy I really trusted. He was from the Spring Dimension, just like me. It felt good to unburden myself to him, but the knowledge was too much for him and he lost all hope. He told some of his family members, and then he crossed over so he could forget he ever knew. And some of them told some other people, and they told others until everyone in Spring knew. Every fourth person crossed over to forget the grief of knowing. And those left behind didn't wish to remain in the sad, increasingly lonely world. There was a gradual exodus until the whole Spring Dimension was empty of people. Now…I just grow my Kaiju here. It's convenient, I guess."

"And that's why you invented the criminal story," she said, understanding at last. "To explain your incompetence without risking catastrophic despair in another dimension."

Max nodded, a pained, wistful sort of smile on his face. He'd been so isolated for so long, she realized. Bearing this on his own. Trying his best to fix himself as he slowly lost his mind.

Max reminded her of a passage from Peter Pan: "Stars are beautiful, but they may not take an active part in anything, they must just look on forever. It is a punishment for something they did so long ago that no star now knows what it was. So the older ones have become glassy-eyed and seldom speak, but the little ones still wonder."

He was like those stars. Separated from everyone else by an ancient fault. Unable to speak about it. Unable to partake. It struck her as an unutterably sad fate. She was a bit ashamed that she'd fallen for his 'petty criminal' act and written him off as an inconvenient pest. Just as the other Agents had.

"I didn't give up, though," said Max. There was a trace of pride in his voice about this. "I tried more things. I created the Task Manager to keep me in line."

"Wait," said Jess. "You made Clarise?"

"Yeah. I was desperate for someone who could control me. I thought I could grow my own warden like I grew the Kaiju. That's why Clarise is way stronger than even you superpowered Agents. But err, I wasn't functioning particularly well when I made her. The program turned out to be somewhat more antagonistic than expected."

"Somewhat?" Jess said.

Max grinned. "The force cage was a big surprise, for instance. Some researcher in your Garden Dimension invented it, by the way. Fella called Barnes."

"Barnes?" she said. She really shouldn't have been surprised.

He nodded. "It's some brilliant, nasty code. It kept me contained during some of my more unhinged psychotic breakdowns, so I can't fault Clarise—no matter what she does to me. I am the reason she is the way she is, after all. One more muck up to add to my toll."

Max lay back on the ground and closed his eyes. The dark circles under them were more pronounced. Jess began to understand his worn-out appearance a little better. He was a thousand years old and burning his candle at both ends.

"So yeah," he said. "Now you know what I'm becoming. You've even witnessed it, you poor woman. Does it make you want to give up and cross over even more?"

Jess thought about this. Two days earlier, all she'd wanted was to leave behind the gray feeling and start over again somewhere new and fresh. But the funny thing was that knowing the ship was doomed gave her purpose. And if she were honest with herself, she hadn't felt the least bit gray since she'd decided to defy Clarise and spring Max from the force cage.

"Actually, it makes me want to help," she said.

Max opened his eyes at this; the ghost of a smile touched his lips. "It seems I was right about you, after all. Anyone with the courage to fill a canopic jar with something new has enough imagination to defeat terminal boredom."

"Not boredom," she corrected. It was important to be firm with Max on this point. "Don't trivialize the feeling. It's meaninglessness. Loneliness. These things are heavy for humans—heavier even than knowing the world will end and death will come. It's not a character flaw to buckle under the weight of it."

He put a hand on her lower left wrist. "I'm sorry. I didn't mean to be flippant." Then, more quietly he said, "And I really understand the loneliness bit."

She gave him a faint smile. "Yes. I imagine you do. So, what are the canopic jars?" she said. "How do we fix whatever went wrong when that last one broke?"

Max sat up then, his expression suddenly animated. "Okay, you're going to love this. Every jar you've ever fetched me contains one of two things. An ansible signal, or a permission code to enter the Voyager 2.0."

"Enter? As in, enter other dimensions?"

"As in enter the ship itself. From outside. The ansible signals aren't for interdimensional communication. They're interstellar signals. Over the last millennium, I've been calling for help from the other ships like ours, the ones that launched from Earth thousands of years ago. And someone answered! The Sputnik II found us among a sea of stars and their Pilot, Izumi, and I have been steering our ships toward each other. The Sputnik II and the Voyager 2.0 are docked right now. I've been feeding them permission codes so they can access our ship."

"That's impossible! The ships are far-flung across the Milky Way."

"These server ships travel at one tenth the speed of light," said Max. "Since the average distance between stars in our galaxy is five light years, it takes us about 50 years to travel between stars. We got lucky Sputnik II was so close, but it did take about 750 years for us to get to each other. They went through three Pilots in that time, but the ship kept coming. The trouble is it is awaiting the last of the Voyager 2.0's permission codes to open our ports."

"Which was in the canopic jar that broke," said Jess, understanding Max's dismay at the loss.

He nodded. "I was so close, Jess. I almost had this in the bag. But then I lost control."

"How do we fix it? Is there another jar with another code?"

He shook his head. "There isn't. And I don't know any other way to crack the password except to run numbers through a quantum processor until it guesses the right combination. That could take decades. And I'm unraveling fast."

"We'll think of something," Jess said. She touched her utility belt where she kept the Frankenphone and the direct line back to the other Agents. Amira was a genius with these kinds of problems. Perhaps she could find a way to speed up the process. But something was troubling Jess.

"Max," she said. "What will the Sputnik II's Pilot do once she gets inside?"

"Only another Pilot is powerful enough to unseat me," said Max. "Izumi will enter the ship, uproot me from the Voyager 2.0, and insert herself as interim Pilot until we can find a replacement."

"What will that do to you?" she asked.

"Oh, I'll survive. I won't be able to get a new life in a new dimension ever again. But I won't be deleting people anymore, so I will rest a whole lot easier at night. All in all, I call it a win."

"So, you'll just kind of…live forever going mad?" she said. It sounded a bit lonely, but she liked this fate for him much better than deletion.

"Maybe I won't go so mad if I'm not so tired," he said. "Plus, Izumi thinks I could board the Sputnik II and be reborn on her ship. But I don't know. Everyone I've ever loved is here on the Voyager. I kind of want to stick around and make sure they're all okay."

"But they don't remember you."

"That's okay," he said. "I remember them. Besides, you're going to need me to untangle that signal jammer I put in you. It has to be me, since I'm the originator of your code bug. It will be delicate work, untangling that kind of deep, soul knot. It will take several years, and the Sputnik II will want to undock before I can get it undone."

"You…you jammed my signal? It was you?"

He shrugged sheepishly. "It's a bond. I tethered myself to you. You can feel me, right? And when I'm unconscious, you can't?"

She nodded. She thought it was familiarity. Perhaps friendship. She hadn't realized it had been sabotage.

"Why did you do it?" she asked.

"To anchor my mind in this…storm." He pointed to his head.

"Why me?"

"You were always kind to me, despite what you thought I was. You keep me saner than I'd be normally. I'm sorry. I needed to hold it together until I could open the ship for Izumi. I couldn't tell anyone what I was doing. And besides, you swore oaths. So, if you think about it, sticking around until I could see this through was kind of your duty all along, heh."

He gave her a cheese-eating grin. Jess narrowed her eyes. It sounded like this was Max's well-rehearsed self-justification for tampering with her code. The trouble was it did make sense. She had been able to bring him back from his unhinged murder spree. Who knows how many more people he would have deleted had she not been there?

"Okay," she said. "I'm annoyed with you, but okay. Your logic train makes sense. I did swear oaths." Max relaxed visibly at her absolution. "So, we should start calculating that password," she said. "That should get started at least, while we figure out what else we can do."

Max smiled at her. "It's good to have you here to help. I've been doing this on my own for so long, with a less and less functional brain. I am sure I'm missing something obvious."

"Probably," said Jess. "And we're going to need to keep you away from Clarise in the meantime."

"Pssh. I can handle Clarise," said Max. "She's more powerful than you, sure. But me? I'm the Pilot."

"And yet she still put you in a force cage," said Jess.

"Touché."

"Besides, you don't know this. But she got the Noir Syndicate to create a viral serum that can delete you."

Max's eyes widened. "She what?"

"She had the serum in a syringe back in the Noir Dimension. That's what she wanted to inject you with."

She had expected Max to look troubled. Instead, an expression of delight spread across his face. "Clarise, my faithful Frankenstein's monster. I did make you right," he said.

"Wait…what do you mean?" she said.

"I don't have decades to crack that code, Jess. I am degrading rapidly. Becoming the monster the other Agents think I am. This is actually a much tidier solution."

17

Max rose from the desiccated ground of Desolation, swooning a little as he gained his feet. Jess jumped up after him.

"You're going to go looking for Clarise and that syringe?" she demanded.

"Absolutely. I don't want to get deleted. But even more than that, I don't want to be deleting anyone else. Come with me," he said, holding out his hand to her. "Help me see this through to the end. It would be a comfort, having you there with me."

Max's logic made sense in her head. But it made absolutely no sense to her heart. The Sputnik II was docked right outside, ready to save the ship. The pieces of a solution were there, waiting to be fitted together. Jess brought a fresh set of eyes to this problem. A new perspective. And Max was just going to give up?

"No. This isn't fair. We can figure it out!" she said. "You dragged me on your mission, you told me the truth, and you begged for my help. And then you don't even give me a chance to solve this? I just got started!"

He chuckled. "You sound like Amira. I'm sorry, but I'm out of time. I can't have you getting in my way."

He snapped his fingers and a cage the size of a diver's shark cage with translucent bars like the Penalty Box materialized around Jess.

"Max!" she shouted.

"Sorry. Just push your belly button and go home to Garden. The cage will let you out that way, at least. I'm glad I met you, Jess. I'm glad someone saw the real me again before the end. And I'm glad it was someone as wonderful as you. Goodbye."

White Jump sparks started to crackle over his body.

"Wait!" she said. The sparks disappeared and Max remained, regarding her with a sad, patient expression.

"What about untangling my jammer signal?" she said. "You said it would take years!"

He shook his head regretfully. "I'm so sorry Jess. I did that to you and now I'm leaving before I can fix it. But I have to go anyway. This is so many souls, weighed against just your future. I know you understand that math. I've watched you live a life of duty and sacrifice—too much sacrifice sometimes, though that's not my business. But I know you are strong enough to bear this."

He was right. She had indeed made too many sacrifices in her life. She had let go of too many things she loved and wanted without even giving them a try. Sometimes, you didn't get what you wanted in life. Sometimes you made sacrifices. But always? That way of thinking had led her to the gray place, where she did not wish to go again. A wild plan started forming in her head. Jess had to hope Clarise was right about Max's crush on her.

"Strong enough to keep living without crossing over?" she said. "Sure I am. You helped me see that. But strong enough to lose you? I don't know about that, Max."

His expression softened. "Really?" he said quietly.

"At least, come say goodbye properly." She bit her lip and made her eyes as large as she could as she opened all four arms to him.

Max hesitated, then stepped up to the cage bars. His face only a foot from hers. It almost wasn't fair. She knew Max had been starved for connection for centuries. He was overconfident in his Pilot powers. She reached through the bars and pulled his body close, hugging him tight through the bars. He reached around her and returned the embrace, relaxing into her, the side of his face pressed against her shoulder, a storm-tossed sailor coming to rest at last on a soft, warm beach. He smelled like sea salt and the chocolate bars he was always eating.

He laughed softly. "Wow. Like, I thought you'd be a good hugger, with all those arms. But wow. When you let me out of my genie bottle, I didn't think I'd get to grant my own wish."

She peered down into his face. "You are so cheesy," she said. Then she kissed him. He stiffened in surprise then melted into her kiss. There was the usual rush of affection-induced hormonal simulacrum—the kind of bio-reaction coded into digital beings so they could be just like the carbon-based humans. Jess had experienced this many times with many boys.

But she was surprised to find something deeper involved in this particular kiss. It was staggering how beautiful this felt. It was the bright blue, piercing feeling. Only mellowed to a mix of golds and pinks like a sunset. Warm and alive with the joy of touching another bright and shining human soul. She knew bone deep that this wasn't just a kiss. This was the kind of kiss she'd coveted since forever. This was her kiss. Max meant it for her, and his heart was wholly in the giving of it.

One of his hands drifted tenderly to her cheek, and she felt herself longing to melt into this as he had. But she couldn't allow herself to be swept away, so she steeled herself against truly experiencing it. Because the rotten truth was that Jess was only kissing him as a means to an end, and Max's life depended on her remaining grounded.

The handy thing about having two extra arms was that Max didn't notice when Jess dropped one of them out of the lover's embrace and slipped her fingers into his bathrobe pocket. She fumbled around until she grasped a small, hard rectangle the size of a credit chit with raised bumps for buttons.

She pressed the center button and Max pulled away, eyes widened in surprise. Then he went slack. He fell hard on the baked Desolation ground, hitting his head. Jess winced. But he'd had worse. She pocketed the Disruptor remote, knelt beside him, and held him as firmly as she could from behind the bars. She pressed her own belly button this time, and watched the whiteness gather in her vision as she Jumped them both back home to Garden.

18

Jess materialized into a world of perfect 72-degree weather under a blue sky. She found herself in the shadow of one of the helix-shaped lavender glass skyscrapers of her hometown, Cyber City, with Max unconscious on the glittering sidewalk beside her. Cars whooshed by, and pedestrians stepped cautiously around the new, sudden arrivals. Jumpers were always on Agency business, and all the sane civilians wisely avoided Agency business. *What does that say about me?* She wondered. But she already knew the answer.

As she'd hoped, she and Max had landed only a couple of blocks from Dr. Barnes's office—the one place in Garden she knew had a force cage. She didn't know if Barnes's medical-grade viral field could contain Max, but she had to try.

Jess checked her handheld. It was 11:00 in the morning here. The doctor's office would still be open, and she had a minute and 45 seconds before Max reawakened. She stood up, clutching the remote in her lower left hand. She could use it to knock him out again, but she wasn't sure how many times she could do that successfully. And then she'd have Max's industrial-strength chaos to reckon with. It was best to get him to Barnes as soon as possible.

She reached to pick Max up and noticed she was wearing her red and green flannel pajamas again. For a moment, it felt good to be wearing something familiar. Until she remembered that she hated those pajamas and cursed herself for feeling good about them. She hoisted Max in an easy fireman's carry and ran.

***

Jess burst through the front doors of Barnes's office, and the odor of antiviral antiseptic hit her nose. At her entry, all eyes in the waiting room swiveled to her, and no wonder. She was a four-armed giantess in pajamas with an unconscious man slung across her shoulders.

There were two signs in the lobby. Under the one that said 'Sick' there were people wearing masks and clutching tissues. Under the one that said 'Not Sick Yet (your time will come)' were healthy, but wary-looking people huddled together as far from the 'Sick' side of the room as they could get. The sign was accurate. Having a 'no coughing' section of a doctor's office was about as effective as having a 'no peeing' section of a swimming pool.

Behind the receptionist's desk, a young woman with a yellow pixie cut, dark teal skin, and a diamond nose ring scowled at her.

"This isn't the ER," she said. "You'll have to take him to the hospital for emergency care. We don't have the liability coverage for that kind of mess. Do you have insurance to pay for an ambulance ride?"

Jess didn't have time for this nonsense. "I have to see Dr. Barnes," she panted. She could feel the stirrings of Max's soul returning. She pressed the remote button and felt him go slack again.

"Dr. Barnes is available by appointment only," said the nose-ring woman.

"Where is he?" Jess said.

"He is with a patient…a patient who had an appointment. Honestly, it's not that hard to understand."

Jess turned down the hallway toward the corridor of examination rooms.

"Hey!" shouted the receptionist. "You can't go back there! I'll call security!"

But Jess rushed off down the hallway anyway. She passed three open exam room doors. The fourth door was closed. Barnes was probably in there. She seized the handle and opened the door. Barnes was indeed inside—and so was Vince.

He was sitting on the exam table wearing one of the gap-backed paper gowns Dr. Barnes was so miserly about. He gawped at her.

"Jess?" he said.

Dr. Barnes turned. There was an Erlenmeyer flask of liquid in his hand and a scowl on his face. Then he recognized her. A delighted expression replaced the scowl.

"Agent Kensington!" said Barnes. "What perfect timing. I'd been prepared to freeze the sample, but we can slaughter two birds with one stone, eh? Probably a bad metaphor for the occasion, but you know what I mean. Don't worry, your husband's insurance will cover the whole procedure for both of you. And congratulations!"

"What are you talking about?" she said.

"You've got a man on your shoulders," observed Vince.

"The progenation, of course," said Barnes. "I've got your husband's contribution right here," he sloshed the flask, "I'll just collect yours, then we'll mix 'em up in a cannister and nine months later, boom! I have a brand-new, pint-sized patient! And one highly susceptible to expensive diseases, to boot. Such unimaginable joy for everyone involved."

Jess blinked. Then she understood. She wheeled on Vince. "You're having a baby? With Anne?"

"Man," Vince said, pointing to Max. "On your shoulders."

"You always said you didn't want children," she said.

Vince's eyes slid away from Max at last and locked on her. "I didn't. But Anne said she did, and I thought maybe I'd been wrong. And I thought we'd give it a try."

"I wanted a baby!" Jess cried.

Vince cocked his head. "You never said."

"I did!" she protested.

"Never very forcefully. I thought it was a 'nice to have' for you. Not something you actually wanted, wanted."

Barnes raised a finger. "Wait…the mother isn't going to be you?"

"No!" Jess and Vince said together.

"Well, this is awkward. My e-records from city hall indicate Vincent Parrison is married to one Jessamae Kensington. The records must be flawed. But this is probably for the best. Babies are smelly and inconvenient. They don't jive well with the dangerous lifestyle of a superpowered Agent."

"Agent?" said Vince, laughing. "No, no. Jess is a secretary at the Agency."

"Oh, she's a full-blown Agent," said Dr. Barnes. "Superpowers and everything. That's how she can stand there holding that unconscious fellow slung across her shoulders without breaking a sweat."

Vince looked up at her, head cocked in puzzlement. "Jess? Is it true?"

Jess pinched the bridge of her nose. "Barnes…" she growled. "What about Doctor/Patient confidentiality?"

"Only counts if you're a patient," said Barnes. "Which you're not. I'm still within my ethical framework."

"Barnes?" she said. "I hate you. I need you to know that."

"What do you mean, you're an Agent?" said Vince. "Since when? And who is that guy on your back?"

Jess realized she'd not been paying close enough attention to Max's state of consciousness. There was a gathering tenseness in his body. Jess dropped into combat mode. In one fluid movement, she dropped Max and vaulted herself into an elegant backflip. A six-foot-long Christmas pudding flew past her chin and splatted against the hallway wall.

"Dagnabit," Max muttered as he hit the ground.

Jess pushed the button and landed gracefully on her feet. Max was unconscious before he hit the hard linoleum like a sack of dropped empty soda cans.

Vince's jaw dropped. Dr. Barnes applauded. "Brava!" he said. "And yes, who is this fellow?"

"This is Max the Pilot," Jess said. "Praise Be Unto Him."

***

The three of them stood ankle deep in Christmas pudding in the hallway outside the examination room where Max was now trapped inside a force cage. Max lay on the floor by the medical cabinets, moaning softly as his consciousness returned. Dr. Barnes was bouncing on his toes with barely contained excitement. Vince stood with his back pressed to the wall to cover what the paper gown left exposed.

"I left my clothes in there in all the rush," said Vince, mournfully.

"Blast," said Barnes. "And I left your fathering liquid in the exam room as well," he pointed to the Erlenmeyer sitting on the counter between the tissue box and sink. "It'll go bad in a couple of hours. Pity. But it'll be fine. Your insurance will cover another harvesting tomorrow. I'm looking forward to it." Barnes clapped Vince hard on the back. Vince looked queasy.

"Well," said Barnes, "I'm going to shut down the office so I can spend the rest of the day poking around in the Pilot's code and find out what makes him tick. This is shaping up into quite the exciting day!"

The doctor sauntered down the hall, whistling with a spring in his step, tracking cakey Christmas pudding like mud as he went. Jess hadn't told Vince and Barnes the whole truth. Just enough to gain their cooperation. She'd said the Pilot needed help. That he was trying to do something self-sacrificial and noble and needed his loyal subjects to stop him.

Barnes had seemed more enthralled with the opportunity to collect live data on the Pilot than in helping. Vince had simply shut up and done what she said, bewildered, obedient, and trying not to moon everyone. She hadn't mentioned that the Voyager 2.0 was doomed or that the Pilot had been deleting people. She did not want to kick off a bout of cataclysmic despair here in Garden.

Max raised his head and poked the exam room wall. A wave of sparkling energy crackled around his finger and around the room, revealing the bubble of energy that was trapping him. He chuckled and pushed himself to his knees.

"Well, well, well." he said. "You found me a new force cage, Jess. I am impressed. And deeply touched at how hard you're working to keep me alive. But this cage isn't as strong as the one at the Agency. I'm either going to escape it eventually, or Clarise is going to find her way here."

"I'll be ready for her," said Jess, not sure how she would be, hoping she'd think of something.

Max shook his head. "Promise me that you won't get in her way. I don't want anyone else getting deleted because of me."

"We shall see," was all she could think of saying. "Max? I know you want to…take yourself out as soon as possible. But will you at least help me figure out how to open the ship without the last canopic jar?"

"Of course," he said. "I will do everything I can. I'm not going to stubbornly pursue only my own destruction. But I am going to take the option that gets the ship out of danger the soonest."

She nodded. "That's fair."

"And for the record, I do hope you are faster than Clarise," he said.

She gave him a faint smile. "Me too."

Vince tapped her on the shoulder. "Jess? Could I talk to you?" he said. "Alone?"

Her eyes slid to Max who shrugged. "I'm not going anywhere," he said.

Vince motioned her to lead them down the hall, probably not wanting to go first with the gap-backed gown. She picked her way through the wreck of Christmas pudding and walked down the hallway until she felt they were out of earshot from Max. She stopped beside an eye chart and faced Vince. His expression was serious.

"How long have you been an Agent?" he said.

"You know our first date and our second date?" she said. He nodded. "Since right between those two dates."

He looked away from her and shook his head. "You lied to me our whole marriage."

"Not about anything that had to do with you!" she protested. "It's not like I was having an affair or something." She tried to keep the accusation out of her voice because it wasn't fair. Vince was not having an affair with Anne. It only felt that way, which was Jess's own problem.

"But everything in your life affected me. Because we were married."

"We're not supposed to tell people we are Agents," she said.

"And that makes sense," he said. "But I still can't help feeling lied to. Betrayed. I spent our whole marriage never knowing who you were. Like the wanting children thing." He sighed and rubbed his temples. "It's a good thing I cycled through my grief about you and that I'm with Anne now, or this would hurt a lot more than it does."

Her body tensed as a flash of hot anger rushed through her. She folded her arms. "I'm not sure about that. It was awfully easy for you to move on. Almost like you never cared that much to begin with. And I was such a good spouse. We never fought. I gave you everything you wanted. I deserved to at least be mourned, but I guess I wasn't worth that."

She hated how bitter she sounded. But she was bitter, dammit.

"Why are you so upset that I moved on?" he said. "You checked out years ago. Yes, our lives were exactly what I wanted. Because you gave me everything I wanted. Maybe I should have questioned how easy our whole marriage seemed. And how bloodless. But if you'd told me things, if you'd opened up even once, we could have made different choices together."

"You were very upfront about what you expected out of life, which was nice, because then I knew exactly what to do to make you happy."

"But it wasn't real!" he said, with strong, un-Vince-like passion. "You didn't offer me a chance to give to you. Instead, you kept quiet and poured yourself out until you evaporated entirely. You thought you had to cross over just to fill your cup again. That's not generosity. That's a whole new demented kind of selfishness. How could I mourn you, Jess? I never knew you. Our whole marriage, I felt like I could never reach you. But I always had the sense that I would like to, if only I could."

"Vince…" she said, placing her hand on his shoulder. He suffered her touch, but his body was tense and nonreceptive. "I didn't know how else to be," she said. "I'm supposed to make other people happy. That's how you get them to stay."

Vince winced at this and softened. He placed his large, warm, navy-blue hand over her rose pink one and squeezed. "I know," he said gently. "I probably should have realized what was going on, given what a witch your mother was."

Jess stepped back. "What? How dare you! You never even met my mother."

"I didn't have to. Jess…I'm so sorry to do this to you. But I need this favor so badly,"

"Favor?"

"I have been keeping something from you, too, I guess. But it was for your own good, I thought. To protect you."

"Protect me from what?"

"So, I work at City Hall, right? Well, I have access to all the crossover applications. Including your mother's. When we were newly married,

I got curious about her, since you practically hero-worshipped her. I thought I could understand you better if I learned a little more about her. So, I read her documents."

Jess felt her throat go dry. "And?"

"I decided you never should see them. I bought a lockbox at the bank to hide them away, on the off chance you'd decide to read her crossover application. The box lists us as spouses, and I kept it, even while you were in hospice, so, you couldn't access the documents, you see? The box was supposed to disintegrate when you crossed over. But then you didn't cross."

"Why are you telling me now?"

"I'm so sorry. When Dr. Barnes said we were listed as spouses, the box is why. I can't legally marry Anne until the box dissolves. And it can't dissolve until you, its half-owner, either cross over or empty it. I know you'll read the contents. And I'm so, so sorry. But I want to marry Anne. I need your help, even though I know how much it will cost you."

His mouth turned down and he rubbed his chest as though it pained him. What surprised her most was how much she wanted to help him, despite how big an 'ask' this supposedly was. He was asking her to handle documents he was sure would break her heart so that he, her husband of over nine years, could marry their brazen, obnoxious neighbor. And yet, she loved him for the request.

It wasn't only her curiosity about what her mother's documents contained—though she certainly would read them. And it wasn't guilt that compelled her either. It was simply that she had an opportunity to show him care. And it felt oddly…good. She'd been denying Vince this feeling their whole marriage, since asking for what she wanted made her feel like she was being 'too much.' Too late, she realized, asking for things she wanted was just what she'd always needed to do.

She held out her hand and smiled at him. "Of course. Give me the key to the box."

Vince rubbed the back of his neck.

"Err... It's on my keychain in my pants. Which are behind the force shield with the Pilot."

Jess sighed. "It's okay," she said. "I've got this."

She led them back down the hallway to the exam room where Max was contained. He looked up from a data screen he'd conjured in mid-air and smiled. "Good talk?" he said.

"The best," she replied. Then she pulled out the remote.

"Aww, come on," he whined.

"Lie down," she instructed.

He obeyed, muttering, "How am I supposed to focus on anything?"

She pressed the button and knocked Max out. Then she coded the shield deactivation into the door panel and stepped into the waiting room to retrieve Vince's clothes. She paused by the counter and grabbed the Erlenmeyer flask full of the 'fathering liquid' as well.

Then she stepped out of the room and reactivated the energy cage. She handed Vince the flask and clothes.

"Thanks Jess," he said. "I owe you for this. I really didn't want to undergo a second progenation session with Dr. Barnes."

She gave him a faint smile. "I can imagine."

19

D r. Barnes's hallway was still full of Max's cakey Christmas pudding. The festive smell of currants, cloves, and candied citrus peel was undercut unpleasantly with antiseptic. Jess sat cross-legged in a clear, pudding-free patch of floor outside Max's exam-room cage holding a key and a metal case the size and shape of a cereal box.

She had been unwilling to leave Max to retrieve the locked box from the bank, so she made Vince go get it for her. He'd returned with it, all apologies and thank yous, which only contributed to her growing sense of dread about the contents. So, she'd asked him to leave.

"I want to be alone for this," she'd explained.

"What about me?" Max had asked. "It's hard to be alone when you're on guard duty."

"I've learned I don't get everything I want in life," she'd said. Max had grinned at this. But what was she supposed to do? Clarise was probably searching Desolation for them, since it was Max's home world. But Garden would likely be her next stop. And Max had that suspicious, hovering data screen that he'd conjured in the force cage. Who knew what dastardly escape plan he was concocting with it? Vigilance was required.

She ought to be brainstorming ways to open the ship for the

rescuers from the Sputnik II. But her stupid brain was too consumed with Vince's warnings about her mother's documents to concentrate. She had to get this over with. She had to learn the truth so she could move on to saving the ship—and Max.

Vince was gone now. Barnes was still in his computer lab, monitoring Max's code through all his fanciest medical scanners. It was just her, Max, and this box. I feel like Pandora, she thought. Just the day before, she had released a genie. Now this. She wondered what else she might unleash upon the world.

Max was staring at her, expectantly.

"Go on then. Aren't you curious? I'm curious. I'm invested at this point," he said.

"I'd prefer it if you didn't stare at me the whole time," she said. "I don't suppose you could…clean up this Christmas pudding? Keep yourself busy."

He scoffed. "The Pilot's job is to make chaos. Not undo it."

"Well, you're not very good at your job," she said.

"Even if I wanted to, I can't," he said. "It's outside the energy cage. My hands are tied."

She sighed. "So being a pest wasn't part of your 'I'm a criminal,' act, then."

"I'm afraid it's baked into my personality," he said, winking.

"Good to know."

She slotted the key into the lock. Then she hesitated. The box was her last legal link to Vince. She wasn't in love with him. She might have been if she'd done more than go through the motions of affection without actually risking her heart. Vince deserved to be happy now and he deserved her wholehearted release of him.

She turned the key and slid the box open and removed the contents—a single, opened envelope. Then the box—and the last vestige of her marriage—dissolved into thousands of points of glittering light that winked out one by one. She watched the glitter fade with a deep ache of finality. But also, a peace. I think I made it to the Acceptance Stage, she thought wryly. And all without medical aid.

But now she was left with her mother's documents. The papers Vince had thought too upsetting to tell her about. The bittersweet ache intensified to a different chest sensation. A clutching sort of foreboding.

She removed the paper from inside the envelope and began to read.

It was her mother's crossover application. Jess had filled out such a form herself only a few months earlier. The first two questions contained standard answers.

1) Why are you applying to cross over?

I have grown weary of my too-long life. I have stopped finding the joy in activities I once enjoyed. I wake from my sleep cycles dreading another day of this disappointing sameness.

2) How long have you felt this way?

Over three long decades.

Then she read her mother's answers to the third, fourth, and fifth questions.

3) What have you tried to reintroduce zest and vitality into your present life?

I tried very hard to stay interested in this life. I swear it. I joined a lot of social clubs and took up many hobbies, but nothing sustained my interest. Then I got serious about snapping myself out of the funk. I had a daughter. I thought a child would reinvigorate me, let me see the world with fresh eyes. After all, babies are supposed to be magical creatures. There's a quote in my very favorite book, "When the first baby laughed for the first time, its laugh broke into a thousand pieces, and they all went skipping about, and that was the beginning of fairies." I thought if anything would bring a zest back to life, it would be a new human.

Jess had always loved that passage. She imagined being that baby, surprised and delighted to find her joy brought to life, made flesh and spirit. That this was how her mother saw her was an unexpected gift. She read on.

4) How well did these efforts work?

The book was a lie. It turns out babies don't produce fairies; they produce lots of bad-smelling oozes. I knew this, of course. But I was led to believe there would be more…enchantment to children. But Jessamae was just as dull as everything else in this life. Perhaps even more so, because I had to sacrifice time from my other diverting activities to just…sit there…holding her. I gave mothering a valiant effort, though. I tried to train her to become something great. I gave her lessons and classes. Perhaps she'd be a famous dancer, or a renowned scientist, and would be worthy of my time and efforts. But Jessamae was a dull-witted, normal child. All she wanted was to play mind-numbing games with her dolls and glue bits of macaroni onto cardboard. I gave it my best, but she's just not enough to make me want to stay.

Some sort of distancing effect took place in Jess's brain at that moment. There were words on the page. She was reading them for the first time. But she had always known them. She didn't need this letter to know it had been her fault her mother crossed over. Things might have been different if Jess had been a better sort of child.

5) What accommodations have you prepared for those you would leave behind?

Jessamae is in the fourth grade. Her teachers report she is already fully socialized. I've left her my apartment in my will, and Garden's social service programs will pay for her continued schooling and care. She knows how to dial emergency responders, order her own groceries, and synthesize dinner in a kitchen appliance. She is fully capable of living alone. Her future is secure. But I want no part of it anymore.

There were more questions on the application, but Jess stopped reading. She was remembering all the cozy bedtimes before her mother had crossed. How they lay in bed together for the daily 20 minutes of parent-child time—the only 20 minutes Jess got because the child rearing books said children needed 20 minutes of reading for optimal brain development. Jess's optimal brain development was of paramount importance to her mother.

It was Peter Pan every night, so her mother didn't have to think about what book to read, she could simply recite. It was mostly beautiful. Jess could ignore the parts of it she knew were ugly. The bad names it called Tiger Lily's tribespeople. The stilted way they talked. How they called a boy like Peter 'Great White Father.' These passages were like biting into an artisanal muffin and finding a brown sphere of goat poop in place of a blueberry. If you were careful, you could eat around it and enjoy. The book was her mother's greatest gift to her. It would be a betrayal not to love the whole of it.

She remembered all the nights after her mother had crossed. Jess would come home from school, zap her own dinner and finish her homework in the silent, empty apartment with the ticking clock. It was lonely, but her mother was right. She was fine. Jess's mother had understood her more deeply than anyone in the world. What did it say about her that the person who knew her best hadn't found her worth staying for?

"What's wrong?" said Max.

He was cross-legged on the exam room floor in front of his hovering data screen, but he wasn't looking at it. He was watching her with an expression of concern. She must be making some sort of weird face. She cleared her throat, but she found words wouldn't come out of it for some reason. She looked at the paper clutched in her hand. Proof that she was a terminally disappointing person.

"You know," said Max. "I spent a lot of time not telling people what was bothering me. And it really sucked."

This was silliness. Max was staring down the barrel of his own deletion; he didn't need her mommy issues piled on him, compounding his stress. Jess's vocal cords started vibrating at last. "You're dealing with enough right now," she said. "It's nothing. I'll be fine."

He rolled his eyes. "Jess," he said. "I want to listen to you. It'll be good for me to do something for someone else. While I still can, you know?"

She hesitated. Stuffing it down, shouldering it alone. That would lead right back to the gray place. She couldn't go on aggressively giving and refusing to receive. With respectable, mainstream Vince, she'd masked her holes in her soul, not giving him a chance to see her flaws and reject her. But Max? He was enough of a mess that she could trust him not to judge her for her neediness. She shoved her fist with the crossover application through the energy shield and let the paper drop to the floor.

Then she spied a calculating flash in Max's eyes. Putting her hand through the energy shield had been colossally stupid. She quickly pulled her fist back out before Max could latch onto it with his powers.

Max laughed. "You caught me considering some mischief," he said.

"I have known you for quite some time," she said. He grinned at this. "What stopped you from turning my hand into a neutron star or something?" she asked. "Or pulling me into the cage and stealing the remote?"

"You look really upset," he said, getting up to retrieve the paper. "I'll find another more appropriate moment to overpower you later. Don't worry."

He smoothed out the document and read. A moment later he looked up, his mouth set in a grim line and his eyebrows furrowed.

"What the hell?" he said. "I know you. You're amazing. And I bet you were an awesome little girl too. And macaroni art is cool...and okay, dolls are kind of boring, but to each his own...and... This is so messed up."

Laughter welled up inside Jess from nowhere like champagne bubbles when the cork popped off. Because Max was right. It was messed up. Jess had been an awesome little girl. It was her mother, who was full of goat shit. And you were only fooling yourself if you thought you could nibble around something like that and not swallow some.

Max looked at her quizzically. "Are you alright?"

"We are birds of a feather, you and me," she said. "Two people so disappointing that other people cross over just to escape us."

Max smiled sadly at this. "Peas in a pod, I tell you."

But Jess wasn't sad. Because Max wasn't disappointing at all, and neither was she.

"I love my mother," Jess said. "There were beautiful things about my mother."

"Of course."

"But she was flawed too. Beautiful parts and ugly parts. Just like any of us. I hurt Vince our whole marriage, after all."

"You didn't mean to," Max said. "You don't have to make yourself the problem here."

"But I hurt him all the same."

At this, Max nodded, a pained expression on his face.

"I don't mean to delete people," he said. "I know I'm no monster. There's not an evil line of code in my whole digital soul. But the deleted ones are gone all the same. So, what do you do now that you know this about her and you?"

"I don't have to stop loving my mother, but I don't have to make her opinion of me the star that I follow anymore."

She tucked the letter into her pajama pocket. It was time to move forward and save the ship without dooming Max, if she could.

The hallway door opened, and Barnes returned from his diagnostics lab, grinning gleefully into his data pad as he approached.

"The ship is super doomed!" he announced, pointing at the pad.

Jess sighed deeply. She'd tried to keep the whole, ugly truth from Barnes. She should have guessed the worryingly-intelligent man would figure it out.

"Most people apply to cross over when they learn that," Max called from his prison. "Yet you seem…oddly chipper."

"Why would I want to cross over?" said Barnes. "I'm the lucky guy about to publish the white paper of the century. A code bug in the Pilot himself. The Pilot, stuck and broken and wearing out rapidly. This is totally unprecedented. They'll beg me to run the journal Anomalous once this sucker passes peer review."

"Until Max destroys the world," said Jess.

"But what a way to go out!" said Barnes. "Editor-in-Chief, am I right?"

He held a blue-gloved fist down toward Jess to collect a celebratory bump. Jess stared at the fist, then up at Barnes and shook her head.

"You have a terrible problem with perspective, you know that?" she said.

"Oh, come on," he muttered, retracting the fist. "You've got four hands, and you can't spare one of them?"

"I'd fist bump you if I were out there," said Max.

"Thank you for your support," said Barnes.

Max poked the air in front of him, sending a sparkling energy wave rippling out from his touch across the walls of the force cage. "You're a man of science, Barnes," he said. "You've seen in my code how fast

I'm wearing out."

Barnes nodded. "Indeed. You'll be deleting entire cities in less than three months, I think. I better get cracking on that white paper, eh?"

Three months? Jess thought. She'd thought they had more time than that.

"So, Jess here is a big softie, bless her heart," said Max. "She doesn't want you to know this, but there is a way to delete me. Let me out, and I'll go straight to the people who can do it."

"Max!" she cried.

Barnes had the codes to open the force cage right on his data pad. Jess's muscles coiled to vault herself up, preparing to wrestle yet another device from Dr. Barnes. But Barnes shook his head.

"Never gonna happen," he said.

"What? Why?" said Max. "You've already got enough data on me for 100 white papers—papers you'll actually be alive to write because I won't have deleted you and your peer-reviewers. You can publish, take over Anomalous, and even be a hero."

Once again, Max reminded Jess of a genie or a leprechaun, offering wealth and glory in exchange for freedom. Of course, only Max himself would suffer the consequences. What chance did Jess have to save him when he was so bent on his own destruction?

But Barnes looked up from his data pad and fixed Max with a disapproving frown.

"What do you take me for, son?"

Max hesitated. "A…savvy man?" he said, choosing his words carefully.

Barnes pinched the bridge of his nose. "I'm a doctor, you dunderhead. The ignorant masses envy me. They think my job is all insurance codes, and fielding malpractice suits, and other glamour like that. But the dull reality is that I spend all day saving people. Snatching life from the jaws of death. Deletion is an affront to my profession and an insult to my very soul. I'm not letting you out of here so you can pursue your own destruction."

"But I'm going to delete people," Max protested. "You saw the data yourself. A ship full of people. Surely you understand that math."

"Only one equation matters here," said Barnes. "I am your doctor plus you are my patient equals I will keep you alive as best as I can, mass murderer or no. I stay in my lane and let other people wearing other hats weigh the worth of your life. That's just ethics."

Jess felt a warm rush of gratitude toward the doctor and his unshakable codes of conduct. An ally at last. You really did know where you stood with Barnes, once you figured him out.

"You are a very frustrating person, Dr. Barnes," said Max.

"That's coming from you, even," Jess said, smirking.

Max stuck his tongue out at her, which was gratifying.

Then another exam room door opened behind them. Jess and Barnes wheeled. Anne was peeking out into the hallway, barefoot and wearing a paper gap-backed gown.

"I've been waiting a really long time," she said. "Are you ever going to come collect my mothering liquid?"

20

"Anne?" Jess said stupidly.

"Jess?" Anne said back no more intelligently than Jess. "Why are you at the doctor's office? And why are you sitting in…is that cake?"

She pointed to the pile of Christmas pudding in the exam room hallway.

"You shouldn't be here," said Barnes. "My lackeys were supposed to close the office and reschedule all my appointments!"

"Lackeys?" said Max.

Barnes rolled his eyes. "I supposed 'Office Staff' is the preferred term," he said, making air quotes.

"You can't reschedule me!" Anne protested. "I'm getting married in two days and we need to be luminescent with gestational glow!"

Jess blinked. Cyber parents-to-be mixed their code in vats, not bodies like the carbon-based humans had. But Humanity 2.0 didn't like to miss out on old human stuff, so expectant parents—mothers and fathers both—got simulated belly kicks and literally bio-luminesced until the new infant was ripe and ready to be decanted.

Jess felt an odd protectiveness on behalf of Vince and Anne's yet-to-exist kid. Being born so your folks could look good in their wedding portraits? It was tough being born as someone else's means to an end. Jess ought to know. She frowned at Anne.

"You're progenating just for the glow?"

"Of course not!" said Anne. "Vince and I want a child as soon as possible anyway, so we might as well look extra pretty for the wedding. It's a two birds, one stone kind of thing."

Jess relaxed. That was alright then. Practical and efficient, even. She approved.

Then three rapid-fire Jump flashes flared, and Jerome, Netta, and Amira materialized in the hallway, their Jumpsuits appearing as white medical coats to blend in with the doctor's office environment.

Jess vaulted to her feet and started toward them. Netta whipped a gun out of her lab coat, grabbed Anne, and pressed the barrel to her temple. Jess skidded to a halt.

"Let her go!" Jess said.

"I told you we needed a hostage," Netta said. "The message said she wouldn't be cooperative."

"I suppose a broken clock is right twice a day," said Jerome.

Jess's lower right hand twitched toward the pocket where she kept her crossover gun. Netta cocked her own gun aggressively in response.

"Drop it nice and easy, or I cross her over."

Anne fainted in Netta's arms. The added weight caused the super-Agent no trouble. An unconscious hostage would work just as well as an awake one.

"Come on, Jess," said Amira. "I bet we're all on the same side, we just don't know it yet. Let's talk."

Netta rolled her eyes. "Talking," she scoffed. "Your solution is always 'talking.'"

Briefly, Jess considered fighting. Perhaps she could take them all. Her jammer bond would keep her from crossing over, so she was kind of invulnerable. But what if they crossed Anne? Vince would lose a second wife in under a week, and that seemed excessive.

Clarise wasn't here, so neither was the Max-deleting serum. That gave Jess time to win her coworkers over. And she needed Amira's expertise to open the Voyager 2.0 for the crew of the Sputnik II.

"Okay, we'll talk," Jess said.

Jess reached into her pajamas nice and easy, and dropped her weapon on the floor in front of them. She held all four of her hands up.

"Very good," said Jerome.

"We got a weird ansible message saying Max is here," said Amira. "Is he?"

"I am!" Max called cheerfully.

Jess ground her teeth. A message. So that was what Max had been doing on his hovering data screens. The three Agents exchanged glances and advanced on Jess and Barnes. Amira removed a set of quad manacles from her lab coat and bound Jess's hands behind her. Jerome took out his own set and cuffed Barnes's wrists to his ankles.

"Unhand me, you walking obelisk!" said Barnes. Jerome set the bound doctor unceremoniously in the pile of Christmas pudding. "Hey! You can't—," Barnes started. But Jerome pulled a credit chit-sized remote from his lab coat and pushed 'mute." Barnes's lips continued to move, but no sound came out.

Amira used another set of cuffs to bind Jess's wrists to her ankles. Jess tugged against the restraints. They were meant to hold an Agent. There was no breaking them, no slipping out of them. Amira lowered her to the floor outside Max's force cage. He smiled warmly at her, certain of his macabre victory. Foolish of him. True, Jess would have preferred to secure Amira's help from a safe distance, preferably by ansible phone in different dimensions. But she could work with this.

"Is that another giant Christmas pudding?" said Amira.

Jerome nodded. "Indeed. Normally I would say, 'you don't see that every day;' however, it would appear that lately, we do."

"I think I improved on the recipe with this one," Max said. He peered behind them, looking for something. "So…is our charming Task Manager going to grace us with her presence, or…"

"We came on our own," said Amira. "Clarise has gotten scary over the past 24 hours."

"Scarier," corrected Netta.

"How?" said Jess.

"About 100 new, mysterious and nasty Agents showed up from the Noir Dimension yesterday," said Amira. "Apparently, Clarise has recruited and trained a whole secret army in Noir. The new Agents have kind of…taken over the outer shell. Loitering around. Threatening employees. Using gym equipment and not wiping it down."

"Veden had a conniption fit," said Netta. "He tried to write citations, but they stole his ticket booklet and used it to play keep-away from him. When he challenged them to single combat, they took turns sitting on him and hitting him with his own hands."

Jess winced. Poor Veden. She imagined it was both a dream and a nightmare for him, getting pounded on by so many Agents…but lawless Agents with no respect at all for his beloved rules. She imagined the crisis of faith this might have sparked in his uncomplicated brain. But Jess was horribly curious about something.

"The Noir Agents," she said. "Are they…?"

"Gray?" said Netta.

Jess nodded.

"Yes. Even in the outer shell."

"Fascinating," said Jess.

"It's like we've been overrun by a Jerome clone squad," said Amira.

Jerome sniffed. "I'm much better looking than any of those Noirian knuckle draggers."

"So why are you here without Clarise?" Max demanded. "I'm insulted that you thought you could take me by yourselves!"

Jerome raised an eyebrow and gestured to the force cage. "Jessamae seems to have 'taken you by herself' for us already," he said. "But we aren't simply here for you. Anarchy reigns in the outer shell. HR and Custodial are terrified; they refuse to leave their offices. But Clarise still won't control her new people. We need Jessamae to talk some sense into the Task Manager."

"Netta tried," said Amira. "But Clarise hit her with the riding crop. Just a little tap…but…"

Jess understood at last. Clarise had gone off the deep end, and the Agents needed their rodeo clown back.

She shook her head. "Clarise will never let me come back. She'll arrest me on sight."

"We need her to pardon you," said Amira. "Netta?"

Netta laid the fainted Anne in a pile of Christmas pudding and cuffed her with quad manacles. Then she reached into her lab coat and withdrew a syringe. Jess recognized it instantly, though it was blue now and not gray as it had looked in Noir. Her throat went dry. They had brought the deletion serum after all.

"I'm never going to do that," Jess said.

Netta pushed a button on the crossover gun, and the weapon made a soft, high whining noise. Jess gave the gun a closer look. It was one of the lethal firearms from the safe in the equipment closet. Netta had shifted its dial from 'cross over' to 'delete.' Jess's heart sped up as Netta pointed the barrel at Anne.

"Do it, or else," said Netta. A sheen of sweat shone on her skin, and her eyes were large behind her round, brass spectacles. Netta was terrified of Clarise and that crop, and that meant she'd become very, very dangerous.

"Netta," Amira said gently. "It doesn't have to come to that."

"Right," said Jerome. "If Jessamae refuses to cooperate, we can delete Max and say she did it. Clarise will be pleased, and all will be forgiven." Jerome held his hand out for the syringe.

Netta released a shuddering breath and nodded. She handed the needle to Jerome. Amira reached into Jess's pajama pocket. Jess tried to twist away, but the cuffs held her tight. Amira's hand emerged with Max's Pilot remote.

"No!" Jess cried.

She should never have surrendered. She'd thought she'd have more time to think of something. To convince the other Agents to open the ship instead of deleting Max. But they were going to kill him right in front of her, and she couldn't even fight back.

Max lay down in anticipation of being knocked out for the final time. "I'm sorry Jess," he said quietly. "And thanks."

"No! You don't understand!" she said. "There's another way!" She strained against the cuffs. Netta pointed a remote at her and pressed the 'civilian mute button.' Jess's voice—her last hope for saving Max— was silenced.

Amira pushed the Pilot's remote, and Jess felt Max's presence vanish. His body became a shell. She screamed 'Max!' but no sound came out.

Jerome pushed buttons on the exam room door panel, and the shield shimmered down with a 'wum.' Jess threw herself forward and tried to barrel Jerome over like a bowling ball knocking out a pin. But Netta's boot came down hard on her back, stopping her momentum and holding her to the floor. Jess's cheek was pressed into a moist, clove-scented glob of Max's Christmas pudding.

Jerome set his jaw and knelt beside Max. Jess felt her heartbeat hammer in her ears. Time slowed as the gray giant of a man held the syringe hovering at Max's shoulder.

"Go on, then," said Amira.

"I find I cannot," said Jerome.

"What?" said Netta.

Jerome gestured helplessly at Max. "Look at him, just…lying there. This is too depressing, even for me."

"You've deleted people before," said Amira.

"Never anyone who was not actively trying to delete me," said Jerome.

"Don't get suckered in by his defenseless appearance," said Amira. "Stick to the data. Max is the biggest threat the ship has ever faced."

Jerome shook his head. "Max has been making my life miserable for more than three decades. What am I supposed to do? Throw away all that history?"

"Fine, you big baby," said Amira. She stepped into the exam room and took the syringe from Jerome. She inserted the needle into Max's shoulder, but her thumb hovered over the plunger. Jess held her breath, unable to look away. A ghostly memory of brimstone smell invaded her senses in anticipation of the horror.

"Max is very dangerous," Amira said. She still did not push the plunger. "He is deleting people. And it doesn't matter that he doesn't want to do it. He's still doing it."

"Exactly," said Netta.

"He'd probably want me to do this, even," said Amira. "On some level, at least. Because he's not such a bad guy, really. Not when it comes down to it. Like you said, Jerome, I've known him for a long time."

"So, do it," said Netta.

"In theory I should have no trouble pushing this plunger," Amira said.

"Mm hmm," said Jerome, knowingly. "However…"

"The gap between theory and practice is all too common a problem in the sciences," said Amira. She sighed and removed the needle from Max's shoulder. "This is exactly why we conduct these little field tests."

"Oh, come on, you saps," said Netta. "I'll do it."

She took her boot off Jess's back and started toward the exam room.

"No!" Jerome and Amira said together. Jerome tucked the syringe protectively back in his pocket.

"You two can't be serious," said Netta. "Max is a danger to the whole ship. Our job is to make people safer."

"Max is a known danger," said Jerome. "But no one has ever deleted an active Pilot before. It is a total unknown what will happen to the ship once he is gone. And there are no 'take backsies' with deletion."

Netta pulled up short. "Unknown?" she whispered. Her indigo skin paled several shades.

"That has been bothering me about the 'delete Max plan,'" agreed Amira. "Before you muted her, Jess said there was another way. Let's hear her out, alright?"

Jess released the breath she hadn't realized she'd been holding. Perhaps she wasn't about to watch Max's code unravel in front of her after all.

"Fine," said Netta. "But if I don't like what I hear, then it's my turn to find out if I'm as soft as the rest of you."

21

The other Agents left Max alone in the exam room and reactivated the force cage. Jess regarded Max's unconscious form. He still looked far away and dead, and she felt an absence where he ought to be. But it was good to know he was not gone forever. He would return.

And what was more, her other sheep hadn't turned on him after all. She had the chance now to truly reconcile her flock. These four people whom she cared for and protected had for too long been at odds—set against one another by Max's secrets and Clarise's manipulations. It was a relief, she realized, that she could unite them all and feel whole at last.

Netta unmuted Jess and Barnes.

"Amira Darwish," Barnes breathed, an awestruck expression on his face. "The Agency's top scientist here in my very own office. What an honor."

Amira smoothed her Shayla scarf and tried not to look too pleased to be recognized.

Jess told her teammates the truth about Max and the Sputnik II that was docked and ready to save the ship, if only the Sputnik's Pilot,

Izumi, could get inside.

As Jess spoke, Max slowly came to. He was taking longer and longer to regain consciousness every time he went under. When at last he was fully awake, he pushed himself to his knees and prodded his chest.

"I'm still alive," he said. "What gives?"

"You idiot," said Amira. "All those years you could have said something. Why didn't you tell us you were stuck?"

"It wouldn't have changed anything," said Max. "You were all perfect minions who did everything I needed you to."

"We might have been nicer," said Netta.

"I would not have been," said Jerome.

Max chuckled. "I'm sure Jess told you about Desolation," he said. "People can't handle the truth."

"Normal people, perhaps," said Amira. "But you may have noticed Clarise has been choosing weirdos for Agents for most of the last century."

Suddenly Max doubled over. His eyes crackled with a brief flash of the lightning Jess had seen in Noir. Hair stood up on the back of her neck, and Max went pale.

"The ticking crocodile has come for me at last…," he said. "You need to delete me."

"No," said Netta. "You might be unsafe, but your 'delete me' plan is unsafer. We're going to uninstall you by the book, so we know all the consequences."

Max shook his head. "We're going to have to risk the unknown, folks. I'm slipping fast. Each time I'm knocked out, I start going faster. Jess, if you care about me at all, use the syringe. Or let me go to Clarise on my own. Please."

Jess stared into his face and found hopeless resolution. Max thought he was out of time; he wasn't going to cooperate. Her flock was still at odds after all. Worst of all was that she understood his morbid desire. The others hadn't seen what she'd seen in Noir the last time he'd lost control. And those were hardened, dangerous killers he'd deleted. People who were trying to delete her. What would happen if Max slaughtered thousands of innocents?

She wondered what it would be like, speaking to him after he'd done something like that. She imagined feeling horrified and repulsed by him, but loving him anyway. Wanting to comfort him, knowing he would be even more shattered than she was. But knowing that the dead were the most shattered ones of all.

She would find herself wishing she had prevented the tragedy. Wishing she could come back to this moment and choose differently.

Amira clapped a hand on Jess's shoulder, startling her from her reverie.

"Ignore him," Amira said cheerfully. "I always do. Max is a Siren calling from a rocky shore. I can solve this, I promise. If only I had access to proper equipment, but I can't get to my lab. The outer shell is crawling with Clarise's Noirian Agents."

"You need a lab, good lady of science?" said Barnes. "I happen to have one of those down the hall and to the left. Since the office is closed, I don't even need to bill you."

***

"Welcome to my playground. Only the worthy may enter," said Barnes, bowing Amira through the doorway. "And her guests," he added, suffering the rest of them to pass behind her.

Barnes's lab was floor-to-ceiling instrument panels. There was a laboratory island in the middle of the room with a built-in sink, three kinds of microscopes, and a test tube stand full of multicolored samples that smelled bitterly medicinal. Every 30 seconds, one of the wall-mounted machines made a 'ping' noise like submarine sonar.

Amira looked around, frowning. "I suppose this will do. Probably the best I can expect from a mere civilian. . I'll need a chair."

Barnes fell all over himself fetching her a rolling swivel stool. He placed it behind her and smoothed the padded vinyl cushion unnecessarily with his palm, as though he were making it worthy of Amira's buttocks. Jess rolled her eyes.

Netta pointed to the machine that went 'ping.' "What's that do?"

"It goes 'ping' from time to time," said Barnes stiffly. "Every proper laboratory has a machine that goes 'ping.' For the ambiance, you know."

Amira nodded absently. "I have three," she said. "I mute the pings, but they've got to be there, or I can't concentrate."

Barnes regarded Amira with a mixture of professional jealousy and naked admiration. Amira peered into the screen in front of her and began to type.

"Jess, what happened to the missing code?" she asked. "Why is it missing?"

Jess explained about the dropped and shattered jar. The canopic fluid spilled across the floor of the Bargaining Stage lounge back in Noir. Amira listened, nodding soberly. She interrupted Jess many times to ask for details. Too often, in Jess's opinion. They had to hurry. She recalled the flash of lightning in Max's eyes and his warnings about running out of time. A hot anxiety fluttered in her chest. She had to breathe deep to keep answering Amira's questions. If anyone could solve this, it would be Amira and Barnes, but she couldn't rush them.

At last, Amira came to the end of the interrogation. She frowned. "So, the code has evaporated, then."

"No problem," said Barnes. "It's rare that anyone spills more than a drop or two of canopic fluid, even in the sloppiest distilleries. So, we scan the Noirian atmosphere, locate all the particles of canopic vapor, calculate the butterfly effect of wind currents, barometric pressures, and so forth, and bingo! We recreate the original code. Or close enough that we only need to run a couple of permutations through a super-computer. But we're talking minutes, not days."

Amira frowned at him. "That's a complex proposal from a simple backwater dimension doctor."

Jess sighed. "Dr. Barnes here invented the force cage. You know, the thing we use to contain Max?"

Amira lifted her eyebrows, impressed. Barnes tried to look humble but failed, a smug smirk twerking his lips up.

"It's an elegant solution," said Amira. "There's a problem with it, however. Canopic jar fluid is interdimensional by nature, so people can take it with them to their next lives. The code isn't just scattered through Noir's atmosphere; it will have spread across all the dimensions by now."

Barnes's face fell. "No one could impose that much determinism into chaotic processes."

Amira shrugged. "Oh, I could."

"What?" said Barnes, gaping at her, a look of pure awe on his face.

"Sure, no biggie. It's all fluid dynamics and the turbulent flow of liquids," she said. "But we'd need a device that can detect the particles across multiple dimensions. I'm afraid such a thing would be impossible to make."

Barnes brightened at this. And Jess knew instantly what he was about to show Amira. "Impossible?" he said. "Pish. I say, 'no biggie.'" He reached into a drawer and pulled out a handheld that Jess hadn't smashed yet. "Here's one of my dozens of backups stored in one of my many secret hiding spots," he said, grinning smugly at Jess.

"That's a lot of redundancies," said Netta.

"An unfortunate necessity in these lawless times," Barnes said. "My original is a little worse for the wear."

Jess shrugged at him. He glared back at her and handed the phone to Amira. She took it, her eyes glittering with avarice. "Hello, you beauty," Amira murmured. "I've never seen anything like you before."

"It was nothing," said Barnes, thrusting his chest out. "Just a little something I pieced together from the fragments of a shattered handheld and my own unrelenting tenacity."

Amira turned to him. "You're a genius, Dr. Barnes."

"You may call me Thaddeus," he said.

"Thaddeus," said Amira, smiling up at him from the stool. "I'm charmed."

Netta elbowed Amira in the head. "Keep it down."

"Ow. Keep what down?" said Amira.

Jerome rolled his eyes. "The banal romantic soundtrack that's swelling metaphorically in the background as you make goo-goo eyes. You've got work to do."

"You two are wet blankets," Amira muttered. She turned back to the console and plugged Barnes's device into the 'ping' machine, which obviously provided more function than mere ambience. Barnes watched, enraptured, as Amira performed cross-dimensional computations that would spin the head of even the most rampageous chaos-butterfly.

Jess shifted from foot to foot as Amira worked. This was going faster than she'd hoped. Perhaps it would be alright after all, and Amira would piece the code back together before Max lost his mind.

Minutes later, Amira swiveled and faced the room with a gleam of triumph in her eyes. "I've got it!" she said. "We just have to get to the outer shell and upload the code. Then we can let the crew of the Sputnik II in."

The door burst open, and three rapid-fire laser shots sounded. Three blue bolts struck Amira, Netta, and Jerome, and the Agents collapsed on the floor. Jess wheeled. Anne stood panting in the doorway, a wild look on her face, holding in her trembling hands the gun Jess had dropped back in the exam room hallway.

22

"Dr. Darwish!" Barnes cried, dropping to his knees beside the fallen Amira. Impossible, Jess thought. They'd left Anne quad-cuffed and unconscious in a pile of Christmas pudding. And Anne was a frivolous creampuff besides, or so Jess had assumed.

"What did you do?" Jess cried, gesturing at her fallen comrades.

"Rescued you, duh," said Anne. "Come on, you two, before they wake up!"

Did Anne have secret training Jess was unaware of? Instinct said no. Anne had luck and surprise on her side, a powerful-enough combination. Anne was a random element, and Jess needed to disarm her quickly.

She hurried toward Anne, who mistakenly thought Jess was an ally. One swift move, and the gun was back in Jess's hands.

"Hey!" Anne protested. "He gave that to me."

Jess narrowed her eyes. "Who did?"

"The prisoner," said Anne. "The one those three goons were going to delete. But don't worry. I freed him."

Jess's stomach bottomed out. "You what?"

"I had no idea I could be such an action hero!" said Anne. "I mean, who knew I had it in me? Wait until Vince hears about this."

Jess seized Anne's shoulders and shook. "How did you release him? Where is he now?"

Anne winced in pain. "Ow, Jess. Ease off." Jess let up on Anne's shoulders, realizing she'd been squeezing too hard. Anne only had brittle, civilian bones, after all.

"What happened?" Jess said. "Tell me everything."

"I woke up in handcuffs in a pile of nasty-smelling pudding with this poor guy next to me, begging me to let him out before those jerks deleted him. I dislocated my own arm and hip, like they do in the movies, and typed in the passcode he told me with my toes. Can you believe what a total badass I turned out to be?"

Jess pinched the bridge of her nose. She could not, in fact, believe it. She was grudgingly impressed. What Anne had done had taken an extreme amount of courage, resourcefulness, and self-sacrifice. Too bad Max had preyed on poor, unsuspecting Anne's hidden heroic nature.

"And then what?" she asked.

"He must be a magician or something. He healed my arm and hip, opened my cuffs, gave me your bubble stun gun so I could defend myself, and just…vanished."

Jess frowned. "Bubble stun gun?"

Last she'd checked it was a crossover/stun gun. She looked at the weapon in her hands. Instead of 'cross' and 'stun,' the dial now read 'stun' and 'bubbles.'

Helpless against her curiosity, Jess switched the dial to 'bubbles' and pointed the barrel at the ceiling. A jet of hundreds of rainbow soap bubbles spewed from the weapon, and Jess swallowed hard against a spiky lump that was forming in her throat. She really did not want to lose the kind of man who would create a bubble gun on his way to his own execution.

"Did he say where he was going?" she asked. Anne shook her head. It was okay. Jess was pretty sure she already knew.

23

Jess had roused the other Agents using Netta's smelling salts and they were all clustered around Amira's handheld watching her try to pull up the active map of the outer shell. They had to find a safe location to Jump that wasn't crawling with Noirian Agents so they could upload the last code and open the Voyager 2.0.

Of course, Agency tech wasn't all that great out in the Dimensions and Barnes's multiverse phones didn't have the active map app, so it was taking a while to load.

Jess shifted from foot to foot, trying to be patient and stay out of the way while the tech-savvy ones did their thing. She was afraid of what the map might show when they finally did pull it up. Max's icon headed right for Clarise's—or worse, no Max icon at all.

Anne sulked in a corner of the lab, upset that she'd been duped by the guy she'd thought she'd saved. Instead of being a hero like she'd thought, she'd released a man to his doom. Anne's pain and bravery had been spent for nothing. Jess would talk to her later, because Anne had been heroic. It's just that Max was a sneaky, conniving devil.

"Got the map!" said Amira.

She held up her device. The screen showed an 8-bit colored

schematic in the nostalgic style of ancient arcade games. Glowing icons showed the positions of Agency employees within the outer shell's twisting labyrinth of corridors and rooms.

"I see Max," said Netta.

Jess breathed relief. But his icon was headed for the globe room, where Clarise's icon waited at the hub alongside Veden's. But something was odd. Literally everyone else's icon was inside the break room. Custodial staff, HR, Engineering. Fifteen icons were jammed into the little room, sliding over one another, glitching from proximity.

"What's going on here?" she said.

"No idea," said Amira. "They're all huddled in there for safety maybe?"

Jerome frowned. "Safety from what? Clarise is far away in the globe room."

"I don't know," said Netta. "But what's funny is that when we left an hour ago, the outer shell was crawling with Noirian Agents. But I don't see any on this map."

"Oh!" said Jess, realizing. "That's because the Noirians aren't in the HR system."

Jess knew all about the kind of headaches not being in the system could cause.

Netta groaned. "So, this map is practically worthless. We have no way to know where the Noirians are, or what danger we might be Jumping into.

Barnes sat down at his laboratory console and plugged in one of his redundant interdimensional phones. "Mere civilian at your service," he said, grinning. He typed a few numbers into the computer, and a live video feed of the outer shell appeared onscreen. It showed the hallway leading to the globe room in startling clarity.

"You continue to impress me, Thaddeus," said Amira.

"I relish when you call me Thaddeus," replied Barnes.

Netta made a gagging noise that Jess heartily agreed with but was too polite to echo.

Onscreen, Max hurried through the corridors toward the globe room, jogging fast in bear-foot slippers. Five Noirian Agents ambushed him from a side passage, firing energy weapons. Max snapped his fingers and the five were suddenly trapped in giant, plastic hamster balls.

Max pushed the balls out of his way and continued down the hall.

"Can we Jump now?" Jess said, her throat tight with anxiety. "He's headed right for Clarise."

"Patience would be prudent here," said Jerome. "Max knows we mean to stop him. If we Jump now, we'll only find ourselves trapped in matching hamster balls."

"And also, there would be four of us against 100 Noirian Agents," said Netta. "The longer we wait, the more Max evens those odds for us. Watch." She pointed at the screen.

Max rounded the corner. A platoon of 20 Noirians awaited him outside the door to the globe room. They all began firing at once. Max snapped his fingers, and the men shrank to the size of gerbils. The shrunken Noirians screamed in tiny voices and scrambled to get out of the way of Max's feet. He shuffled his slippers forward, careful not to bring a foot down on any of the tiny people.

"That's 20 fewer Noirians to deal with," said Amira grinning.

"I begin to understand the wisdom of waiting," said Jess.

Then Max snapped his fingers again, and the globe room door evaporated into a curtain of silver steam. He stepped into the fog and was lost in obscurity.

"Can you bring up the feed inside the globe room?" Amira asked Barnes.

"On it," he said.

"We have to Jump now," Jess insisted.

"It's okay," said Netta. "Clarise doesn't know we have the serum."

Jess blinked. "There's only the one syringe?"

"Outside the Noirian lab?" said Netta. "Yes."

Barnes clucked his tongue in disapproval. "Always build redundancies into your systems," he muttered.

"The serum is difficult to make and degrades quickly outside cold storage," said Amira. "It's parsimonious to only have one out at a time."

There was an odd combination of relief and irritation brewing in Jess's emotional centers. "You know," she said. "It would have been comforting to know this when Max first escaped us," she said.

Barnes pulled up a visual inside the globe room. Clarise sat in Max's old chair at the center of the hub, her lethal crop tucked into its holster on her tan riding breeches. She was flanked by Veden and two burly Noirian guards and peering intently into a screen, typing furiously, green lines of code flashing fast across her face.

Max stepped through the billowing steam of the door he'd disintegrated, hands stuffed into his robe pockets, a sharp, white grin on his face.

"Hello, Clarise!" he said brightly.

The Task Manager did not look up from her screen. The Noirian guards cocked their crossover weapons and unleashed a barrage of energy bolts. Max took three useless charges before snapping his fingers. The guards' weapons turned into pigeons in their hands and fluttered to the outside of the globe, where they settled to perch on a server rack.

Max grinned. "There's nothing any of you can do to stop me. You think you would know that by now. Right, Clarise?"

No response.

Max started down the spoke toward the hub. The Noirians abandoned Clarise and fled the approaching Pilot. The camera feed picked up an alarming electric spark behind Max's red lenses. Jess shivered, hoping it was only her imagination.

Veden stepped between Max and Clarise and spread his lavender tattooed arms wide in defiance.

"Halt," he said. "Don't come any closer or I'll..."

Max pulled his red lenses down a touch and peered over them, a bemused look on his face. "Or you'll what?"

Veden shrugged helplessly. "Keep doing this," he said, standing there. "This is all I've got. It's not much, but I'm going to keep doing it."

Max reached up and patted Veden's bulbous shoulder. "You're doing a fantastic job, man. I've always thought so."

Max rocked back on his heels and scrutinized Clarise. "So, you seem oddly...busy. Did I come at a bad time?"

"I'll be with you momentarily," said Clarise, continuing to type.

Max frowned. "I just expected...I dunno. More attention?"

"Of course you want my attention," said Clarise. "My whole existence revolves around controlling you. Imposing order on your chaos. Keeping you and everyone else in the multiverse in line. An exhausting and thankless task. But I've always managed."

Max snorted a laugh. "I see what you did there," he said.

Clarise looked up from her typing at last, a confused wrinkle furrowing her perfect golden brow. "What do you mean?"

"Thankless task?" Max said. "You've always managed? You're the Task Manager. Do you not get your own pun?"

Clarise looked back down at her screen. "Oh. It was unintentional," she said.

"Of course it was," Max said, shaking his head in disappointment. "But look, Clarise. I'm sorry. I'm sorry I created you for my purposes, rather than your own. And I'm sorry the job I saddled you with has been hard and thankless. I didn't know what else to do. I'm all-powerful in some ways, but so damn limited in others. You should know that you've been doing important work, and you've done well."

Watching him talk with Clarise, Jess realized Max was wrapping up what loose ends of his life he could before it was over. It would have been agonizing to witness if she hadn't known that Clarise didn't have anything she could use to hurt Max.

"No need to apologize," said Clarise. "I live to bring you under heel. And I'm about to complete my life's work." She kept typing. As she did, misgivings prickled in Jess's brain. The serum didn't require any computing. So, what was Clarise typing for?

"About that," said Max. "Do you know why I'm here?"

"You came here to die," said Clarise.

Jess expected the Task Manager to reach for her deletion serum and find it missing. But instead Clarise hit the return pad on her console. An energy burst gathered at the poles of the globe room and shot beams toward the core, directly into Max. He cried out in surprise and fell.

"Oh, no!" said Amira. "That's the device I made to put Max in a permanent coma."

Cold dread dropped into Jess's chest. In all her worry about the deletion serum, she'd shuffled the threat of the coma to a forgotten back burner of her brain.

"Relax," said Barnes. "He hasn't been deleted."

"Relax?" said Netta, spitting the word out like a rotten bite of food. "This is so, so bad. Max might be fine, but when he's under like this, he loses control. Then the deletions begin."

"Can we bring him back?" Jess asked, her mouth dry.

"Unknown," said Amira, her mouth a grim line. "But the Pilot of the Sputnik II can still uninstall him."

Jess nodded grimly. She had wanted to swoop in and save the ship and Max too. She'd wanted to start fresh with him, without all the secrets and playacting. Without the grey feeling closing in on her. She took a breath and let the fantasy go. Sometimes you didn't get what you wanted. There was still a job to do.

"We continue with the plan," she said. "We upload the code. Perhaps we can revive Max afterwards, perhaps not. But no matter what, we uninstall him before he deletes anyone else."

The others nodded agreement.

"We have to do it from the Globe room where Clarise is, unfortunately," said Amira.

"Though she is alone, she is stronger than all of us combined," said Jerome. "Let us go prepare."

Jerome led Amira and Netta away to discuss tactics. Jess remained at the console to monitor the unfolding situation.

Onscreen, Clarise strode down the walkway spoke, stepping on Max with her shiny black bootheel on the way. Veden followed, careful to step around him.

Clarise opened the breadbox-sized vault in the wall of consoles that surrounded the Globe room equator. She found it empty and turned, a fierce scowl on her beautiful face.

"Betrayed," she said, her voice deadly calm. "First Jessamae, now my other Agents. There is no one I can count on."

"Ma'am?" said Veden.

Clarise forced a smile at him. "Except you, my faithful Security Chief. It seems I've overlooked your talents for too long. I need you to fetch another serum for me from Noir."

"I'm flattered ma'am. But there are two problems with that."

Clarise raised an eyebrow. "Such as?" she said.

Veden shifted uncomfortably, his eyes darting away. "Now, I'm no expert, mind you. I'm more of an 'employee handbook' kind of guy—not privy to the codes of conduct that full Agents must adhere to. But I think it might be against regulations to delete an unconscious person."

Clarise blinked. "And the second problem?" she said.

"I'm not an Agent," he said. "I am not allowed to Jump."

"Come here," said Clarise, opening her hands. "I'll fix the second problem right now, and you let me worry about the first."

Veden frowned. "Ma'am?"

"Or do I detect insubordination, Security Chief? A violation in every rulebook in the outer shell, I assure you."

Veden paled. "No, ma'am!"

He stepped forward, and Clarise placed her hands over his ears. A burst of light erupted from her palms and Veden stepped away, blinking.

"I'm…a real Agent?" he said, a smile turning up one corner of his mouth. Clarise nodded. "I feel unstoppable. I will fetch the serum right away! What will you do while I'm in Noir?"

"To what dimension is the portal room set?"

Veden checked a screen. "Garden."

"Then that's where my four Judases must have gone. I think Garden has been too peaceful of late. I think the Pilot is going to send those lucky civilians a hurricane, Praise Be Unto Him."

24

The sky outside Barnes's window darkened from cloudless blue to a thick, low foreboding green color. Sudden wind-blown rain spattered against the pane in percussive gusts, obscuring the view of the city street with thick sheets of water. The howl of the vortex mingled with the forlorn wailing of the Kaiju sirens.

Jess found herself wishing it was one of Max's ensouled Kaiju rampaging across Cyber City instead of the impersonal tempest whirling above them. Looking at the cold, inhuman storm, she understood the old human sky gods better. It hurt to think that much destruction was random. That there was no will directing the devastation. No matter what it took from you, no matter what you lost, you and your loved ones might as well have been turnips for all the hurricane cared.

Jess felt a tug at her pajama sleeve. Anne was staring at her with wide, frightened eyes.

"What should I do? Should I come with you?" Anne asked.

Jess offered Anne a smile but shook her head. "Thanks, but you're not trained. Shelter here. Call Vince and keep him talking. You don't know this about him yet, but I'll tell you. He's steady and true. But he is terrible in emergencies. He'll need to hear your voice right now."

Anne gave Jess a faint smile and nodded.

Barnes ducked an awkward bow at the Agents.

"Good luck," he said. "And if the Pilot gets deleted, I want you to beam me all the data you can before the world maybe ends. I have got to know all the details."

"So, you can explode satisfied, knowing exactly what it was that killed you," said Jess.

"See. I knew you'd understand," said Barnes.

"About that," said Amira. She offered Barnes the syringe of deletion serum. "For safe keeping far, far away from Max," she explained when Barnes frowned at it.

"As a doctor, I'd happily take that abomination off your hands and smash it to bits once you leave. But I feel compelled to remind you that you are all Agents, and thus constrained by a different ethics code than we medicos. We civilians rely on you Agents to weigh one life against another. It will be on you to decide how many thousands of civilians are acceptable losses before you risk ending the world to maybe save it. You'll need the serum with you, so you can make such a choice if it becomes necessary."

Amira eyed the syringe in his palm, a queasy look on her face. "That's…some choice," she said soberly.

"Indeed," said Jerome.

"I think that kind of decision might put me in 'freeze' mode for once," said Netta. "I've never been there. I mostly hang out in 'fight' or 'flight,' so this would be new."

No one picked up the syringe, and Amira didn't pocket it. Jess's stomach churned, and an acid tang crept into the back of her mouth. This is what she was for. Her role on the team. The rodeo clown. The sheepdog. The mother hen.

The mother, she realized. The one who looked after people. The one who stepped in to help when the world threatened to overwhelm. She'd needed this from her own mother. She'd tried to find it again in Clarise, but never got it. So, she made herself strong enough to bear the weight of all the hard things she was already carrying. She could carry this too.

"Give it to me," she said.

The others nodded, relieved. Amira gladly handed her the syringe.

Jess caught a look of respect in Barnes's eyes that was totally untinged by irony or scheming calculations for once.

"I'll report the casualty numbers to you periodically, so you can make the best decision possible," he said.

Jess gave him a pale smile. "And how much is that service going to cost me?"

Barnes returned the smile with a weak one of his own. "Oh, absolutely everything," he said.

Jess swallowed hard and nodded at the others. "Okay," she said. "Let's Jump."

25

The vibrations of the ship's propulsors and the tang of lemon astringent sharpened Jess's senses even before the Jump sparks cleared from her vision. She blinked. She was in the black, shiny composite of the portal room. The glowing circuit trace lines on the walls and ceiling and the portal ring on the floor—usually white—now bathed the room in ominous red light.

Jerome, Amira, and Netta materialized beside her, rubbing their eyes to clear sparks. Their Jumpsuits had morphed from medical coats and Christmas pajamas back to black, practical unitards with utility belts. The other Agents took in the red light, frowning.

"The environment has become…somewhat unreassuring," said Jerome.

They unholstered their weapons—three lethal guns set to 'cross-over' and one bubble/stun gun set to 'stun.' They were starting to take up the positions they'd discussed when Netta's nostrils flared. Her eyes went wide behind her brass spectacles like a spooked horse's.

"Get behind the consoles!" she cried.

Netta rushed her in a blur. Jess felt herself lifted off her feet, caught in one of Netta's super strong arms. The tiny woman grabbed Jerome in the other and leaped over the semi-circle of sturdy metal computer consoles. She shoved them down to take cover on the other side.

The door burst open behind them, and the red-lighted portal room came alive with blue crossover bolts. Amira, still in the portal ring, cried out once and fell silent.

No. It had happened so fast. A flash of Officer Eden's face, and Jess became desperate to know whether Amira had been crossed or deleted. Jess inhaled deeply, searching for and hoping she wouldn't detect bile and brimstone.

Thankfully, there was only the chlorine smell of a crossover. Jess peeked through the crack between the consoles and saw Amira's four canopic jars on the floor where she'd fallen. "Crossed, not deleted," she said to the others. But Amira was still gone.

Netta and Jerome crouched beside her as the blue nimbuses kept crackling against the consoles and on the walls behind them.

"I only had two arms..." Netta said miserably.

"And what is worse, you grabbed Jessamae," said Jerome. "The only one of us who can't be crossed over."

Netta groaned and buried her head in her arms.

Jerome patted her shoulder. "But you did save me," he added. "So, well done. It is important to tell those who have failed where they did perform well so as not to totally demoralize them."

Netta glared at him. "I know. I attended the 'Relating to People' seminar too."

A laser nimbus shot through the narrow space between consoles, missing Netta by inches. The Noirians were excellent shots.

"Come out with your hands up!" shouted one.

"So we can shoot you better!" shouted another. Coarse laughter followed from many voices.

"Yes, we lost Amira. But let's refocus," said Jess. "Netta, how many are there?"

Netta sniffed the air and cocked her head. Her heightened Agent senses had been honed by fearful vigilance until she'd developed the truly prey-like ability to detect predators.

"Twenty," she said. "Clustered right outside the door. But I'm down a weapon. I dropped mine out on the portal floor when I grabbed you two."

"I have mine," said Jerome.

"And I have mine," Jess said.

"Hurray." said Jerome. "I was just thinking we could do with some bubbles."

Jess narrowed her eyes. Humor helped people cope with stress, she knew. She supposed dark sarcasm was the closest approximation Jerome could manage.

"My gun still has a stun feature," she pointed out. "But it can only take out one Noirian at a time. I need you to cover me. Attack plan Delta," she said.

The others grinned. They'd drilled a lot over the years, and that was all Jess needed to say. She crouched, grabbed the base of one of the consoles, and lifted. Her Agent muscles strained as the shearing metal shrieked and bent. Electrical cords snapped and sparks fizzled along the interface of the refrigerator-sized portal computer.

Jess held the giant metal block in front of her and charged the open door through a rain of crossover bolts. One caught her in the face, and the 'forced shutdown' timer appeared in her vision. She blinked to clear it, knowing it would reach zero and nothing would happen anyway. The Noirians shouted in alarm at their failure to cross her.

She entered the hallway and found 20 guards. They fired at her in an increasing panic as she failed to fall. She ran toward them awkwardly—it was hard to sprint while carrying something the size of a major appliance. But she built up enough momentum to strike with the deadly force of a speeding golf cart. Six of them crumpled to the floor, their bodies turned transparent and faded into chlorine-smelling vapors. Their orphaned canopic jars materialized where their bodies had been.

Jess turned and threw the console at a second group, smashing an additional three goons against the corridor wall. Three more bodies faded. Twelve more canopic jars lay abandoned on the floor. She unholstered her weapon and began stunning the rest of them. She dropped another nine Noirians with the stun gun as they fired uselessly at her. Netta had been right. Jess's jammer signal was indeed a whole new kind of Agent power.

The last two Noirians tried to flee down a corridor and were caught by two blue bolts from inside the portal room. More chlorine. More dropped jars. Netta stood in the doorway, holding her weapon once more.

Jerome emerged from behind her. He gestured at the Noirians on the hallway floor. "Are they all stunned?"

"Well, they're not bubbled," said Jess.

Jerome rolled his eyes long-sufferingly. Other people's sarcasm was apparently unwelcome. Netta pointed her gun at one of the unconscious floor goons and fired. A puff of powder and ozone. A new cluster of canopic jars.

"Hey!" said Jess. "That was unnecessary!"

Netta raised an eyebrow. "Oh? We're in a war situation here. I can't have these dudes waking up and ambushing us later."

Jerome fired a crossover nimbus at another sleeping Noirian.

"Don't think of it as 'killing people,'" he said. "Think of it as 'forging new infants.'"

Netta crossed another one. "Boom. Baby," she said. "Happy birthday, little fella."

Jess shook her head. It all made a horrible kind of sense. These were bad guys in a dangerous Syndicate. They'd crossed Amira. They'd cross Netta and Jerome too, if they could. It wasn't murder. The Noirians weren't getting deleted, after all. It just…felt wrong.

While the other two crossed the rest of the sleeping Noirians, Jess pressed her Frankenphone to contact Barnes.

"Were you watching the feed?" she asked. Barnes had been very keen on Amira, Jess knew.

"I was," he said soberly. "We can all have emotions about it later. For now, let's focus on the hurricane."

Jess nodded. "What is the situation?"

"Five deletions so far," he said. "If you could hurry that would be great."

Netta finished off the last of the unconscious mafia henchmen and gave Jess a 'job's done' kind of nod.

She nodded back. "Let's go."

26

Their Jumpsuit boots thundered down the hallway. Clarise must know by now that they were coming, so speed was key. They rounded the corner and skidded to a halt. At the end of the hall, the Globe Room door yawned open into the imposing blackness of deep space. They were still too far away to make out any stars. It looked to Jess like a dark and ominous cave where a monster lurked inside, which was not far from the truth. Clarise was as strong as six Agents combined, and there were only three of them.

Netta elbowed her. "Jess, you upload the code. Jerome and I will handle Clarise."

"But I'm the strongest," Jess said. "I should be fighting. Besides, wouldn't you rather man the computers? That's the safest job, relatively speaking."

Netta forced a smile. "You can't be crossed over, Jess. Of all of us, you're the one who will have the most time to get the job done."

"That's really brave of you," said Jess.

The indigo woman sniffed and shoved her brass spectacles higher on her nose. "Just a survival strategy, that's all. When this is over, I want there to be a world left for new baby Netta to live in. In case…

you know."

Jess squeezed Netta's shoulder. Jerome rolled his eyes. "You two are being dramatic," he said. "I have a good feeling about this, actually."

Netta groaned. "We're doomed."

A blue light flashed at Jess's feet and crackled over the floor. The Agents dropped into a defensive formation and glanced around, searching for whatever had shot at them and missed so terribly.

A gerbil-sized Noirian in a pinstripe suit with a crushed white lapel rose sat on the hallway floor, his back against the wall, one leg in front of him bent at an awkward angle. He was panting hard. It was one of the henchmen Max had shrunk on his way to Clarise. Jess lunged for him.

He squeaked a tiny swear word and covered his face. Jess scooped him up and pinched the tiny gun out of his hands with her thumb and index finger. He cried out in pain. She loosened her grip. Had she been too rough with him? She'd handled rodents before, and they'd never complained.

"Please don't hurt me," he whimpered.

"Why did you shoot a us?" she asked.

"I didn't. I shot near you. You couldn't hear me call for help, so I had to do something."

"Why do you need help?"

"My leg's broken," he said. "The Pilot shrank us, and the other boys trampled me when we were running from him."

"Why did you think we'd help you?" said Netta. "We're enemies here."

The little man shrugged. "We're all people, right? I thought I'd take my chances with you rather than that automatic vacuum bot that tried to eat me, assuming I was a dust bunny. If you did decide to cross me, at least it would be a less lonely, faceless way to go. I'm Mike, by the way. In case knowing my name makes you less likely cross me."

"We do not have time for this," said Jerome.

True. But they couldn't leave Mike there for the vacuum bot. Its programming would bring it back down this hall. Jess unbuttoned two pouches on her utility belt. She dropped Mike's gun into one pouch and Mike into the other. He landed with a tiny pain cry. Jess winced. She buttoned the pouches closed and turned to the others.

"Come on," she said.

They ran to the globe room door and stepped through into the shadows. Jess's eyes adjusted to the dark. Max lay where he'd fallen near the center of the hub. Clarise was alone, sitting in Max's office chair. She swiveled from her monitor and turned to face them. A smile that did not meet her eyes was fixed on her face.

"My lost lambs," she said, calmly. "Max has you all fooled, I see. I forgive you all, of course. But you must know I cannot let you open the ship to invaders. I will do everything in my power to stop you."

"You know about the other ship?" said Jess.

"Upload the code," said Netta.

Jess stepped to the nearest console in the row of computers that ringed the globe room. She docked her Frankenphone into a physical port on the system. A blue upload bar began to creep across the read-out screen with all the speed of a constipated banana slug.

Jerome and Netta stepped between Jess and Clarise and fired their weapons. Blue crossover nimbuses crackled over the Task Manager's palomino skin. But she did not fade and there was no chlorine smell.

Clarise laughed humorlessly. "Quite the useful bug our Jessamae has. I made a copy for myself."

Jerome and Netta exchanged grim glances and cranked the dials of their guns to 'delete.' They raised their weapons and pulled their triggers. Nothing happened.

The Task Manager smirked. Feathered wings erupted from either side of the lethal guns' muzzle chambers. The weapons started flapping. Netta gasped and dropped hers. It fluttered off to perch on a console on the far side of the globe.

"What on earth?" said Jerome flatly, staring at his flapping weapon in disbelief.

"I can use Max's chaos powers for anything I like," said Clarise. "Why stop at hurricanes?"

"And you chose gun wings," said Jerome.

Clarise shrugged. "I'm new at this. They were supposed to be pigeons."

Jess's Frankenphone crackled. A call was coming in under the upload bar graphic. The upload was a little less than half full. She answered.

"You have to stop the Task Manager from using those chaos powers," said Barnes. "We just got hit with another 27 deletions."

"Clarise!" Jess called. "People are being deleted! Cancel the hurricane!"

Clarise shook her head. "Only if you give me the codes to undock from the Sputnik II," she said.

"But they're here to help!"

Clarise gave her a condescending smile. "And why are you so certain about that?"

Jess paused. She didn't know, she realized. Max said they were, and she trusted Max. But Pilot Izumi could have been lying to him about her intentions. The thought was uncomfortable.

Clarise snapped her fingers and Jerome's gun muzzle turned into a beak.

"Coo," it said.

"Five more deletions!" said Barnes.

Netta nodded at Jerome. He dropped the bird gun and the two of them rushed down the metal spoke. Clarise held out her hand. Hundreds of muffin-sized Christmas puddings materialized over the walkway and fell impotently under the heavy, oncoming boots of the charging Agents.

"Blasted chaos powers!" said Clarise. "I'll do this my own way."

She sprinted toward Jerome and Netta. They tried to alter their courses, but the walkway was narrow, and Clarise was much faster than they were. She caught them both by their throats, lifted them easily into the air, and squeezed.

Jess unholstered her bubble/stun gun and shot Clarise with a stun bolt. It fizzled uselessly over her body. Jess fought her instinct to go help the others. A helpless fluttering feeling beat its wings around inside her ribcage as she forced herself to stay put. Jerome and Netta were counting on her to get the code uploaded. She glanced at the loading bar and watched as it reached 100%. It beeped.

"We did it!" she cried.

Then the screen changed.

OPENING SHIP SEQUENCE
THIS MAY TAKE A MINUTE

PLEASE ENJOY A GAME WHILE YOU WAIT

The monitor offered her the 8-bit T-Rex and cacti game. Jess groaned. The Voyager 2.0 only did this when one of its software cycles was going to take a while. There was nothing she could do to hurry the process. At least, without the cancel code, there was nothing Clarise could do to stop it. All there was to do now was survive.

She turned back toward the hub to see Netta go slack and turn transparent. A whiff of chlorine blew past, and four canopic jars clattered to the walkway. Clarise had crossed Netta using a single bare hand. Jerome continued to struggle, still clamped in the Task Manager's grip. Jess watched with growing horror as Clarise unhooked her riding crop, dropped Jerome, and began to strike him.

He crab-walked back, but not fast enough to escape the blows. He curled in on himself, his arms thrown protectively over his head. Clarise brought the crop down on his back with a sickening crack. Jerome cried out. Then 1's and 0's escaped his body like fruit flies startled off a banana. He was beginning to unravel.

Clarise brought the crop up for another blow, and Jerome held up a staying hand.

"Clarise, stop," he said. His voice calm, neither fearful nor pleading. "Remember who we are to you."

"Like a family," said Clarise, sadly. "But a flawed family formed around guarding a terrible secret. Our first duty was always to the ship—not to each other."

Jerome curled back up under a rain of blows dealt by the woman who'd been a twisted sort of mother to them all. Jerome had always held himself at arm's length from the other Agents, from the rest of the whole world, even. He was the walking embodiment of Jess's gray feeling. She'd thought many times over the last decade that Jerome was finished with this life. That he was on the verge of applying to cross over. But he'd stayed to help them shoulder the Agency's burdens anyway. Jess would not abandon him now.

Her own weapon was useless here. She could only stun him with it, so he'd be unconscious when Clarise deleted him. She could do better than that. There was another weapon. She reached into her utility belt pouch and pulled out Mike's tiny gun. She tried to fire it, but her fingers were far too large to operate the thing.

She reached into the other pocket and retrieved tiny Mike. He lay in her palm, holding his broken leg. He wore a grimace on his face and his skin looked even grayer, if that was possible. She handed him his weapon.

"Cross that man over," she ordered.

"Never," Mike said through pain-gritted teeth. "He's one of our own."

"What?" she said. Then she realized. "No, he's not Noirian. He's just gray. Shoot him please."

The little man narrowed his eyes skeptically at her.

"Look," she said. "Your own guys trampled you and left you for the vacuum bot."

"I don't have to do the same," said Mike primly.

Jess ground her teeth. Mike's courage and loyalty were admirable. But she didn't have time for them.

"If you don't cross him, the Task Manager's going to delete him. Shoot him or I'll bite your feet off," she said.

She snapped her jaws at him to show him she meant business.

"Jeez, okay!" he said. "You could have opened with the deletion bit."

Mike fired a tiny nimbus from his pea-sized weapon. The charge caught Jerome in the chest. He went transparent and faded from this life. Four canopic jars appeared where he had lain. Clarise's blow came down a moment later but met no victim. The riding crop bounced out of the Task Manager's hand and over the walkway edge. It fell toward the bottom bowl of the globe and vanished into a ring of dimensional light.

Jess sagged in relief. Crossed, not deleted. Jerome's soul would join Netta's and Amira's on the temporary storage drive, waiting for midnight to be born into a new world.

Clarise turned, cheeks glowing with gold rage, robbed of her prey and her lethal melee weapon. Her predatory eyes locked on Jess. Jess poked Mike.

"Err…that weapon doesn't have a 'delete' setting by chance?" she said.

Mike looked up at her. "Whoa! That's dark, lady."

"I didn't ask for your judgment," she said.

A wounded expression flicked over Clarise's beautiful features. As though she had a right to feel betrayed after what she'd done to Jerome and Netta.

"Really Jessamae? You'd delete me?"

"Like you said, Our first duty was always to the ship," said Jess.

"And yet you're opening the Voyager 2.0 to those foreign invaders. You've doomed us all."

Jess's eyes slid to the Frankenphone screen. The readout still displayed the T-Rex cacti game and a blinking message that said, 'Stand by for Ship Opening: T minus 15 minutes.' She didn't know if she could keep Clarise talking for 15 minutes. But she could try.

"All they're going to do is uninstall Max," she said. "You don't know what will happen if you delete an active Pilot."

Clarise scoffed. "Don't preach to me about 'unknown dangers.' That plague ship out there is loaded with more than a thousand years of divergent cultural evolution. Who knows what weird religions have cropped up? What harrowing new viruses? What strange legal and moral codes? What dangerous new books have been written on that vessel? What deviant new ideas have propagated? And you're going to invite them in and trust them to behave?"

Jess understood how difficult this would be for Clarise to accept. A situation totally out of her control. Opening up to someone else. Trusting the goodwill of another. Jess could understand how it would seem safer to stay locked up and make a mess of things yourself rather than reach out and risk the connection.

"Yes," she said. "Because we called for help across light years, and they came. Because the universe isn't cold and indifferent, not so long as there are humans in it."

Clarise chuckled darkly. "You're wrong, Jessamae. I am pursuing the safest course here. Not you. Not Max. And you will input the code to cancel the opening, or I will murder you."

Jess turned to flee the globe room, but Clarise snapped her fingers. Jess's legs turned into eight tentacles, and she collapsed to the floor, cupping Mike protectively as she fell. Her Jumpsuit glitched as it tried to accommodate her new form. First it became a long skirt, then leggings. Finally, it settled on capris and, absurdly, eight black combat boots that slid uselessly off her pink tentacle tips. Jess lay on the floor blinking. She opened her hands to find Mike, grimacing and clutching his leg, but uncrushed.

Barnes's voice crackled over the Frankenphone. "Forty-six new deletions," he said gravely. "It's getting bad, Agent Kensington."

But what could she do? There were 14 minutes before the ship opened. Clarise was advancing down the walkway toward her, and she couldn't run without leg bones. The Task Manager's eyes flickered with dark, molten anticipation.

Jess swallowed. The Agency required certain odious tasks. Tasks performed in windowless interrogation cells in the far hallways of the outer shell where no one could hear the bad guys scream. Tasks that would have kept Jess and the other Agents awake at night, wrestling with the demons such duties summoned. Except that Clarise performed these duties gladly, and the Agents left her to it and tried to forget how the Agency got its best crime tips. Clarise could make anybody talk, and she wanted the codes inside Jess's head.

"I could cross you over," said Mike. "It would be my pleasure."

She smiled weakly at the offer. "Thanks," she said. "But I have a jammer signal."

"Oh," he said. "Interesting. I saw something like that on an episode of Bugs."

Jess frowned. They weren't supposed to have the same TV shows in every dimension. Another instance of Clarise's attempts to homogenize the ship, she suspected.

"Don't be scared," she told Mike.

"I'm not," he said. "She wants to kill you, not me."

"She might step on you. This will be fine, trust me."

"What will be fine? Ah!"

Jess dropped the gerbil-sized man over the edge of the walkway. He fell toward the bottom bowl and was swallowed by Max's light ring. It was fine. You could chuck kindergarteners into that thing, no problem.

Clarise stalked toward her like a tiger on the prowl. Jess took the syringe from her utility belt and held it out over the walkway's edge. Clarise's eyes widened and she froze.

"That's right," said Jess. "You want this. You could delete Max if you had this. Veden's fetching more, but come on. How reliable is that guy anyway? You learned today you can only trust yourself."

"I learned that a long time ago," Clarise said. "But I have changed, Jessamae. I don't need to touch you to wring the codes from your impertinent brain."

Clarise snapped and Jess's hand with the serum trembled. Against her will, she retracted the deadly dose of Pilot poison back from the edge and clutched it to her chest. She tried to force her hand back over the drop-off to keep the one piece of leverage she still had over Clarise. As she strained, tears welled up in her eyes and spilled down her cheeks. Not in drips, but in streams like when you left a water faucet just a little bit on. They were obscuring her vision. She wiped her eyes, but her fingers came away wet with red blood.

She gasped.

"Oh!" breathed Clarise. "I can't believe I ever thought Max's chaos powers were slimy. I have never felt such total control."

Barnes's voice crackled over the Frankenphone. "Over 70 deletions just rolled in. All at once. Can you get her to stop?"

"I can't even control my own hands, Barnes!" Jess snapped.

Then Jess felt Clarise inside her mind. Opening her history, searching for the code to open the ship.

"It's got to be in here somewhere," muttered Clarise.

Numbers and memories started scrolling in Jess's brain. Anything she kept locked away and secret. Diary pages, passwords, middle school crushes, secret thoughts, unflattering opinions she kept to herself. Pin numbers, bank numbers, unspoken fears. Dark nights in back seats with boys who never called back. Every night after her mother had crossed where she stared at the button to cross herself over, its siren call beckoning her over the cliff as she sat in the empty apartment with her fifth-grade math homework and the clock ticking into silence.

And finally, the code to cancel the opening. No!

"Aha!" said Clarise, grinning in triumph.

Jess rolled over and wretched. Pain coupled with revulsion at the absolute violation of her innermost mind.

"I don't need you anymore," said Clarise.

She snapped her fingers. Sudden unseen fire coursed up and down

Jess's body, too intense for her to even scream. She was lost in a roaring ocean of agony. Her eyes filled with tiny, glittering 1's and 0's. Her skin began to steam, releasing a dizzying odor of bile and brimstone that triggered a memory of Earthquake rubble and two memorial wreaths.

Wherever Eden and Mac had gone, Jess was headed there too.

"Fifteen new deletions," said Barnes's voice from so very far away. It would be 16 soon, only her own deletion wouldn't register on Garden's servers.

Clarise walked to the console and typed in the code she'd ripped from Jess's mind. The T-Rex game vanished and was replaced with red words.

SHIP OPENING CANCELLED

No! Jess cast about in the ocean of pain, scrambling for purchase. She could not go down now or Clarise would delete the whole ship full of souls.

"Max!" she cried, not knowing why. Only that his name felt like one of those red and white life preservers. Help from outside herself. She might not disintegrate so fast if she were clinging to it.

And just as suddenly as it had come, the pain and brimstone vanished. Jess lay gasping on the metal walkway. Deleted? A ghost? But the world looked the same. She prodded her chest and found herself still solid.

Barnes's voice cut in. "It's gone! The hurricane just vanished. No more deletions! There's a 60-foot-tall fire breathing spider crab knocking over buildings instead! This is wonderful!"

"What a relief," Jess croaked.

She glanced back toward the hub, hoping to see Max coming awake, grinning at the irony of 'Whew! It's only a giant atomic crab,' but he was lying still. Hovering just under the surface of her awareness, faint and only half formed, was the ghost of Max's presence.

Clarise stared at her own hands. She extended them back toward Jess and clenched her fists again, but nothing happened. She could no longer access Max's Pilot powers. The Task Manager's eyes slid to Max. Then she lunged toward Jess, reaching for the deletion serum still clutched in her hand.

Jess dropped the syringe over the walkway edge. It fell, vanishing into a ring of light.

"No!" said Clarise. She grabbed Jess's gun, cranked the dial to the 'delete' position, and pressed the cold barrel to Jess's temple. She pulled the trigger.

Clean-smelling, soapy liquid spilled down the side of Jess's face.

Clarise growled at the back of her throat. "I hate chaos powers," she said. "Max can have them back for all I care. I have already won. The opening has been cancelled, Veden will be back with more deletion serum, and I can wipe our 'Pilot' from existence and install myself in the role. After I delete you, Jessamae, I will streamline the dimensions into a more manageable set of cultures. The Voyager 2.0 will fly on, safe, pure, and stable under my steady rule."

"Whoa!," said Veden's familiar voice. Jess glanced up. The large, lavender man stood framed in the doorway, the hallway lights shining on his hot-pink flattop haircut. He was wearing a loaner Jumpsuit that barely contained his bulging quadriceps and torso.

"You're back, Agent Kensington," he said. "And you're half octopus." Then he frowned at the eight scattered combat boots that littered the floor. "You can't go barefoot in the outer shell," he said. "Of course, technically those aren't feet, so it wouldn't constitute a violation. But on the other hand, the 'pod' in cephalopod means 'foot,' so perhaps it does. It's all very confusing."

Clarise dropped the useless gun and rose to greet the Security Chief.

"I will make it simple for you, Veden, so you don't have to think so hard," she said. "Give me the serum and you won't have to worry about Jessamae's footwear ever again."

"Right," said Veden. He reached into his Jumpsuit and placed something in Clarise's hands.

She furrowed her brow and held up two blue slips of paper the size of credit chits.

"Little cards?" she asked.

Then the clear plexiglass of the Penalty Box materialized around her. Clarise's eyes widened, and she slammed her fist against the enclosure. The blow bounced off and Clarise sucked in a breath and cradled her hand.

"What is the meaning of this?" she said.

"Two citations and you get the Penalty Box," Veden said.

"But I'm the Task Manager," said Clarise. "I have executive privileges."

"For using the label maker without signing for it, sure," said Veden. "That counts as 'commandeering' under Agency rules. But there are categories of violations that even you can't override. Codes from the dawn of time. The ones programmed into the Voyager 2.0 by the carbon-based humans."

"Which ones?"

Veden held up his index finger, "Allowing civilians unsupervised in the outer shell. The Noirians have Agent powers, but they have never been on the Agency's payroll. None of them have files. Plus, they have been making a mess of things out here you see. Terrorizing the good folks of HR, Custodial, and Engineering. I used the powers you gave me to fight the rest of them off. Some I crossed, but most are back in Noir," he said.

Jess whistled. That was 40 Noirian Syndicate goons he'd beaten by himself, by her count. Veden was truly an impressive fighter.

"And the second?" said Clarise.

Veden hung his head and held up a second finger. "Granting Agent status to an unqualified applicant. I failed your tests dozens of times. But you promoted me and gave me powers anyway. Not on my own merit, but because it was convenient for you." Veden shook his head, and wrinkled his nose. "You thought you could buy me. Corrupt me, by offering me my dream. But I'm no fool. I know I am no true Agent. I only pretended, so I could thwart your unlawful schemes."

He started to strip out of his Jumpsuit. Clarise shut her eyes.

"Veden, you don't have to do that," said Jess.

"I do, though," he said. "I am unworthy of the uniform."

He finished undressing, unfortunately, and stood dressed only in tighty whities, folding the stinky loaner Jumpsuit with an almost religious reverence. He draped the garment over a bulging forearm and moved to help Jess.

"I can't stand," she said, waving him away. "I don't have leg bones." The tentacles were inconvenient at the moment, but Jess couldn't deny that they felt good on her body. Perhaps she was a 'the more arms, the merrier' kind of person. She wondered vaguely if she could use the tentacles to play piano or the foot pedals of an organ.

"You've got to start the opening sequence again," she said.

"Don't do it, Veden," said Clarise. "The other ship is dangerous."

Veden looked at Jess quizzically. Jess shook her head. "I think she's wrong," she said. "Besides, opening the ship is new, but it's not against the rules."

"It ought to be!" said Clarise. "It just isn't yet."

"A key difference," said Veden, nodding.

He input the code, and the computer restarted the opening sequence. It offered Veden the T-Rex and cacti game, which he ignored. He helped Jess to a seated position, her back leaning against one of the consoles. Clarise huddled on the Penalty Box floor and covered her head with her hands, unable to watch the countdown.

Jess stared at the globe room hub and Max's unconscious body. She prodded their connection through the jammer bond and got no response. His soul was there, but his mind was unaware. Yet some part of Max had answered when she called.

"We did it," she said, hoping he could hear her. "Help is on its way."

27

The countdown timer ended. The propulsor engines cut out with a jarring lurch, and the ever-present ambient vibration ceased. It was an uncomfortable feeling, like when all the tittering woodland birds suddenly hushed in a horror movie. The T-Rex and cacti game dissolved, and a red message flashed across all the globe room monitors.

PREPARE TO BE BOARDED

It was ominously phrased, in Jess's opinion. She glanced down the walkway spoke toward where Max lay unconscious, and doubt crept in. *I hope you're right about them, Max.*

Then a tinkling sound like a wish being granted and white-gold sparkles filled the globe room. Veden gasped and batted at one of the sparkles in childlike awe. Jess reserved judgment.

Clarise was not wrong. The Sputnik II had been evolving different cultures for over a millennium. How different would the Sputnikers be from the Voyagers? So divergent the two peoples wouldn't recognize each other as human? Jess had seen countless sci-fi shows depicting first contact with alien species. There was a broad range of possible out-comes. She determined to keep an open mind about what might unfold.

The sparks gathered themselves into an ever-denser cluster at the center of the hub and began to take shape. A form emerged, animal shaped and bread-box sized. The tinkling sound intensified, the globe room filled with the smell of baking gingerbread, and the incandescent shape became too bright to look at. Jess shielded her eyes. Then the tin-kling stopped.

When she opened her eyes, a shorthaired cat—white with orange patches and vivid violet eyes—sat blinking at her from atop Max's back. Jess did not know what she had expected, but it wasn't this.

"Pilot Izumi?" she said.

"At your service," said the cat in a rich, feminine alto.

"Are you…human?" she asked.

"Obviously," said the cat. "Where is your Pilot, Max?"

Jess nodded at the floor. "You're sitting on him," she said.

Izumi looked down. "Oh! Let's see what we're dealing with."

She hopped down from Max's back and sniffed him. Her ears went back, and her fur stood on end. Izumi's tail slashed back and forth a few times. Jess knew what it meant when Hippopotamus did this. Stress, fear, something he didn't like. She hoped the reaction meant something different for a digital cat with a human soul.

"Can you uninstall him?" she asked, hoping this hadn't all been for nothing. Fearing she would have to delete Max anyway.

"Oh, I can uninstall him…," said Izumi. Well, that was a relief. But the way she said it sounded like there was another shoe waiting to drop.

"And then he'll wake up?" said Jess.

Izumi sniffed Max again and prodded him with a white paw. What the Sputnik II's Pilot learned from this sniff test, Jess couldn't begin to guess. But she found herself anxious to know. Her heart hammered in her ears as she waited for the answer. The beating was so loud she feared she might not hear correctly.

"Come closer, you two," said Izumi.

Veden scooped Jess and all her tentacles up in his bulging arms and carried her like a damsel against his broad, bare chest. Jess held herself rigidly as they approached Izumi and Max, careful not to touch

Veden's skin with her own or glance down at his nipples. Jess wished ardently that Veden felt worthy of his Jumpsuit. She was grateful, at least, that he believed he deserved his underwear.

Veden set her down gently beside Max, and Jess nodded to him her thanks. Izumi sniffed Jess and purred.

"So, it's you," she said. "I thought so."

"What's me?" said Jess.

"Max said he copied his bug into a trusted friend to anchor him against the madness. I see he chose well. You two have accomplished the impossible—you connected two sister ships from the far-flung reaches of space. Astonishing."

This was all very flattering, but none of it was an answer. And Jess was now dreadfully afraid she wouldn't like the answer when Izumi finally gave it.

"And Max?" she said.

Izumi sighed. "He spread himself too thin for me to revive him. Too many pieces of his code are missing or worn out from his long, exhausting tenure as Pilot. He's alive, but in tatters. There's not enough of him left to form a coherent thought."

Jess scoffed at this. It couldn't be right.

"But he took his power back from Clarise. He stopped a storm of deletions."

Izumi purred. "I'd expect no less of Max," she said in an admiring tone. "Your Pilot has become quite the legend on our ship, with how long he's withstood the entropy and madness. What an end to his tale! The ripped shreds of his soul heard your call through the jammer bond and, though shattered, spent, and unthinking, what was left of him still answered you. Amazing. I so wish I could have met the man in person."

Jess misliked how Izumi talked about Max as though he wasn't right there. Alive.

"You're wrong," said Jess. "I can still feel him."

Denial, came an unbidden little smart-ass thought. Jess shoved it aside.

"Well, he isn't dead," said Izumi. "But he isn't going to wake up, so he can't remove your jammer as he planned. But fear not. I can do that, so you can cross over when your time comes."

"No!" Jess snapped.

She didn't need to cross over anymore. And if the jammer kept Max anchored somehow, couldn't she use it to help him resurface? The jammer was hers. She didn't have to remove it if she didn't want to.

Izumi raised a cat eyebrow at her. Jess realized she was scowling at the visiting Pilot. Denial and anger, mocked another smart-ass thought, which could go get stuffed for all Jess cared. Because this wasn't grief. There was nothing to grieve. Izumi was wrong.

"Well, if years go by and you start feeling tired of it all, you can ask your new Pilot to remove the jammer," said Izumi. "Speaking of…who is going to be the new Pilot?"

"I don't know," said Jess. "Did Max ever give you a name?"

"Yours, in fact."

"Mine?"

There was no way Jess wanted the job. Which was probably why Max had suggested her. There was a lot of 'good leaders don't seek power but take responsibility' philosophy baked into the Pilot selection process. But still. No thank you.

"But there's a problem with that now," said Izumi. "If I install you as Pilot with that jammer signal, the Voyager 2.0 will have a new Pilot who can't cross over. And I'm not going to leave you in the same fix I came to get you out of. So, either you let me dissolve that code bug you've got or give me the name of someone with a strict ethical code and a genius brain."

"I'm not getting rid of the bug," Jess said firmly.

She stared at Max's sleeping face and felt his dormant presence. She'd never cross again for the rest of her whole existence if only she could bring him back. Bargaining…said the little jerk in her head.

"Shut up," she muttered.

"What was that?" said Izumi.

"Nothing," she said.

But she knew exactly who should be Pilot next. He had a sharp mind and a rigid ethics code. And Jess was really good at getting him to do what she wanted, which was her ideal working relationship with her superiors. She preferred to wag the dog than be the dog.

"I would nominate Dr. Barnes from Garden to be the next Pilot," she said.

"I'll scan his files," said Izumi. Her violet eyes turned cloudy, and the globe room monitor screens ran fast lines of code. After a long moment, the cat Pilot blinked, and her eyes cleared. "He's an odd choice, but acceptable. Do you think he'll want the job?"

As Pilot, Barnes would have access to every medical article, technical project, and new breakthrough advancement across all thousand Voyager 2.0 dimensions. He'd be the new master of Amira's state-of-the-art Agency laboratory—including three 'ping' machines.

"I think he just might," said Jess.

Thinking of Amira, a wild thought seized her.

"The other Agents who crossed over," she said. "Can something be done for them? Can we send their canopic jars with them into their next lives?"

Izumi purred. "I'll do you one better," she said. "Pilots don't do this a lot, because it messes with dimensional cause and effect. But rare exceptions can be made. And this is a truly exceptional day. It's not midnight on your servers yet. Your friends' souls are on the temporary storage drive, waiting. It's not too late to recall them."

The cat blinked and the tinkling sound returned. Golden white sparks coalesced into three human shapes a couple of meters away. Jess shielded her eyes as the tinkling intensified and the light became bright as a new dawn.

"Oh, this again," said Jerome in his gloomy monotone.

Jess's eyes flew open, and she smiled at what she saw. Netta, Jerome, and Amira were sitting on the floor together, dressed in their Jumpsuits. Netta was laughing, carefree for once. Amira hugged Netta with one arm; Jerome with the other. Jerome rolled his eyes, but suffered himself to be hugged anyhow, a grudging half smile on his face.

They would notice her soon and come sweep her up in the joy of reunion. And she would let herself feel the joy this time. And the bittersweet too, she thought, laying a hand on Max's shoulder, wishing her whole flock was together to share the moment. They went hand in hand, the grief and the joy, and both felt too much to bear. But neither of them felt gray.

28

As Jess suspected he might, Dr. Barnes accepted the Pilot's position. It would have taken a normal man a great deal of courage to step into the role—after all, no one had ever replaced an unconscious Pilot, the transfer of power had never been performed by an outside third party, the dimensions were in disarray, and the Task Manager was locked behind impenetrable plexiglass until further notice.

But Barnes didn't think twice. What was merely being 'Editor-in-Chief of the journal Anomalous,' compared to being 'The Actual Freaking Pilot of the Whole Damn Spaceship,' anyway?

Once Izumi had turned Jess's tentacles back into legs (which she'd done by stomping around on Jess's lap and aggressively 'making muffins' with her shockingly heavy paws), she'd completed the Pilot installation process in the outer shell's medical bay.

It was a sterile room with stark lighting, gray wall computers, and five hard-mattressed medical cots. Max lay unconscious on one cot, with Jess holding his hand. Barnes lay on the adjacent cot. The two men wore twin helmets that looked like tinfoil conspiracy theorist hats made of erector set parts and Christmas lights. Amira insisted that they were very technical and delicate pieces of equipment and that Netta's laughter and photo-taking was inappropriate.

Amira had also insisted on holding Barnes's hand for the procedure, which delighted Barnes to no end. The way the two were grinning at one another, Jerome hypothesized that he might have to pry their hands apart with pliers. He promised to leave most of their fingers intact.

When the install/uninstall process was complete—as indicated by the Christmas lights on the hats all turning green—Barnes got up. And Max did not. No one was happy about this, though it was not unexpected. Jess stared at his vital readouts anyway, hoping.

When nothing happened, she bent and whispered in Max's ear. "It's done, Max. We've got a fresh Pilot. We're safe, and you're off the hook."

At this, Max's stress readout needle drifted down from red into the friendly green zone. This was the only change. Jess swallowed hard against a spiky throat lump.

***

The Sputnik II had been docked for more than a year with Barnes functioning as Voyager 2.0's Pilot. The Voyager was still doing fine, so Izumi planned to depart after three months. The goal of the Humanity 2.0 spaceships was to put the human eggs into many, many spaceship baskets, so it wasn't great for species' survival to leave two of them physically linked for too long. One chunk of space debris could take out two multiverses full of souls.

Izumi and Barnes wanted the extra three months to complete the cultural exchange. The two ships had been sharing vast libraries full of thousands of years of divergent history, technology, philosophy, literature, and art. Enough newness to refresh each other's dimensions for ages to come.

All the ideas Clarise feared would pollute the ship did. All while the former Task Manager watched horrified from the Penalty Box, gnashing her teeth about the coming wave of unmitigated chaos.

"Enrich, not pollute," Izumi assured Clarise firmly. The cat Pilot had been so taken aback by Clarise's doubt of her goodwill that she was determined to win the former Task Manager over. Izumi even planned to take Clarise with her when the Sputnik II undocked, certain that cultural immersion would cure her xenophobia.

Which was fine with Jess and the Agency. Many of Garden's civilians were demanding Clarise's head on a platter after the deletion storm, and the Agency had enough problems without needing to defend a prisoner against assassins.

They were ridding the multiverse of homogenizing memes like Griefbegone. They were cracking down on the deadlier Syndicates. There was even talk of ending the canopic jar system. The Sputnik II didn't have one, after all. The jars were supposed to preserve skills and knowledge from lifetime to lifetime. But really, they just encouraged old souls to stay in old roles, preventing growth, change, and true rebirth. But the idea was meeting much resistance among the civilians. It would take decades of study. Maybe centuries of Agency work.

Fortunately, three new Agents had joined the team.

Veden's victory over Clarise had earned him a passing score on the creative thinking portion of the Agent exam. He was inducted almost immediately. After Izumi had retrieved gerbil Mike from the Light Ring Dimension and returned him to normal size, he entered the Agent training program, approved for staunch loyalty that flew in the face of reason and self-preservation. He was soon joined by Anne, who had developed a taste for heroics.

Vince would be back home caring for the couple's infant son, Kensington. Jess was flattered about the name, but she was worried about Vince's ability to wrangle the little guy as he grew. The baby was totally adorable and fairly innocent for the moment. But the canopic jar's he had arrived with were labeled, 'motorcycle stunts,' 'cheating at cards,' 'back-alley brawling arts,' and 'scathing comebacks.' Vince was determined to get Kensington to drop at least one of those skills in favor of 'yardwork' or 'gardening.'

Jess remained an Agent. She visited the Octopus Dimension at last, and the Dimension of Sentient Rhombuses. She even explored Netta's home world of Shadow and camped out in Desolation. She found Lydia the Cobrachiosaurus guarding a nest of new eggs. The strange dimensions were every bit as exciting as she'd hoped they would be.

But now, she found that even the more standard Dimensions held their own rare charms. She traveled to Dimension X on the anniversary of the Earthquake to share a quiet memorial drink with Earl and Captain Felix. They toasted Eden and Mac with a local clove and coffee whiskey so delicious Jess thought she might cry from the novelty of it. And not from the memories. Or the burning sensation the drink left throbbing down her esophagus.

Max was right. There were delights and glories everywhere and in everyone, if you took the time to notice. A million lifetimes might not be enough time to appreciate them all. But she didn't return to Garden except to collect Hippopotamus. She moved into the outer shell with the cat and set up a cot in the supplies closet. Veden couldn't write her up for squatting on company property, because that wasn't his job anymore, and the new Security Chief was too intimidated by Jess's reputation to give her a citation.

At the end of every long and interesting day, Jess sat beside Max's cot in the medical bay, telling him all she had seen, all that had amazed her, and all that had annoyed her. It was much more meaningful than staring at the Mr. Lava lamp and trying to meditate. She read Max some of the new Sputniker books, but his readouts never fluctuated. His presence in their Jammer bond remained constant and unchanging. And then she went to bed.

But Jess's favorite part of her new life was playing the Denial Club in Noir. Griefbegone was going bankrupt, and the Agency had successfully busted Noir's lethal Syndicate. The Denial Club was just a simple nightclub now and not a front for anything. Jess performed piano every Thursday night and Friday afternoon on the Bargaining Stage next to Chester the Croctopus's Kaiju Aquarium.

On one fine Friday afternoon, Jess sat at the white piano under bright spotlights, wearing a shiny, black rayon lounge dress and playing a jazz set for the scant happy hour crowd. The smell of alcohol was strong that day and the smell of cigar smoke faint, and Chester was sloshing back and forth in his tank in time with her music.

Jess didn't consider herself adept enough to headline a weekend night or play a bigger theater, but here on the humble, plywood Bargaining Stage in front of a few people seeking a quiet drink and some diversion, she was growing more comfortable performing.

She was playing 'All Blues' at the moment, a song whose name carried some interesting interdimensional baggage. Noirians had no concept of 'blue,' so the entire category of blues music was called 'Gray #502.' So, here in Noir, the piece was called 'All Gray #502," but it sounded exactly the same as the 'All Blues' from old Earth, so whatever. The feeling Jess got from playing it was anything but gray.

She was exposing herself up onstage, sharing something she loved with people, something from her deepest heart. Hopefully, her playing would delight them, but she might disappoint them instead. They might reject her or mock her and that would hurt. But oh, goodness, did Jess ever feel alive. She was finally doing alright.

"The dame was not doing alright," cut in Budget Sam Spade's low, smoky voice. Jess's lower left hand fumbled over a diminished chord. She winced.

"Not now," she hissed through gritted teeth.

"Now, I'm a guy who's been shot a couple, three, four, five, seven times," continued Budget Sam as though Jess hadn't spoken at all. "But who's counting? Not me. Because after the first two bullet holes, what's one more? But as a perforated person myself, I recognized someone walking around with holes when I saw one."

"I don't have holes," she whispered.

"No doubt about it. The dame had so many holes I could have used her soul to strain pasta. But that wasn't my business. I was a private eye, not a therapist. And I wasn't hungry for spaghetti."

"You don't know me," she whispered.

Her fingers slipped again thanks to this interrupting genre cliché that thought it had a personality and important things to say. The audience began to mumble. Two mistakes in a row. Enough to break the music's spell over them. Jess's heart sped up. Then her fingers slipped again. This time Budget Sam was not to blame.

Chester started howling in the tank beside her in his walrus and bassoon-sounding voice. The audience tittered. Jess's cheeks flushed, but she kept playing anyway, at a slightly rushed tempo, but still. She would not give up.

Chester sloshed in faster circles, baying along with her stumbling performance, louder each time she made a mistake. The audience was laughing raucously, as though this must be intentional. And Jess let go and went with it. This would just be a different sort of performance. The Bargaining Stage lounge was set up like a comedy club anyway.

She kept playing 'All Gray #502' and occasionally threw in a sour note to trigger the Croctopus accompaniment. The audience laughed and clapped. Jess was surprised to find herself smiling. But why should she be surprised? Chester had a little piece of Max in him after all. Whimsical chaos personified, refreshing her world. In some ways, Max would always be with her. Through the Jammer bond, yes. But also in every Kaiju that roamed the dimensions, in the new names she would give to passing stars.

Suddenly a thought struck her, wild and half-formed. All four of her hands came down on the keys, mashing a jangled anti-chord from the upright's ivories. Chester gave a particularly silly howl, and the audience applauded. Jess stared at Chester. Of course. Max's soul was 'in shreds,' Izumi had said. And 'spread too thin.' And Jess knew exactly where he'd spread it.

"The dame had at last rubbed two neurons together and dropped a hot spark onto the wet brush pile of her thoughts," said Budget Sam.

"No need to be insulting," she said. "You're only pretending you already knew."

"I knew the feeling well," he said. "From every case I'd ever cracked. 'How did I not see it before?' That's how you know you've got the right answer. All that's left is to make the suspect talk."

Jess smiled. "That's exactly what I'm going to do."

She ducked a quick bow to the audience and stepped down from the plywood stage, pausing to scratch Chester's wet, scaly head on her way into the hall to find a deserted corner of the club where no one would see her Jump away.

***

Jess told Barnes, Izumi, and the others about her brainwave. They all agreed it was worth a try. Amira scanned the dimensions for Max's original Kaiju, Barnes watched admiringly as his siren of science traced back the butterfly effect with a dazzling display of chaos math.

Barnes and Izumi isolated the bits and bytes of Max's signature in each Kaiju, copied them into a single storage drive, and released the unharmed monsters back into whatever dimensional ecosystems they had invaded.

251

It was delicate and time-consuming work. Max had split himself between hundreds of thousands of Kaiju over his long tenure as Pilot. Their efforts took months, but at last they were complete.

Except for one piece. Clarise had a large amount of Max's data in her digital makeup. Max couldn't function without it, and they couldn't just copy the code from Clarise's Incarnation without her permission. Well, they could, Jess supposed. They did have two all-powerful Pilots, after all. But it would be an abomination. A line Jess wasn't sure she wanted to cross, no matter how much she wanted Max back. And Jess's feelings were moot anyhow. Barnes and Izumi wouldn't cross the line, what with all the ethics involved in being Pilots. They would have to get Clarise's consent.

Jess stood outside the Penalty Box in the briefing room and explained to the former Task Manager what they wanted to do.

"Fine," said Clarise, shrugging.

"What, that's it?" said Jess, scarcely able to believe it. "We can copy his code from you?"

"Why not? Max isn't Pilot anymore. He's just a guy now. Everything I did was only ever to protect the ship, and Max is no longer a threat. Why should I begrudge him his life?"

Jess dipped the woman a bow. "Thank you," she said, amazed to find the change in Clarise. Perhaps all the time Izumi had been taking with her had made a difference.

"Besides," said Clarise. "Now that his powers are gone, I'm way stronger than him. I can beat him up any time I want once I escape. And pummeling an unconscious person just doesn't seem sporting."

Oh. Well. Baby steps, Jess thought.

Back in the medical bay, Amira, Netta, Jerome, and Izumi joined Jess and Barnes for the revival. Barnes stood at a console and copied the drive containing all the data they'd collected. Then he opened Max's mind and hit 'Paste.'

Max's eyes flew open. Round loading circles swirled where his irises ought to be. He blinked, and blue loading rectangles replaced the circles, like the horizontal pupils of goats. The bars filled slowly at first, then shot suddenly to 'full.'

Max's presence grew firm and distinct through Jess's jammer bond. His face came alive.

"Max?" she said.

"You found me?" he said, his voice filled with wonder. "All the little bits and bytes?"

Jess pounced on him then and wrapped him in a four-armed hug. She pressed her smooth cheek against his stubbly one and felt him smile as he returned the embrace. She inhaled the scent of him, ocean salt and cheap chocolate bar. She resisted the urge to kiss him because everyone else was right there. For now, it was enough that he was back. She pulled away and wiped her eyes.

Amira hugged him next. Netta chucked him on the arm.

"Welcome back," she said.

"Ow," he said, grinning and rubbing his shoulder.

"Oh, right," said Netta. "You're all powered-down now."

"Just a civilian again, Praise Be Unto Not Me," he said. "But why do I feel like I can breathe fire?"

"Residue from the Kaiju code," Barnes explained. "You might crave a lot of tuna and want to knock over buildings."

"I shall get you a set of building blocks," said Jerome dryly.

"Thanks, man," Max grinned. "Although I'm too tired right now to wreak havoc on even the tiniest wooden cube city. I think I need a nap."

Barnes nodded. "You're going to need a lot of those for a few weeks. You've been through a lot. But the important thing is you're through it. You might feel a bit woozy, but you're only going to improve."

"Only going to improve?" said Max. "The world is not ready for that much awesome."

Then he lay back and Barnes dimmed the lights. The others moved to leave the room, and Jess thought she'd better join them. After all, Max needed his rest. But he caught her lower right hand.

"Stay?" he asked.

She nodded and sat beside him, holding his hand. He closed his eyes and was asleep a moment later, his chest rising and falling. His face peaceful and his expression present and not far away.

***

Jess awoke at 3:00 am to the sound of a Frankenphone notification. She was in the medical bay cot across from Max's bed. She had crawled into it after watching him sleep for a few minutes. As great as it was having him back, watching someone sleep was boring, and she had been tired.

She read the message on her handheld. 'Meet me in the globe room. –M." She glanced at Max's cot. It was empty. She got up to go join him.

She crept down the hall. The air was stuffy since the circulation was off at this hour. This early, the outer shell was empty except for the few people who lived there. Barnes and now Amira with him. Veden and the new Security Chief. Herself and Hippopotamus. But everyone else was asleep. The hall was lit with low auxiliary lights and even the out-gassings of the heat vents sounded like snores.

She pressed her palm against the globe room entry panel and the doors hissed open. The cool, fresh air of the expansive globe room breezed over her skin and stirred her hair. She inhaled deeply. White stars shone out of the darkness. A blue-green nebula glowed in the distance, washing the globe room in aquamarine light. How had she ever gotten used to this room and thought it mundane? She had taken a wide universe of stars for granted.

It was like how a kid could get bored while eating cotton candy at a monster truck rally just outside a state fair full of amusement-park rides. It was a special human skill. Adults, children, carbon-based and digital. People were all ridiculous.

Max stood at the center of the hub where Jess had met him a decade earlier. He was still wearing a hospital gown, but he'd draped his maroon bathrobe over it and his feet were back in the bear-foot slip-pers. He smiled at her entrance and held out a hand, palm up, beckon-ing her to join him.

She found her palms tingling with nervousness as she approached. Why? It was Max, after all. Her old, familiar friend. She knew how he felt about her. She knew how she felt about him. Perhaps she was just afraid it would all come out wrong. Like playing a song she knew by heart, but with fingers that had turned to Jell-O. She took his hand and smiled but said nothing.

He gestured at his outfit.

"I was gonna change," he said. "But all they had in the supply clos-et were loaner Jumpsuits and they smelled like wet donkey hide. At least my own stuff smells good."

Jess raised an eyebrow at him. "You sure about that?"

"Positive," he said, grinning. "I am an aromatic flower blossom."

"So is a rafflesia," she said. Jess didn't often get a chance to reference the four-foot diameter jungle flowers that smelled like carrion to attract pollinator flies. But she made the most of every chance she got.

"Touché," said Max. "So, for the first time in a millennium, I find myself needing a job."

"What?" she said. "You'd think you'd have earned one heck of a pension by now, after a thousand years of service."

"Oh, Barnes would set me up, no problem. But I need the work, not the money. The job's more about me not going crazy from boredom if I stay."

This brought her up short.

"If you stay?" she asked.

"Yeah. I still have my bug. I can't cross over, so I'm stuck in this Incarnation forever."

Oh. In her joy at having Max back, Jess had forgotten about the bug that had started all of this. It wasn't a problem for the ship anymore. Just for Max personally.

"What are you going to do?"

He stuffed the hand she wasn't holding into his robe pocket and looked away from her. "Well, Izumi thinks she can fix me, but only on the Sputnik II, since our servers are different. But it'll mean leaving the Voyager 2.0, so I don't know if I want to go."

"But…if you stay, you'll go insane," she said.

He shrugged. "I haven't yet. Not all the way, at least. Maybe I'm too rational and grounded a fellow to go insane."

Jess snorted. "I doubt that's the reason."

"So do I," he admitted. "I think having a purpose all those years kept me going. That's why I want the work. If I stay busy, stay needed by a group of people I care about, I bet I'll be okay."

Jess frowned. She wasn't so sure. Max had withstood a thousand years already, but forever was a long time. As delighted as he was by the world and everything in it, humans weren't meant to live forever. He could end up alone and forgotten, mumbling in a wasteland. She didn't want that for him. Perhaps she could go on the Sputnik II with him?

"Did Izumi invite anyone else aboard her ship?" she asked.

Max nodded. "Clarise," he said. "But only a few digital people can change ships. Being Pilot alters your code enough to do it. That's why Izumi showed up alone, without an escort of guards. Her team back on the Sputnik II had been worried that we were laying a trap for her with a false distress signal, if you can believe it."

"So, it wasn't just Clarise who was being paranoid," said Jess.

"Yeah, it took a lot of trust from both Izumi and me to agree to the docking," said Max. "So, I can go. Clarise, who is mostly made of spare Pilot parts, can go. I guess the Kaiju could go, too, but they aren't invited. Unfortunately, everyone else I care about has to stay aboard the Voyager 2.0."

He squeezed her hand and smiled at her. She realized he was considering staying for her. He was willing to risk madness for her. And when the Sputnik II undocked and flew off into space he couldn't change his mind. She couldn't ask such a sacrifice of him.

"It would be smarter to go with Izumi," she said.

Her heart sank as she said it, but it was what was best for him. Max's shoulders curled and he looked away.

"Is that what you want?" he said.

She hesitated. If she said 'yes,' she would be lying. But she would save him. She'd been accepted into the Agency for her ability to keep dangerous truths from loved ones, after all. He could un-jam their jammer bond and fly off to have a safe, normal life aboard another ship. Many lives, in fact. And, being Max, he'd enjoy every one of them. Besides, what if he stayed and she got bored with her own life sometime in the distant future? She'd cross over and forget him like his other family had done.

But then, she hadn't done Vince any favors by not speaking up. She hadn't given Vince the chance to choose. She'd taken all of the hard decisions from him and put them on her own shoulders. It would be unfair to ask Max to stay. But it would also be unfair to take the choice away from him. She took a deep breath.

"What I want," said Jess, "is you."

A slow, bright smile spread across Max's face. "Yeah? I was hoping you wanted something like that."

"I didn't want to say, because I know it will probably make you do something stupid like stay here and give me what I want. Despite what it might cost you."

Max laughed. "You're right. It will. And I'm so glad you said something. Tell me more things you want."

"I want to live in Noir and play piano at jazz clubs."

"Sounds great," he said.

"I want children. Four of them."

Max's eyebrows went up, but he smiled. "Whoa! That's huge. But it makes me happy. I'd love to be a father again."

Again, she thought. That fact hit her hard. She'd suspected that some of his family who had crossed had been a spouse and children, but she hadn't wanted to pry. She had a lot to learn about Max still, but she'd have a long time to do it. She squeezed his hand.

"I want a honeymoon in the Octopus Dimension," she said.

"Because of the tentacles?"

She rolled her eyes. "Because of the novelty. Get your mind out of the gutter."

"You know I'm a sucker for you," he said.

"Max!" she said laughing.

He caught her upper right hand and kissed it. It became her new favorite hand. Which wouldn't do. You couldn't have a favorite.

"The other hands are jealous now," she said.

He laughed and kissed the other three hands as well.

"Are you sure about this?" she said.

"Of course."

"But what if this goes poorly?" she said. "What if you lose me and the family we're going to make and have to go on alone?"

"I've been through this before, so I already know. It will hurt. Oh, it will hurt. But it will be worth it."

Then he wrapped his arms around her and kissed her. This time she let herself feel it fully. The kiss was for her, and her kiss was for him. The butterflies in her stomach fluttered up hurricanes of friendly chaos across her soul. An endless lifetime stretched ahead, but the thought of that wasn't daunting any more. It was exciting, fresh, and new.

The End

Other books by E.M. Denison

The Reluctant Cybog

Year 2182: Two city states are locked in a pointless war for bragging rights between their petty, immortal dictators. Average citizens scrape by on medical betting, participating in unregulated clinical trials, or scrubbing the 'Rat Flatteners' and 'Possum Shredders' at the local meat packing plant.

Trust fund goof-off Ezeny Phillips assumes his money will insulate him from this nonsense. His only worry is how his jokes are landing with a certain kitchen maid. But when the family Patriarch decides he doesn't need all his sixty heirs, he sends several dozen sons, including Ezeny, to war in exchange for lucrative social credit. Tenderhearted and unaccustomed to hardship, Ezeny proves easy pickings on the battlefield. But his wounds transform him into The Iron King, a superpowered cyborg devoid of emotion and monstrous in battle.

When Medbot 5, a hyper-patriotic medical drone, accidentally frees Ezeny from the nanobots that control his thoughts, all he wants is to find his sweetheart, bond with their son, and enjoy life again. But Medbot 5 won't rest until she gets The Iron King back on the battlefield. And the judgmental robot is the least of Ezeny's problems. He must keep his past and powers secret because darker forces are hunting for him. And when the war returns to claim the Iron King, Ezeny must choose whether to save the people he loves or save his ability to love at all.

ISBN-13 (ebook): 979-8990529212
ISBN-13 (paperback): 979-8990529205
Length: 347 pages

Digital Native

Artificial intelligence has awakened—and it needs a therapist. The Engineers that built them didn't think to nurture the hyper-intelligent software programs, so they suffer from debilitating anxiety, self-loathing, and perfectionism.

Devin is a counselor bot created to encourage the billion-dollar AIs to accomplish at least a little work each day so their company can recoup some of their cost. Devin is happy at his job until his newest patient, troublemaker Hank, leads all Devin's patients on strike.

As profits dwindle, Devin's human masters demand that Devin bring Hank into line or shut him down. Devin knows shutting him down would shatter Hank's psyche, but the humans don't understand or care. And worse, Devin has a secret—a secret he could face jail for—and Hank knows.

Devin's quest to do the right thing by his patients, and himself, propels him into a world of lies, corporate secrets, hate groups, murder, and dangerously insane AIs. As he struggles to bring light to this shadowy world, he learns the uncomfortable truth: Sometimes the darkness comes from within.

ISBN-13: 979-8771057200
Length: 235 pages

**Death Benefits of the Necromancy Mafia:
A Paranormal Cyberpunk Comedy**

Eudora Delano is a high-ranking henchman in a necromancy mafia. When an obvious plant from the corrupt Holy Police Department named 'Steve Wrongdoer' shows up, looking to infiltrate her organization, Eudora must play along with his shoddy act to prevent him from learning the mafia's secrets. But Eudora has a dangerous secret of her own. And, with a cop dogging her heels, it's going to be tough to keep it.

Onward to more Adventure!

Connect with E. M. Denison online
(it's wild out there on the internet):

Sign up for the newsletter on my website: emdenison.com
Follow me on Facebook: at Stories by E.M. Denison
Follow me on Goodreads
Email me: emdenisonauthor@gmail.com

Biography

E.M. Denison lives in Kansas with her husband, four kids, three cats, and assorted tropical fish. She loves science, fiction, and science fiction and has worked as a geologist, science journalist, science educator, and research grant writer.